PENGU

Dead to Me

Gytha Lodge lives in Cambridge with her son. *She Lies in Wait*, her debut novel, was a *Sunday Times* bestseller, a Richard & Judy Book Club pick and an international bestseller. Set in the New Forest and the surrounding area, Lodge's highly-acclaimed DCI Jonah Sheens series also includes *Watching From the Dark*, *Lie Beside Me*, *Little Sister* and *A Killer in the Family*. She is also the author of standalone thriller, *Dead to Me*.

By the same author

She Lies in Wait
Watching from the Dark
Lie Beside Me
Little Sister
A Killer in the Family

Dead to Me

GYTHA LODGE

PENGUIN BOOKS

PENGUIN BOOKS

UK | USA | Canada | Ireland | Australia
India | New Zealand | South Africa

Penguin Books is part of the Penguin Random House group of companies
whose addresses can be found at global.penguinrandomhouse.com

Penguin Michael Joseph, Penguin Random House UK,
One Embassy Gardens, 8 Viaduct Gardens, London SW11 7BW

penguin.co.uk

Penguin Random House UK

First published by Penguin Michael Joseph 2025
Published in Penguin Books 2026
001

Set in Garamond MT
Typeset by Falcon Oast Graphic Art Ltd
Printed and bound in Great Britain by Clays Ltd, Elcograf S.p.A.

The authorized representative in the EEA is Penguin Random House Ireland,
Morrison Chambers, 32 Nassau Street, Dublin D02 YH68

A CIP catalogue record for this book is available from the British Library

ISBN: 978–1–405–95706–9

Penguin Random House is committed to a sustainable
future for our business, our readers and our planet. This book is
made from Forest Stewardship Council® certified paper.

FSC www.fsc.org MIX Paper | Supporting responsible forestry FSC® C018179

For Kath Vlcek, aka Little Wolf's Books. I'm dedicating this to you in honour of all your constant, brilliant support – and not at all because you told me I had to do this . . .

1. Anna

From: Anna.Sousa@fleetfoot.com
To: rmurray@met.police.org.uk
24/06/2025 22:32
Subject: Help

Hi Reid,

So if you're reading this, it's just possible you might be the only person who can save my life.

Sounds pretty extra, doesn't it? It feels ridiculous to write it. But if I'm honest, I'm actually kind of scared. I think I might have screwed things up in a big way.

I'm well aware you may have deleted this without even reading it. I'm crossing my fingers that if you have, I was overreacting. That the email wasn't necessary.

Obviously, things between us ended badly. Worse than badly. And you're doubtless finding this as comfortable to receive as I'm finding it to write.

But you're still the one I've found myself writing to. I think that's because I still remember the whole of you, and not just the angry, grieving man who broke up with me.

I remember the man I trusted right from the start. Not because a colleague told me you were a good guy. It was because there was no ego when I asked for your help. No hesitation when you heard I wanted to blow open a human-trafficking ring. And more than that, because you had a total, dogged determination to help the victims. Even if you never got any credit for it.

I remember you, too, as the guy who bought a seriously expensive coffee machine for his team because they were all unhappy about the crap they were drinking. One you paid for yourself, even though you prefer Douwe Egberts granules and never used it. The guy who battled with the building management at his apartment block to get extra recycling bins for everyone so all the plastic didn't end up in landfill. And I remember that you never took credit for either of these actions.

I also remember you as the boyfriend who never minded when I was late, or I forgot something, or I made a mess of your place and didn't even notice. Even when I got totally distracted by a thing on my phone in the middle of a conversation. You were the one person I've dated who understood it wasn't that I don't care. That I do, in fact, care an awful lot.

You understood how I work, I think. At least for most of our relationship.

I used to love the way you'd quietly put things away, or offered to help on my terms. How you seemed to genuinely love watching me get suddenly hyper-focused on something, and would ask me about it when I was ready. And how you once gently but firmly defended my lateness to Dad when he made a sarcastic remark about it. Nobody else has ever done that.

So I'm hoping that *this* person is still in there somewhere. The one I met. And that he hasn't been totally consumed by the angry asshole who hurled abuse at me and then left. Because I'm only going to send this as a last resort. Like, if all is lost.

Let's just hope I'm right about you, huh?

2. Seaton

The sun was blazing through the conservatory of Midsummer House, winking off the wine glasses and well-polished silverware. Despite many of the windows standing open, Seaton was sweating slightly underneath his tailored jacket and there was an uncomfortable moisture beneath his tightly trimmed beard.

He probably should have suggested somewhere else. Dining at Cambridge's only double Michelin-starred restaurant meant sitting in the conservatory. Given that it was twenty-nine outside and climbing, that conservatory was beginning to feel like a furnace.

Anna would probably be hit even harder by the heat. She would inevitably be hungover after last night's May Ball.

There was movement by the door. Seaton glanced up, only to look straight back down. It was an elegantly dressed couple. Not her.

Elegantly dressed is unlikely, was his next thought.

He couldn't help a twitching smile at the memory of their last lunch here. Anna had been late, obviously. He'd never known her to arrive on time. But she'd also been dressed in rowing kit, fresh off a sculling outing on the river. The rowing had, of course, overrun. It was in Anna's nature to make things overrun. Brief coffees would become accidental three-hour heart-to-hearts. Short walks across town would somehow end up encompassing half the city. Errands could last an entire day – or be forgotten entirely.

Lateness, he'd expected; wearing sports gear to Midsummer House, he had somehow – in spite of everything – not. The trouble was that Anna's work as a journalist tended to spill over into the rest of her life. She would get wrapped up in it, and so had turned up to expensive restaurants dressed variously as an eco protestor, a wellness influencer and – memorably – as a high-class escort He was *still* getting odd looks from the staff at Rules after that one.

And now, here in Cambridge, she was pretending to be an American-born postgraduate student. She didn't answer to Anna, but to Aria. As far as anyone here knew, she was his god-daughter, who had used her dual nationality to give herself a second chance at rowing in the Olympics.

Anna had been playing the part of Aria for the last three and a half weeks, living it up as the young and athletic heiress to the Lauder dynasty. It had been a simple, quick way of becoming accepted by a small but significant group of wealthy students. Seaton had been uneasy at first. He'd worried, if being brutally honest, that she didn't have the upbringing for it.

It was something he felt entirely to blame for. He should have anticipated what would happen if he told her American-born mother he didn't love her. His ex-wife, Mona, had been bound to take Anna back to her family home in Coney Island.

Seaton knew, too – had always known – that he could have tried harder to see Anna even so. He'd always had the money to fly out there, and even in the later years of his career, he hadn't been so very busy.

The problem, really, had been the way it made him feel. The shame of it all, particularly when his ex-wife looked at him like she hated him. And perhaps worse still was the next man Mona had chosen to marry. Frank was a straightforward, slightly macho restaurant owner with conservative morals who insisted on taking the family to church every Sunday. He commented when women were 'wearing too much make-up', and policed the lengths of their skirts. There was a distinct note of ridicule in Frank's tone, too, whenever he spoke to Seaton. He sometimes looked at Seaton's well-tailored clothes as if they were actually offensive to him.

Cowardly as it was, Seaton had found himself avoiding the whole experience. He'd flown out there very little, and Mona had never once been persuaded to bring Anna to him. Which meant his daughter had grown up almost entirely free of his influence, in a small, down-at-heel house. She'd had as little of an upper-class-heiress upbringing as could be imagined.

But now that Seaton had spent some time getting close to his daughter (shamefully late, at their respective ages of twenty-six and fifty-seven) he'd realised that she was a consummate actress. Not only that, but her sudden obsessive interests, her natural talkativeness, her sensitivity to everyone's moods and her swift ability to adapt were all real blessings when it came to working undercover. Anna was made for this work, and he'd felt enormous pride witnessing even a small part of what she did.

He also found himself watching her Cambridge life with an odd nostalgia. She was getting to do so many of the formative student things that he'd experienced here: the dressed-up formal dinners in ornate halls. The college parties. The rowing. The wine society. Even attending the ultra-privileged Pitt Club, which he'd briefly joined, to his later sense of shame. And last night, she'd been to Trinity May Ball, one of the best (and most expensive) nights out Seaton could remember.

Elements of student life had changed since his time, of course. But some of it remained a carbon copy of his own experience, and it was both fascinating and a little sad to see Anna go through it all for herself.

He glanced at his watch. She was now twenty-five minutes late. Pretty much as expected. She would presumably have been up until dawn, technically working but also – obviously – eating, drinking and dancing. And probably also clambering onto fairground rides in a dress that was far too expensive for that kind of behaviour.

He gave in to the urge to look towards the doorway, but it remained empty. They clearly should have booked for two o'clock instead of twelve thirty.

The Belgian waiter came by again to ask whether he wanted another glass of Krug, and Seaton decided he might as well, despite it being his third on an empty stomach.

'Some more still water, please, too,' he said. 'Hopefully my daughter will make it shortly.'

The waiter gave a perfectly non-committal smile. It was one that could be read as condemnation of Anna's lateness, or indulgence, depending on what Seaton wanted. And not a jot of *Oh, we've been stood up, have we, sir?* It was the kind of pitch-perfect attitude you paid for here.

Once the waiter had gone, Seaton was left with just two couples, the only others in the restaurant. The empty seat opposite him felt ever more obvious.

He sighed and retrieved his phone from his jacket pocket. No messages, but that wasn't unusual. At some point in her distractable mode of operation, Anna usually realised that she'd lost track of time and went into a panicked frenzy of motion. In neither distracted mode nor frenzied mode did she generally manage a message.

He put the phone down on the thick white tablecloth, then picked it up again quickly to send her an Everything all right?

He felt impatient for her to arrive. He wanted to know how last night had gone, and to tell her about his own activities, which had been stressful but also, he had to admit, rather good fun. It was strange how much all this had started to feel like *his* investigation, too. How invested he was in the answers.

He remembered mocking her gently in the past about her obsessive focus on each story. He'd seen it when she'd first dragged Reid into helping her. The two of them had been determined to break open a sex-trafficking ring she'd stumbled on, and Anna had barely slept during that time. When she hadn't been undercover (getting alarmingly close to one of the women who was meeting and grooming young girls) she'd been trying to help Reid work out where the young women were being brought in, and where they were being moved to.

Seaton had eventually realised that her feelings towards Reid ran beyond the work they were doing. It had been clear from the way she'd talked about him that she idolised him to a degree. It had been somewhat inexplicable to Seaton, her interest in this man who was so much less brilliant than she was.

But Reid was firmly out of the picture now. Everything had ended very badly between them and she hadn't seen him in – what, a year and a half? Longer? And despite writing an increasingly lengthy email to him over the last few weeks, she didn't seem to have ever actually sent it.

The waiter came with Seaton's third glass of Krug and Seaton took a small mouthful. It didn't, he thought, taste quite as good as the last one. It was now thirty-five minutes since Anna should have been here, and there was no reply to his message.

I'll give her another five, he thought.

But eight minutes later, the rest of the champagne was gone without him tasting it at all, and Anna had not arrived.

At 1.13, forty-three minutes after their agreed meet time, Seaton finally gave in and called his daughter. Instead of ringing out, the phone went straight to her voicemail, though the message said, '*This is Aria. Leave me a message, and if you're good I might reply.*'

It was only then that Seaton felt real unease creeping up on him, souring the champagne and chilling his skin.

With a feeling of a line crossed, he scrolled until he found his daughter's own number: the one for the phone she kept hidden away in her student house and which was registered under her own name. This time it rang, but after ten rings the call ended with an automated, anonymous voicemail message.

Seaton rose, then, and with an instinct born more out of the hope that he was wrong than anything else, he walked past the waiter and out through the front door of the restaurant. The tiled path opened on to the great expanse of Midsummer Common, where a few families were picnicking in the sun and a handful of others were out walking dogs.

He shielded his eyes from the glare, trying to make out everyone who was walking the various paths. Anna would probably come on her bike, but it was clear that none of the cyclists was her.

Seaton walked back inside with a slightly dizzy feeling and found himself drinking a glass of water standing by his table, staring at nothing.

'Is everything all right?' the waiter murmured after an unspecified time, startling him out of a circular round of thoughts.

'Oh,' Seaton said. 'Yes, I . . . I'm sure it is.'

But as he sat down once again, Seaton had to admit to himself that everything was far from all right. Because it was clear that Anna wasn't coming.

3. Anna

I'm very aware that you might have stopped reading already, even if you opened the email. And more aware that you might stop at any future point.

I obviously can't make you read on, but I figure we're long overdue an actual conversation about what happened. About the night when you suddenly seemed to forget who I was and think something totally different of me.

I could see that something had happened. I know I got things wrong, and I should have stepped forward to comfort you. From your pale, empty-looking face in the hallway light. From the way you came in and started to tidy up the counter and then wipe it down like you always did before you could talk about anything emotional (do you still do that? The little comfort routine before you can access your feelings?), except you got it all in the wrong order, with things not put away and the cloth in a drawer, and then you just stalled. Stopped. Like something in you had stuttered and broken.

I should have been there for you. But the truth is I was frozen in fear. Terrified that someone else was dead.

And in fact what you told me was almost as bad, Reid.

'Tanya did it to herself.'

Because how could you believe that? How could you accept that your amazing, driven, and above-all *collected* sister would have taken a cocktail of drugs? I can see now that what happened to us that night was the terrible conflict between your grief and mine: yours the burrowing kind of grief that wanted to wrap itself in guilt and responsibility for what happened; and mine the stubborn, furious, fighting kind.

At least, that's how I've come to make sense of the fact that when I tried to argue with you, you turned on me and accused me of heartlessness and virtually whoring myself to get at a story. Things I'd never, ever thought would cross your mind.

I was so angry with you about what you said, Reid. The hurt of that: it felt like the worst possible betrayal. You were supposed to know me. To love me.

But I've had to try to make my peace with it, in the absence of a chance to talk to you. And I hope you can make a little peace with it, too. Enough, at least, to listen when I tell you that I've stumbled on the death of another young woman and that it's put me in danger.

It all kicked off three months ago. At a party.

It was one of those charity events at the Victoria and Albert Museum, with tiny little canapés and themed cocktails (which were *universally* bad) and dozens of Gucci-dressed leaders of the world all scattered amid exhibits they clearly had no interest in.

I mean, a few of them were doing that thing where they'd drop in something obnoxious like, 'Oh, the Gormley is on loan from the Tate, actually. We sponsored the original exhibition there.' Or maybe some of the guys would look at a seriously ripped version of Achilles and say, 'I do love classical sculpture. It's a window back to a time when men could be unashamedly *men*. I feel as though few of us really live by their values any more.' I was itching to ask if they spent a lot of time getting naked and singing songs to their boyfriends in tents. A basic education in the classics will get you a long way.

To summarise the party, it was the kind of event that makes me feel uncomfortable, even now that I've attended dozens of them in one role or another. So I'd had to put my professional mask on for the night and swallow down all my real feelings.

I was there to help a Crown Court judge condemn himself, which I was doing by pretending to be a very earnest young human rights lawyer named Alexandra. You know the kind: wide-eyed, hanging on his every word, not long graduated from Harvard. And . . . well, I had to let him flirt with me. But it wasn't what you're imagining. Just, you know, laughing at his jokes and letting him put his hand on my arm.

I probably don't need to tell you that the Right Honourable Mark Taylor was putty in my hands. I don't know what it is about that kind of man, but they always, *always* want to shock the innocent young girls.

I'd attached myself to his group a half-hour after arriving. I hadn't even needed to lean into the part. Mr Taylor had made all the assumptions he wanted to about me instantly. Obviously, the barrister who introduced me to him had no idea that I'd given him a false name and occupation. People at these parties work on the assumption that you'll exaggerate your achievements a little, not flat-out lie. So it didn't matter that I knew *none* of the people they were talking about and had never drunk the wines they were into. I just laughed along and let them assume.

Anyway. I was there pumping Mark Taylor for information, and at some point during the rounds I was introduced to a young woman named Cordelia Wynn. She stood out, because she was younger than everyone else there. She'd clearly come with her intimidating mother, who I was also fleetingly introduced to. Cordelia also looked uncomfortable. I could see her shifting and grimacing while Mr Taylor boasted about all the borderline inappropriate things he'd done as a judge.

Sadly, the inappropriate things were what I was here for. I'd had the nod from a defence barrister that Taylor was known to manipulate juries, and here he was, admitting to it. My microphone was recording every word from inside my clutch bag, and all I needed now were the specifics.

As Cordelia eventually looked nauseous and left, Mark Taylor began to explain in glorious detail how he'd helped a jury to make the *correct* decision about a defendant who was, and I quote, 'the scum of the earth'. It was job done for me, and given I was by then sick of trying to pretend I didn't find the Rt Hon. Mark Taylor repulsive, I pulled my bag onto my shoulder and started to look for my exit.

Mr Taylor seemed to pick up on the signal. He leaned flesh-crawlingly close to me and murmured that we should go to his hotel. This despite his status as a very much married man who boasted online that he put family life above everything. One hundred per cent the cliché.

I told him I was going to find the bathroom, and squeezed between a group of financiers and a statue of a man clubbing another one to death (nice touch). I was within sight of the door, and out of view of the sleazy judge.

But just as I was almost home and free someone touched my arm and said, 'Sorry, could I – could we talk?'

It wasn't really surprising that it was Cordelia. For one thing, there weren't a whole lot of people at that party who would have asked anything hesitantly. For another, there had been an aura of desperation to talk about something coming off her.

What was a little surprising, up close, was how fierce she looked. It was one of those expressions that twanged hard at my instincts for something that needed telling, but also made me feel immediately guilty. At a guess, Cordelia wanted to tell me about a miscarriage of justice. Something she thought a human rights lawyer could help her with.

I think, you know, there might have been other people I would have happily lied to in those circumstances. At least initially.

I'm out to be honest here, Reid, so this is the no-bullshit account of my actions. I'm not going to try to pretend I wasn't tempted to go along with it to get the story out of her and worry about the truth later. After all, telling her the truth risked blowing my cover and possibly getting me lynched before I could get out.

But I'd seen Cordelia's face when Mark Taylor was talking. She was a young woman with morals. And I didn't want to let her down.

'I'd like to help you,' I said, as quietly as I could. 'But before you say anything else to me, I need you to know that I'm an undercover journalist and not a lawyer. I deal in injustices, too, but not in the way you might be needing.'

Cordelia blinked at me, something hardening slightly in her eyes. And then she nodded at me, slowly.

'OK,' she said. 'I . . . I'd still like to talk.'

Her dark eyes moved around the room, taking in the manifold expensive suits and beautiful dresses. The hard social smiles and Business Eyes. The kind that would rove away, looking not for a personal connection but the next networking opportunity. The next step up on the ladder.

Those people, honestly. They're gross, and they don't even know it.

It was weird watching Cordelia, though. I suddenly realised that she could see them, too. The social smiles and Business Eyes. And I liked her a little bit more.

'Yeah, we should totally go outside to talk,' I said, just as she opened her mouth to say the same.

It was goddamn freezing in the V&A's Exhibition Road Courtyard. A cold March night is not the right time to stand in a windy courtyard in a sleeveless dress.

But it was also empty, and that meant Cordelia felt free to tell me everything. At least, everything she knew about a vibrant, clever, talented young woman named Holly Moore – and how she'd died.

'We met at St Paul's,' Cordelia told me. I could already tell it was one of *those* schools without needing to look it up. The kind where just going opens all sorts of doors that most of us would have mistaken for smooth walls. 'We were the outsiders: her the orphan who could only afford to be there because of her parents' life insurance policies; and me the rabid socialist who couldn't stand anything the place represented. Or my family, actually. Originally it was us and another friend, but mostly just the two of us. Outsiders.' She gave a ghost of a smile. 'I don't think most of the students understood us, and the staff all either loved us for being smart or hated us for our politics.'

I realised that I already knew the crappy punchline to this story: that talented, bright, promising young Holly had died at the end of her second year of university. Had died, in fact, at one of the biggest and most prestigious events of the year.

Holly had gone to Trinity May Ball, along with hundreds of other students. She'd gone to have the time of her life, but had somehow died without anybody noticing.

It was a story I knew because of the job I did, but one I probably should have known more about. I don't know if you were the same when it happened, Reid, but I couldn't handle it: the way Holly's death became *everything* to the media, because she was slim and beautiful and had a tragic backstory.

And it wasn't fair on Holly, a young woman whose death was senseless and awful, but every time I saw those blonde curls of hers I felt nauseated. Because Tanya – our wonderful, gorgeous Tanya – had barely been worth a subhead on page ten.

I still had to work on myself to listen to Cordelia that night.

To squash every broken-hearted thought over Tanya and give Holly's story the attention it clearly deserved.

'We both applied for Cambridge, just different colleges,' Cordelia said. 'She ended up at St John's near the centre, and I was with lots of the feminists out at Newnham.'

Holly had been a great natural sciences student and a promising runner – already a bronze medallist at the five thousand metres in the under-twenties World Athletics Championships. At St John's, she'd met an English student named James Sedgewick, who she'd quickly fallen for.

'The thing about James is, he sort of straddles two worlds,' Cordelia explained. 'He's an actor and climate activist and is very uncomfortable about capitalism. But he's also part of a wealthy family that's been going to Cambridge for years. His dad and his grandad and everyone were all members of the Pitt Club, so he obviously had to join, too.'

'Right,' I said. 'The Pitt Club is . . .?'

'Oh, it's . . . like an exclusive members' club,' Cordelia explained, with a note of slight embarrassment. 'You have to be rich or well connected. For years it was all boys, but recently they realised they needed to start letting the girls in if they were going to survive. James's sister joined, too, actually. She's a bit older.'

'Got it.' I tried folding my arms round myself at this point, wishing I'd chosen a dress with goddamn sleeves. 'I guess it's kind of like a fraternity.'

'I think so?' Cordelia didn't sound sure. Maybe the world isn't quite as obsessed with American college culture as we like to think. 'It's definitely about who you know and how much you're worth. But a few of those guys have something about them and it was the more worthwhile ones who James was drawn to, and Holly in turn. So we all ended up being friends.' She shook her head impatiently. 'Anyway, that's . . . only relevant because they all went to Trinity May Ball together.' I know I must have given her a blank look, because she said, 'It's one of the really big events. Black tie, lasts all night. Fireworks, drinks, you know. And they hold it at the very end of the year, after exams are done, during May Week. Which is in June, just to be confusing.'

'Sounds like a big occasion,' I said. Honestly, I was so cold by then that thinking of anything to say was difficult, but something told me I should keep listening. That this was worth the whole-body shivers and agonisingly painful hands.

'I don't know exactly what happened once they all got there, but somehow – during the fireworks – Holly drowned,' Cordelia said, her voice tight. 'She drowned in four feet of water. And nobody saw.'

Cordelia's face twisted, and she turned away, her eyes blinking furiously and her lips pressing together.

'I'm so sorry. That's such a terrible thing.' After a beat, I tried, 'Was there any investigation into what happened?'

Cordelia nodded. Breathed, and then said, 'The post-mortem . . . they found ketamine. A really huge dose of ketamine. They think she pretty much overdosed, climbed over a fence and then fell into the river while the noise of the fireworks was going on. Everyone was . . . looking up. They wouldn't have seen someone face down in the water.'

I felt something in me twist as she said that, Reid. I didn't remember reading about that. In resenting this other student who'd had all the attention I thought Tanya deserved, had I really missed that she'd also died of a drug overdose? At the same age, in the same university?

But Cordelia wasn't done.

'But you need to understand several things,' she said, her voice determined in spite of the clear emotion. 'The first is that Holly was an athlete. She barely even *drank*, right? And with drugs, she and I were the same. We lost a friend to an overdose at fifteen – Rheanna. She died on the green outside school after one of a series of stupid nights where she tried to fit in, and Holly was heartbroken. She's obviously never touched anything before or after. We lost our other outcast. Our friend.' She shook her head, eyes glittering but her expression unflinching. 'She used to get worried any time James was persuaded to take MDMA by the rest of that group. There is just no way that she would have taken a load of ket voluntarily.'

I looked at Cordelia, trying not to let her see what this meant to me. It reminded me so much of what I thought about Tanya. The fact that you only had to know her to realise she wouldn't have done this.

On some level, I knew I had to be a good journalist, still. I had to ask the right questions.

And luckily, I knew exactly what to ask, because you'd asked it of me.

'I guess – I know that after a stressful time, people can sometimes behave differently,' was what I chose, in the end. 'Particularly if they're under pressure. Can you imagine how those factors might have made her act out of character?'

Cordelia lifted her chin, her jaw set. 'Holly wasn't a pushover, and of all the drugs she would have taken, that was the last one. It was what Rheanna took. Like, she would never have risked even a *try*, never mind enough to OD.' And then Cordelia looked around her, again, to check the empty courtyard – even though nobody in their right mind would be standing out there in that cold – and she said, 'And the thing is, the day she died, she messaged me to say that something had happened. Something really bad. And she needed advice about what to do.'

4. Seaton

Seaton stepped back out on to Midsummer Common, the Krug paid for and the table abandoned. It was the kind of thing he would normally have been anguished over but he found himself caring not a jot about it.

Everything seemed overexposed outside, fear turning a perfect summer's day into something stark and unsettling. Fear, and a terrible sense of guilt.

If something had happened to Anna, Seaton knew he was complicit in it. There was no question. He'd been involved in all of this from the start, and at no time had he stepped in to try to protect her.

You tried to protect yourself, though, didn't you? he thought wretchedly. *You did that, as usual.*

He found himself remembering that one, singular dinner at Rules of London where she'd turned up looking the part: elegant navy cocktail dress on, and hair beautifully styled and dyed a rich, full blonde. He'd narrowed his eyes at her, and she'd laughed, and said, 'OK, OK, I do want something. I actually want your help setting up an undercover identity as a Cambridge student. But I think you'll be on board.'

Seaton's initial reaction had been one of discomfort. His position as Emeritus Fellow of Christ's College was not one he was inclined to take lightly. He might not have full duties, but he was still very much involved with the college, and highly respected within the university as a whole. If she was expecting him to jeopardise his standing and reputation by lying for her, then things were going to get very awkward.

But then Anna had begun to explain how she'd been asked to look into Holly Moore's death, and in spite of his reservations, he'd been fascinated. It just hadn't been for the reasons she might have predicted.

Seaton knew all about Holly's death. Philip Sedgewick, the father of Holly's boyfriend James, was one of Seaton's oldest friends. The incident at Trinity May Ball had torn into the Sedgewick family.

Philip and his wife, Marcie, had mourned Holly in their own right; their son had been barely able to function for months after her loss, and was far from back to his old self a year later. He felt as though he'd let her wander off and die.

That night in Rules, listening to his daughter talk, Seaton had felt a flicker of hope. If Anna was right, and Holly had been murdered, James would be freed of his guilt. He'd have someone else to blame.

And so he'd listened, transfixed, as Anna took him through details of the post-mortem and the extent of the police investigation.

'Holly's friend Cordelia is absolutely right,' Anna had told him, her eyes alive. 'The amount of ketamine in Holly's blood was more than double the lowest likely dose that would have killed a woman of her weight. Like a seriously big overdose. Doing the math on it at Holly's bodyweight, that comes out at around five grams, too. So that's a hundred and fifty pounds' worth of ketamine, all injected by one person during a small window of time.' She'd raised an eyebrow. 'Like, who would do that? Holly didn't have money like some of these others, and I don't even see why one of *them* would choose to buy that much ket for fun. For reference, a tab of MDMA like all of her friends probably took, would have cost around twenty pounds in Cambridge at that point and been a *lot* easier to hide in a bag or something than the syringe you'd need for a ketamine injection.'

Seaton had blinked at her. 'I, er . . . how have you done all your workings?'

'Oh. By her weight and a calculation of blood volume,' Anna had said with a shrug. 'Cordelia Wynn is a medic and I got her to go over it all. She agrees. I've also checked that math against known amounts that have caused an overdose versus concentrations found in blood. It all holds up.'

'Right,' Seaton had said. 'That's . . . good work.'

'And there were two injection sites on her arm, too,' Anna had continued. 'Police statements say she'd taken nothing before she left the group, and I'm pretty sure that's true because they wouldn't have wanted to stand in a group in a very obvious place while one of them injected a load of ket. It's unbelievably risky. If she *had* been going to take something with them, it wasn't going to be ketamine anyway. The group is into MDMA and occasional cocaine. So, fully sober at ten fifteen, the last time anyone saw her.' She'd paused to finally eat a mouthful of her mackerel pâté and drink a gulp of wine. 'And we know it was ten fifteen because the police checked what time the burlesque show wrapped up, which is where they last saw her. All good?'

Seaton had taken a moment to process all of this, and said, 'Yes, OK.'

'But,' Anna had said with energy, 'she was found floating face down at ten forty-eight. Now ketamine takes at least half an hour to wear off once it hits. You're not going to take a second shot of it unless you feel it fading. It often *is* used in multiple doses because of its short half-life. But assuming that Holly left them all at ten fifteen, then had to go and find her supplier, *then* find a quiet spot to inject herself . . . there wasn't *time* for it to have worn off. She can't have dosed up before ten twenty at the absolute earliest. And somehow, less than half an hour later, we're expected to believe that she'd had time for it to hit, then wear off, to inject herself again with a huge dose, fall into the water and drown, and be discovered.'

It had taken Seaton a few moments more to work through those timings for himself, but he'd realised that she was right. And he'd found himself watching her with a renewed sense of her intelligence. It gave him a rush of pride mixed with a twist of regret that he was only getting to see her in her element now, when she was twenty-six years old.

He'd nodded, unable to keep from smiling, and she'd gone on to explain the other significant facts: the fact that nobody had ever found out who'd given Holly the ketamine. The fact that Holly had messaged Cordelia the day of the ball, explaining that she was preoccupied with something that had happened which she was seeking advice over. And the fact of there being only four real suspects.

'Cordelia Wynn is exactly the kind of person you want as an informant,' she'd said. 'Right after it happened, she got hold of a list of Trinity May Ball guests. And having done a seriously thorough job of cross-checking, she's positive Holly only knew four people from the university who were actually there that night. So given her message about something having happened, our pool of possible murderers is almost definitely just these four students.'

'Who are they?' Seaton had asked her immediately, feeling a twist in his stomach.

What if she thinks James might have done it? he thought.

At that point, for the first time, Anna had looked hesitant. 'So this is where there might be a conflict of interest. I don't know. They're all Pitt Club members, and a lot of the parents are, too.' She studied his face for a few seconds. 'The students are Kit Frankland, Ryan Jaffett, Esther Thomas and

James Sedgewick. James's dad was in your year at Cambridge. I know you didn't like most of them, but presumably you still speak to a few . . .?'

Seaton sighed. 'I guessed James might be on the list.' He drank a hefty mouthful of Barolo and swallowed it before going on. 'Philip Sedgewick is the one Pitt Club member I still talk to. He's my oldest friend, and a good one.'

'Oh.' Seaton had watched his daughter's face fall, briefly, before she masked it with her usual half-smile. 'OK, that's not going to work.'

Seaton had felt a jolt of loss, as though something was being taken away from him, and he'd put a hand out towards her.

'No, look. I *want* Holly's killer found, whoever that is.' He put his glass down carefully. 'Her death tore that family apart. I don't think James can have been involved, but whatever the truth is, I'd like to help find it out. You just need to promise me that you'll tread carefully. Her death has already caused a lot of pain.' He'd fixed her with a very direct look after that. 'And promise me you won't do anything to embarrass me, of course.'

'Absolutely. Scouts' honour.'

'And . . . this is all official?' he'd asked, tentatively. Anna had been known to throw herself into stories before getting full approval in the past, and he was eager to know if that was what he was looking at here.

Luckily, the question had made her laugh.

'It's totally official,' she'd told him. 'I didn't even have to convince the *Ensign*. Gael was sold the moment he heard it was a chance to take down rich white kids, and Maria somewhat horrifyingly looked up all the previous stories about Holly's death and said she was in because "Pretty dead white girl stories always sell".'

Seaton had grimaced at the same time Anna had, and that had made him smile.

'I think there might be a nicer side to it, too,' Anna had added. 'I mean, she might have been a Cambridge student and an athlete, but she was also an orphan and an outsider. Her only money was inherited from her parents, and she used it all on attending an expensive school. *Their* only family was a sister in Baltimore who clearly had neither the money nor the interest to come over and raise hell.' Anna had shrugged. 'I think the *Ensign* would probably want to fight for her, anyway. Particularly if she was killed by a bunch of rich kids who were supposed to be looking after her.'

'Well, that's somewhat heartening,' he'd said. 'What's your budget?'

'Whatever I need for accommodation,' she'd told him. 'And then a credit card for clothes and entertainment and stuff, but, like, that will be seriously itemised. I can't go crazy. So I've borrowed a lot of clothes off Imogen at work. You know, the new hire? Grew up with private yachts and a pony, that one.' She gave him a broad smile. 'I don't think they've realised yet that I'm not some kind of a champagne socialist like the rest of the staff.'

The comment had made Seaton a little uncomfortable. It was still hard for him, knowing that Anna was not wealthy, and that he had the means to help her. But her mother had made it *abundantly* clear that Anna did not want his guilt money.

But this story, and her place in Cambridge, was something he *could* help with. And so Seaton had stepped in to smooth her path. He'd used his contacts to find her a hard-up postgraduate English student to talk her through the academic side. He'd advised her on pretending that she was a Jesus College student, because he knew enough fellows there to give her the jargon she needed to talk convincingly about the course.

He'd helped her get set up as a rower, too. Anna had wanted to seem exactly the kind of talented, athletic young woman who might come across from the States to be able to row here. It had given her a perfect excuse to have been barely seen by anyone in her college over the course of the year (because rowers trained pretty incessantly) and also a reason to be desirable to a group that liked status. So he'd hit up an alumnus who was now a boatman and got her access to a sculling boat and blades at Jesus College Boat House.

It had been the rowing angle that had led him to find her a whole new identity, in fact, something he'd felt immensely satisfied with. After the Rules dinner, he'd gone away and mulled over the difficulty of faking a really high-profile rowing pedigree. It might once have been straightforward, but in this day and age competitors' names were easily available online. If you'd never rowed at any events, it would show.

Anna was, herself, an extremely able rower, which was why she'd chosen that sport to fake. As a tall and strong young woman, she'd ended up rowing crew while at Colombia and had achieved some national success. Since moving to the UK, however, she'd become a weekends-only rower at one of the London clubs, a much less intensive lifestyle. But with a few weeks to put some extra muscle on at Cambridge's intensive F45 gym, she would undoubtedly look the part. Which just left her track record.

He'd realised that the best thing would be playing a part that already existed, and after a lot of digging he'd happened upon a persona that had fitted perfectly: that of Aria Lauder.

Aria was a twenty-three-year-old member of the Lauder dynasty, a seriously moneyed family with a lot of land in Vermont. She'd gone to Yale, where she'd rowed crew and ended up competing in the world championships. She had all the prestige Anna was looking for.

But – and this was where he felt as though the fates were shining on them – during her final term at Yale she had come close to overdosing on cocaine, which had turned out to be a serious addiction problem. She had ended up behaving erratically, and crashing out of the rowing programme in disgrace. She had been sent to rehab some months ago.

Even better than all this, Anna's team at the newspaper had found out that Aria was back in rehab again, having removed herself and been readmitted. This information was *not* online and had taken a lot of careful work to discover.

With all her social media deleted and a reclusive family except for a senator brother who wanted nothing to do with her, Aria couldn't have been a better pick. And she'd been all Seaton's discovery.

He'd even been able to find a perfect house for 'Aria' to live in – the end terrace of a row that looked out on to Jesus Green. It sat right next to a series of student houses occupied by Jesus College students but was privately owned. It had status, of the old-fashioned kind a wealthy American family would likely look for, but it also didn't look too much for a postgraduate student. All of this was the kind of thing nobody else would have got right. It had taken intimate knowledge of the university and its colleges, and of the status signalling that went on in these families.

Even better than feeling he could help, though, Seaton had got to spend time with Anna. He'd felt as though they were at long, long last getting to become a real father and daughter. As though he'd started to make up for two lost decades.

So why did you let her walk into danger? he thought to himself now as he hurried the last steps across towards Anna's house. *You knew she was taking risks. Why didn't you stop her?*

But as he grew close enough to see the number on Anna's little green front door, and the net curtains in the blank windows, he realised that there was a simple answer to that: he hadn't wanted to risk Anna retreating from him. He'd been afraid of driving her away – again – and so he'd kept quiet and played along.

He found himself in front of the door, less than twenty-four hours since he'd last stood here but with a very different feeling coursing through him. He didn't really expect his knock to be answered this time, but he still made a point of picking up the hinged brass knocker and rapping it three times.

He was very aware of the sounds around him as he waited: of the rhythmic *thock* of tennis balls at the courts close by on the green. Of a group of students talking on the grass. Of riotous birdsong, and a hum of background traffic.

From inside the house, however, there was nothing. With a sick feeling, he pulled out one of the two shiny brass Yale keys he'd been given by the lettings agent. They'd agreed that he would keep one, in case she needed him to pick something up for her. But he'd never yet had to use it, and the idea of letting himself into his daughter's space made him feel uncomfortable.

A sudden, awful thought occurred to him at that point: that she might be here, but not answering because she had company. Could she have stumbled back home with someone after the ball?

Seaton imagined a half-naked, muscular male student standing in the hallway, and he winced. He bunched the keys into his fist and hammered on the green-painted front door, a no-nonsense sound much harder to ignore than the knocker. He waited another minute and still gave it another sharp rap before he eventually let himself in. Even then, he felt it necessary to call out once the door was a few inches open, and then again when it was open all the way. He remembered, just in time, to call her Aria. His anxiety was making rational thought challenging.

There was silence within the house. His view inside was of the slightly dim hallway, and it was empty of life. It did, however, contain Anna's backpack, which was leaning up against the wall. On the coat rack there was a range of jackets, the mid-sized Staud shoulder-bag she wore when required to be slightly more formal, and beneath them a selection of sports shoes, heels and everything in between. None of them had been left in any kind of order.

Seaton moved past them, heading for the large living room, which at least had only a few cups, plates and books scattered around, along with a vase of wilted flowers from Seaton's own garden that she'd failed to put enough water in. He tried not to take their unloved state personally. This was just how she was.

When Anna had moved in here, Seaton had arranged for a cleaner to come in two days a week, acutely aware that she might be hosting the Pitt Club group here. Anna had been outraged by the idea at first. Having someone clean offended all her ideas of independence, personal space and social equality. But she'd later admitted that it was actually wonderful when the pragmatic Moira come in to just *sort* everything, and she wasn't sure how she was going to manage once she went back to her London flat and had to do it all herself.

'She puts laundry on,' Anna told him, early on. 'And then she *hangs it out.* Like, immediately. Without it having to go through another two times because you forgot to take it out and it reeks. I'm not sure she's actually a human being.'

Seaton moved through to Anna's study-bedroom, which was pure chaos. The bed was unmade, the thick down duvet and pillows piled up in total disarray and the sheet half off. Any visions he'd had of being able to tell whether she'd slept in it died a death. Anna was obviously not someone who ever made her bed, which he should have predicted.

He looked for other clues to interpret instead. Her desk, which she'd propped a mirror on, had a jumble of cosmetics. Although he wasn't familiar with the specifics, Seaton recognised the brands: Dior. Yves Saint Laurent. Helena Rubinstein. He knew that Anna hadn't used them for her May Ball make-up routine, at any rate. He'd paid for her to have her hair and make-up done in town by a stylist. He'd been impressed at how Hollywood she'd looked afterwards, though he'd also been a little disturbed at how unlike his daughter she'd suddenly been. As if she'd been replaced by a glamour model or an actress.

What was missing from the desk was Anna's laptop, which usually sat there, whenever she hadn't carried it out to some coffee shop or taken it to London with her. Seaton found himself frowning at the empty space. Was it downstairs, perhaps? In her backpack? Or at the kitchen table?

A quick hunt showed him that it was in none of those places. And that added to his worry considerably. It might be password protected, with hidden files, but it wouldn't be impossible to break into.

It would be a disaster, Seaton thought with a rush of cold. *Everything she'd found out . . . Who she was . . .*

He tried to stop himself panicking. To think rationally. She might have taken it somewhere, but he was certain she wouldn't have taken it along to the May Ball. The photo she'd sent from the queue had shown her holding only a black-and-silver handbag to match her dress, with a pair of hot-pink shoes poking out of the top. Flat shoes for later in the night, he'd guessed.

Did she come back here? he thought. *Did she wake up normally, start working and stumble onto something, then forget about meeting me because she was pursuing it?*

It was the kind of thing she'd do, but she'd have taken her phone with her. Her real one.

Pulling his own mobile out again, he rang her original number. For a moment, there was no sound – and then he heard an unmistakable buzz from somewhere upstairs.

He felt his heart squeeze as he hurried to the first floor, chasing the sound until he found its hiding place: a Prada sunglasses box in the bottom of her wardrobe. He had to slide all of her dresses to one side to see it, and crouch down to pick the box up.

With the phone in his hand he began to feel a real, creeping sense of fear. It was here, and she was not.

And into his subconscious crept the other thing he hadn't quite registered along the way.

The dress, he thought. *The dress isn't here.*

The Dolce & Gabbana dress that Anna had spent a fortune on – *his* fortune on – and which she'd been wearing when he'd last seen her – it wasn't here.

Which meant that Anna had gone to the ball and had never made it home.

5. Anna

One and a half weeks later I was walking into a Cambridge college with a whole new identity, all ready to crash a party hosted by Kit Frankland and Esther Thomas: two of the four people Holly had been with the night she died.

I'd already found out as much as I could about the four of them during the preceding days. Cordelia and I had met up several times in the American Bar of the Savoy Hotel, selected by her because it was convenient when she was on her way to or from her mother's house or the centre of the city, and because nobody connected was likely to be there. And by the way, Reid, that place has *the* most intensely patterned carpet I have ever experienced, and looks about as un-American a place as you can imagine. Major colonial British vibes.

'I have to warn you,' she told me during our first mini interview, 'that I don't have any inside information on them now. After what happened, I asked them all a lot of questions.' She pulled a face, looking down into her coffee. The tables in there are all shiny gold, which I do *not* understand. Who the hell wants to look down and discover what the underside of their chin looks like? I'd covered my side of the table with my laptop case to make sure I didn't catch sight of it by mistake. 'They one by one stopped talking to me, and then it became a united front, and that was it.'

'I'm sorry,' I said, trying not to wonder if she was looking at her drink or her warped reflection. 'That sounds tough.'

Cordelia shrugged. 'In some ways, it made it easier. The

decision to leave Cambridge and come to UCL. Which was the right thing to do.'

I watched the set of her jaw as she said it, and I wondered if she really thought that, but I felt like I should leave difficult subjects and focus on the actual job.

'Tell me about the four of them, then. As much as you know.'

And, in fact, Cordelia knew a lot. Kit Frankland was, by her account, the ringleader of the group: the handsome, charming, athletic and effortlessly clever son of a highly successful City lawyer who'd gathered them all together. He studied law at Downing, played rugby for the university, and allegedly socialised for England.

'He also, in my opinion, likes to collect damaged people,' she added. 'He could easily have made friends with whoever he wanted, and on the surface of it, he selected people with status. But in reality, there were a lot of other students with status who he just wasn't interested in, and I think it's because they weren't fragile enough for his liking.'

I narrowed my eyes at her. 'You think he likes to feel better than they are?'

Cordelia considered this, and said, 'Maybe. I think he definitely gets a kick out of feeling like he can make their lives better, but I wonder whether that's also to do with control.'

I nodded, thinking about this. Holly had definitely counted as a girl who was damaged. She'd been orphaned and had lost a friend to drugs. She was also a misfit in their group. She would have been easy for him to manipulate if that was what he'd wanted.

'Esther is his right-hand woman,' Cordelia had gone on. 'Huge mummy issues. Single-parent upbringing, and her mother is an ultra-ambitious member of the UN General Secretariat who likes to tell Esther she's not good enough.'

I winced. I'd met parents like this at numerous events. The kind who thought their children should live their lives to fulfil their own ambitions.

'I guess she's a lot less confident than Kit?' I asked.

'Rigidly self-controlled,' Cordelia said. 'And a tough one to crack. Esther liked Holly, but I think she found my friendship with her a threat.'

'She and Kit aren't together?' I asked Cordelia, scrolling through social media photos of Kit and Esther. They appeared time and again, but interestingly there were also other group shots where Kit's arm would be slung possessively round one of a series of petite brunettes; girls with dimples and a less flawless veneer.

'No, it's never been like that,' Cordelia replied. 'They're not each other's type. Kit likes them little, brunette and exuberant. Whereas Esther is super together and collected, and wants . . . well, I think she finds it hard to decide what she wants because her dearest mama is so set on her marrying a rich boy with status. But I've never seen her look at Kit as anything more than a brother figure.'

This all made sense of the fact that a young woman named Sarah Lafferty seemed to crop up in a lot of Kit's recent photos. She was presumably the latest of the petite, exuberant brunettes. She was easy enough to find online. Her social media taught me that she listened to a lot of Taylor Swift and watched tennis of all kinds, so at least we'd have something to talk about if I met her at the party.

'Esther was the first one to tell me I wasn't welcome in the group any more,' Cordelia added. 'I was suspicious of her at first, but later I thought . . . well, she took Holly's death incredibly hard and I don't think she knew how to deal with questions about it. Difficult to know what's underneath when everyone grieves in different ways.'

Ain't that the truth, Reid?

'James was more straightforward,' Cordelia went on. 'He's always been pretty emotionally open. After Holly died, he was angry at everyone and everything, and he basically oscillated between wanting to listen to my questions and storming off, like it was too much.' She shrugged. 'He seemed to me absolutely like someone who was hurting and didn't know what to do with the feeling.'

I got where Cordelia was coming from, not least because the anger and shutting down sounded a lot like your coping mechanism. But I also had other thoughts about James Sedgewick.

However much I understood the bereaved urge to lash out, I also knew the figures on how often women are killed by their romantic partners. Anger can be down to many things, and one of those is guilt. But it sounded like Cordelia had decided he was innocent, so any of that was a conversation for another day.

'How about Ryan?' I asked instead.

Cordelia considered this. 'He stopped socialising half as much after she died. He was always out, before. He'd hit bars with Kit's crowd, and then go out with the rugby guys the rest of the time. But then in third year, after Holly, he was suddenly staying in and working. I don't know if he's still like that, but it clearly hit him somehow.'

I logged this, too, as equally likely to be guilt or grief. I was intrigued to see how the four were now, and whether any of these emotions still told on them almost a year later. The party wouldn't necessarily provide instant access to their innermost thoughts, but it would tell me something about how well they were coping on the surface.

My sort-of invitation to the party had been engineered by Cordelia's older brother Luca, by the way, who used to be a Pitt Club guy himself and still gets invited to student parties.

I wasn't too keen when Cordelia first suggested him being the one to introduce me.

'It would be a great idea if he weren't related to you,' I told her. 'But if they think I'm some friend of yours, after they pretty much excommunicated you for asking too many questions . . .'

But Cordelia shook her head. 'Luca doesn't have the same surname, and looks nothing like me. Better still, back while he was at Cambridge we weren't really talking. I think I *may* have written him a letter formally disowning him because of his chosen career path and morals.'

'What does he do?' I asked, intrigued. 'Conservative MP?'

She laughed. 'He's in finance. Which is almost as bad. I told him exactly how many people were killed every year by the hoarding of wealth.'

I couldn't help laughing at that, and Cordelia looked momentarily offended. 'Sorry. I just . . . I love that you wrote to disown him. I would literally rather die than admit I was angry with someone.' I shook my head. 'It's . . . impressive. And I basically want to be you when I grow up.'

'Oh god, don't be like me,' she said, shaking her head. 'It makes friendships hard work. I've had to learn to ease up on my principles sometimes and . . . you know. Accept people for what they are.'

It was funny. I'd been thinking how alike Cordelia and I were, but right then I realised that she actually reminded me of you, Reid. Because although we'd both lost people and got a little hooked on finding out the truth, her way of looking at morality is a lot closer to yours than mine. She is a person of absolutes.

Even the thorough, clinical way she'd analysed everything to do with Holly's death was your style. Obsessive, yes, but not in the random-ideas-and-leads way I looked at things: it was the dogged, checking-all-the-bases way you work.

Learning that you worked like that surprised me about you, you know. Because the way we talk ridiculous crap and make jokes that go off at weird tangents is so similar. I kind of thought you'd work the same way I did.

But we're chalk and cheese: me all diverting round corners, and you straight down the line. And yet you're so damn smart with it. The first rule-following, structure-and-systems person I've ever met who I've thought was seriously clever.

Sorry, this was a digression. I was talking about getting to that party.

The one other piece of planning I'd done with Cordelia had been about my way into the group. Both Cordelia and Gael had been adamant that I needed to basically seduce one of them.

'They're about to leave university,' Gael had told me, with breezy pragmatism. 'They won't care about making new friends at this point. But if you're a possible girlfriend, they'll care.'

And I know, I know, Reid. I know this is the stuff that's most distasteful about my job. I hated that it had to work like that, too, but I felt beaten down by their logic.

So I listened as Cordelia told me my target should be Ryan Jaffett.

'He used to be a full-on fukboi . . . umm . . . womaniser, you know,' she said in a rare moment of what looked like embarrassment. 'But then during second year he seemed to just get tired of it all and he really sorted himself out. It's very clear he really wants a proper girlfriend. Plus his type is posh but a bit alternative and, ideally, sporty.' She gave me a luminous grin. 'He's going to *love* you.'

I found myself hoping fiercely that she was right as I walked into Downing College towards the party. I at least felt the part of Aria Lauder, in a very short and very casual-looking bohemian dress Cordelia had picked out ('*Nobody* dresses up for anything unless they have to.') and with a strong application of the obligatory eyeliner and strings of little necklaces that the young women with money here wore. Cordelia and I had already discussed at length that I needed to cue rich as well as different, and I hoped I was getting it right.

Tonight wasn't really the first test of my persona as I'd already engineered a few coffees and encounters in Jesus College, where I was supposedly a postgrad. But it still felt like the first real hurdle. All the bedding-in meant nothing if I couldn't convince these four friends to let me close.

I felt my adrenaline rising a little as I made my way into the grounds of Downing College. It's one of those places that is designed to intimidate. Big, neoclassical buildings around a huge grass lawn. It's actually very reminiscent of Columbia, though on a smaller scale, which was unhelpful just then, given how much I'd struggled to fit in there.

But I reminded myself that I'd become a very different person to the Anna who walked onto campus at eighteen. I've taken people down by charming them and seeing through them. I've been in dangerous situations and brazened my way out of them. I wasn't going to let a bunch of undergrads make me feel anxious.

Luca had sent directions to Kit and Esther's building, and I followed them with as much performative certainty as I could manage. The music from their party became audible by the time I was a hundred yards away, and I could see a few people milling around on the grass at the back. That was the advantage of a ground-floor room, I figured: easy access to the grass outside through the windows. Though I suspected this wasn't something the porters would endorse. College lawns were, I'd learned, sacred spaces, reserved for fellows and high-ranking college staff only.

The main door to the building was locked, so I had to wait until a couple exited to slip inside. After that, I followed the sound to an open doorway at the back.

The party turned out to be a mass of people crammed into the sitting room of Kit and Esther's 'set'. I'd never come across this term before Cordelia used it, but a set was simply two student rooms which were linked by a living area. And of course, this being the abode of two students from generational wealth, it was pretty big, beautifully decorated, and had candles scattered around in a genuine fire-hazard kind of a way.

I took a minute to hover in the doorway on arrival, semi-transfixed at the fashion choices going on. Cordelia had explained in detail that the last few years had really shifted female fashion towards dressing down, but it was fascinating to see in the flesh. It was almost all wide-leg trousers and chunky shoes, unbrushed hair and big, owlish glasses. A few of the young women or non-binary crew were sporting A Look, with frills and fishnets, but the only people who looked formal in any way were a few of the guys who were inexplicably still wearing chinos and shirts, as though the last fifty years hadn't happened.

The other thing Cordelia had explained to me was how little the students actually partied these days: how historic drinking societies had folded since Covid lockdowns had broken with tradition; how few of them partied hard; and how many of them preferred to stay in and craft.

It was a good thing she'd warned me about the crafting thing, actually, because otherwise I might not have known how to deal with the sight of someone sitting on the arm of a chair, in the midst of a student party, crocheting something and barely making conversation.

What Cordelia had stressed, though, was that Kit, Esther,

Ryan – and to some extent James – *did* party. They were some of the few who had arrived at the university with a clear mission to enjoy themselves. And that meant a lot of other people ended up getting drawn towards them. Hedonism with a plan is always kind of magnetic, particularly if you were never the type of kid at school who went out and partied, which I'd guess was most of the others here.

It was already crazy hot and extremely crowded by the time I slid in through the door with an offering of Absolut Elyx vodka. It wasn't a brand I'd even heard of, but Cordelia had handed me the bottle the day before, in the know even about this despite being a non-drinker herself. And isn't that in itself fascinating, Reid? That she's twenty-one and *British* and teetotal? And not even alone among her peers?

'They don't do Smirnoff,' she'd said with one of her wry grins. 'Just don't ask me how it tastes.'

Even standing in the doorway, I was wondering where I could go to get more air. I could see in glimpses that the large Georgian windows of the living room were wide open, which was how everyone had been getting out onto the grass. There were (I saw later) bare patches on the paintwork of the window frames where someone – Kit or Esther, presumably – had unscrewed the security locks.

I'd been hovering there for maybe a minute before the familiar face of Cordelia's brother emerged through the throng. I only knew Luca from photographs, but he stood out pretty clearly. It wasn't just that he was older, with very slightly receding hair at his temples; it was also the totally corporate air of the guy. He looked absolutely not like a student.

Luca caught sight of me and slid through the crowd with his glasses flashing and a beaming grin, doing what I had to admit was a great job of looking like he knew me.

'Hey, Aria. So glad you came,' he said, as though we'd known each other for years. Such corporate bullshit, and so useful just then.

He took me by the arm, and dragged me into a conversation with an incredibly monomaniacal law student who must have been only eighteen, and then, shortly afterwards, smoothly caught the elbow of Esther Thomas as she squeezed past.

I could feel my heartbeat pick up at the sight of her. It was a little bit about anxiety, but also excitement. I was bored with prepping and wanted to meet the guys I'd been poring over at last.

'You look bloody fabulous, as always,' Luca said, leaning in to kiss her.

'Thanks, Luca,' Esther said without any real warmth.

I got the impression from their interactions, actually, that Luca had a bit of a soft spot for Esther. But for whatever reason, Luca wasn't what Esther wanted. Which was interesting, given Cordelia's comments about her being pushed to marry for money and status. Didn't Luca have both?

Esther's glance fell on me after that, and Luca asked if we knew each other.

'Don't think so,' Esther said, just loudly enough to be heard over the music.

'Aria Lauder? She's an English postgrad at Jesus. Also an amazing rower, but don't let her hear you say it or she'll be insufferable,' Luca said easily.

Esther gave me a searching, considering look and then smiled very slightly. When she did, it was hard to look away. I found her immediately compelling, in the same way that an exquisite statue is compelling. My eyes kept wanting to go over and over her features, and over the short, impeccably styled hair. She was undeniably beautiful, but I was also instinctively looking for the real person under there. She was so poised, so polished, that it was almost impossible to read more. It was like any analysis kept glancing off.

'Do you know any of the third-year English students at Jesus?' Esther asked me. 'My friend Tilly's there.'

It was only a polite comment, I was sure. An attempt to find connections. But I was suddenly very aware of how thin my facade of being a student was. And even more aware of the little recording device I was wearing underneath the dress.

Luca, totally unfazed, gave a laugh. 'No chance. Even the postgrads hardly see her. She's always fucking rowing.'

I couldn't help grinning at him, while pretending to be outraged. He was a natural at this.

'I do talk to people *sometimes*,' I protested. 'When they're not being boring.'

I felt as though I'd somehow slid past the difficult moment and into my character. It's always better after the first lie's been told. Just like I always used to feel more comfortable after I'd delivered my first line in a college play or spoken my first words in a debate speech.

Esther asked me a few questions that I answered easily. Fluently. She spoke to me for long enough to find out about my apparent family, and she warmed up a little more. Clearly I'd passed some kind of social status test as far as she was concerned. She even got a blandly handsome boy – Cosimo, maybe? The recording isn't clear – to make me a cocktail. I wondered whether this was, in fact, a boyfriend, but she seemed uninterested in what happened to him once he went to make the drinks.

I would have gone on to ask her about what she did, as though I didn't already know she was a social and political sciences student, but a figure I recognised as Kit Frankland pushed through the crowd.

I found my eyes locking onto him, and felt as if he'd caught me out. For a moment I genuinely thought he was about to eject me from the party for being a fraud.

But instead of looking my way he drew Esther aside with only a brief glance in my direction.

Calm the heck down, I thought, taking a very large mouthful of sickly-sweet cocktail. *They're just a bunch of kids at a party.*

But I found my eyes following them and saw Kit glance back at me again as Esther said something. I gave him a small smile, the kind of smile you might give if you were aware you were standing in someone's room, and then I turned to grin at Luca.

'I'm so glad I made it out,' I told him. 'It's genuinely nice to see you.'

Luca gave me a nod and said quietly, 'I'll give it a minute before I do any more intros. You good?'

'I'm good,' I said.

And he turned to talk to someone next to him in such a way that I could almost look like I was involved without having to be.

I half watched them, but glanced over towards Kit and Esther again repeatedly. Their eyes were no longer on me, which helped ease my ridiculous anxiety. They were huddled together with someone, and as I shifted slightly I realised it was Sarah Lafferty, Kit's girlfriend.

I watched him hand something to each of them. They both put their hands to their mouths straight afterwards, swiftly and subtly.

A tab, I thought. *MDMA, maybe? They're getting high.*

I made sure I was looking anywhere else after that, as the last thing I wanted to do was get caught watching them take it. But it interested me that Kit had a supply of drugs. I wondered if he was essentially acting as a dealer to the others. If so, that might make him more likely to be the one to have drugged Holly with ketamine.

I thought, too, about how Cordelia had ended up ostracised by the group. He could have engineered that just as readily if he'd been worried he'd get exposed as a dealer. There was a huge threat to his career – as well as his place here at the university – if the wrong people found out.

What if they do actually work out the connection between Cordelia and Luca? I thought, suddenly.

I detached from him and moved towards the stereo system. If they saw me with other people they wouldn't associate me with Luca too closely.

The stereo system was, obviously, elaborate and clearly expensive. Pale oak tower speakers on either side of the two windows and a huge sub-woofer next to a desk on which someone had perched both an amplifier and a laptop. There was a tall, broad figure hunched over it, strawberry-blond head nodding to the beat, and it was only as I got closer that I recognised him as Ryan Jaffett.

I came to a stop, figuring I'd take an opportunity to watch him while he was engrossed, but it turned out Ryan was more anxious about what everyone thought of his tastes than he wanted to let on. He glanced up and around the room and caught my eye.

It's too early to talk to him, I thought, giving Ryan a vague smile and letting my gaze slide away. *You can't seem like you're here to move in on them all.*

I tipped my glass back and turned to ask one of the girls next to me if she knew where the bathrooms were. It took two goes for her to hear me, long enough for it to hopefully seem like a proper conversation. Enough for Ryan to lose any interest and go back to lining up playlists.

But when I squeezed my way towards the door I found

Ryan standing right in front of it, his gaze boring into me. He was *so* much taller than I'd realised, taller than me in my heels, and intimidatingly powerful-looking in his tight T-shirt.

I felt my stomach twist as he stared down at me.

'And where do you think you're going?'

6. Seaton

It became increasingly obvious to Seaton that he needed the police. Step by step, he was exhausting every avenue he could think of.

While at Anna's house, he messaged to ask James if he knew where she was. James was the one member of that group who he knew independently, and whose number he had. Of course, as far as James knew, Anna was his god-daughter rather than his daughter, but it wasn't unreasonable to be concerned about a no-show for lunch.

James replied quickly, but with a message that made Seaton's heart twist.

> She left the ball pretty early with some friend of hers. Kit's been trying to call her too, but she's not replying. We haven't seen her since eleven last night. Hopefully she's just crashed out, hung-over.

A few seconds later, he messaged again to ask if Seaton needed help tracking her down. Seaton was already messaging back to ask who the friend she'd left with was. But James's reply was more than disappointing.

> Sorry, I don't know him. Saw the two of them at a distance and honestly couldn't tell you. Are things ok?

Seaton tried to still his anxiety while he thought for a minute, and then messaged:

> Thank you. Could you ask around? A bit worried for her. Call me if you hear anything, please.

He stepped outside the house, and paused. Should he be saying more? Should he be insisting that he needed a description of this friend, and an exact account of where Anna had been and how she'd seemed?

Perhaps he should call Philip Sedgewick, too. Ask him to step in. He was the sort of person who always, always knew what to do in a crisis.

But he stopped short with his phone in his hand, too afraid of bringing Anna's whole house of cards crashing down. Something that would be terrible for him, and possibly dangerous for her.

What *should* he be doing? He was standing on her doorstep now, immobile, and he had to act.

He wanted to try calling that temporary phone of hers again but he was worried about that, too. If she'd ended up stuck somewhere, he might just drain her battery. And if she was hiding, he'd only bring attention to her.

Just as he lifted his head from his phone with a sigh, he caught sight of a retreating figure striding away towards town. It looked, he thought, like Kit Frankland, dressed in a polo shirt and jeans.

He tried to make out the young man's profile as he turned the corner of the terrace, but he still wasn't sure. All he'd seen of Kit was a series of photographs on Anna's laptop, and the figure wasn't close enough for his features to be clear.

And surely if it *was* Kit, he'd be here trying to track Anna down. He would have knocked on the door. Wouldn't he?

Seaton hesitated and then decided it was time to make all this official. He had an old university acquaintance who was an assistant chief constable at Cambridgeshire Constabulary. He was the man for this.

Gerry and he hadn't exactly been close, but when your daughter was missing, a high-ranking officer was exactly the kind of man you wanted on your side.

Seaton's call was answered by some admin clerk who told him they couldn't put him through to specific officers if Seaton didn't know their extension. They were then particularly obtuse about passing on a message.

So Seaton decided to go to the station in person. He'd file a missing persons report, he decided, then ask to see Gerry and have it prioritised.

The first thing that went wrong was the wait. By the time he'd sat for thirty-five minutes in a stifling-hot reception area at the police station, with the dehydrating effects of the lunchtime champagne kicking in and increasing levels of real hunger, his anxiety had morphed into anger.

When he was then faced with a slow-moving constable who took almost ten minutes just to take down basic details, he found himself snapping.

'Look, is there someone more senior I can talk to?' he'd said, his voice tight. Irritable. 'This really is quite urgent.'

The constable, a man probably in his late twenties, had raised an eyebrow at him. 'This will obviously go to someone more senior, and if your daughter is deemed high risk, it'll be treated urgently.'

'Well, of course she's high risk,' he snapped. 'As I said, she was undercover, in the middle of investigating a murder. She was last seen with the people who killed a young woman last year.'

'So you said,' the constable replied. 'I just need to go through the process . . .'

'Look, I'm sure there are faster ways,' Seaton said, before the constable could go on. 'I'm a Cambridge fellow and a friend of Gerry Siegland's. You just ring him, and I'll explain this to him. I'm sure he'll understand the urgency.'

For Seaton's entire life, his position in the university had opened doors. It had gained him respect. But for some reason, as the constable looked up from his iPad, Seaton felt a shiver of uncertainty. Because the PC wasn't looking at him with respect. Instead there was . . . something else.

'Sorry,' the officer said with a very forced-sounding politeness, 'do you mean the former assistant chief constable?'

'What?'

'Former Assistant Chief Constable Siegland?' the PC asked flatly.

'I . . . I had no idea he'd retired,' Seaton said, feeling his uncertainty growing.

There was a flicker around the PC's eyes, and Seaton was suddenly certain that Gerry Siegland had not, in fact, retired. That there had been some kind of scandal.

'Perhaps there's someone else . . .?' he tried.

He saw the way the PC's mouth tightened and he knew he'd played this wrong.

You've messed this up, he thought. *Why couldn't you actually keep in touch with these people? You would have known about Gerry.*

But he hadn't kept in touch with Gerry because Gerry was an obnoxious, bullying ass. With a sinking sensation, Seaton imagined the kind of trouble Gerry might have got himself into in a position of authority. The kind of trouble Seaton now appeared to be associated with.

After a brief pause, the PC said – in a very measured voice that Seaton suspected was an attempt to hide disgust – 'Everyone who comes into the station will be listened to with respect, no matter who they know. Your daughter's case will be taken as seriously as it needs to be.'

But it became clear that it *wasn't* being taken seriously. That Seaton had lost credibility with the PC, and that he'd lost it further when the PC presumably caught a whiff of the champagne on his breath and asked him if he'd been drinking, to which Seaton stiffly admitted that he had.

It only got worse when the constable tried to ask him where Anna might have gone. Who she might have contacted. And Seaton had to admit, with a miserable sense of shame, that he didn't know. That he only had one contact number for someone she'd been investigating – James's number – and her editor's phone number. That was it.

'With the two of you being . . . not all that close,' the PC said after a pause, 'is it possible that she just decided she didn't want to see you? She is twenty-six.'

'But we *are* close now,' Seaton objected angrily. 'I keep explaining. She's been updating me with all this, and that ball – she was in danger!'

'*The college May Ball*,' the PC had read back to him. 'A social event she went to with this group of friends? The ones you want us to pretend she's called Aria to?'

And Seaton could tell that he'd lost.

He was ejected from the station shortly afterwards with a very clear idea of what was going to be done to find his daughter: nothing. Nothing at all. A form filled in somewhere and no action taken.

He'd failed her. That was what he now realised with a terrible, heavy certainty. He'd failed her both by not keeping up with the right kind of people and by not being close enough to her.

He'd failed her before that, really. From the moment he'd admitted to her mother that he didn't love her, and was sure he never could. Failed her again when he'd let her mother walk away instead of asking what she intended on doing.

He'd probably failed Anna again a hundred times since. All the times he'd considered flying over to visit on a whim but been too afraid of a hostile reception. Over the money her mother and stepfather had refused to take, leading to Anna growing up too proud to take *anything* from him unless he hid it somehow. And by his inability to really talk to her as an adult now that she'd chosen to come back to England.

And he'd failed her last night, when he'd let her walk into that ball without backup or protection.

He was now standing beside the great, open expanse of Parker's Piece, facing full into the bright June sun, with no memory of having crossed over the road from the police station. He closed his eyes against the glare.

This is your fault, he thought. *Now what are you going to do to fix it?*

By the time he opened his eyes again he'd remembered that he still had Anna's phone. The phone he'd meant to tell the police about but had lost track of in the mess of the questions he'd had no answer to.

If he could just unlock the thing it would probably track her other device. The one she'd used as Aria. Knowing how useless she was at keeping track of objects, he was confident she'd have risked adding them both to her Apple account and would have assumed nobody would find out. If he could just get into the phone, he might be able to find her – assuming, that was, that the phone was still on her.

He had a sudden, horrifying image of her lifeless body being bundled into the river. Weighted down this time so nobody could find her. Killed because she'd found out too much and had never known when to back off.

Stop it, he thought, squeezing his eyes shut. *You can find her. You can find her.*

He remembered, in a vivid rush, Anna sitting at her laptop in his kitchen on one of the nights when she'd stayed over. He remembered asking her, 'What are you doing?'

And then her half-focused reply, eyes still on the screen, 'I'm writing to Reid.'

It had startled him, that response. 'Why?'

'Because I was right about everything, and he was wrong.'

Seaton had stood watching over her shoulder. He'd read a little of what she'd been pouring out into the email and it had made his heart ache.

In the end he'd said gently, 'Listen. Break-ups are . . . they're hard. Sometimes the hardest things. Like grieving, really. But . . . nobody *owes* you being in a relationship with them. And they don't owe you any of their time once they've broken it off, either.'

He remembered how she'd stopped typing and had given a long sigh. 'I'm not asking him to change his mind, Dad. I'm telling him about all of this. The Holly stuff. All the *other things* . . . I'll edit them out. It's just cathartic.'

Seaton had nodded, hoping she was being honest with him. 'Why are you telling him about Holly?'

'Because I know he'd do something about it if everything went wrong,' she'd said, and looked up at him with an unusually vulnerable expression. 'And it's good to have a backup, in case. You know.'

Seaton had sat himself next to her. 'You do realise I'm . . . you know. Happy to be your backup.'

Anna had half smiled. 'I know. But it's also good to have someone who can start a full-scale manhunt if they need to.'

Remembering the phrase felt like a punch in the stomach. She'd known, on some level, hadn't she? She'd understood what she'd stirred up. And a full-scale manhunt was what he now needed.

But Reid Murray? he thought with a surge of anger. *The man who broke her heart over nothing?*

Anna hadn't told him everything about their break-up – their relationship didn't have the kind of easy openness for that. But Seaton had been the one to pick up the pieces when Reid had dumped her without warning, and what little she *had* told him had made him want to drive round to Reid's house and lay the man out.

Of course he was biased towards his daughter, but how had Reid believed all those things? How had he decided that Anna had betrayed him, and cared only about her career?

Reid hadn't been the man she'd thought. That was clear. He'd let her down, badly, at a time when she'd already been fragile. He wouldn't have blamed her for hating him.

So why did she write to him?

It made him feel angry on her behalf, that she'd still chosen Reid when he'd let her down so completely. And perhaps angry on his own, that she'd picked Reid over him. But on some level he knew why: she'd written because she still trusted him. Even after everything he'd done.

He found himself pulling his phone out once again, poised on the verge of doing something that might be exactly what Anna had wanted . . . or might be a huge betrayal of her trust.

If she hadn't sent the email to him, and she hadn't spoken to him in a year and a half, did he really have the right to call Reid in?

But if she never had the chance to send it I might be the only one who can do the right thing, he thought.

And with a sigh he unlocked his phone.

'You'd better not let her down again,' he muttered to himself, as he searched for Reid's number.

7. Anna

I think the moment when Ryan stood a fraction closer than I wanted, waiting for me to reply, was the first moment in all this that I felt afraid.

It's a hard thing to really explain to anyone who's never experienced it: how much the size and presence and aura of a guy can cut through all the layers of social assumption you've learned and make you realise that you'd be powerless if he wanted to hurt you. Totally powerless.

Even in a room full of people.

I guess it's in some ways lucky that we're all of us used to appeasing when under threat. My instinctive reaction when challenged on where I was going was not to give anything away to him but to laugh and say, 'Well, I may be going home. But that depends.'

Ryan listened to my answer, glanced around, and then said, 'You should stay. You haven't even talked to me yet.'

He gave me a grin, and I realised that the way he'd accosted me had been an effort at flirting. He hadn't been accusing me of anything, or trying to scare me.

I let out a breath that I hoped he couldn't see was shaky.

I caught his eye, I thought to myself. *This is a good thing.*

Cordelia had clearly been right about his type.

I gathered myself together and managed to say, 'I might be persuaded if you're going to be fascinating enough.'

'Well, I'll . . . do my best.' Ryan gave a laugh, and the admission that he wasn't infallible was somehow a little touching. 'To start with, let me get you a drink.'

'Oh, that's . . .' I glanced towards the crush of people near the drinks, considered and then gave in with a smile. 'I wouldn't mind one.'

'OK. Don't go anywhere,' he said, and headed to the drinks table.

Obviously, I fleetingly thought about the dangers of taking a drink from a strange man who might be a poisoner, but dismissed my anxieties pretty quickly. He didn't know who I was and would be an idiot to drug someone at a comparatively small party.

I came a little way back into the room, and caught Luca's eye. He raised his eyebrows, clearly checking in, so I gave him an 'All OK' smile.

And then Ryan reappeared, squeezing in that little bit closer than most people would have done. It was less intimidating this time, and seemed more about an attempt at cosying up to me. Or just a lack of awareness of personal space maybe.

I thought about Cordelia's description of Ryan as a reformed womaniser and wondered whether he wasn't so great at social cues. Whether he got himself a bad rep by getting things like personal space that little bit wrong. I'd worked with a guy like this in the past, and at first felt uncomfortable and then after a while sorry for him as I'd realised he just didn't understand.

But anyway. I took the glass – which had what looked like another Margarita in it – and then thought about how easy it would have been for him to lift a petite woman like Holly Moore into the river, and I felt the hairs rising on my arms.

'Thank you,' I said.

'It's the full-fat version,' Ryan said as I took a tiny sip. 'Real alcohol. In case you were, you know . . .'

I gave him a grin. 'That's OK. I'm drinking tonight. A little, anyway. No training tomorrow.'

'Oh, what training?' Ryan asked me, taking a big gulp of whatever he was drinking. Vodka tonic, maybe?

'Rowing.' I pulled a face. 'I'm back in again after an injury and it's boring as hell. Everything hurts.'

I watched his interest sharpen. Cordelia had been *so* spot-on. The sports stuff totally hooked him in.

Ryan quizzed me about the rowing, then started telling me about his rugby, and actually it turned into a decent conversation. And somehow, even though someone handed him another drink and asked if he was doing shots, we didn't break off.

'Why rugby?' I asked him, after a while. 'I mean, you'd make an amazing rower. Just saying.'

'I don't know,' he said, shrugging. 'I guess . . . my brother and I were always into it. And then he became this star player. He's playing for England now, you know?'

'Seriously?' I asked, and then, reading his expression, I added, 'What an asshole.'

Ryan gave a surprised laugh. 'That's . . . kind of how I feel about it. He's made it seem like any other success isn't good enough. At least, that's the way Dad talks about it.'

He shook his head, and I felt a weird little twist of sympathy. I realised that this kid had grown up with everything being handed to him financially, and yet felt . . . not good enough.

Well, there was at least one side of that which I understood. And Aria would have understood all of it.

'Tell me about it,' I said quietly. 'Try having a brother who's made it to the Senate before he's thirty. Particularly after I . . . You know. Left the US and came here.'

I deliberately sketched over the reasons for coming over here. At some point, if I got to know them better, someone was probably going to google me. And if they did, they'd find out about Aria being an addict.

The real Aria might have wanted to keep it quiet at first. But in the long run, it gave me something to confess. And an aura of vulnerability. Which would be helpful if Cordelia was right about Kit and his habit of collecting broken people.

It was that thought that made me look around for Kit, and I realised when I found him in the crowd that he was already watching me. So much for thinking he'd moved on to other things.

He held my gaze with an expression I couldn't read, and it gave me a slightly sick thrill of anxiety.

I was the one who looked away.

'. . . when you're doing Olympic rowing,' Ryan was saying, shaking his head. 'Surely your parents must stan that.'

I laughed, enjoying the sudden Gen-Z slang in his otherwise impeccably posh speech, all the while trying not to think about that gaze of Kit Frankland's. I'd prepped for this, anyway, and the words came easily enough. 'Oh. My mom thinks sport is frivolous. She thinks *I'm* frivolous, actually. And Dad has never understood how he managed to father anyone so disorganised and willing to make a spectacle of myself.'

Give them a story that's pretty much the truth, Reid. That's how to do this job.

'Sounds like our parents should hang out,' Ryan said with a weird, unhappy little smile. 'Mine could tell yours how important sport is and how they wished I was better at it. They could share anecdotes about our inadequacy.'

He gave a laugh, and drank suddenly, and I got the impression he was embarrassed at oversharing.

'They can hang out on an island somewhere,' I said. 'Fuck 'em. If they aren't proud of us, they're idiots. Look at us.' I raised my arms and gave him a brilliant smile. 'We're awesome.'

Ryan gave a slow smile, and then clinked his glass against mine, but whatever he opened his mouth to say next was lost to the arrival of a couple of older-looking guys. They bounded up to him, and one of them got Ryan into an almost immediate headlock.

I watched a switch go in Ryan. The unguarded, fragile side to him was immediately shut away, and he became a loud, bantering, backslapping *lad.* And it didn't take me long to realise why.

These were his older brother's friends. A pair of twenty-eight-year-old ex-rugby-playing lawyers.

It was easy enough playing along with their noisy camaraderie. I recognised their type more readily than I did the rest of the students here. I'd had to flirt with enough guys like this during my time.

They were the kind who would continue to be hard-drinking, slightly bullying wielders of power, and many of them would go on to break laws. And they would all of them be willing to share way too much to a spellbound, innocent-seeming young woman they were trying to impress.

One of the two (I can't even remember their names, Reid. I want to say Hector, maybe, but in my head they're all Hectors or Percies or something) – one of them went to get a cluster of shot glasses. Eight of them. They were full of tequila, and it was clear that I was expected to have two of them as well.

It slightly surprised me that Ryan held up a hand. 'Not really drinking tonight, fam.'

'That's simp talk,' the guy with the shots said. 'Seriously, take a look at yourself.'

I saw Ryan hesitate, and then take the two offered shots without more argument.

He can't stand up to them, I thought.

The shots were a clear end to our conversation. Ryan was too much into competitive drinking and rugby anecdotes now.

I slid away, not sure Ryan had even noticed, and looked

for a quick way to escape the crush. Which basically meant the window.

Getting over the windowsill was an interesting climb in a short dress, but I think I managed it without showing the *entire* room my newly bought (and actually quite nice, by the way, Reid) underwear.

It was a relief to be out there, away from my immediate worry that I wasn't going to be able to do what I came here to do. Ryan was supposed to be fascinated by me, not by some friends of his brothers.

I sighed and tried to breathe out the doubts. There were only a few students hanging around outside, despite the fact that the air was a wonderful temperature and you could still hear the music with perfect clarity. It was also beautiful out there, with that huge, open lawn and the colonnaded buildings around it.

I found a free spot along the wall between a couple of windows and leaned back against it. Should I just leave at this point? Try again on another occasion? But how many parties were there going to be? These guys had exams going on. Finals. They'd be studying more and partying less, and I only had three and a half weeks until the end of term, at which point I'd lose them all to home and vacations and future lives.

I needed them to let me in. Quickly.

I was on the point of braving the crush again, this time to go and talk to Kit, when a puff of exotic-fruit vape smoke made me glance around. I hadn't looked properly at any of the students out here, I guess partly because I figured I'd seen most of my targets inside. So it caught me a little by surprise to recognise the undeniably handsome face and long, floppy fringe of James Sedgewick from his social media photos.

I couldn't help taking a longer look. He was very much on his own, and seemed profoundly closed off to everyone else.

He had the look of someone who'd been on the verge of leaving for some while. There was a 'done with this' vibe to him.

I sensed a possible rift to exploit, and so I moved in. And, Reid, please don't try to pretend you wouldn't have talked to him, too. I know you, and you would have been in there as determinedly as I was.

'Jesus, it's hot in there,' I said to him after a second or two to gather my thoughts. 'I still don't understand why air conditioning can't be a thing around here.'

James gave a little snorting laugh and then said, 'It would ruin the authentic Cambridge experience. Remember, if it was good enough in 1760, it's good enough for us now.'

'True – why change?' I agreed. 'In fact, I'm shocked Kit doesn't have a live lute band. Kind of killing the vibe with his sound system.'

'Oh, but that's the thing,' James said, glancing over at me, and then away. 'Some of us still have to be the nobility, and some of us still have to be the plebs. Kit is the nobility. So he has towers made in Sweden from three-hundred-year-old oaks and . . .' He waved his hand, searching for an appropriate addition to this.

'Speakers crafted from moose gut?' I suggested. 'With electronic circuits put together by elves?'

James gave a smile. 'That kind of thing.'

The whole conversation gave me a deep feeling of satisfaction. It was clear that James felt disillusioned by his friend, and in that disillusionment there lay the chance of driving a wedge between them.

But as I was working out how to continue the conversation another male figure appeared through the window.

In sharp contrast with the awkward way I'd clambered out, he slid out through the opening athletically, all while holding what looked like a Tom Collins.

It was Kit Frankland. He probably jumped out of that window most days. Home advantage.

I was hoping he'd move off towards the other couple of people standing on the lawn, but he looked over towards us and then moved in.

'You OK, Jamie?' Kit asked as he closed in, but somehow I could tell his attention was actually on me.

Up close, I became aware of exactly how big he was. He might not have been a wide front-row rugby player like Ryan, but he was taller than I'd realised – probably six three – and clearly powerful. Despite the good-natured smile he was now gracing us with, I found myself thinking that I would go a long way to avoid getting in trouble with him.

'I'm good,' James told him, with what sounded like slight defensiveness. 'Just having a vape.'

Kit turned to me. 'Sorry, I don't know . . . Did you come with Luca?' I was sure Kit knew the answer to this already. I felt instinctively that what he'd really come to do was give me the third degree. I was an outsider, and that was, I guessed, dangerous.

I gave him a brilliant smile, and said, 'I did. I got talked into crashing. For some reason he thought it was a good idea for me to try an undergrad party.'

Kit shook his head slightly. 'Not just *an* undergrad party. This is *my* undergrad party,' he said. 'It's going to spoil all the other ones for you.'

'Oh, sorry,' I said. 'I should have realised. Is that what all the candles were for? Like, offerings for us to be grateful for your generosity?'

I said it with a grin, and Kit had the good grace to laugh. 'Exactly. We'll take whisky or blood sacrifices, depending.'

'Shit, I forgot the whisky.' I glanced towards the window. 'Given that . . . is there anyone you wouldn't miss? If I offed them?'

'Ha. Several people, actually.'

There was a sound from James at that: a short, impatient sigh.

'I'm heading off,' he said.

I turned towards him with a strange feeling of looking away from a bright light.

'Really? Already?' I asked. That was my plans busted. He seemed closed off now, and I realised that bantering with Kit had probably lost me ground.

That said, there is always power in making people feel like they have to compete for your attention. And again, Reid, I know you do this too. So quiet with the moral judgements.

'I should be revising,' James said. 'Nice to meet you . . .?'

'Aria,' I supplied. 'Nice to meet you, too.'

James glanced towards his friend, and then said with his eyes still on him, 'Don't let Kit talk you into anything stupid.'

Despite the slight smile, I felt like there was more to that statement than light-hearted fun. I thought inevitably of Holly, and I couldn't help a slight shiver as Kit said, 'But that's my one real skill.'

James didn't bother to go back into the party. He just drifted off across the lawn, heading for the front gates. His hands were in his jacket pockets and his head was down, a picture of sadness.

'I'm usually the one who leaves first,' I commented as I watched him go.

'Why's that?' Kit asked me.

'Early training,' I told him, looking back at him and secretly trying to assess whether this young man was really capable of murdering his friend.

I saw the way his interest picked up. 'Rower?' he asked.

'Good call,' I said. 'Exactly.'

'So . . . CUWBC?'

That, Reid, is the university women's boat club. And by the way, a lot of those young women go on to have professional rowing careers, so he wasn't undervaluing me.

'More national,' I told him. 'I'm on the high-performance programme.'

'Wow, nice.' Kit looked genuinely impressed by this. 'That's basically my dream. Only with rugby.'

'Oh, national stuff?'

Kit nodded. 'Five-year plan is to graduate then get a pupillage in some well-paying law firm while training so I have a backup. Probably get fired for not working enough hours . . .'

'Aren't you too pretty for professional rugby?' I asked him, grinning.

Kit laughed. 'I play at number seven. I don't have to get my face involved too often.'

'You could try using it as a distraction technique,' I suggested. 'I'm pretty sure that's how I've won several races. I get my game face on, it makes them laugh, they can't concentrate . . . I win.'

'OK, I need to see your game face now.'

'I can't just do it off the cuff,' I told him indignantly. 'I'd have to be competing at something.'

Kit looked around. 'We could do competitive jumping.'

'Oh, game on,' I said. 'Are we doing distance? From a standing start?'

'I think so,' he said. 'Given there's no bar to jump over.'

You will be able to predict entirely that at the prospect of a game to play I was totally all in and almost forgot what I was really there to do. Within seconds I was practising my crouching posture, planning how to get the best forward momentum, and working out whether I could sabotage Kit's chances.

'OK, I'm going to need some of your drink,' I told him, straightening up after a few moments.

Kit handed it to me without complaint, and I sank at least half of it before saying, 'Ready.'

Obviously, the game was enormous fun. I did, indeed, do my game face, which Kit found hilarious, and I beat him a couple of times, and got beaten a couple of times. We both fell over through overreaching and ended up laughing hard enough to not be able to breathe.

And of course, equally obviously, by the time we'd ended up laughing too hard to continue I'd passed whatever test he'd set for me. As I excused myself to go home, he said, 'Thanks for crashing. See you soon.'

And I knew, at that point, that I was in.

8. Reid

Reid so very nearly didn't answer the call.

It came at half four while he was pulling running kit on. He was rushing to get ready, impatient to finally leave the flat.

He'd been trying to go for this run since 8 a.m., but had ended up helping his DS out with intel on a stabbing (Reid somehow always ended up looking at the WhatsApp chat on his days off) and had then made the mistake of answering a knock at the door. It had proved to be his upstairs neighbour, Pjotr, needing help with his heating, which was stuck on. Cue two hours of Reid sweltering in what would have been a warm flat anyway as he tried to turn off a valve that was inexplicably boxed in behind a cabinet. He'd ended up sawing a misshapen piece out of the back of the cabinet, all the while thinking that Tanya would have done this better. That she'd always been the practical one.

After that, his parents had rung him for tag-team rambling conversations, and Reid had only just managed to get them off the line, answer another query from his DS and change into his kit when the new call came through.

He growled at the phone. He was itching to get out of the flat and into the twenty-six-degree afternoon. It was glorious outside, and the last thing he needed was yet another phone call.

This one wasn't a number he recognised, though. A mobile that wasn't saved into his phone.

That didn't necessarily mean it wasn't someone known to him. Reid had changed both his phone and his SIM eighteen months ago, and he was still occasionally getting flak for not updating people. People like Tanya's friend Midda, or his cousin Pete.

He hesitated with the phone in his hand, briefly imagining one of his team in danger. Maybe he hadn't saved the number of one of his new DCs. Maybe they needed him.

With an exasperated sigh, he answered the call. 'Reid Murray?'

'Ah, Reid. I . . . Sorry to call out of the blue. I managed to get your number from your parents. It's Seaton Laws. Anna's father.'

Reid felt a surge of adrenaline so strong it was almost like electricity. It drove him up onto his feet, his running shoe falling to the floor with an unheeded thud.

Seaton. What the fuck?

Fast on the heels of that jolt of adrenaline came a feeling of nausea. He couldn't get himself together enough to answer. Couldn't even think. It was shameful how much it affected him: both the voice and the sound of Anna's name.

He tried to walk away from it, unconsciously gravitating towards the kitchen. The shrapnel of his hurried lunch was still on the worktop and he found himself tidying the plate away and reaching for a cloth to sweep up the crumbs while his mouth failed to form words.

'Ah . . . I hope you don't mind me calling?' Seaton said into the silence.

'Right,' Reid said in the end, pausing with the cloth in his hand and realising that it was shaking. 'Nice to hear from you.'

Which wasn't true. Wasn't true at all.

He wanted to ask why the hell Seaton was getting in touch, but he also didn't want to form the words. He wanted to shout, instead, *Why now? Why, when things are just about normal again, and I don't think about Anna every bloody half-hour any more?*

'Good to speak to you, too,' Seaton said, as awkwardly as ever. 'Look, I know it's in many ways unfair to be calling, but I'm . . . I'm worried about Anna. She's gone missing. I know that . . . I know that things didn't end well between the two of you, but you were the one person she still trusted, believe it or not.'

'She's . . . missing?' Reid asked, his eyes still roving over the counter, looking for something to clean. A stray crumb to wipe away. He couldn't quite identify what the feeling tumbling through him was, but it was messy and painful and unpleasant. 'For how long?'

'Since last night,' Seaton said. 'She was looking into something. A murder, actually. And I think she might need your help.'

Reid found himself leaning against the counter, the cloth balled up in his hand and a tight feeling in his stomach.

'Tell me,' he said.

9. Anna

I set out to write everything down, and not just the stuff you might have wanted to hear. But I've still found myself shying away from admitting to some things.

So here's the full truth. I didn't spend my first weeks in Cambridge looking solely at Kit Frankland, Ryan Jaffett, Esther Thomas and James Sedgewick.

I also started looking at Tanya's death again.

And I know – I *know* – that you told me to stop. But how am I supposed to do that when I still don't believe it was an accident?

It didn't necessarily start as a conscious thing. I'd be looking over photographs of Kit's group at events and find my eyes drifting to the background, almost willing one of the girls in dresses to be a slim, strong sportswoman with ruddy cheeks and short-cut blonde hair. A young woman who never stopped moving, and organising, and helping everyone.

It would make me burn with a need to see the places Tanya had been. On one occasion I packed my laptop up and headed over to Selwyn College instead of Jesus, where I found a café and homed in on a chatty-looking pair of undergrads in their third year. I asked if they'd known any of my friends in the year above, and then I dropped in names of a few of the other students who'd done geography alongside Tanya.

'Oh, I kind of knew Pete,' one of them said. 'I think he's out in Chile now, isn't he?'

'Is he?' I asked with a laugh. 'That's so bad that I don't know. I am not a good friend.' While inside I wanted to yell at them for not remembering the one important person. The only one who mattered.

On my way home I felt a sense of terrible anxiety at the danger I was running. Admitting to other people that I'd known Tanya's friends could so easily get me found out. I lacerated myself for it. Promised myself I'd stick to online research from then on.

But as I dug further into Holly's life and found images of her at a few athletics events, I was painfully reminded of all those photos Tanya would send over of her matches, and of the couple of games you and I actually went to watch together. And somehow after a few days I was looking up the university hockey club to find out whether they had any friendly matches on now that the main season was over, and when I found that there was one – over on the fields beyond Newnham – I got on my bike and cycled over, filled with an urgency to meet some of these girls and find out more.

It felt strange to see the same stands and banners and kit on a warm summer's day that I'd seen at Tanya's matches in the driving rain of winter. Stranger still to realise that she would never be at another of these matches.

I took myself over to where the Cambridge supporters and subs were standing and spent forty-five minutes cheering the Cambridge side on before I eventually got up the courage to talk to one of the students watching. He was a young guy in a polo shirt and shorts, and he seemed to be alone.

'Which one are you supporting?' I asked him as he gave a roar of triumph at a goal.

'Oh. Min,' he said, clapping and giving me a fleeting smile. 'She's the . . . Black headband? Tall?'

'Oh, she's great,' I said.

'How about you?' he asked me.

And of course at that point I hesitated and told him that I'd come in remembrance of a friend. That it was weird but kind of nice. I told him about Tanya and asked if he'd known her.

I watched him tense, looking awkward.

'That's . . . I'm so sorry. I heard about that. Min was on the second team then.' He shook his head. 'This fucking place, huh?'

It was said with a dark ferocity to it, but no matter how gently I tried I couldn't get any more out of him. And though I tried to wait and speak to some of the players and the coach at the end of the game they were too much caught up in victory. Too elated to reach right then.

And so I slunk away once again, dizzy with anxiety and also furious with myself for failing.

The truth is that I can't stop looking, Reid. And I've never understood how you could. It's one of so many things I wanted to say after you told me I was a terrible person and then cut me off.

There were other things, too. Things about how grief can twist you up and make everything seem bitter and wrong. About how there's a massive difference between wanting the *truth* and wanting a *story*.

About how I was grieving, too, and didn't handle it perfectly.

And that you aren't fucking perfect either, Reid.

I thought for a long time about what I wanted to say. I rehearsed and wrote out most of it. But the tide of need to tell you rose and eventually fell. I accepted that I wouldn't get to say most of it. But after that tide receded I was left with an aching anger that you thought I never loved your sister.

And that was so very unfair.

I know it's not the same as how you felt. Of course Tanya could never mean as much to me as she did to you. She was your sister. The buddy you'd grown up with, with whom you'd sighed over your good-natured, impractical parents. She was the one who'd always organised you all, even as a small girl, and made everything more fun. I know this.

But I loved her too, Reid. From pretty much the first time I met her.

There are some things about you and me that are weirdly similar. Our sense of humour. Our taste in movies. Our love of a puzzle.

But the one thing that will always divide us is your solid, loving family unit. The cluster of relatives that's always been happy to see you.

That's never how it's been for me. Even when my mom was still with Dad, there was an undercurrent of anger in the house, which means my youngest memories are of trying to make everyone happy. And once we left, I have memories of Mom looking at me like she'd made a mistake taking me with her. Like she couldn't stand the sight of me.

This isn't supposed to be a pity party. All I mean is, when I walked into your family home and Tanya wrapped me in a hug that smelled like violets – all that blonde fringe of hers falling onto my forehead in a tickly mass – it did something profound. And as much as I loved meeting your parents, too, it was Tanya who started making me tea and ushering me into the nicest chair. Tanya who gave me laughing asides about the things you and your parents said.

She made me feel one hundred per cent like I belonged. And honestly, it was the first time I'd ever felt that.

I can't think about her without remembering how much constant energy she had for fixing things. For fixing people. And whenever I think about her, everything in me rebels against the idea that she could ever, ever have taken that overdose. Not just because she was always so in control of things like timings and medication, but also because I can't imagine a world where Tanya wasn't on top of her work.

You know that time we went to see her in Cambridge? A few weeks after I first got to meet her? That would have been, what, Lent term the year before she died? Do you remember that?

I do. I remember all of it. Because it felt all of a sudden like I had a sister of my own.

We'd only managed to spend an hour having lunch with her at Bill's when you got called away. One of those situations when you could have done with being more selfish about your free time.

I could see Tanya giving you a resigned smile as you ducked out onto the street to answer the phone. I now know that the street outside is called Green Street, and isn't all that far from my Cambridge house. It's a weird thought.

'That's him out for the rest of the day,' Tanya said once you were gone, and then she leaned forwards and pulled a piece of fluff out of my hair. It was one of those things she did so easily and instinctively that it never made me feel embarrassed, despite the fact that she was younger and I was supposed to be the Professional Working Woman.

'It had better not be,' I told her, feeling a drop of real disappointment. 'I'm having fun.'

'Oh, you don't have to go if he does, do you?' she asked, blue eyes a little pleading and voice its usual husky tone. 'We can hang out until he's back. I'll even spill the tea on how annoying he was as a teenager.'

'That's pretty hard to say no to . . .'

'Good,' she said, smiling at me. 'I'll show you my room if you're down.'

'Definitely down.'

And so after you came to tell us that you were needed back in London for a few hours – which I know you must remember, as you looked genuinely upset about it – Tanya and I went back to her square little room at Selwyn College. It was nothing like the rooms I've seen more recently. No expensive sound systems. No huge drinks cabinets. A tiny floor space, and limited natural light. But it was also absolutely organised, something I later realised was a feature of Tanya. There was no mess, and all her work was in orderly, labelled files. She had a scheduler on her wall, with a to-do list on the side.

Everything on the to-do list was ticked off, Reid. She was just . . . amazing.

That afternoon Tanya made me tea and began telling me very openly about the break-up she'd just been through. I'd only heard a little about Matt from you before that, so this was all a real window onto their relationship.

'I knew something was up,' she said, her cheeks even more red than usual as she bent over the kettle. 'He had mentionitis about this girl Rachel, right? Like, just kept on talking about things she'd said. And then I started finding out they'd gone for coffee together and stuff when he'd implied he was busy.' She shook her head. 'He tried to say they were just friends and it was good for him to have other people to hang out with while I was so busy with hockey. But then there was this – this dinner thing that I couldn't go to.' She swallowed, and I could tell it was hurting her to talk about this. 'It wasn't a big thing. Just a choir dinner. They have them every term. I said I was so sorry but I was away training. Matt was all, "Never mind, next time."'

'Suspiciously chill about it,' I said.

'I know, right?' Tanya brought the filled mugs over and bundled herself in on the bed beside me as though we really had grown up together. 'The dinner happened while I was away training,' she went on. 'He said nothing else. But then some pictures appeared on other people's social media, and there was Matt, with Rachel. Who isn't in the choir. And when

I asked why she was there he said he'd invited her instead.' She came to sit opposite me, her eyes a little reflective in the uplighter she'd installed in the room.

'What an asshole,' I said with feeling. 'That's not just . . . that's not even private cheating.'

'Exactly,' Tanya agreed. 'It was rubbing it in my face.'

'I'm guessing there was more?'

Tanya gave a snorting laugh. 'He obviously denied it, but before confronting him I'd done a deep dive on his phone. There were messages talking about things they'd done. And I mean, things.' Her lip curled, and she shook her head.

'He's an idiot,' I told her. 'I've already decided you're about the best person in the world.'

Tanya laughed. 'Thank you. Right back at you.' She blinked for a second, and then said, 'It's good he's out of the picture. He spent a lot of time guilt-tripping me for prioritising work or hockey, even when I spent a lot of time with him.'

'Sounds like an envy thing,' I suggested. 'Like, he didn't want you being more successful than he is?'

Tanya tipped her head on one side. 'I . . . maybe that's true.' She gave a small smile. 'Well, he's only helped my hockey game. I'm enjoying visualising his face on every ball I hit.'

And I think that's the point I'm trying to make. She was a survivor, Reid. The state-school kid who'd fought for her place and was flourishing. And it made me so angry, reading that coroner's report, seeing his assumption that she'd died because she wasn't good enough. That she'd been driven to drugs because she 'wasn't coping'. That because she wasn't some private-school kid of bankers or doctors she'd been destined to fail. That's what it said to me.

I don't think she was ever, ever failing. Even when she decided to get back together with Matt after all, it was on her terms. And I know you were angry about it and thought it was the wrong decision – I know – but I could tell she'd made him crawl through mud to be with her.

And actually, now I think about it, that was more of you being you, wasn't it? More of your inability to see people as shades of grey. You made it into a moral thing right at your dad's birthday party, when everything was supposed to be a celebration.

I remember Tanya arriving. How she bounded in with her slightly flushed cheeks and her thick wool sweater, looking just the picture of health. It would have been early March, wouldn't it? Only a couple of weeks after that weekend in Cambridge with her. Still miserable wintertime, but Tanya always seemed like she'd been out in the sun somewhere.

'Shit, sorry. Traffic nightmare. Am crap,' she said as she hugged your dad and then you in turn. I was beginning to notice and to love that she didn't stop talking for at least the first minute while entering a room. 'Hummus and crisps for you. Literally the most original person ever. Anna, you look so nice! Why are you wasting time on Reid? Give me a hug. Oh, the wine's in Matt's car. He's about fifteen minutes behind me. Wow, little cousin Seb, you've grown your hair! You're starting to look like a proper Murray man. Anyone got a bottle open? I need one basically right now. Yes! Large. Larger. That one. You're a ledge.'

You must remember this next bit, because you were staring at her. And you interrupted her stream of words to say, 'Matt? As in –'

'Matt!' I could see the way Tanya avoided looking at you as she said it. 'My boyfriend Matt. You know.'

She scooped up the large glass of red she'd been handed and started drinking it while she gave you a meaningful look over the top.

'So no longer your ex-boyfriend?' you persisted.

Tanya gave a small eye-roll and put the glass down with a clink. 'Obviously not.' She grinned over at me as if sharing a joke and moved to the table to start cutting a French loaf that had been left out there. 'I'm not in the habit of bringing exes to family events.'

'No, but . . . it seems a lot to get past,' you said, following her and hovering. 'The cheating.'

'Sounds like they've talked it all through,' I murmured at you as soon as I'd closed in. You didn't seem to be able to hear me.

'But . . . Twice, though, Tan. He cheated twice.'

Which was true, to be fair. But it was still her decision.

Tanya turned, chewing on the piece of French bread, and breezed straight past you to the drinks counter. 'Shall I get more ice out, Dad?' she called. And then she said to you, 'Matt is getting some therapy. He's accepted that he was being insecure about me not being around all the time. Having my own life. I've put clear boundaries in place, and it's going to help. He had to grow up a lot when I broke up with him, and we're in a much better place now.'

By the time she'd finished delivering this she was already vanishing into the pantry, where the full-height freezer lived. She reappeared holding a bag of ice, and I found myself wishing I had her easy competence. She always knew what needed organising. Whatever the situation. From the moment she walked in the door things just got more together instead of – well, less so.

Why would she need all those drugs, Reid? How would someone so together, so competent, need Ritalin? There are plenty of us who might possibly benefit from a concentration aid, but Tanya? She was born focused.

Anyway, this wasn't about that. It was about you and your rigidness. I have such a clear memory of the next part. There was the sound of a car, and Tanya came back to stand in front of you and said, 'That's probably Matt. It's all fine, OK? We've worked stuff out. Be nice.' And she gave you a squeeze on the arm and one of her slightly wonky smiles.

But you weren't nice, were you? You were being her over-protective big brother. I know it must have been hard not to. She was eight years younger, and you'd always felt like you had to protect her, but what you did wasn't fair.

You looked very levelly at Matt when he came in – and yes, it annoyed me, too, that he was carrying the wine as though it were a gift just from him. But still.

I distinctly remember what you said when he asked how work was going. 'Oh, you know. The usual. Trying to make sure good people get justice and the arseholes get what they deserve. But it doesn't always happen that way.'

And then the way you just . . . turned away from him and put your arm round Tanya. It was brutal. I hated how awkward it was and how you'd ignored your sister's wishes. She'd asked you to welcome Matt in and you'd done the opposite. If she'd been any less tough, I don't think she would have been able to laugh at you and slide away to stand with her boyfriend like she did.

The other problem with being absolute about your loyalties is you can end up writing people off. I mean, Matt probably wasn't worth wasting time on, but we didn't know that for sure. He was young and still had a lot to learn. If Tanya wanted to give him a second chance, that was up to her.

You've never really dealt in shades of grey, though, have you? In your world, there's right and there's wrong, and people are good or bad. No mitigating factors. No understanding.

Maybe that's what you end up thinking when you've grown up in a happy family instead of a dysfunctional one. When nothing has ever been that hard in your life.

Until you hit twenty-nine and lose your only sister.

But I lost her too, Reid. I lost the young woman I'd started spending every free weekend with. The friend who loved hearing about my work, and was a rational head to talk to when I felt like I'd screwed things up. The almost-sister I'd supported when she found out she'd been cheated on once again, and had accompanied to at least two events she'd intended on going to with Matt.

Having written this far, I realise I was kind of naive, actually. I should have expected that, one day, I'd find myself standing on the wrong side of your line of good and evil. And maybe part of me did expect it. I just didn't think it would happen while I was trying to do everything in my power to help you.

10. Reid

Reid had always prided himself on being the calm one. The focused one. The one who knew exactly what to do in a crisis. Where civilians and even some of his colleagues would cease functioning, Reid was always, always the one who quietly did what was needed.

And yet here he was, slumped on the sofa with a mass of uncertainty running through him. His calm had deserted him, wiped out by a simple phone call about the woman who'd broken his heart.

Perhaps it wasn't just about the emotional side of this. Perhaps it was also the uncertainty he felt.

He knew Anna well. As well as anyone, and possibly better than Seaton did. He knew that her disappearance might not be anything to worry about.

Whatever else he'd got wrong about her, Reid knew that Anna's ability to get distracted had been both profound and genuine. It was something that got in the way of her life (and infuriated people) so often that he was positive she wouldn't fake it. It was entirely possible that Anna had just rushed off after a line of enquiry and would turn up in a few hours with an explanation.

He could still vividly remember his disbelief three weeks into their work together, when they'd met for dinner. It hadn't been a date, however clear the chemistry between them had been. They'd just been meeting up at The Real Greek to brainstorm on her sex-trafficking case. The one that had become *their* case the moment she'd laid it all out in front of him.

The conversation that night had ended up diverging, as it so often had, onto ridiculous invented concepts and deceptively light-hearted sharing of their lives. He wasn't sure why he'd found himself talking to her when he usually found it so hard not to deflect, but somehow it all just poured out when they were together. And he hadn't felt stupid about sharing, either. Though he'd had ample time to feel very stupid in the eighteen months since.

Halfway through the main course – when they'd been in the middle of discussing the film *Tornado* for some reason – Anna had left the restaurant table to go and use the bathroom, taking her phone with her.

She'd then disappeared for the next two hours.

'Oh my god, I'm sorry,' she'd said contritely when he'd finally, finally been able to get her to pick up her phone. 'I actually forgot we were in the middle of eating. I suddenly realised that the warehouses might not be as much of a dead end as we thought, and I needed to go and talk to someone. It was honestly worth it, though. I'll explain when I get back.'

He'd told her, bluntly, not to bother, because he was going home. He'd been waiting in that restaurant the whole two hours, more and more convinced that she must have been abducted. It had been humiliating, stressful, and a waste of his time.

Anna being Anna, she'd ignored the brush-off and had turned up at his house twenty minutes later to apologise profusely, to the point where he'd started to feel she really did mean it. And then, after a pause, she'd given a tiny quirking smile and asked if he'd like to know what she'd found out.

He'd caved and let her in, and then found himself caught up in her story. Not only caught up in it, but actively working with her once again.

In spite of himself, he started reliving the rest of that night.

He could picture their matching poses, hunkered over his coffee table as they'd pieced everything together and drunk more wine than they should have drunk. And then how they'd somehow been next to each other, with her intense energy drawing him in.

He wasn't actually sure, to this day, who'd been the one to initiate that first kiss. But he did know it had been a long time coming.

For a moment he was really remembering the kiss, and then the heated, abandoned sex that had come after. And how utterly, terribly afraid he'd felt in the morning as he'd realised he was falling for her. Really, properly falling for her.

In daylight, after she'd left for home in a rush (of course), it had been so clear to him that it hadn't meant a thing to her. That she was only in it for the fun.

So he'd met her that evening and done the mature thing. He'd told her it had all been a mistake, and that they should keep things professional. He'd convinced himself that he could shut everything away and just work with her from time to time.

It had only been once she'd downed her cocktail and got up to leave that he'd realised she might have some feelings tied up in it, too.

'It's a no to keeping things professional,' she'd said. 'It wouldn't work for me, trying to pretend there wasn't anything else. Better to have proper boundaries and just . . . not.'

She'd turned and left, and he'd felt the most horrible tearing sensation. One that had stayed with him for the next month.

For fuck's sake, he thought now, as he realised that he was giving free rein to all the memories he'd spent so much time packing away. *You don't need this. Any of this.*

He got to his feet, making a mental effort to shut everything emotional out and put his professional hat back on.

This wasn't *his* missing persons investigation. It belonged to Cambridgeshire Constabulary and, technically, he should leave it up to them.

But he couldn't help agreeing with Seaton that Cambridgeshire weren't concerned. The constable Seaton had spoken to sounded convinced that she'd wandered off somewhere, and although Reid thought it a possibility, she also might be in danger.

The protocol would be the same for Cambridgeshire as it was for the Met: as a missing person, her case would only get passed to someone senior if it looked high risk. So in all probability, the constabulary wouldn't action this until tomorrow.

He sighed. However much he didn't want to see or talk to Anna ever again, there was no way he could just ignore it if she'd got herself in trouble.

So what to do?

There were procedures you could go through if you suspected someone was missing. Steps to take. You could do them before anything became officialised. He didn't have to go in guns blazing or put anything on the books until he'd taken a few of those steps.

The first thing was to try the people and places nobody had thought to check yet. Seaton had already been in touch with at least one member of her group of Cambridge students and asked him to speak to the others.

Reid would probably go over that ground again to make sure they weren't keeping things specifically from Seaton, but before that there were other avenues that hadn't been explored at all. Seaton hadn't checked her London flat. Hadn't checked the *Ensign* offices where Anna worked. Hadn't called round the hospitals and checked for her, under either her name or her pseudonym, or for any unknowns who'd been admitted.

Reid tried to suppress a crawl up his spine as he thought of

Anna lying seriously ill or injured somewhere since last night, with nobody apparently aware.

The *Ensign*, he thought. Let's start there. She might be in some meeting for all anybody knows.

He googled the number, then asked the switchboard operator to put him through to Anna. He could feel his stomach squeezing as he waited, not sure whether he wanted her to answer so he could dismiss this whole thing, or for her *not* to so he wouldn't have to talk to her.

After six interminable rings her voicemail cut in, and he hung up.

She could still be in a meeting, or making coffee.

Dialling the same number again, he asked to be put through to Gael.

As investigative editor, Gael was the one person who would know where Anna was at any given moment. He also knew Reid from the meetings they'd had about the sex-trafficking story, so Reid wouldn't need to establish his identity.

Two rings in, Gael picked up. Reid felt a flood of strange nostalgia the moment he heard his markedly Costa Rican accent.

'Gael, hi,' he said. 'It's Reid Murray. I know it's been a while.'

'Reid,' Gael said, sounding genuinely pleased to hear from him. He guessed that was probably in anticipation of a story coming his way and braced himself for a less enthusiastic response in a moment. 'How are things?'

'I wondered if you knew where Anna was,' he said. Realising how it sounded, he then added hastily, 'I'm not stalking her. Her dad wanted me to track her down.'

Gael gave a relaxed laugh. 'Her dad? Has she stood him up for lunch again?'

Reid couldn't help laughing too at how close to the mark this was, and yet how much it failed to summarise what was going on.

'That's exactly it,' he said.

There were sounds of movement from Gael, and Reid guessed he was looking something up. 'Ahhhh, she's not here at the moment. She's doing some financial stuff. Her worst nightmare. She's had to go and talk to a bank or something today.'

'Was she around yesterday?' he asked, as lightly as possible.

Gael paused a second, before saying, 'I . . . Yes, she was in first thing yesterday before she went to this meeting with one of the finance people.'

'OK,' Reid said. 'That's good to know. Thanks.'

'No problem,' Gael said, as if he were already on to the next thing. 'Hey, Reid? You know the Met Commissioner personally? Well enough to put me in touch?'

'Ahhh, no,' Reid replied. 'Sorry.'

He decided not to add that he was about as far from the commissioner's acquaintance as a burger flipper was to the owner of McDonald's. It was probably better to keep Gael thinking he was useful.

'Hey, no problem,' Gael said. 'Take it easy!'

Reid hung up, feeling his unease increase another step. Gael had said Anna was involved in something financial. No mention of a murder in Cambridge. Maybe she'd ended up with two investigations on the go and really was at a bank somewhere.

Or maybe Gael knew very well that Anna was supposed to be in Cambridge, and had fed Reid a load of bullshit to avoid spilling their secrets.

He sat back to think about this. *If* her father was right about what she'd been doing and she'd been trying to uncover a murder, then the fact that she hadn't turned up for lunch, the fact that she wasn't answering her phone, and the fact that she hadn't been into the office . . . all of these things together weren't great.

Twisting it round and imagining Anna had been a detective looking into a murder, if she'd missed those contact points, he would have been concerned. Genuinely concerned.

Should he be calling Cambridgeshire up and asking them to take this seriously? Let his colleagues there take this on and do their hopefully efficient work? He could spur them on and then stand back.

That would be the *right* thing to do, procedurally. If he gave them enough of a reason, then Cambridgeshire might step up and get a couple of actual detectives on it.

Beyond that, Anna was no longer his problem. She was his ex-girlfriend, and she'd seriously let him down. He should be calling Cambridgeshire right now, and letting someone else deal with this.

He looked out of the living-room window for a moment, at the sunshine pouring down past the sycamore tree outside. It was almost five-ten. The park would be a perfect temperature now. If he called Cambridgeshire and left in ten minutes for a run, he might just get out before the post-work runners descended.

Sunny days off were so precious, and he'd wasted so much of this one already. Did he really want to waste the rest of it on an ex-girlfriend he would prefer never to see again?

He looked at his phone, and kept looking at it. He somehow couldn't quite bring himself to make the call.

It's the right thing to do, he told himself.

But it didn't feel like it. For the first time he could remember, the right procedure felt like totally the wrong thing to do as a human being.

If Reid left this to Cambridgeshire Constabulary, and they did very little – if he did that and harm came to his ex-girlfriend as a direct result – Reid knew that he wouldn't be able to forgive himself. And somehow, in spite of how much she'd angered him and how little he ever wanted to see her again, the idea of a world with Anna *not* in it was achingly wrong.

He drifted through to his bedroom again and looked down at the discarded running shoe. Then he sighed and started changing into his suit trousers and shirt.

'You win, Anna,' he muttered. 'You win.'

11. Anna

I need to tell you about what happened next, I know. But I'm back here, and all I've been thinking about on a loop is what it was you thought you saw in me to make you fall out of love with me so fast.

After the first time you decided that you didn't love me I got a little obsessed with that thought. After we'd finally hooked up, only to have you say, 'That shouldn't have happened, I'm sorry,' it cut me surprisingly deeply.

I couldn't work out exactly what it was that you'd decided *not to love*, even though with every other break-up I'd always been kind of 'screw it, we just weren't compatible'. I guess it's harder to take rejection when you've stupidly let yourself fall hard for someone. You start searching for the *how* and the *why*. Looking for what you can do to stop it happening again.

It has a weird effect, thinking like that. You suddenly find yourself having these little anxious moments in conversations with other people. You wonder whether you've talked too much about something, or gone off on too much of a tangent, and whether they secretly think you're a tiresome freak. You start to imagine that all those cupboard doors you've left open in your life have been a black mark against you, as irritating as your mother said they were. And you wince at the times you've forgotten birthdays, or told a terrible pun at a bad time, or drifted off in the middle of important events. You become convinced that everyone must secretly be keeping score, and that you just never knew.

I think I'd only just managed to get back to my normal 'who

cares?' self by the time you walked back into my life. I was half tempted to tell you to fuck off, because I didn't want to feel like I wasn't good enough again. But I'd missed the way you spoke straight to my oddness. You'd always made it feel like you actually *valued* all those things about me, and wanted me to be one hundred per cent myself.

I never felt like I had to try to be anyone else around you, actually, and that was one of the things that really worked. Also one of the things that made it a heap of shit when you broke things off again.

The *real* kick in the teeth was that it wasn't any of those things that you broke up with me over. It had never even occurred to me to worry that you'd think I was a bad person.

And here I am, writing all of this, and part of me is wondering whether you weren't right in some ways. And it's . . . not helping.

OK. Enough. Let's just get on with the facts.

The party had done everything I wanted it to, even though I hadn't seduced Ryan or got James on my side. I'd still been invited in.

Kit messaged (via Luca initially) to ask me to come for drinks with them all on the Saturday night, and it was clear that this was just the chosen few. The Pitt Club elite, with me a potential new member.

The whole dynamic of that invitation fascinated me. I was made welcome because Kit Frankland had decided I should be there. Whatever test I'd passed that night had opened doors, though a small part of me was alert to the ease of it. I'd sometimes catch Kit looking at me with an indulgent kind of approval and feel a thrill of worry that I wasn't the hunter I thought: that I was somehow his prey.

We met for those drinks at Downing Bar, right where

Esther and Kit lived and only a short bike ride for me, James and Ryan. I'd obviously by this point worked out where everyone's rooms were. College porters will give you an unholy amount of information if you act like a student trying to find your friend's room. So I knew that James lived high up in an attic on St John's Third Court, and that Ryan was in a Corpus Christi-owned townhouse on Trumpington Street called, imaginatively, T-Street.

I arrived at Downing Bar late, obviously, fully expecting to have to work hard to charm everyone. I was particularly worried about getting Esther onside, but to my surprise, her face lit up as soon as she saw me. She rose to give me a surprisingly enthusiastic hug in greeting and then sat me down next to her.

I wasn't quite sure how to take this. Esther had seemed so closed off during our brief conversation at the party. Was this all an act? Her mother's diplomatic role rubbing off on her?

Ryan, contrastingly, gave me a stiff nod and turned his whole body to talk to Kit's girlfriend, which made me blink. I'd been expecting him to be friendly again, and couldn't help losing my thread for a second. But Kit covered things smoothly by leaning in to ask me about rowing. Work. And then he chatted nonsense about his supervisor and a feud about essay submission while Esther laughed and interjected explanatory notes for me. It felt almost rehearsed, at the time, and it was difficult to really relax into.

Kit's petite brunette girlfriend, Sarah, watched and laughed. She seemed in two minds about me being there. I felt like she was the one person who was straightforward wary about a newcomer, but prepared to like me if it turned out I was OK. So I set about proving that I was. Mostly by dropping in a comment about my experience at an Eras tour concert, and bonding a little over Taylor Swift. It was gratifying that Esther got on board with this conversation too.

But I was still very aware of Ryan in the background, a nagging sensation of something being wrong. And between comments, I tried to work out what the issue might be. Whether he was angry I'd been invited in. Whether I'd offended him somehow.

Once James finally arrived, at close to 10 p.m., I was relieved that he seemed to be OK with me being there. After he'd talked to the others for a while he gave me a grin, looking at me from under his fringe, and then ducked his head to take a drink.

It was weird, you know, seeing someone so objectively attractive feeling apparently so underconfident. I found myself trying to suss him out, wondering whether the whole shyness thing was just a facade.

'Hi,' I said eventually, realising he wasn't going to start a conversation.

'Nice to see you again,' he said after a second. 'Did you enjoy the rest of the night?'

'Of course she did,' Kit said, suddenly appearing across the table with a drink in each hand. 'How could anyone not enjoy chatting to Cambridge's most talented leading man, and then getting beaten at competitive long jump by a renowned rugby player?'

He handed the glasses over and then sat with an eager expression.

'Beaten, my ass,' I protested. 'I left you standing.' And then I halted for a moment, and said, 'Wait. Who's the leading man?'

Kit shook his head. 'James is. And no way did you beat me.'

I turned to James and said, '*In. Heels.*' And then said, 'Are you really?'

'Umm . . . Not really.' James ducked his head again.

'One hundred per cent,' Esther corrected him, putting her hand on my arm as though we were close friends. The change in her was still disconcerting. 'He was Hamlet at the ADC last term and it got such amazing reviews they've got funding to tour it, and Steven Berkoff is apparently super interested in getting him into the RSC. And on top of that, his *Who's Afraid of Virginia Woolf?* performance at the Fringe won an actual award.'

'Ohhh. That's amazing.' I gave him a sheepish look. 'Sorry. I should probably know. I don't think I've made it to any shows.'

'Don't be silly. It's not big stuff.' He took a slug of his drink. 'Anyway, the main thing is you beat Kit at sport.'

Kit had put his arm round Sarah proprietorially. She turned to look up at him, but his focus was all on James now. 'Stop glorying in my failure, James. Wait. Alleged failure. Victory.'

'Humiliating defeat,' I put in, and Esther gave a delighted laugh.

'Right,' Kit said, sitting forwards. 'We clearly need a rematch.'

'Fine,' I said. 'But only if you wear heels, too.'

James downed the rest of his drink and said, 'I'd better go. I promised myself I'd only be here half an hour.' He gave me an apologetic grin. 'I'm madly behind on work. Please don't take it personally.'

'I fully will,' I told him.

James laughed, but there was a trace of embarrassment to it. I had to stand up to let him slide out from behind the table, and he seemed to want to avoid looking at me the entire time, even when I had to hand him his jacket.

'Are you going to come tomorrow?' Esther asked, her voice keen with disappointment.

'I'll see,' James said. 'I'm going to get my arse handed to me if I don't do some secondary reading for the Tragedy paper. And then I'll get someone else's arse handed to me if I don't sort out American lit, too.'

I couldn't help laughing at that, and James at least met my eye briefly, with something of a grin, before he made his way out, pulling his vape out as he went. I remembered that he hadn't been part of the MDMA distribution at Kit's party. Was the vaping his replacement drug now that Holly was gone?

'So . . . I know he *said* that wasn't about me,' I said, once he was too far off to hear, 'but was that my fault? Did I make him feel *super* awkward?'

'Oh, no, don't worry,' Esther said with what might have been an attempt to reassure me, or might possibly have been a patronising note, I wasn't totally sure. 'He's . . . had a hard time. That's all.'

'I'm sorry.' I glanced towards his undeniably dashing form, which was now vanishing through the doors. 'Has the college been down on him about work? It must be hard fitting it all in.'

'It's – not really that,' Esther said. She looked profoundly uncomfortable, suddenly, and it was interesting to watch. 'More . . . personal stuff.'

'Ah, OK.' There was a tension in all of them now, I realised. Well, Ryan and Kit and Esther were tense. Sarah just looked distracted.

The tension made me want so badly to prod at it, Reid. But I knew, for certain, that I couldn't do that tonight. That if I did, I would never get to be a part of this group. So I looked at the glasses on the table and said, 'Oh, hey. I should get a round in.' I grinned at them. 'See? Certified card-carrying Brit already. And it's only been ten months.'

To my surprise, when they all gave their orders, Ryan asked quietly for a plain tonic with lime, and I wondered whether the G and Ts I thought he'd been drinking all evening had actually been non-alcoholic.

I nodded and started to head for the bar. Ryan jumped up and offered to help me, which was a second surprise.

And then, when we were at the bar, away from everyone, he said awkwardly, 'I just wanted to . . . to check whether I was a dick . . . the other night.'

I blinked at him, remembering how he'd got carried away with talking to his brother's friends. It had been enthusiastic and a little boring, but not obnoxious.

'Not at all,' I said. 'I didn't think you were anything but nice to talk to.'

'Oh.' He blinked, as if surprised. 'That's – that's really good.' He looked away from me, and then back. 'I was worrying about it. I'm, you know, not supposed to drink. I . . . I turn into a real twat most of the time. When I do.'

I frowned at him, trying to read his face. 'You did some shots, but you seemed fine. Just kind of rowdy.' And then I looked at the two cocktails on the bar. The bartender was busy pouring a glass of wine for Kit and a vodka tonic for me. 'So you're basically teetotal?'

Ryan nodded. 'Yeah, as of this year. I really need to be.' He shook his head, and when he met my eye it was with a look of real sadness. 'I got sick of finding out that people were angry with me the next day. I don't think anyone likes drunk me.' He gave a humourless laugh. 'I definitely don't.'

I could feel my pulse in my neck as he said it.

He'd have been drinking at the May Ball, I thought. *And maybe lots of times before that. When Tanya was here . . .*

I looked back at the drinks, trying to think of what Aria would say, instead of what Anna would.

And with a thrill of exhilaration I realised that I knew how to talk to him about this. How I might get him to open up about what he'd done.

'Isn't it . . . hard?' I asked, after a beat. 'When everyone else around you drinks so much?'

Ryan gave a shrug. 'Nah, it's mostly OK.'

I met his eye. 'I . . . had a problem with that kind of thing,' I said. 'Not alcohol.' I looked towards the bartender and realised he was waiting for me to pay. 'Actually, can I get one of those elderflower tonics with ice, too?' I asked. 'Sorry.'

The moment the bartender had gone I said quickly and quietly, 'It was cocaine. I . . . I wasn't rational on it. And I couldn't *not* take it.' I shook my head. 'It was all a fucking mess. But the hardest thing was trying to be around the people who were still using it.'

When the bartender came back I paid, and then I pushed the vodka tonic I'd originally ordered to one side and gathered together all the other drinks. I didn't look at Ryan as we split them between us to carry. But I could tell that he was watching me with absolute attention.

'I had to ask them not to use it in front of me,' I said, once the drinks were in my hands. 'And even now, I think it'd be hard if I was around people who were getting high all the time.'

I did look at him then, and there was a painful kind of understanding in his expression. It was difficult to see, actually. Because while part of me was still wondering whether this guy who was bad with alcohol had killed two young women while drunk, I was acutely aware that I was lying to someone who had addiction problems.

It's a good thing, I was trying to tell myself. *This is a real connection. You can use it.*

'It is kind of shit,' he said. 'I mean, these guys aren't too bad. They don't pressure me. But it's still . . .' He shook his head. 'I guess I just need to be tougher.'

I raised an eyebrow at him. 'Or you need an ally.'

I walked back to the table with him, and didn't make a big deal out of drinking my non-alcoholic tonic. To be honest, getting to drink something soft was a relief, Reid. I *cannot* drink as much as those guys and still function the next day, even at only five years older. You'd think a few years of hanging around with Dad and his 'Oh, I thought it was a good excuse for champagne' style of living would have prepared me, but no. They are on a whole other level.

At that point, I'd only had a single non-alcoholic drink to break up the cocktails, but it clearly made an impression on Ryan. After that, he started making eye contact and talking to me. Even smiling and directing his jokes toward me.

And you know the nice thing, Reid? Instead of having to seduce him like everyone wanted, all I'd done was be a friend. It felt a mixture of good and like the worst kind of betrayal.

Nothing is ever simple.

It was probably only ten minutes after I got Ryan on my side that Esther asked me to go to the bathroom with her. I guessed this was a girl talk, which meant her sussing me out further. Esther wasn't the kind of person to do things for no reason.

But when she bundled herself into the same cubicle as me, slid a notebook out of her bag and laid out two lines of white powder on it, I realised my mistake.

For a second, I was genuinely frozen. It wasn't the drugs themselves, it was the timing, and the fact that this was cocaine. Had Ryan betrayed my secrets within minutes? Was Esther testing me?

But I shook myself and gave my pre-prepared excuse for exactly this type of situation.

'Oh, I can't, I'm really sorry,' I told her. 'If I get drugs-tested for the trials and I come up with anything in my system, I'll be out. Doesn't matter what it is.'

And you know, I think my anxiety might actually have added an accidental aura of naturalness. The panic of a former user. If Esther *did* know what I'd told Ryan, or found it out later from googling, it would all make a sort of sense.

But either way, Esther didn't react with suspicion.

'You poor thing,' she said with what looked like sympathy, and snorted up both lines herself.

It gave me a squeeze of worry, watching her do it. I thought of Holly, drowning in that river. And inevitably of Tanya, dying alone in her university room.

That was too much.

But Esther seemed fairly immune to the effects. Twenty minutes later, she was simply more animated. And she still seemed determined to keep her arm through mine and to ask my opinion on everything.

I saw Kit and Sarah excuse themselves to the bathrooms not that long afterwards, and it occurred to me that snorting lines or taking tabs was just something they did, as naturally as drinking a cocktail or eating a hot dog. Despite the possible damage, and the unbelievable expense associated with making it a regular habit.

Ryan, though, stayed at the table, and when I glanced over at him he gave me a small nod. Which made me think maybe he hadn't told Esther anything. That actually, he was trying to be an ally to me in return.

I gave him a crooked grin and downed the last of my alcohol-free tonic.

I excused myself at 11.15, in spite of Kit's best efforts to make me stay. Of the three who'd taken coke, he seemed the least wired, which I found interesting. I wondered if he liked to see others out of control, without ever losing his own.

I also had the flash of a thought, as he leaned away from Sarah and towards me to talk over the sound of the music, that Kit's power might come from being their supplier. I found myself unconsciously stepping away slightly, and I saw a flicker of something cross his face as I did. A little look of surprise and displeasure.

He's not used to being crossed, I thought. *He's always been able to pull everyone's strings, whenever he wants.*

How else would he feel confident enough to lean that close to me, with his arm still round his girlfriend?

'You're really going?' he asked, after the tiniest of pauses.

'Absolutely,' I told him. 'I'm not doing a seven a.m. outing on any less sleep or any more alcohol.' Which was an entirely true statement. I was quietly dreading the next session of the river-based torture I was putting myself through in the name of realism, despite having got a lot fitter and stronger. It still hurt like hell and the blisters on my hands weren't yet hardened into painless callouses, either. A look I was only getting away with having told everyone I was just back from an injury.

'Surely you have to let loose sometimes?' he asked. He tilted his head, and a very small smile twitched at his mouth.

I gave him a considering look. 'I pick my times.'

And then I turned very deliberately to Sarah and hugged her goodnight, before moving away from them both.

Esther was talking animatedly to Ryan now but broke off when I approached. Ryan's expression dropped slightly, but Esther hugged me close.

'Ohhh, come tomorrow,' she said, squeezing me tightly. 'This was so much fun.'

She seemed genuinely sad to relinquish me, and I wasn't quite sure how to react to it. I'd spent all night watching for the break in her routine, and now wondered whether this wasn't the real Esther. Whether the overcontrolled, glossy version of her wasn't the side she struggled to shake off. It was confusing.

When she finally let go I was drawn into a sudden, slightly suffocating hug by Ryan.

'Good luck with the outing,' he said into my hair. 'See you next time.'

'Good luck with these guys,' I said with a laugh as I drew back.

It was weird how I knew, even before I checked, that I was being watched closely as I left them. Kit Frankland had turned to lean against the bar, leaving Sarah to stand awkwardly alongside him, and was watching me steadily with an expression that was at total odds with the cheerful, sociable smile he presented to the world.

It was the expression of someone who wanted me to know he wasn't fooled. And it made part of me squeeze in worry.

12. Reid

The feeling in Reid's stomach as he looked up at Packington Gardens was more than simple unease. He hadn't laid eyes on Anna's flat in more than a year and a half, and to be here, now, made him feel lost between the past and the present.

He could almost, almost believe that if he crossed the road and rang the buzzer he would hear Anna's voice telling him to come on up. And that she would be warm, and welcoming, and *here.*

It took him a while to go over and press the button for number fifty-two. He'd half hoped that he might see a light on up there; enough to free him from worry. But the fact that there wasn't a light didn't mean that Anna *wasn't* there. It was still sunny out on the street, and she could easily be sitting in the reflected light from the houses opposite, laptop out and phone off as she worked away at something. Perhaps at figuring out this murder.

Reid realised that he didn't even know whose murder it was yet. If Anna *wasn't* here, then he was going to want a lot more from Seaton. Though 'want' was maybe the wrong word. He didn't *want* anything to do with this.

It wasn't just that he was anxious to avoid Anna. It was also the fact that this was all based around Cambridge. She'd managed to make everything worse by getting involved in the city his younger sister had studied in and then died in. And everything he did seemed to involve painful memories.

He'd decided to call Trinity College to ask them for CCTV around the time Anna had left the May Ball, and it had inevitably reminded him of the tickets Tanya had bought for the same event in her third year; tickets she'd never got to use. He'd had to contact the college a few weeks after her death, asking them to gift them to a student who couldn't afford them, and it had been profoundly painful. Though after the college had got back in touch, sympathetically and with huge gratitude, to tell him the students they'd chosen – two of their access students from a state-school background, there on hefty financial support – it had done something to ease the bleak despair he'd felt.

He'd also called Addenbrooke's Hospital to check whether Anna might be there, and that had taken him right back to the time Tanya had been admitted with a concussion after a hockey match. Reid had called the hospital switchboard on that day too, beside himself with worry after a message from his dad. He'd been pacing one of the Finsbury Park meeting rooms as he'd waited to be put through to the ward, and had felt only slightly relieved that she was conscious and talking.

Reid had still got himself onto the King's Cross train and taken a taxi to the hospital to see her. He'd ended up feeling like a spare wheel because Tanya had been surrounded by three hockey teammates who'd all been talking animatedly about the remainder of the match while Tanya laughed, an ice pack on her forehead and a slightly drowsy expression on her face.

This had been after she'd broken up with Matt for good. Not so very long before she'd left them all. So there had been no boyfriend there to look after her.

But Tanya had seemed in good spirits nonetheless.

'Reid!' she'd gasped as she saw him, somewhere between delighted and appalled. 'You did not leave work just to come see me!'

'Too right I did,' Reid said. 'Literally the only good excuse I've had to skive this year.'

The hockey mates had made room for him, and he'd ended up joining in their conversation, before the on-call doctor had arrived and politely suggested they might limit their numbers. The three girls – who had all, Reid thought, seemed like nice, thoughtful people in spite of their unbelievably posh accents – had scurried away, promising to see Tanya later. Reid had stayed on to talk to the doctor and had insisted that his sister needed more painkillers while they waited for her CT scan.

'I'm fine!' Tanya had protested.

'You can't pull that on me,' he'd said quietly to her. 'Not after the broken arm you pretended not to have.'

'Not the same!' Tanya had argued, half sitting up, but then had flinched afterwards, and Reid had grinned in victory. The exchange had done what he'd hoped and got Tanya some proper painkillers. She'd grumbled, and then grumbled again that having a scan was ridiculous, but submitted anyway. They'd established that there was no fracture but that she had some swelling and was going to have to take some days off. It hadn't gone down well.

In the nineteen months since her death, Reid had often thought back to moments like this. He'd been a good older brother to her just then, hadn't he? He'd *seen* her pain, and he'd done something.

But he'd somehow missed the more profound pain in his baby sister: the kind of pain rooted in fear which had driven her, only four or five weeks later, to take a cocktail of medications and suffer heart failure. He knew the signs must have been there, and he'd rehashed and examined memories trying to find them until he was no longer sure what had been the truth.

It was all this that Anna had managed to stir up today, totally aside from his feelings about their break-up. And the number of pain points he was hitting made him begin to think she'd done all this on purpose to torture him.

At least checking the north London hospitals for Anna's two identities had been less confronting. He'd been able to get through it without thinking about Anna or Tanya in any great detail and had established that none of them had an Aria Lauder or an Anna Sousa, and neither did they have any unknowns matching her age or description. So if her flat was empty, he would need to start looking among these Cambridge students and the work she'd been doing. Assuming he really, truly was going to try to find her.

With that in mind, and the buzzer of Anna's flat still unanswered, Reid sent a one-line message to the mobile number Anna's father had used, asking where Seaton was in case he needed him.

Seaton's reply was swift and – strangely – almost welcome.

> Already on my way to London to see you. There in half an hour. Finsbury Park?

Reid's mouth twisted in a wry grin. It was somehow very Seaton to get on a train *before* checking whether Reid actually wanted him to.

He messaged back.

> Good idea. How about the Blacklock Inn? Give me an hour.

He looked back up at the buzzer for number fifty-two, and the word 'SOUSA' next to it. Nothing was happening. He'd pressed it twice now, for a lengthy time. She wasn't there – or if she was, she wasn't replying.

He let out a very long breath, wondering what to do next. How far to go.

He knew that Anna had hidden a spare key, including a key fob for the front door of the flats, under an ornamental stone a little way along the wall from the door. It was a necessary move for someone who frequently forgot her keys and also came and went at strange times of night. She'd told him she had to be very careful not to get seen using it or her building management would give her hell.

'So unfair of them,' Reid had commented. 'It's not like you're leaving easy access to the entire building out for anyone to use.' But although the idea of doing this had made him itch, he'd said it with a grin. He'd understood pretty quickly that a lot of Anna's life was about coping mechanisms.

Reid was confident that the key would still be there. Anna was not someone to have become magically organised over a matter of months.

He peered through the glass entrance door into the empty hallway and then checked over his shoulder before he moved along the wall with his eyes on the ground. It didn't take him long to find a recognisable sparkly grey stone. It lifted easily, revealing a muddy key with a grey and yellow disc fob.

He smiled to himself. A simple victory for once. And then he went to open the door.

The experience of letting himself into Anna's flat was as painfully disconcerting as he'd expected. A distinct voice was telling him that he shouldn't be here. This was her space, which he had no right to be in any more.

Another voice was trying to hurl at him every painful memory of that last terrible argument they'd had here: the scathing way she'd spoken to him after he'd begged her to just stop, and let him mourn Tanya properly at last.

'You're the one who asked me to look into this.'

'And now I'm asking you to stop looking,' he'd snapped back. 'Can't you just respect my opinion as a detective and accept that you don't know more than I do about this?'

'Oh, I'm so sorry for not immediately bowing to your superior intellect.'

He found himself pausing in the doorway, fists clenched as though he was readying himself to fight her again, his eyes very firmly closed. He could picture the rage rising up in him. What he'd felt as he'd spat his response at her.

'Jesus. You don't care about anyone, do you? You're just a cold, career-hungry bitch.'

He swore that he'd see her there when he opened his eyes. The absolute implacability of her expression. The total lack of empathy as he drowned in grief.

But instead, he saw a hallway full of mess. The few square feet of floor around the door was full of shoes, reusable shopping bags with unknown contents, empty cardboard boxes, letters that had clearly never been opened and assorted sports gear. There were also a fair few coats that for some reason weren't on the coat rack he'd painstakingly installed for her but were instead flung onto the floor with their sleeves inside out.

He felt ambushed. Wrongfooted by a rush of strange, infuriated affection. It was disarming to be reminded of the chaotic, flawed woman he'd fallen for instead of the hard, unassailable figure he'd broken up with.

He couldn't quite put his finger on why it made him feel so uncomfortable. Was it because her erratic personality had appealed to him in some strange way? Or was it that he'd so thoroughly pushed that side of her from his mind that he was only now facing the full picture?

He'd asked her once if she'd ever had an ADHD assessment. It had seemed bizarre that she hadn't mentioned it, considering that she was probably the most categorically ADHD person he'd ever met. From her scatty brain to her lack of awareness of time; from her fits of energetic talking and activity to her sudden quiet as she became hyper-focused on something; from her profound inability to sit still without fidgeting combined with the way she would forget entirely what she'd just been doing and wander off – all bundled up with the incredibly fast and unique connections she made.

'Oh, I was convinced for, like, a year that I was ADHD when I was seventeen,' she'd told him. 'But my mom told me not to be stupid, and then when I asked my schoolteacher he said probably not.'

Reid blinked. 'Did he . . . actually assess you? Or put you forward for a proper assessment?'

'Well, no,' Anna had said. 'But he pointed out that I was probably overinterpreting things that everyone was talking about a lot at the time, and he had a point. Neurodiversity had become this big hot topic. He said we're all disorganised or fidgety or a bit random sometimes, but that didn't mean it needed a label. He said he'd taught ADHD kids, and they threw chairs across the room and picked fights.'

'Er,' Reid had said, thinking of one of the boys in his class. 'That sounds a bit of an exaggeration. One of the ADHD boys I knew was incredibly people-pleasing. He sat and doodled and talked nineteen to the dozen but missed half of what we were supposed to be doing and could never, ever find his homework.'

Anna had laughed, and shrugged. 'Well, if I *am*, then it doesn't matter now, I guess.'

Except, Reid had thought, *that it might help people not to blame you for things that you can't help. The wandering off. The failure to remember life events. The sudden hyper-focus that makes you forget that other things matter.*

A small voice in his head raised a counterthought now: *But you blamed her anyway . . .*

And he silenced it, brutally. What he had done – what he

had judged her for – it hadn't been the same. He'd *accepted* all her scattiness and eccentricity. He'd loved it, truth be told. It had been the cold, hard, selfish actions at the end he'd been so hurt by.

Just find her, he thought, exasperated with himself as he realised he was standing still again. *Everything else can wait.*

It was hard to know exactly what he was looking for in the flat. The frazzled pot plants were no guarantee of how long she'd been gone. Nor was the fact that there seemed to be very little food in the fridge, as she'd always been erratic about shopping, and he couldn't read much into the dates on the unopened letters.

There was no sign of her laptop, he noted. It hadn't been in Cambridge, either. Seaton had one of her phones, but the other one didn't seem to be here.

So laptop, phone and Anna were all missing. A point he tried to note to himself while ignoring a fizz of real worry.

He stood looking around the kitchen, trying to see more. Anna's usual workstation at the kitchen table held only newspapers (the latest from a week ago), more unopened letters and several plates with crumbs on. He could see no backpack of the kind she usually carried the computer in.

He looked at the chaos of open cupboards and vividly remembered her joking, 'Don't judge me for the open cupboard doors. You'll be able to follow them if I ever get kidnapped . . .'

It had been a throwaway remark that had turned into a running joke, because Anna hardly ever closed a cupboard once she'd opened it. Somehow she was always on to the next thing, too impatient or too distracted to take the millisecond to shut any door behind her.

But now, here he was, living the reality of her disappearing. And the trail led nowhere.

13. Anna

The strange mood as I left the bar on that first Saturday night gave me an edgy, anxious aftertaste. Back at the Jesus Lane house, I went over everything I'd said, wondering if I'd screwed up and given myself away (I do this a whole lot more than I was ever willing to admit to you, Reid) and then googling increasingly stupid stuff until 2 a.m.

I badly needed something to counter the anxiety, but I was coming up blank. There was still no sign of any link between any of the four and Tanya. There was also nothing online about Ryan or any unnamed students attacking women when drunk, or doing anything violent, which was disappointing. I was so sure his words to me had implied a past awful event. Though I have to admit I found myself hoping he *hadn't* attacked Holly or Tanya, because there was a vulnerability and willingness to change in Ryan Jaffett that gave me hope in the guy.

I spent a while looking up more about James Sedgewick and Kit Frankland, too. James, because he'd been so uneasy at my presence. Whatever Esther had said, I felt like I'd unbalanced him by joining the group. Logically, the most likely person to feel threatened by an outsider was someone with a guilty conscience.

Kit I had different concerns over. There were obvious reasons to suspect the guy who seemed to supply them all with drugs. He was clearly also someone who liked to exercise power, and the way he'd watched me as I'd left had, to be honest, given me the creeps.

The last searches I did were for weird events in relation to Esther Thomas's name. She seemed, of them all, the least obvious candidate, but I knew I couldn't discount her. Poisoning was often the choice made by a woman without the strength to kill in another way, and with no other options left open. But Esther was as hard to read online as she had been in person. The only thing I really concluded was that she'd grown very close to Holly Moore before she'd died. There were increasing numbers of photos of the two of them with arms round each other over the two years, and Cordelia had featured, I noticed, in fewer and fewer. An interesting note.

I eventually gave up when I realised it was now gone two, and went to bed, only to lie awake thinking about it all. I wished I had more access to the group instead of having to wait an unspecified number of days till the next social event. But I couldn't push. I knew that instinctively. They had to pursue, and I had to be the one who was hard to convince.

I ended up feeling gritty-eyed and sluggish as I took my borrowed scull out on the water at seven the next day. I'd been warned to wear my sneakily sourced GB kit and not to use any college blades as, technically, students weren't allowed on the river on a Sunday morning. A rule it was good to know.

Did I tell you it was Dad who arranged my sculling boat? I can't remember. He's done a lot for me here, and in return he demanded regular updates on everything I was doing so he got to feel involved.

It's totally clear to me that Dad has been both bored and lonely since he retired and that all this has been giving him something to do. But actually, it's been weirdly nice getting to spend time with him. I've started to feel like I know him a little better, you know? Beyond the surface stuff about him.

So despite my tiredness, I was looking forward to our

arranged brunch after the sculling session. It was our third meet-up since I'd arrived in the city, and this time I had a few things to report.

Dad picked the Ivy as the venue. Not where I'd go for a big plate of food after a rowing outing, but I wasn't paying. I managed to be only twenty minutes late, and I'd changed into clothes that didn't smell. But I was tired and distracted and he gave me a very shrewd look after we'd ordered.

'You look exhausted,' he said. 'Are you putting too much into the rowing?'

'Oh, not really,' I said. And then amended, 'I might taper it off slightly and focus on the gym sessions, which are more balanced. I'm kind of bored of everything aching all the time.' I rolled a shoulder and sighed. 'But mostly I just didn't sleep well.'

I took him through the previous night's work in an extremely low voice, leaving only James Sedgewick out of it. It wasn't too hard when I had hardly anything to say about him anyway.

It was useful to be rehearsing all this before I had to go and tell it all to Gael the next day. We have a weekly scheduled Monday check-in, with the option to add other catch-ups, and I don't think I've looked forward to a single one. It reminds me of when I used to learn piano and had never done enough practice to satisfy my teacher.

'It's annoying,' I finished, in the end, 'because I'm so short on time I can't think of any way of making more progress today. I mean, I could maybe go and look into some of the sports stuff Ryan and Kit both do. Maybe see if I can track down someone who knows them that way. Happen to bump into them. But it's a long shot and probably a waste of time.'

'You know,' Dad said, slowly, 'if you wanted to meet sports folks, there's a pretty good opportunity today. The BUCS cricket final is today at Fenner's. A lot of the sportier students like to go for a social event, and it's a sunny afternoon.' He raised an eyebrow at me. 'We could take a picnic.'

Now this, Reid, immediately made me perk up. And not just because of the free food. Despite everything I'd promised myself, I was still aching to look into Tanya's death, too. Anywhere sports folks were gathered offered me a chance, and I wanted to take it.

'Well, if you're sure you're not busy . . .' I said.

'I was already planning on going,' Dad told me.

But I wondered, actually, whether that was true. The moment I agreed he looked totally psyched. He was suddenly sitting up straighter and talking with more animation. See? The man needs more to do with his time.

I had to message Cordelia for fashion advice on the cricket match and inevitably ended up late. Mostly because I had to wait for her to finish morning lectures to reply.

And I know it's pathetic that I can't do this stuff for myself, but honestly, would you know what these guys would wear to a cricket match? Who's even *seen* a cricket match? You have to come from a very specific cluster of countries to have even been close to one growing up, and after that there's a load of class in there, too.

Anyway, my video call with Cordelia resulted in the selection of a cute little ruched Christopher Esber minidress in olive green with a cropped, fitted white blazer over the top. I of course also had my wireless voice recorder clipped to my bra, out of sight.

'I can't believe that these people wear blazers for real,' I told Cordelia as I looked at myself in the small image on the Zoom call. 'It's like they think they're still at school and there's a uniform.'

Cordelia gave a laugh. 'You should see them at Henley. Seriously. All cocktail dresses, blazers and hats. At least this is quite casual.' She gave me a critical look. 'Anyway, you don't have to completely fit in. You're the slightly rebellious one, so no formal heels. Oh, you've got those ankle boots . . . try those.'

'That's great,' I said, 'because my legs are so tired I don't think I can balance in big heels.'

The ankle boots worked, Cordelia decided. I was ready except for hair and make-up.

I probably still would have been on time for the cricket match, except we somehow got talking about life in general, and I found myself – to my surprise – telling Cordelia about Dad. While wandering around my room, ineffectually gathering and applying make-up, I gave her the run-down on Mom taking me to the US when I was five, how I'd thought we were just going on vacation, and how weird it had been starting over in Coney Island.

'What was different about it?' Cordelia asked me as I drifted around trying to find make-up without really concentrating on it.

'I guess . . . money,' I said. 'There was so little after we left. Mom didn't want his "guilt money", whatever that meant, and I think Dad eventually felt too proud to offer. And . . . she's really different from Dad.' I shrugged. 'It was a weird dynamic.'

'Did you miss him?' she asked me.

The question surprised me. 'I . . . don't know. I guess I used to like the way we made up stories and joked around.' I couldn't help smiling to myself at the thought. 'There wasn't really any of that with just me and Mom. I guess she was finding life hard, but also . . . she's not built that way, you know? She's a straightforward, serious person. And then, when she married Frank, who's this even more straightforward, serious guy who works hard and likes quiet and controlled environments . . . honestly, we barely seemed to talk at all. Unless it was about groceries or home repairs or something someone had said at church.'

It's weird, isn't it? That must be the most I've said about any of that to anyone, except maybe you. And here I was telling Cordelia, who was basically a client.

'Do you like him? Frank?' she asked me, and I found myself turning to look at her on screen.

'Not a whole lot. I mean, he isn't cruel exactly . . . and he doesn't dislike me, I don't think. But I think he finds me incomprehensible.' I laughed. 'Suddenly the fact that I was messy and disorganised and always making random comments were seen as bad things. I was being told to sit still and be sensible, and Mom went along with it. It only got worse when Ben came along, and turned out to be pretty much Frank's idea of the perfect child.'

Cordelia gave me a small smile. 'They tried to squash you to fit,' she said. 'No wonder you ran away over here.'

I couldn't help laughing at how true that was. 'Yeah. I kind of escaped to London thinking I'd find my people. My mom made me think Dad was like me. Which turned out to be not *quite* true. Like, he's got this sideways brain, too, I think. But he's all in control and nicely turned out and tidy . . . I think he sometimes wonders how he managed to produce me, if I'm honest.'

'Honestly, fuck him if he isn't proud of you,' Cordelia said, simply. 'You're doing more with your life than most people are. I decided years ago that if my mum didn't like what I was doing with mine, that was her problem to deal with.' She paused, thoughtfully, her expression distant but not unhappy. 'So now we just coexist, really, and it's actually better.' She looked back at me again, with that direct, piercing gaze of hers.

'Do you still talk to yours? Your mum?'

I took a moment to breathe out, because this was weirdly hard to admit to. 'We've not really spoken a lot since I left. It's almost like she's decided that Ben is *their* child, and I'm . . . Dad's . . . Though I keep trying. And I will always want to talk to Ben, who may be unimaginative and a little dull at times but is the sweetest boy alive.'

I don't know why I'm sharing this with you here, Reid. I mean, you know all about Mom and Ben and Frank. Maybe I'm saying it because it tells you a little about Cordelia and how she's both insightful and also kind. Or maybe because it's late and I'm on my own in this house and I feel like dwelling on it.

Anyway, she helped me. In lots of ways, beyond just getting ready for the cricket match.

The event itself started out feeling like a disappointment, you know. Although there were a lot of folks scattered around the stand and grass to watch, they were largely seated. That made it difficult to make any new connections, and I was immediately worried the only thing I was going to get out of it was the amazing free picnic provided by Dad.

He'd bought champagne, too, obviously. Taittinger, this time, with a whole specially shaped bucket with its own integral ice packs. It's unsurprising that he has paraphernalia to enable him to drink a bottle at the right temperature anywhere, given how much of the stuff he drinks. He reminds me of those people who treat themselves to an iced coffee whenever they've done anything, only with twenty times the disposable income.

Tough day? Open a Moët. Written a difficult email? Better buy Veuve. It's a warm Tuesday? Time for Taittinger.

I sometimes wonder whether there will ever be an occasion

when champagne doesn't seem appropriate to him. I imagine something bad happening to me and Dad somehow still dealing with it by opening champagne.

Which makes him sound monstrous, doesn't it? And it probably isn't even fair. I guess I'm just fixated on dark thoughts tonight.

I appreciated the Taittinger, anyway, even while I worried we'd be drinking it alone. But somehow Dad just drew people in. I don't know if it's because he's kind of famous for his semiconductor invention stuff or because he keeps his distance a little, but a series of mostly men of varying ages came over in ones and twos to seek an audience.

What fascinated me watching their interactions, though, was that Dad didn't actually seem to like any of them all that much. And I wasn't totally surprised. Several of the older ones dropped snobby, acid or just horrible comments about other people during the conversation, and I was glad when each of them eventually ambled back to their own seat.

'Is everybody you know an asshole?' I muttered to Dad, after the fourth round.

He gave me a twitching smile. 'Only the ones I introduce you to.'

I didn't hold out much hope for the next acolyte to come over, this one a tall but heavy-looking man of probably forty-five. But this guy actually turned out to be gold, because he mentioned that his daughter was with him, in an obvious brag.

'Obviously, with all the championship stuff, she's more into athletics than cricket,' he added. 'But she has to have a day off sometimes.'

I instantly went from disinterested to laser-focused. 'Oh, sounds like she's training at a high level?'

The guy looked delighted that I'd asked. 'Yes, she'll be at the World Championships in August.'

'That's awesome.' It was easy to say it like I meant it, because this was someone who had a serious chance of having known Holly.

And maybe Tanya, too, I thought.

'You know, we should probably introduce Tess and Aria,' Dad said, totally understanding the assignment. 'My god-daughter is an obsessive rower. I feel as though they'd get on, and it might be nice for Aria to actually socialise for a change.'

His friend – whose name I honestly can't even remember, Reid – seemed enthusiastic about this idea. It then turned into serious excitement the moment he realised I was apparently both a Lauder and an Olympian in the making. Without me needing to say a word, the guy led me over to where his wife and daughter had a picnic blanket spread on the grass outside the boundary.

His wife was long and leggy like he was and had linen trousers that I remember thinking were staying unbelievably creaseless considering she was hunkered on the ground. She gave me a smile and then lowered her sunglasses to look back at the match, the only one of the three who actually seemed interested in the cricket.

Tess turned out to be in training for the heptathlon. She had a tall, strong physique that was much more like mine than Holly's, and a cheerful, slightly self-centred way of talking to everyone that reminded me of the particularly rich and talented girls from Columbia.

She talked at me for some while about her achievements and was actually pretty easy to steer onto the subjects I wanted. After a little while, I told her I'd made friends with someone whose girlfriend had been a promising athlete. I said James Sedgewick's name, and Tess's eyes widened in the way of someone who has a personal investment.

'Oh, god, poor Holly,' she said. And her reaction was at that fascinating point between emotional and *This is one of my favourite subjects*. 'I used to talk to Holly at meet-ups and ask her advice on running. Because, you know, she was good. Genuinely talented.' She blinked. 'I learned things from her.'

'Aww, I'm really sorry,' I said. 'It must be so hard, losing a friend like that.'

Tess nodded, her mouth twisting slightly.

She wasn't a friend, I thought with a buzz of satisfaction. *She's got something to say.*

Tess glanced away at the match, half-heartedly applauding. It looked like someone had just been bowled out, and I did my best to applaud, too, while having no idea whether this was our side or theirs.

'I mean, we weren't the closest ever,' she went on, dropping her voice. Her parents were now talking to each other, and I guessed Tess didn't want them hearing this. 'I didn't hang out with her or anything. Like, I think she saw me as competition after a while, yeah? And you know, she wasn't *totally* this sweet person they all went on about in the news.'

'Oh, really?' I asked. Then I added, 'People are so rarely that perfect, though, are they? Everyone just hates talking badly of the dead. Which seems . . . disingenuous.'

'Exactly,' Tess said.

'Interesting that she saw you as competition,' I said. 'Did she try to stop you succeeding?'

'Well, she refused to keep helping me with my running after I started placing in races,' Tess said with a hint of a smile. 'And she was pretty annoyed that I was given more funding than she was at one point.'

I'd been hoping for more, obviously, Reid. And it occurred to me immediately that if I'd been Holly, an orphan who'd apparently burned through her inheritance on paying the remaining fees on a public school, I'd probably feel frustrated that someone whose parents could have bought a whole athletics track got more funding.

I think my doubt must have shown, because Tess quickly threw in, 'And she had a temper, too. The whole good-sportswoman thing fell down in the changing rooms. She got tripped in a race once and helped the other girl up, checked she was OK. But afterwards she kicked a locker door so hard it had to be replaced.' Tess gave a much more obvious smile. 'And she was *vile* to her boyfriend sometimes.'

'To James?' I asked, with genuine surprise.

'Absolutely,' Tess said. 'We'd see it sometimes, out on the field. Her having a go at him and him just taking it. He's too soft-hearted to argue back. And once I overheard a whole row up close. She was furious with him because he'd uploaded something and tagged her in it and it made her look bad. She was spitting. It didn't matter how many times he said he'd taken it down now, she kept on going.'

Now this, Reid, was finally something useful, and exactly the reason it made sense to talk to someone who didn't idolise Holly.

But it also made me feel really uncomfortable. Do you ever feel like that, Reid? Because here I am, trying to find Holly's killer, and all the while I'm kind of putting her on trial, too. Looking at the reasons someone might have killed her like she might have deserved it, even though I don't think anyone deserves to be murdered. Least of all a talented, twenty-one-year-old orphan.

Anyway, I decided not to push any further on the Holly angle with Tess. It was partly that weird discomfort and partly pragmatism. The last thing I wanted to do was seem too curious and for word to get round. Kit and his gang might not be here, but they'd probably know people who were.

What I asked next was . . . it was maybe stupid. But we'd come this far towards the subject that I could feel it opening out in front of me and just drawing me on. The whole thing within touching distance.

So I sighed, and said, 'It's so sad seeing another Cambridge athlete die, anyway. There was the hockey player too last year. Tanya . . . Morris, was it? Something like that? I read about it, and it was just the worst.'

'Oh, yeah . . .' Tess said, her expression thoughtful. 'That was awful, too. I didn't know her, but a girl in my college was on the team with her and was a mess about it. Felt like she'd let her down.'

'Let her down how?' I asked.

But at that point I have to admit that I lost track of what Tess was saying in reply. Because having let my eyes drift around the cricket grounds, my gaze had suddenly landed on a very familiar face.

Probably only a hundred yards away, standing in a small group up in the stands, was James Sedgewick, and he was looking at us with a flat, furious stare. The kind of stare that makes your stomach feel like it's falling out of your shoes.

Whatever Tess was saying got cut off, anyway. She followed my gaze and just . . . stopped. Broke off in mid-sentence.

And when I looked at her face, she looked terrified, Reid. Genuinely terrified.

14. Reid

Seeing Seaton Laws in the flesh was another punch of giddy, painful nostalgia for Reid.

Eighteen months hadn't changed Anna's father a whisker. His short-cropped beard was shaped exactly as it had been the last time Reid had seen him, which he guessed must have been at Anna's birthday dinner the September before they broke up. Seaton might, Reid thought, even be wearing the same suit. It was hard to tell, though. He seemed to have a whole range of blue or navy suits that were difficult to distinguish from one another.

It was stifling in the bar. Seaton had commandeered a high-backed armchair alongside a fireplace that fortunately held only flowers. When Reid arrived he was sitting in there with his legs crossed, his chin propped on his hand, with an untouched coffee on the table in front of him. He was the picture of a distracted academic. But the picture didn't last long. He noticed Reid quickly and rose with clear agitation.

'Reid, hello.'

Despite the probable urgency of the situation, Reid felt himself slipping into an awkward social mode as he took Seaton's hand.

'It's good to see you,' he said, half truthfully. 'I . . . how are things with you these days? I didn't ask before.' There was a brief pause, while Seaton shrugged, and Reid tried, 'How's the garden?'

'Fine, fine,' Seaton said, immediately. 'Blooming. Would you, er . . . like a drink?'

Though feeling that it was wasted time, Reid accepted the offer and asked for a pint of Diet Coke. He felt like he needed both the hydration and the caffeine.

Reid sat in the free chair, discovering that it was a great deal lower than Seaton's. The Reid of a few years ago might have felt humiliated, but years of interviews in all manner of situations had removed any such concerns. It was possible to perch on a wobbly stool and still dominate a conversation if you wanted to.

And that went for situations when you were unofficially interviewing your ex-girlfriend's dad about her disappearance.

Seaton returned a few moments later carrying the pint of Coke and, somewhat unexpectedly, a packet of salted kettle chips and a glass of water. Reid wasn't quite sure what he'd expected Seaton to buy, but for a man who was generally into champagne and fine dining, there was something disconcerting about it.

'Should probably eat something,' Seaton said as he sat. 'I got through three glasses of Krug waiting for her, all on an empty stomach, and I've still not managed to rectify the situation.' He tore open the crisps. 'It's not exactly Michelin-starred fare, but it'll do.'

Something about the sight of Seaton willingly consuming crisps when he could have stayed in Cambridge eating gourmet food was unexpectedly touching. He'd somehow expected Seaton to just want all of this sorting out. He hadn't anticipated her father's own determination to help her, or the shake in the man's hands.

'I've been to Anna's London flat,' Reid said, assuming his professional voice. 'I was able to access it, which was helpful. No sign of Anna. It's hard to say whether she's been there today. I'd guess not, but that's not necessarily much use if you were expecting her to be in Cambridge. Also no sign of the laptop or this phone you say she's been using.'

Seaton picked the water up. His hand shook a little more as he drank. 'So no leads at all is what you're saying?'

'Can you tell me more about what she was doing?' Reid asked. 'This murder she was investigating. Am I right in thinking it was the death of Holly Moore?'

Seaton gave him a look of mild surprise. 'Yes, it was. How did you happen on that?'

Reid couldn't help smiling. 'Well, you did give me the names of Kit Frankland and Esther Thomas. I looked them up on the way over here. They both gave quotes to the press about Holly.'

He decided not to add that connecting people with crimes was basically his job.

'Oh.' Seaton gave this a moment of thought. 'Yes, it was fairly high profile.'

'Can you tell me how Anna ended up investigating it?' Reid asked, thinking of Gael's comment that Anna was working on a financial piece. 'Did the paper send her, or was this her own thing?'

'Oh, they agreed to it all,' Seaton said, 'but it was Anna's investigation. A young woman approached her, positive her friend had been murdered but nothing had been done about it, and Anna realised she had a point.'

Reid gave a slow nod. Hearing that there had been enough evidence for a full *Ensign* investigation was, if anything, worrying. Of all the scenarios about Anna's disappearance, the idea of her having waded into a covered-up murder was the most concerning. Generally speaking, people will do a lot to keep murders from coming to light.

And the fact that Anna had vanished a year to the day after Holly had died at the very same event made his spine crawl. It was the kind of crawl that happened when a dive team reported they'd found something in a lake, or when he was played a terrified 999 call that cut off halfway through. He'd never thought he might experience that kind of reaction to news of Anna.

'I'd like the name of this friend of Holly's who approached her,' he said, as neutrally as possible. 'And any messages you have from Anna.'

'Of course,' Seaton said. 'Holly's friend is called Cordelia Wynn. She's a second-year medical student at UCL. I don't have her phone number saved, but I can spell her name for you.'

Reid watched him write it down in looping script that was at odds with his constrained behaviour. He'd added, Reid saw, *2nd-year UCL medical student*, presumably in case Reid forgot what he'd said. Which was surprisingly helpful, if a little patronising.

'Oh,' Seaton added after that, reaching into his pocket. 'I brought you Anna's phone. Her real phone. But I can't get into it. Maybe your cyber people could, you know . . .? If you pretended it was someone else's?'

Reid looked at the very familiar, battered phone in its robust star-patterned case and felt dizzy for a moment. Had she really not upgraded it in the last eighteen months? Somehow not lost it? Or smashed it?

He remembered, vividly, picking up that same phone to create a playlist for their road trip up to Scotland. Anna had been driving, and when he'd picked it up she'd said urgently, 'Mind the cable! Ah, shit,' as the satnav had disappeared off the screen.

'Sorry,' Reid had said, not sure what he was apologising for.

'Not you,' she'd said, laughing. 'The cable is a piece of crap. You have to get it at a precise angle, and, like, sacrifice to several gods to keep the connection alive. Do you think you could try putting it flat and then . . . Bingo!'

The connection had returned, and Google Maps had

reappeared in a few button presses Anna had made while allegedly concentrating on the road. Reid had spent the next twenty minutes trying to make a playlist while leaving the phone completely flat. He'd ended up looking down for so long that he'd felt sick and had to open a window.

Anna had immediately, without asking, signalled left and pulled off at the next services.

'Let's take a short break while you recover from me making you almost puke,' she'd told him, and he'd felt the strangest gratitude that he hadn't had to admit that he felt ill. He was, in many ways, made of the same stuff Tanya had been. Always determined to mask any troubles. To pretend nothing was wrong.

He found himself staring, now, at Anna's phone, with Seaton waiting patiently to hand it over. With a twist in his stomach, Reid took it.

It felt strangely warm in his palm, as though it had some of Anna's energy in it. Though, in fact, it had probably just been next to an overheating fifty-seven-year-old man all the way from Cambridge.

'I'll . . . see what I can do,' Reid said. He didn't feel equal to disappointing Seaton right now by admitting that there was no way he could hand it to the cyber team.

This wasn't his investigation, or anything to do with the Met. And if he got caught lying about the provenance of a device in order to track his ex-girlfriend, his career would be over. There were very good reasons – including reasons of stalking and abuse – that officers were never allowed to do that.

If he could somehow find a way of turning this into a Met investigation, then he'd be able to hand it over. But at that point, he'd be handing the whole case over with it. He couldn't be SIO of an investigation into his own ex-girlfriend's disappearance.

The one thing he *might* do was try to unlock the phone himself. It was dodgy, and the idea made him feel nauseous, even though he had zero intention of using it to snoop on his ex.

But there might be messages on there that made it obvious where she was. If not, then it might still contain an excuse for the Met to take over. There might even be messages that were so obviously threatening, Seaton could go back to Cambridgeshire and force them to step up. But it was still dubious, and worse, felt like a huge invasion of privacy.

He put the phone into his pocket and realised that Seaton was still sitting forwards, his expression hesitant. There was clearly something else he wanted to say.

'I . . . may actually have another device,' he said. He cleared his throat and then went on, 'Hypothetically, if someone were to have discovered a device hidden in a murder suspect's room . . . and inadvertently picked it up in a hurry . . .'

Reid shook his head with a sigh. 'Would the person picking it up be Anna?'

'Ahhh, not quite,' Seaton said. 'Say that person were, in fact, me?'

Reid couldn't help giving a startled laugh. 'You . . . what?' As Seaton gave a sheepish look, Reid narrowed his eyes and asked, 'Seriously. She managed to drag you into this?'

'I offered some assistance,' Seaton said with dignity. 'I made the decision myself. She didn't have many other people to rely on, when it came down to it.'

Reid felt that comment like the barb it was, and then experienced a rush of anger. Did Seaton really expect him to be there for Anna a year and a half after they'd broken up? After what she'd done? What she'd revealed herself to be?

He took a breath, determined not to let on to Seaton that any of this was bothering him.

'So this device . . . is a phone, I take it?' he asked, and as Seaton nodded, said, 'Taken from a student room?'

'*Accidentally brought out* from Ryan Jaffett's room. One of the four she was looking into.'

'Did Anna ask you to look for it?' Reid asked, his thoughts grinding through this.

'Not for a phone, specifically,' Seaton said. 'She said she was positive he had something hidden and that it was significant. She suspected a second phone or a pen drive or some such item. And . . . ah . . . she suggested a few places to check.' He cleared his throat. 'Someone . . . someone else came in, just after I'd picked it up. A young woman. I'm sure she was looking for the same thing. I had to hide in the shower. But anyway. It all went well in the end.'

Reid shook his head, in part at the idea of Seaton hiding in a student's bathroom in a position that would have been impossible to explain, and in part at the shadiness of Anna's methods. Though he had to admit it sounded like she'd known something significant. Why else send her dad there, and how else would she have guessed the phone was going to be hidden?

'She didn't explain why?' he asked.

'Unfortunately not,' Seaton admitted. 'I – we were sharing information, to a point. But you know Anna . . .'

Reid gave a wry smile. He did, indeed, know Anna.

'All right.' What should he say? So much of him wanted to tell Seaton to keep hold of it and tell him nothing more.

But what if it's the key to everything? What if it shows where she's gone?

'An unlawfully taken phone is difficult. But . . . if it arrives in my possession in a way that isn't quite clear, then we might be able to take a look at it, if it comes to it.' Reid felt detached from his own body. Was he really saying this? 'If, for example, you were to tell me the phone was left somewhere for you with a note saying it might be of interest, then we'd have a reason to look. On the basis it could be Anna's.'

'Wonderful,' Seaton said with a beaming smile. 'Coincidentally, it happened exactly like that.'

He reached down into his bag again and handed another phone over. This was also an iPhone, though it was a lot newer-looking than Anna's and wasn't in a protective case.

Reid felt a surge of real anxiety as he took it. He had a sense of having stepped into the water for a paddle and then been dragged miles out to sea by a rip tide.

There had always been things Anna was willing to do that he wouldn't. That he couldn't. He had to follow the rules. More than that, he *wanted* to follow the rules.

And now here he was, pocketing a stolen phone and offering to lie to his colleagues. All for an ex-girlfriend who'd betrayed him entirely.

It's only wrong if you actually go ahead with the lie, he told himself. *Just taking the phone isn't a crime as such.*

'All right,' he said, suddenly eager to move. To go. 'I'll . . . see what I can do. Obviously, if you do think of anything she told you, or if she contacts you . . .'

'I'll let you know straight away, yes,' Seaton agreed.

It was as Reid was rising to go that Seaton said, abruptly, 'Thank you for doing this, Reid. I . . . I know it's asking a lot. But I hope you realise that she'd do the same for you. Without question. Even now.'

Reid was already tired of feeling wrongfooted by all of this. He wanted so badly to go back to his normal, safe, everyday thoughts.

And yet, as he blinked at Seaton for a moment, he felt a rush of some long-forgotten warmth.

15. Anna

On the second of June, I arrived at my Monday check-in with Gael feeling like I was made of anxiety, even having written up the fragments of information I'd picked up at the cricket match. I'd listened back to all of it on the Bluetooth recorder and made as much of it as I could, conscious of needing to prove I was getting somewhere now that I was fully a part of the group, and equally conscious that my four-week deadline had already been reduced to three weeks and a half. Two and a half weeks of term, and a week of debauched revelry in the madness of what was known as May Week after it was officially over.

But Gael was clearly satisfied by the story of Ryan's drinking, and even more so by my explanation of Tess's story and James's death stare.

'When are you seeing them again?'

'Tomorrow,' I told him. 'Wine tasting.'

I said it with breezy confidence, but after Esther had messaged to invite me, I'd spent the train journey racked with anxiety about the event. Wine is obviously something I know zero about, which wouldn't be so bad if upper-class people with money weren't *so* hot on knowing all about it. And Aria Lauder's parents were known as big buyers of wine. The idea of turning up and saying totally the wrong thing was making me sick with nerves.

The trouble was, I felt totally unable to admit to anyone that I hadn't actually got this. I couldn't destroy the image I'd built up at work of being the Cambridge professor's daughter from an Ivy League university; and the idea of asking Dad or Cordelia for more help was just humiliating. I'd leaned on them both a heap already and was beginning to worry they thought I was incompetent.

And to be honest, there was a limit to how much either of them could teach me in thirty-six hours. I wouldn't have a chance to taste a bunch of wines with them, which was the only way I was going to get half decent at this stuff. So I'd done as much googling as I could about *terroir*, and region, and length, and then I'd looked up the wines we were going to taste.

Gael seemed totally pumped by the concept, anyway.

'It's perfect,' he said. 'They'll be inebriated and easy to direct. Ryan may get drunk again, which will let you see what he's like or get him to confess what he's done before. And the others might have something to say about Holly. James, too, maybe, if he's pissed off with you for talking to this other girl at the cricket.'

'Great,' I said, trying to catch his enthusiasm for it all. It *was* an opportunity to find out more, and things could so easily kick off. I'd make progress.

Though as I remembered James's flat stare all over again, I felt a flicker of worry.

There was nervous energy running through me as Esther led me into what was apparently the smaller dining room at Magdalene College (which, by the way, is pronounced *nothing like* it looks. This place, Reid). We'd met at the college gates, and Esther seriously wasn't helping my nerves by talking at length about a Haut Lafitte tasting she'd been to earlier in the year.

'I really hadn't expected some of the palates,' she told me. 'Have you ever tried their white Bordeaux? It's extraordinary. Almost crystallised.'

'I have not,' I told her, with as light a laugh as I could manage. 'But I believe you.'

I was momentarily rescued at the doorway by Kit calling from across the dining room. He and Ryan were standing alongside a table covered with different-shaped glasses. No Sarah tonight, it seemed. But then, it probably wasn't surprising. Cordelia had told me that Kit's girlfriends were only add-ons rather than core members of the group. Which might be healthy, or might be about Kit keeping a level of control over the people in his life.

I scanned the room and realised with a flicker of further anxiety that James was already here, too. He was deep in conversation with an expensively tailored man who must have been my dad's age and an extremely pretty, dark-haired woman of probably close to my own. I braced myself. There was every chance James had told the room I'd been gossiping behind his back.

After this thought came another one: I realised my expectation that the wine tasting would be students only was way off. It was run by the Wine Society, which was a student society officially, but only half the occupants of the room looked to be undergrad age. The rest were a whole spread of other ages, and some of them were at least in their sixties.

Ryan gave me a warm hug as I arrived, but I could sense tension in him, and I realised that this event might actually be worse for him than it was for me.

'Hey,' I said. 'I didn't know you were coming.' Which was basically my tactful way of saying, *Why is a teetotaller at a wine tasting?*

He gave me a tight smile. 'Yeah, Esther talked me into it.' He added, more quietly, 'I won't be swallowing any.'

I blinked at him, thinking that this sounded like the craziest test of willpower I'd ever heard. But I couldn't say a lot else without embarrassing him. So I changed the subject to rugby.

While we spoke, I was half listening to Kit teasing Esther for the amount of work she was doing. It was gently done, but I sensed a serious undercurrent.

'I'm honestly doing hardly any!' she eventually protested, with what almost sounded like a note of stress. 'Around all the social stuff we're doing, it's barely ten hours in a day, and my nightmare exams are on Thursday and Friday. I shouldn't even be here.'

That comment drew my attention. She'd been talked into coming out *in the middle* of her exams? With only two days until the next one? I would have been cramming in a panic at that stage, with at most a brief pint of soda with my friends before returning to my room.

At the same time, I wondered whether ten hours was a usual amount of study for her, because it didn't leave much room for other stuff. I really wanted to join their conversation. To ask questions and find out what made Esther tick; what might tip her over the edge. I wanted to see under Esther's surface and work out whether her affectionate side could turn obsessive.

There was a loud laugh from James's group, and we all of us ended up stopping to look over. It was the well-tailored older guy, guffawing at something the pretty dark-haired girl had said.

James, I thought, looked embarrassed to be there. I wasn't sure if it was the company or the event, though he definitely fitted the aesthetic. His Greek-statue face, tumbling hair and slim build suited his old-fashioned tuxedo perfectly, and I suddenly saw how he must be on stage.

The pretty young woman leaned over to talk to him, and James visibly relaxed a little. I wondered whether she was a new love interest. If she was, she would apparently be the first person James had considered since Holly's death. His social media and Cordelia agreed on this. But as the rest of my group started to talk again the girl detached herself and moved away across the room, leaving James to drift over to us.

I saw James look towards me and then away, and was sure there was a grilling of some kind coming. It couldn't have been clearer that he'd disliked me talking to gossip-loving Tess.

I decided I needed a glass of wine to calm the roiling nerves in my stomach. There were a few people already drinking champagne and near us on the table was what looked like my kind of light red, so I reached out to take one and offered a glass to Esther, too.

'Oh,' she said, quietly, turning towards me. 'I . . . do you really want to drink a red before a tasting? I don't even know why they've served it.'

I felt the jolt of a misstep. It was like they'd set up a trap for me to walk into.

'New secretary,' Kit said, leaning in. 'Doesn't know the rules.'

There was something about his expression that challenged me, and you know I can't say no to a challenge, Reid. I laughed and knocked a large mouthful of the (actually really nice) wine back.

'As far as I'm concerned,' I said after I'd swallowed it, 'the rule is "Drink what you feel like drinking right now". I have a day off training tomorrow for the first time in two weeks. Screw saving my palate for a load of wines I'll probably dislike.'

Kit gave a slow smile, and then – slightly to my surprise – picked a glass up, too.

'I'll drink to that.'

After a moment, Esther glanced at the second glass I was still holding, and said, 'You know, I like your rule better.'

Ryan glanced towards a cluster of older men and shook his

head with a smile. 'I'm not going to join in. You're all making me look like a pleb.'

I couldn't help giving a shocked laugh. 'Nobody actually says "pleb".'

'Only a pleb would say that,' Ryan countered with a grin. I shook my head at him, sure that this was all just an excuse not to drink but also thinking the language was a little . . . off. It was, I realised, the first time I'd heard any of them sound snobby about anything.

James had drifted over to us by this point, and was watching us consideringly.

'I'll leave you all to it,' Ryan went on, 'and go and chat up the elderlies for a bit. Get it out of the way.'

He squared his shoulders and moved towards the cluster of fifty- and sixty-year-olds, where he was immediately accosted by the well-tailored man who'd been talking to James.

'Ohhh, is that Ryan's dad?' I asked, delighted. 'Explains so much.'

'Er, no,' James said after a momentary pause. 'That's *my* dad, trying to charm everyone, as usual.' As I looked at him, startled, he added, 'Sorry. Can't really . . . do anything about it.'

I wasn't sure if Kit's expression was pure amusement, or also glee at my mistake. But either way, the only thing for it was to apologise to James without any visible embarrassment. I was clearly already in trouble with him, anyway.

To be fair to me, Reid, there was virtually no similarity at all between the powerful, skiing-and-horses build of Philip Sedgewick – a man who seemed to ooze confidence – and the delicate handsomeness of the son. I guess they were both handsome, in their way, with Philip still young enough to be a looker. But the dad was all broad cheekbones and merriment. None of James's delicate poet-from-a-bygone-age thing.

Now that I'd seen Philip Sedgewick for myself, I was also

surprised at Dad still being friends with him. He seemed like the kind of ultra-connected ex-public-school guy he'd been avoiding at the cricket.

I watched Philip for a few moments and then told James, 'You have to be a changeling.'

'I've often hoped so.' James gave me a smile, which was a positive note. He didn't seem angry, now I came to think of it. 'There's worse, you know.' He nodded towards the very pretty young woman I'd seen him with before. 'That's my super-in-every-way sister.'

I couldn't help staring. 'Wow.' I shook my head, looking her over again. 'She looks great, but you're prettier than she is, you know.'

'Thanks,' James said. 'I think.' There was a pause in which Kit moved to murmur something to Esther, something I badly wanted to hear. But James was saying, 'I'm . . . sorry I didn't come to say hello on Sunday.'

'Sorry?' I blinked at him, and then realised what he meant. 'Oh, at the cricket? That's OK. You were with friends.'

'Honestly, it wasn't that,' he said. 'I would have come and got you. It's just . . . I had a bit of a falling-out with Tess Withnell a short while ago and I didn't want to make things awkward.'

'Ohhhh,' I said. 'Is that because she's a shit-stirrer?'

And there's a big irony in that, Reid, because obviously I was only saying it because I was, myself, shit-stirring. But in my defence, I was doing it for a good reason.

James's mouth tightened, and then he sighed. 'Yes,' he said. 'So I'm guessing she told you her usual crap about me and Holly?'

I gave him a grimace. 'Yeah. I'm sorry. I shouldn't have mentioned that I'd met you, but I was just trying to think of something to say that wasn't "Wow, you're so athletic."'

James gave a short laugh and said, 'It's honestly not your fault. But for what it's worth, she knows very well that what she's saying isn't true. The conversation she loves to share was about someone *else* tagging Holly in something, not me. Holly was totally justified being angry. It was a girl at Holly's college trying to make out that Holly was friends with a right-wing commentator just because they'd been standing near each other at a dinner the college had hosted. It was a really gross attempt to make her look bad. She was furious and angry, and I was there for her, because that's what you do when you're someone's boyfriend.' He looked away from me, his expression flat. 'I also asked Kit, as our pet lawyer in the making, to threaten the girl who shared it with legal action, and she took it down. But it caused Holly a lot of hurt at the time.'

'I'm sorry,' I said, both because it was the sensible thing to say and because it was the right thing to say. It was hard to tell whether James was telling the truth or spinning me a tale and acting it perfectly. But I both needed to make him trust me and felt how hard it must be to lose your partner. 'For what it's also worth,' I added, 'I've met people like Tess before. The kind who are dying to tell you gossip about everyone you mention. I've learned not to listen to it, so you don't need to worry.'

I put a hand briefly on his shoulder, and he gave me a half-smile.

'Good,' he said. And then, lifting his head, he added, 'Do you want to meet the family? Mum's here somewhere, too.'

'Of course.'

I gave James a smile but felt a returning jolt of anxiety. Pulling off the Aria Lauder act in front of James's well-connected family was, in many ways, likely to be a harder job than managing it with the students. And the friendship between Dad and Philip Sedgewick made it feel more risky.

But I was also keenly interested to meet the parents of these absurdly privileged kids. It had struck me already that covering up a crime was a difficult enterprise and that a wealthy, well-connected parent might have stepped in to help. I think most of us would do more than we'd like to admit to protect the people we love.

I followed James towards the silver-haired man, and Philip lit up with delight the moment he heard my name.

'Oh, you're Seaton's god-daughter! What an absolute pleasure to meet you.'

'Thanks,' I said, taking his offered kiss on the cheek and feeling incredibly grateful that Dad had thought to lay proper groundwork. 'I'm surprised he's willing to admit to the connection.'

'Not at all, not at all,' Philip said, warmly. 'He's immensely proud of you. He's told me all about your rowing achievements. What an impressive thing, to be rowing for Great Britain.'

I felt a strange little twist just then, realising that Dad had been boasting to Philip about achievements of Aria's when he'd clearly never told him anything at all about my own.

'Well, I'll only be rowing GB if I can stay in the squad,' I countered, wryly, trying to keep my head in the game. 'Which means both being faster than three other bow-siders and not pissing Nat – our head coach – off so much he drops me.'

'Always the hardest challenge,' Philip said with a twinkle. 'My daughter used to row for the university,' he added. 'Olivia,' he called, to James's curly-haired beauty of a sister. She was currently talking to a group of what looked like PhD students. 'Come and meet my friend's god-daughter. You two can bore each other about rowing.'

'I'm only ever fascinating about rowing,' Olivia said, coming over with a grin. 'But I do miss it like mad. Want to go out in a pair in the morning?'

My concerns about being found out evaporated quickly amid the warm and lively welcome of James's family. His mother, Marcie, who drifted over after a few minutes, was a quieter, softer version of the others. A decade or so younger than Philip at what I guessed was mid-forties she also looked fascinatingly like James, her dark hair longer and her height a couple of inches shy of his but her eyes and cheekbones just the same. There was a warmth in the way she watched her children that made me feel a little pang of longing. I don't think Mom has ever looked at me like that.

The Sedgewicks were, in summary, all easy to talk to and hard to dislike. This despite the way they mentioned trips to the Caribbean and their house in the south of France as if these were normal things. Like James, they wore their wealth lightly, and I immediately enjoyed the way they challenged and gently ribbed each other over everything. All except gentler Marcie, who largely tutted and smiled at them and told them not to be such bullies.

'I do try with them, you know,' she muttered to me in resigned amusement after Olivia had been harsh to her brother about his hair. 'But Philip's genes won.'

'Well, James got your looks,' I told her. 'Which is a win.'

'Don't let James hear you say so,' she said, conspiratorially. 'He'd much rather believe he looked like his soldier uncle. If he has to have the Buckley looks, you can see why he'd choose gruff, military captain Eddie over looking, well . . . beautiful, I suppose.'

'Ahh, come on!' I protested. 'James is, like, the handsomest man on the planet!'

Marcie gave me a slightly thoughtful look, and I realised she probably thought I was *interested* in James. I decided on a quick subject change, and because I was there to work I decided to bring up Holly. It seemed safe enough, now that both James and Esther had mentioned her to me.

'I'm sorry he's had such a rough time,' I said, quietly. 'It must have hit all of you, what happened to Holly.'

I saw Marcie's eyes go from thoughtful to glimmering.

'It – it did,' she said, looking away from me. 'You know, I struggled a lot with feeling selfish after she died. I missed her for myself, as a friend. It was so nice having another young woman around who hadn't grown up with all this.' She waved a hand at the lushly decorated room, somehow summing up the ridiculous extravagance of it all with that one gesture. 'We were the two outsiders. The ones who didn't ski or sit on a horse from five years old.' She shook her head. 'Anyone who can make their mother-in-law feel like they have an ally is a special person.'

'Well, it sounds like she was lucky to have you, too,' I said. 'Having a family welcome you in is pretty special.'

The trouble with *that*, obviously, was it was right back to sounding like I was trying to be James's new girlfriend. Something I only realised after I'd said it.

It was a relief when Philip interrupted us straight afterwards.

'You must let me escort you to your seat, Aria,' he said, holding out a hand. 'We're in danger of stopping you from sitting with your friends.'

I glanced toward the tables and saw that they were beginning to fill up. Kit, Ryan and Esther were already sitting, and James was squeezing his way past the line of chairs on the far side. There were only two seats left near them, and Esther was looking round at me anxiously.

'Oh, thanks,' I said to Philip, taking his hand formally.

I could still feel Marcie's thoughtful gaze on me as he led me away, but Philip himself seemed to assume I must want to sit next to Ryan rather than James, and I decided to leave him with that impression.

'It's been a pleasure to meet you,' James's father said,

pulling the chair out for me. 'I'll look forward to seeing you again soon.'

'Thanks,' I said, giving him a brilliant smile.

To my surprise, the last seat was taken a moment later by Kit's girlfriend, Sarah. My guess about this being a core-group-only event had clearly been wrong.

I smiled at her as she sat down, realising that she was looking over at me.

'I didn't know you were coming,' Sarah said, immediately. And I felt a jab of fellow feeling, the two of us for some reason being kept out of the loop.

'Esther got her a ticket,' Kit said, breezily, apparently unconcerned that Sarah was not next to him. After that he sank quickly into outraged banter about being accused of plagiarism over a mock exam essay he had – in fact – plagiarised. This seemed fairly typical of Kit, from what I'd learned so far.

Sarah laughed, but I saw her eyes cut across to me again and again, whoever I was talking to. Her opinion on me seemed to have shifted since the last meet-up, and I couldn't quite suss out what was going on there, or why my presence specifically bothered her. But I knew it was something that could go either way: something I could use in my favour, or something that might ruin everything if I wasn't careful.

The wine tasting itself ended up being a lot less stressful than I'd predicted, anyway. Now that I'd made a stand as someone who didn't care about the theory, I felt free to resist all efforts at giving flavour notes and instead commented on whether I liked them or not. Or as I decided to put it, 'Bullshit or not bullshit.'

Somehow my refusal to play along had a direct effect on Esther, too. Her earlier anxiety over spoiling the taste had evaporated, along with her comments on *terroir.* And when she refused to drink any more than a sip of one of the reds, giving a definite 'Not my thing,' I saw Kit looking over at me with a very considering expression. It made me wonder whether I was infringing on his little kingdom of influence too far.

The weird thing was that, as the wine hit them all, they didn't turn nastier or less forgiving, like I'd been expecting. There were no scathing comments about people who didn't know their *appellations*, and no remarks about people poorer, or stupider, or in a minority, or any of the casual sexism I'd experienced from some of the guys at Columbia. There was actually a social awareness to this crowd that made me understand why Holly Moore had wanted to spend time with them, and the drunk versions of them were only more fun.

Ryan seemed to be spitting most of his wine out, to do him credit, though there were the occasional moments when I saw a glass that had been half full suddenly empty. I was on the alert for any behaviour changes, but he seemed much as normal, if an increment louder and happier.

I guess the one uncomfortable note to it all was Sarah's behaviour. She was no longer looking over at me but instead away from us all, in an increasingly unhappy silence. When Kit occasionally leaned round James to murmur a comment to her, it seemed that she was unenthusiastic about replying. *Definite trouble in paradise*, I thought, which was much better than trouble directed at me.

In between all of this, I was constantly looking for a way to introduce the topics of Holly and Tanya. It took until dessert before I found my opportunity, and, in fact, it was James choosing to leave early – despite his family still all being there – who gave me the chance.

'I wish he'd stay and let us cheer him up,' I said. 'But I guess if you guys have spent all year being there for him, maybe it's not about that. Maybe it's just a matter of time.'

'He needs to date again,' Ryan said, shaking his head. 'It's time.'

'Ryan!' Esther's response was shocked. Even, I thought, hurt. 'You can't . . . Holly wasn't just anyone. You don't just *find someone else* when you were with your soulmate.'

Ryan gave an exasperated sigh. 'I know she wasn't just anyone. But he's twenty-one. He can't rule himself out of dating forever. And I think if he could date, then he'd believe that life wasn't over. It'd do him good.'

'It's not forever,' Esther said, stiffly. 'It's only been a year. Not even a year.'

I suddenly saw an opportunity opening up: a chance to mention Tanya, and with a familiar, headlong feeling of risk, I took it.

'I don't see how you could go through that and not blame yourself,' I said. 'It's impossible to lose someone and not feel like it's your fault. I met a girl from here, a natural sciences student, who was over in Vermont for the summer. My mom made me go and talk to her so I was prepped for Cambridge, and I kind of liked her so we stayed in touch even when I . . . postponed. And then she fell off the map, and I found out later she'd died of an overdose once she'd been back over here a while.' I had to take a little pause then. It was harder than I'd thought it would be, telling them about Tanya. About the guilt I'd felt. I hadn't expected to feel like I was using her story when, in fact, it was essentially true. And I'm sorry, Reid, if you feel like I was using it, too. 'I didn't really know her. Not really. But she was this super-talented hockey player, and it seemed like such a waste. I felt like I should have helped her. You know?'

I looked up at each of them, finding a strangely tense silence, and I realised that Kit was staring at me with none of his usual composure. His mouth was slack and his expression shocked.

It was Sarah – no longer looking away from us but looking right at me – who finally broke the silence. 'Wow, was that . . . was that the girl from Selwyn?'

They know something, I thought with horrified triumph. *They know her.*

'It . . . yeah, it was,' was all I could manage.

'That's so weird,' she said, her eyes wide. 'Kit and Ryan met her, too. Didn't you? Tanya, wasn't it?'

I felt it in my stomach, Reid. The twist of bitter triumph.

I looked sharply at the two boys and had to hold in the immediate hard questions I desperately wanted to ask. It was only reasonable to be surprised at this point. Not anything else. But I could feel my hand shaking against the tablecloth as I asked, 'Whoa, seriously? You knew her?'

Kit was shaking his head. 'No, not really. Just met her at a dinner. Only the once, but . . . like you say.' He held my gaze for a moment and then rose with what was a very un-Kit-like clumsiness. 'Back in a second.'

I stared after him, and then said, 'God, that's so strange. The same Tanya.'

Ryan shook his head, frowning. 'I mean, he didn't really *meet* her. Neither of us did. She was at the same formal exchange. The rugby first eleven went to Queen's formal hosted by the first hockey girls, so you can imagine how chaotic it was. We didn't even talk to her. She was down the other end of the group and she left early.' He looked towards the door, and I realised that his eyes were a little unfocused. 'He's kind of rinsing it for a story, to be honest.'

Sarah pulled a strange little face and took a long pull of wine before rising to follow Kit, and I suddenly wondered whether this was what Ryan did when he was drunk. Whether he lost all of his social filters and said the things nobody wanted to hear. Whether he was a bit of an asshole.

If he does, then that could be seriously useful, I thought.

Esther was shaking her head at Ryan.

'He's not rinsing it,' she said, quietly. 'It just shook him up. He was right there, and didn't notice that she was struggling. And then the next day, she was dead. Of course he felt bad. You felt bad, too, didn't you?'

I had to take a long drink myself at that point to hide the dizzy, nauseating understanding that flooded through me.

Shit, I thought as I swallowed it down. *They were there with her the night she died.*

So you see, Reid? I was right.

After everything you said to me, *I was fucking right.*

16. Reid

It was 7.15 p.m. and Reid was walking towards the tube station once again, with no clear idea of what he was doing. Despite the heat, he felt shivery with cold.

Every part of what Seaton told him had made him more afraid for Anna. Totally aside from it approaching twenty-four hours since she'd vanished – a deeply worrying fact in itself – hearing the methods Anna had been employing set off resounding alarms in him.

He couldn't explain why it made him feel so wretched, the idea that something had happened to her. She'd let him down. Treated him terribly.

But in spite of that, he found himself remembering the Anna he'd first met. The Anna who had been almost half an hour late to their initial meeting, despite having asked him to help her with something, and still managed to utterly charm him.

He'd been leaving the office, just to make it clear he wasn't going to be messed around, when she'd turned up in the entrance hall. And somehow he'd stopped being irritated between one breath and the next. Because instead of the pushy, driven or possibly arrogant journalist he'd been expecting he'd been confronted with a frantically apologising, rapidly talking hurricane of rain-soaked energy.

'God, I'm so, so sorry,' she'd been saying, before he'd even fully acknowledged her. 'The tubes were a bit messed up, but I was already running late anyway because there was one of those work meetings where everyone has to have *an opinion*, and you just feel your life *draining away*. And then I couldn't find my Oyster card, which I didn't even *need*, obviously, but I got obsessed with finding it because otherwise you look like a tourist in front of a bunch of strangers you'll never see again. So that was clearly stupid, and my fault, and then I suddenly realised it was dumb and ran out but forgot my coat so I'm kind of soaking. Anyway. I'm here. Do you still have time?'

She'd stared imploringly at him, rain dripping off her hair and into her eyes, with just the slightest of smiles, and he'd found it impossible to turn her away.

'We're OK for time,' he'd said. 'Depending on how much of your drained-away life you can still spare. I mean, you might have fun things to fit in, too . . .'

She'd blinked at him and then given him a high-wattage grin. 'Oh, well. We've probably got, like, forty-five minutes before I expire. And you seem a good use of my time.'

'Does . . . that mean I'd have to deal with your corpse at the end of the meeting?' he'd asked, letting her through the barrier and starting to head up the stairs. 'Because I already have a few of those to manage today. And, in all honesty, I'm crap at it.'

He wasn't sure whether it was the laugh she'd given in response or the way she'd said, 'It's OK. We have people for that. Just ring the office,' that had sealed it for him.

Though maybe it was the moment he'd looked back at her and seen that . . . warmth of hers. The fun. The skewering intelligence in her eyes, and her genuine joy in the conversation.

Whatever it had been, he'd known that he was probably in trouble way back then. Even when she'd told him that some of the evidence in her sex-trafficking case *may* have been gathered using slightly underhand methods. He'd shaken his head at her, and for the first time in his life found himself accepting that maybe the ends might justify the means.

'I need to prove it the right way, now,' she'd said. 'I know I should have done it the right way the first time, but I had to have enough to get my boss on board. I really had to stop them, you know?' Her eyes had been full of a much more serious expression than usual. 'One of the reasons I want you involved is to make sure nothing happens to those girls while I'm busy building a story. It's not worth sitting back and waiting while I get all my sources right. So I'm going to give you the details of one of the sites and hope you might get someone to put surveillance on it while we find out who's bringing them in. And if they look like they're moving them, can you just go in there and rescue everyone who needs it, and we'll worry about my editor later?'

The memory made him feel dizzy. Was that . . . had she really said that? Had he forgotten? Or misremembered?

It didn't make sense. Not with what she'd done over Tanya. With her obsessive chasing of the story at the expense of everything else.

He reached the steps to Finsbury Park tube station and stopped there, trying to make some sense of the Anna he thought he'd known. He had no idea what he really thought, and equally little idea of where he was going or what he was going to do next. He had no excuse to bring this to the Met yet, and nothing to spur Cambridgeshire on, either.

The one thing he really wanted to do right now was ask someone's advice. But the one person he might have talked to was no longer an option. Not since that person had been sanctioned for what was basically corruption.

Dom Davies was Reid's fellow DI at Finsbury Park and had for a long time occupied the spot that would have been reserved for a best friend. Their close working relationship had come crashing down when it had turned out that Dom had failed to report a series of WhatsApp messages that had been unquestionably sexist and profoundly inappropriate. If he *had* reported them, the two officers sending those messages would have been investigated and would never have been free to continue to sexually assault young women in their custody, as it had later turned out they were doing.

Much of Reid's anger had been directed at the two offenders, but of course he'd been angry with Dom, too. His friend had turned a blind eye, in a way that so many people did. He'd been complicit and let those two arseholes get away with it for longer.

Reid had been shattered to learn that his closest friend wasn't the man he'd thought. And, at that point, Anna had been . . . she'd been there for him, now that he thought about it. But she'd also provided another take on Dom's behaviour, one that had taken him aback.

'When it's your friend, you probably see these slightly inappropriate things and wince but tell yourself they're all right really,' she'd said gently. 'And when it keeps happening, it must be like being in an abusive relationship. Where's the line? When do you suddenly decide that enough is enough? At what point do you start thinking you've let it happen for too long and have missed your chance of complaining?'

Stop it, he told himself, taking a few steps along the pavement and back in an effort to clear his mind. He pushed all this away again. Pushed away the memory of Anna's hand ruffling his hair and her head leaning against his. Of her breath tickling his temple.

He needed to work out what to do next, without Dom's help or anyone else's. Cambridge was a forty-five-minute train ride away, with probably a taxi at the far end after that. So with the tube ride to King's Cross, it was realistically an hour and a half to see any of the four students Anna had been looking into.

If he started now, he might get a response from the Trinity porters about CCTV during the journey, and maybe even be able to follow up on what they found. But there was also one person in London who might know if Anna had decided to deliberately run off somewhere, someone Seaton hadn't yet contacted.

That was Cordelia Wynn.

Reid took out the piece of embossed notepaper Seaton had so carefully inscribed for him and decided that his best bet would be to call UCL in his official capacity. Doing that was still totally legitimate within the early-stage asking of questions.

The UCL staff were helpful. He was told without trouble that Cordelia lived in an accommodation block off Pentonville Road named Dinwiddy House.

It took him only seventeen minutes via the tube to get there and, looking around the place, he realised that Cordelia Wynn might actually be a slightly less overprivileged person than he'd been assuming from her name. Dinwiddy House was a very large, unattractive, nineties-looking building spread over four storeys. It had row after row of windows that indicated the students were packed in pretty tightly. There was a large brick courtyard at its centre with a few straggling plants and an inexplicable semicircular paved construction that seemed to provide neither shelter nor seating.

The place was clearly inexpensive, and given that Cordelia was in her second year, she'd presumably had other options. Not a snob, then.

With so many different entrances, it took Reid a good few minutes to locate Cordelia's room. Fortunately the doors were equipped with buzzers and labelled with surnames, and he found C. Wynn on the fourth door he tried.

He felt a flood of relief when Cordelia Wynn's hesitant voice came over the intercom with a 'Hello?'

'Hi, this is DI Reid Murray,' he told her, aware that she could see him through the doorbell camera while he could see nothing in return. 'I'm a detective with the Metropolitan Police, though that's not anything to worry about. I'm just trying to track down Anna Sousa and I wondered if you could help at all.'

There was a pause of a few seconds before Cordelia said, 'I'll buzz you up,' and he wondered about that pause the whole way up the three flights of stairs to her room.

Cordelia gave him a very searching look as she let him in, and he felt the need to show her his badge and look as professional as possible. She still kept her face towards him as she backed away and sat down, though, and he got the impression she was someone used to assessing people carefully. There was none of the ready self-confidence of the posh hockey girls Tanya had made friends with.

Her student pad was as small and unassuming as the building indicated, though there were signs of her family's money here even so. She'd illuminated the gloom with two beautiful lamps and replaced what had presumably been a bare overhead light with a giant, gold-tinted bulb with a spiral filament. There was a painting on one wall, too, and photographs on others, along with a framed quote in blocky stamped ink that read *happiness is only a choice if you can afford to pay for the freedom to choose.*

Reid smiled at that, and then found his eyes drawn to a collage of pictures in a big black frame. Each one portrayed Cordelia with a girl he realised must be Holly Moore. She was recognisable from the photographs that had been used after her death.

Tracking through, he could see the two of them ageing up through school and then into university. At times there were other girls with them. He recognised Esther Thomas from the Instagram photos he'd looked at on his way over. She was impossibly glamorous in all of them and seemed to have the most curated of pouts for the camera no matter where it captured her.

In contrast, Holly seemed full of warmth. Open and caring. And although Cordelia had chosen these photos he felt as though the love between the two friends was clear as day, too.

He could sense Cordelia watching him keenly still, her body tense despite her casual sports gear. It seemed there was something she wanted to say but perhaps was wary of telling him.

'Why are you looking for Anna?' she suddenly asked, as if she couldn't wait any longer.

'I'm a little bit worried about her,' he told her, quietly. 'Her dad got in touch because she missed lunch today. He told me you'd been helping her, and I thought you might know more than anyone else.'

There was a momentary pause, and then Cordelia asked, with a trace of tension, 'When you say she missed lunch, you think she's missing?'

Reid gave her a nod and a sympathetic grimace. 'I was hoping she'd turn up somewhere unexpected, but she isn't answering her phone, and nobody's seen her since last night. Which is . . .'

'Since the *ball*?' Cordelia's words were sharp.

'Yes, exactly,' Reid agreed.

'When?' she asked, her gaze harder now.

'The last sighting we have of her was at around eleven. After the fireworks. I'm in the process of checking CCTV.'

He saw Cordelia put a hand out to the desk. He wondered if she was feeling dizzy; whether this had hit her almost as hard as the news about her best friend only a year before.

'She didn't . . .' Cordelia's throat seemed to tighten on her, and she stopped, swallowed and tried again. 'Did anything happen?'

'Someone allegedly saw her leaving with a man, but not someone known to the group.'

It clearly took Cordelia a moment to process this, but then she asked, 'Was she with Kit? Before?'

'It seems as though she left Kit Frankland's group and exited the ball with this other man,' Reid told her.

There was another moment's silence, and then Cordelia rose and said, explosively, 'For fuck's sake. What was she thinking? And why are you only coming to talk to me now? She's been gone almost twenty-four hours! Anything could have happened to her. Did it really take you that long to get over yourself and help?'

She was almost squaring up to him, her eyes very wide and very slightly over-bright, and it gave Reid a strange pang of guilt. He supposed he should have expected something like this. Anna was by nature an open person, and it made sense that she would have shared some of her history with Cordelia Wynn. But he'd been thinking of her as a confidant about professional business: about Holly Moore and her investigations. He'd gone in unprepared for anything more personal, and felt like he'd taken a hit to an unshielded part of himself.

He took a breath and tried to strike a professional tone. 'I'm afraid Mr Laws only told me about the situation a few hours ago. I've been trying all her usual contacts since. Work, her flat, hospitals . . .'

'She's not in a fucking hospital, is she?' Cordelia snapped. 'Someone's grabbed her.'

'I'm afraid I don't know,' Reid said, trying to calm her. 'Could you tell me more about what was going on? I know she went to Cambridge to look into Holly Moore's death.'

Cordelia slightly surprised him by giving a sharp laugh. 'She may have looked into it, but that's not why she *went*.'

Reid stared at her for a moment, his mind spinning. 'Sorry,' he said with a half-formed idea that he might not want to hear what she had to say. 'Why else would she have been there?'

'Because she was still trying to find out how your sister died,' Cordelia told him, her arms folded. 'She became convinced Holly died because she knew too much about Tanya. She'd never given up on all of that, and when I realised she cared more about your sister than she did about Holly, I nearly blew her cover myself.'

17. Anna

I know what you'll be thinking, Reid. I can hear your Detective Reid Murray thoughts.

Just because Kit and Ryan were there, at the right time, that doesn't mean either of them were involved in Tanya's death.

But lack of definitive proof means nothing. And, in fact, it means less than nothing in the face of a litany of coincidences which stretch too far: Tanya and Holly both dying of a drug overdose. Both having spent the evening with the *same people* before they died. The two of them talented young athletes. Both deaths being dismissed as accidental overdoses, despite a lot of questionable features.

Kit and Ryan claimed Tanya left that dinner early; that they'd never talked to her. But the more I thought about that, the more unlikely it seemed. Tanya was a magnetic young woman and a star athlete. She would have been exactly the kind of girl they'd be into, even if she was maybe a little too blonde and a fraction too tall for Kit's usual type.

Tanya had a reputation as a sportswoman, too. She was popular with her teammates, and making waves. There was no way they wouldn't have known who she was, and they would have wanted to impress her.

As I walked rapidly away from the wine tasting, presumably crossing the river at Magdalene Bridge even if I forgot how I'd done it within a few seconds, I found myself thinking that we could find other witnesses to what happened that night. Witnesses the police clearly never bothered to find.

There would, I knew, be students who remembered whether Kit and Ryan had talked to Tanya, and whether they'd left with her. Ryan had said their first rugby team had been hosted by the university women's hockey team. That gave me a list of people to identify and covertly contact – as long as I could work out who'd been playing last year.

I found myself thinking again of Holly, and how she'd wanted to get advice the day before she'd died. Was there a chance the advice could have been about something she'd only just understood? Something that related to Tanya's death six months before?

The moment I was back in the Jesus Green house I loaded up the WhatsApp files Cordelia had sent me and trawled back to the date of Tanya's death. I'd obviously already checked these dates, but I hadn't known what I was looking for then. I wondered, now, whether there was something significant that I'd missed.

But the only thing that stood out to me was from a week after Tanya's death, from Holly to Cordelia.

We want to cheer Kit up. He's still a bit stressy-depressy. Xx

It was the kind of phrase that would have sounded heartless to anyone not firmly Gen-Z, but talking lightly about mental health stuff is something I'm fully familiar with. Holly just meant, basically, that Kit was anxious and sad. He'd seemed that way when we'd talked about her death at the wine tasting, too.

There were three reasons he might feel like that, as far as I could tell. The first was that he'd simply been sad about the death of a girl he'd failed to help. It was, I had to admit, possible. But it seemed more than weird that this kind of death had happened around Kit twice.

The second reason was that he'd done something to harm

Tanya directly and been racked with guilt, or anxiety over being caught, or both. That was the kind of thing that might make someone stressy-depressy for a long time.

The third option was that he'd failed to stop someone *else* harming her. He'd been at that dinner with Ryan, who had been quick to dismiss Kit's guilt over the event. Could he have attacked Tanya when drunk and then killed her to cover it up? Was it possible that Holly had found out about it and died, too?

You know as well as I do that there was no examination of Tanya's body for sexual assault. No attempt to identify whether she'd been the victim of something worse before those drugs got into her system.

Having thought about what might have happened, I then tried *not* to think about it. I wondered about the others instead. James and Esther hadn't been at the dinner, theoretically, but they still might have met up with the other two later on, perhaps with Holly.

James had seemed unaffected by the conversation about Tanya, which was maybe a point in his favour. Esther, though, had grown all but silent later on. She'd kept glancing around as if looking for an escape, and then suddenly said that she was tired and wanted to go home.

Maybe she's the one I should be interrogating.

I scrolled back through the screenshots of Cordelia's WhatsApp messages to the night Tanya had gone to sleep and never woken up; the night of the formal exchange. There was that brief, apparently unimportant conversation about drinks to reread. It had started with Cordelia:

Hey, Holl! What are you up to? Evening plans? Xx

And then Holly replying:

I'm on deadline, but I'll probably get finished up in time to get drinks in with Kit and the others. Xx

So it sounded like Holly could have been there for after-dinner drinks, and that 'the others' could have included James and Esther.

There were no more messages that evening, but I noticed now that twenty minutes later, Cordelia had called Holly. I hadn't really registered this before.

The conversation had lasted for fifteen minutes, and that meant Cordelia might, just might, have some idea of what Holly had decided to do. I needed to find a way of asking her about it.

I picked up my phone and, after hesitating, messaged Cordelia to ask if we could meet up the next day. And then after a little consideration I sent Esther a message, too, telling her how much I'd enjoyed the night and finishing with Let me know if you want coffee tomorrow! I have a day off training and I'm determined to actually be sociable. Xx

Esther replied before Cordelia did.

Thanks for the fun. You have to come and keep me company with the boys more often. I'd love to have coffee but unfortunately with exams looming I only have time for a brief break, and I've promised an old flame I'll see him for breakfast. So sorry, darling! A drink after my next exam? X

The mention of an old flame interested me. It sounded to me like Esther wanted to talk about it, or she'd just have said she was busy. So I took the bait, and said:

You're on for post-exam drinks! Thursday evening? And old flame sounds exciting. Tell all if you have time. Xx

I could see her typing for a little while before her reply came through. A message arrived from Cordelia agreeing to meet before Esther had finished.

When Esther's message came, it was short, suggesting that she'd been writing and deleting.

> Oh, it's not really that exciting. I probably shouldn't be going. There's no future in it. But somehow you always want to see the inappropriate ones, don't you? X

This was interesting, too. An inappropriate ex could have been someone she'd been dating when both Holly and Tanya had died. Could he have been at the May Ball? Or was he totally outside their social circles?

And by the way, Reid, I noticed then, as I've noticed since, that Esther has a weirdly old-fashioned way of talking and messaging. It's like she's fifty instead of twenty-one, and already married with kids. I think, you know, that it makes it hard for her sometimes. She doesn't instinctively gel with anyone her age, and because of that she puts barriers up to avoid getting hurt. Which only makes it all worse.

I decided I was going to have to ask Cordelia more about Esther and the ex-boyfriend. If she'd been dating someone inappropriate and it had gone badly wrong, that was more than interesting.

Before I finally fell asleep at a half-reasonable time, I found myself thinking about James Sedgewick all over again. I had to admit, it was harder thinking about him as a killer now I'd got to know his very normal-seeming family. The easy banter between them all was a lot more like the relationship between you and your parents and sister than like the messed-up stuff I've witnessed in troubled homes.

I'm including mine in that, by the way, even though I have yet to kill anyone.

But saying all that, there can be an unconscious pressure in having a brilliant family. One that a younger son might feel unable to live up to. And I wasn't going to assume that the public face of the Sedgewicks was everything there was to know. They might be warm and friendly on the surface and cruel and controlling behind closed doors.

Though, actually, the thing I ended up wondering right before I drifted off was: *What would they do if James killed his girlfriend?*

And I somehow knew for sure, Reid, exactly what they would do: They would close ranks and protect him, convinced they were doing the right thing.

I felt more optimistic about everything in the morning, once I'd finally had a proper night's sleep. Though that was followed by a not very productive day hanging out in an amazing coffee shop called Bould Brothers which I'd heard Esther and Kit talking about. It was near Downing College, and I could see why they liked it. Totally aside from the decor being lush, it served *the* nicest coffee, and I was jittery with too many cups of it by the time it hit twelve.

It kind of surprised me, you know, that they didn't hang out at specific Pitt Club locations. My vision of the club as being a fraternity was not quite right. It seemed more like somewhere they would go occasionally for dinners. Which was making me a little anxious about being able to get a story about the place as backup if I didn't uncover a murder, if I'm honest. Something I badly needed to keep Gael happy.

Anyhow, none of Kit's group stumbled into the coffee shop, and my research into who'd been on the previous year's hockey and rugby teams proved to be grindingly slow. By the end of the day I'd only managed to find out one set of hockey girls' names from a fixture list and I'd made little progress in working out which colleges any of them went to or how to make contact.

I was suffering caffeine withdrawal and feeling grouchy by the time I went to change for my London meeting with

Cordelia. She'd asked me to come for a drink at her mother's club, like that was a normal thing, and wanted to meet at six, because it was the only way she'd have time to fit me in before a 7.30 mother–daughter dinner. Unlike the third-years I was infiltrating here who were in the midst of exams, Cordelia, as a second-year medical student, was very much still working a full-time schedule at this point and had practicals most days. Which meant, apparently, shadowing doctors or attending classes or practising diagnosing patients. It sounds like genuine fun to me and I can see why Cordelia enjoys it.

An hour later, at the Caledonian Club, I found her waiting for me in the tartan-carpeted members' bar with a whisky sour (mine) and a matching mocktail (hers). And by the way, another rich venue, another insane choice of carpet. Someone should give the money to people with actual taste.

I couldn't help grinning at Cordelia as she lifted her drink at me, her expression managing to be both wry and curious. I was definitely thinking of her more as a friend than as a source of information by then.

'I've got forty-five minutes before I'll need to be getting into the shower,' she told me as she led me away from the bar to a table in the very far corner. It was screened from view by a glass partition. Useful in case someone relevant happened to recognise us, which I'd learned was weirdly possible with Kit Frankland's kind of people and this kind of place. 'Mama has booked me a room, so at least I've got facilities on standby.'

It hit me, all over again, how different life must be if you had money. How much less time you must spend dragging dresses over your head in restaurant bathrooms or taxis. How much more elegantly made-up it would be possible to look because you could rely on good lighting in a proper mirror.

Cordelia seemed to catch what I was thinking. 'You should

get your dad to stump up for membership somewhere for you,' she said, wryly. 'He must have a club somewhere.'

'Oh . . .' This was an awkward point. Dad did, indeed, have club membership, though he'd chosen the much more modern Pavilion Club. Membership was his way of having a home from home when he stayed in London, which he did a crazy amount of the time. Bored and lonely, like I said.

But Dad had obviously never offered me membership, or any other financial support beyond dinners out, and I was equally obviously never going to ask. For all Dad and I were in many ways closer than Cordelia and her mother, it just didn't work like that for us.

'Yeah, I guess so,' I said, as breezily as possible. 'Maybe I should arrange it.' And then I went on, 'I wanted to ask you about Esther. She told me she was meeting up with an old flame for breakfast. Do you know who she might mean?'

Cordelia raised an eyebrow. 'Well, she's dated a few Cambridge boys,' she said. 'Any specifics?'

'Yeah,' I said. 'She mentioned it having no future because he was inappropriate.'

This seemed to genuinely surprise Cordelia. 'That's . . . interesting. I mean, Esther's mother is totally determined for her to marry a rich boy. And the right kind of one, too, and Esther pretty much lives to do what Mummy says.' She chewed her lip for a minute. 'I can't think of anyone I know about. And Holly would have told me anyone *she* knew about, so maybe this is someone from the last few months. Though "old flame" is . . .'

'It implies before that, doesn't it?' I said.

'So maybe school?' Cordelia suggested.

'But why inappropriate?' I asked. 'Surely she went to *the* best school.'

'She went to Cheltenham Ladies' College,' Cordelia said.

'Girls only. So anyone she met wouldn't have been a school-friend. And she's definitely straight.'

'She said "him",' I agreed. I'd listened back to the recording to make sure.

'Teacher's kid?' she offered. 'Local boy?'

'Could be,' I agreed. 'I'd be really interested to know, though. I'm guessing he wasn't at the ball . . .'

'I'm pretty sure not,' Cordelia said, 'but then, I don't know his name.' She gave a shrug. 'Sounds like we need to find out more about him.'

'I hard agree with that,' I said. 'OK, I'll see if I can get her to tell me.' I took another swallow of cocktail. 'There's something I wanted you to try and remember, too,' I told her. 'Something from eighteen months ago, so it's a reach, but . . .'

I could see Cordelia sitting up, her face alive with interest. 'I can try,' she said. 'About Holly?'

'Yeah.' I mean, it *was* about Holly. Even if it was about Tanya, too. I wasn't being deceptive, Reid. 'There was a thing that happened. The death of another student, which was . . . well, it was, like, *crazy* similar to the way Holly died. An overdose that made no sense in someone who just wouldn't have taken those drugs. The police not investigating enough.'

'Who? A Cambridge student?'

'Yeah,' I said. 'She was called Tanya Murray, and she died nineteen months ago. And the reason I'm asking is, I just found out Kit and Ryan were at a formal exchange with her the night before. Nobody's clear on what happened that night, but I think Holly might have seen something.'

There was a beat. A pause. And then something in Cordelia's mouth twisted.

'Sorry, but she didn't see anything,' she said. 'She didn't say a word to me about witnessing a crime, and she would have done.'

'She might not have shared the details,' I pushed. 'These were her friends. She thought they were good people. If she witnessed something and really, honestly thought it was just an accident, she would have wanted to hide it. To protect them.'

'No, she wouldn't,' Cordelia said, flatly. 'She would have told them to go to the police. She was a sympathetic person, but she was also an intensely moral one.'

'Well, what if it wasn't something that even *meant* anything at the time?' I tried, realising that I'd gone about this the wrong way. Of course Cordelia didn't want to hear Holly criticised. Of course she didn't. Holly was so much on a pedestal to her that this was too much.

I could see that she was watching me with a totally different expression now. The kind of expression reserved for an animal you don't trust.

'Maybe something happened that just looked like one of the boys being full on and then getting rejected by Tanya,' I said, slowly. 'And then they said something incriminating that made her realise they'd tried to go after her. Maybe Kit, I don't know . . . said he'd walk her home and then . . . then said the wrong thing later about what had happened. Maybe that's why she was killed.'

Cordelia was shaking her head at me, her jaw set. 'You don't know what she was like,' she said, quietly. 'She wouldn't have let them follow some girl home.'

I wanted, so badly, to argue with her just then. To say that there was *something* wrong with Ryan when he drank, and that Kit was pulling all their strings. And that Holly had been happy to overlook that. She would forgive a lot in her friends.

It occurred to me, suddenly, that there was a whole part of Holly's behaviour that had never quite made sense if I believed Cordelia's account. Holly had always said she'd hated the overprivileged, wasteful side of the way these people lived.

And yet what had she done with her parents' inheritance? She'd used it to pay for the most exclusive of schools. Had that been her guardians' idea, or hers? Because she surely must have gone along with it if that money had been left in trust.

Then, later, she'd gone to Cambridge and, instead of distancing herself from the rich crowd, she'd sought them out. That rich crowd had enabled her to live a glamorous, expensive lifestyle that was beyond her means. The lifestyle she'd always claimed to hate but which she hadn't really, had she?

What would she have been willing to overlook, to keep living like that? I wondered.

I looked back at Cordelia, at the defiant expression, and I knew I could never say all this to her. She'd doubled down on this absolute devotion to her lost friend, despite being shaken by those actions, too.

You can't go up against her faith in Holly, I thought. *But maybe, instead, you can appeal to her sense of what's right.*

'Look,' I said, calmly. 'Holly deserves justice. She deserves it so much. But so does Tanya. She didn't deserve to die, either. And if you can help me with this, even if it *isn't* about Holly, then maybe we can solve the murder of another brilliant young woman.'

Cordelia blinked, and I could see that she was thinking this over. I thought maybe, just maybe, I'd reached her.

But then, as she spoke, I realised that I'd really, really underestimated Cordelia Wynn.

'The way you talk about her . . . about this Tanya . . .' She looked at me, searchingly. 'She's not just another student, is she? She's Reid's sister.' And then she leaned back in her chair and gave a harsh, bitter laugh. 'You are a piece of fucking work.'

I genuinely didn't know what to say for a moment. I hadn't expected her to work it out, but then I'd been too open with her, hadn't I? I could only blame myself. Why had I told her so much, when all I should have done was my goddamn job?

'I'm not – I'm so sorry,' I told her. 'This *is* about Holly. I'm not just interested in Tanya.'

'I need to go,' Cordelia said, and she rose, quickly, but with a strangely impressive dignity in her anger. 'Can you show yourself out, please?'

'Cordelia –'

'No,' she said, firmly. 'I need you to leave me to think about this.'

Fuck.

That was the main thing I thought as she left.

There was so much that was bad about this. My career was under serious threat, for one. Cordelia could make a complaint to Gael and the *Ensign*, and that would land me in serious shit. She could also tell the group who I really was and put an end to all this.

Why did you do that, you idiot?

Over and over I thought about what I should have said and berated myself for getting carried away. I must have sat in that chair for a full quarter-hour, on a self-lacerating loop, and I was only kicked out of it by a loud shout of laughter from the bar.

As I peered over the glass screen I realised with horror that one of the two men standing there was Philip Sedgewick. And as I drew in a quick breath he turned and looked right at me.

18. Reid

This was what he'd been avoiding for eighteen months. This toiling mass of frustration, confusion, doubt and worry.

Reid had walked away from Cordelia Wynn. He'd had to.

As a detective, as a professional, fleeing had obviously been ridiculous. He'd come to her with questions, and got answers. Just because they were answers he hadn't expected, that was no reason to go to pieces. He should have been able to adjust.

But somehow hearing everything had been about Tanya had knocked the breath out of him. He'd felt like he might suffocate in that little room.

Cordelia's face had been drawn with surprise as he'd mumbled something indistinct and run for the door.

He'd relived, on the way down those stairs, that last conversation he'd had with Anna. The one where he'd begged her to stop arguing with him about Tanya's overdose and accept that she'd done it to herself.

Anna hadn't listened. She'd kept on and on telling him that it made no sense.

He still remembered how he'd tried to reiterate the facts.

'You know how much her degree and her hockey career meant to her,' he'd said. 'She was already on sertraline for anxiety; we know that. It's not hard to believe that she would have turned to other drugs, too, when she felt like she had no other option.'

'But why so much, Reid?' she'd asked him. 'Why take four times the amount of Ritalin the average person her size would need? And why take enough modafinil to keep her awake for a week when all she was trying to do was finish an essay?'

'Because it wasn't working,' Reid said. 'Because she'd been taking more and more for months and she still couldn't focus!' he'd snapped, hating Anna for making him say this. 'Look, the coroner sought a doctor's opinion, and he said the problem with these drugs is that people self-medicate on higher and higher doses, not understanding the damage they're doing to – to their heart.' He'd had to swallow and move away from her to go on. 'One of the dangers of an overdose involving modafinil is also that it can bring on delusions and hallucinations which stop someone from recognising what's happening to them.' He'd felt his mouth trembling as he'd tried not to give in to tears. 'She wouldn't have known to save herself.'

'She wasn't stupid, Reid,' she'd snapped back.

'Neither am I!' he'd ended up shouting at her. 'What right have you got to think you know better than fucking everyone? It's so – arrogant!'

'Oh, I'm so sorry for not immediately bowing to your superior intellect,' she'd said, her voice dripping with sarcasm.

Had that been it? The moment when he'd realised he'd been wrong about her all along?

He shook his head. He was sure it hadn't. He'd felt hurt, but not . . . not like his whole world had twisted.

And then it came to him, suddenly, as he stepped out into the courtyard. He knew what had made him look at everything differently.

It had been when she told him what she'd done that night.

'Reid, you have to listen,' she'd said, standing there in her tight black dress, which he'd already known must be for work. Anna didn't buy clothes like that for herself. 'The whole investigation was inadequate. I got all dressed up tonight and chatted up DC Polwich in the bar the Cambridgeshire detectives go to. And he told me they never even tried to find out where the drugs came from. Never checked CCTV . . . nothing. It was barely an investigation, like you said in the first place. And we both know that's not right.'

It had hit him so hard, what she'd said about going and flirting with an officer. He'd always known she used methods like that when she had to, but she'd said they were *Gael's* methods. The *Ensign*'s methods.

And there she'd been, his girlfriend, willingly flirting with another man, and telling him as though it was totally OK.

He stopped in the middle of the courtyard, next to the brickwork sculpture, and tried to control the adrenaline flooding through him as he remembered it all in full. How he'd erupted. Told her every terrible thing he thought of her.

He remembered the hurt and anger on her face. How she'd told him she'd been trying to help. But her protests had come up against his absolute conviction that she'd been fooling him all along. That the real Anna didn't care about him, or Tanya, or anyone else, as long as she got her story.

She'd seemed like a different person to the one he'd spent a year with, as if her mask had fallen away. He'd seen her tight, closed-off expression and it had been easy to say, 'You're just a cold-hearted, career-hungry bitch, aren't you?'

He remembered the way she'd made a small sound as he'd said it, and it had felt like a point finally scored against an unassailable opponent. Like a victory.

It didn't feel like one now, somehow.

In the eighteen months since he'd walked away she'd thrown herself back into finding Tanya's killer all over again – into finding Holly's killer, too. She'd ignored what he'd said . . . but it hadn't been about her career, had it?

Anna had taken a big risk to do this. She must have lied to her boss, and everyone else at the *Ensign*. They would never have let her go off investigating something related to someone she knew so closely.

She'd been doing this for Tanya.

Maybe for me . . .

He recalled Seaton telling him that she would have rescued him if he'd needed it. And he tried to remember exactly what had convinced him she was a master manipulator, rather than someone using every possible means she could to help. Exactly why he'd been *so sure.*

But somehow, all he could remember was her hurt. And his own.

'Fuck!' he said, explosively, hearing it echo out into the empty courtyard. He felt like tearing at something with his hands. At this feeling, maybe.

Because he knew it wasn't the frustration, confusion, doubt or worry that was cutting through him. It was guilt, pure and simple. Guilt, and a feeling of having ripped his own life apart for nothing.

You have to get it together, he thought, after a few minutes of wheeling inactivity. *This isn't helping anyone.*

She hadn't necessarily been right about Tanya. That was the thing he needed to remember. Tanya had been struggling for months. Perhaps for years, really. She'd been his baby sister and yet hadn't been able to tell him when something was wrong. She had been a perfectionist who was impossibly hard on herself.

It was something he'd had to come to terrible, heart-rending terms with after the coroner's verdict. Little by little, he'd acknowledged that the flashes of odd behaviour he'd seen in her had been desperation. The way she'd suddenly travelled to Paris on the Eurostar when she should have been in lectures, and then called him, laughing about it. Her abrupt conviction that she needed to move rooms to a higher floor in order to be happy. The change to a vegan diet, and then the absolute rejection of it a week later.

Even the last time he'd seen her: when she'd arrived at Finsbury Park station with no warning a few hours before the end of his shift.

'Heyyy, big brother,' she'd said, as one of their DCs had shown her to his desk. 'How goes?'

He'd scanned her face, worried that she'd got into some kind of trouble while in London. Why else would she be here?

But she'd looked bright-eyed and merry, her cheeks flushed pink as usual and her short blonde hair wind-blown. She'd looked healthy and happy and glorious.

'Everything OK?' he'd asked. 'Did you get mugged?'

She'd given a laugh, one that he'd taken as carefree then but which he'd later remembered as almost out of control. 'Oh, is that the minimum requirement to come and see my brother?'

He'd given her a grin. 'No, but you don't usually seem so keen.'

At Tanya's shrug he'd wondered whether there was something she'd wanted to talk about. He'd glanced at his computer clock, acutely aware that he had two and a half hours left of the day's work and a lot to squeeze in. He and his team had been under pressure, running a big surveillance op, which would hopefully precede the arrest of a string of violent thieves.

'Can you . . . hang around a couple of hours?' he'd asked. 'And we'll go and get dinner?'

'I . . . sure,' Tanya had said, glancing around.

'There's a relatives' room you can use,' Reid had volunteered, getting to his feet.

'Nahh, you're all right,' his sister had said. 'I'll go and get a drink. If you're lucky, I'll have one waiting for you.'

She'd looked as though she couldn't wait to leave, but then, at the door to the stairs, she'd turned and said, 'Just a couple of hours?'

'Yeah, I'll be quick as I can,' he'd promised.

Tanya had skipped off down the stairs surprisingly lightly in her boots, and Reid had got his head down and worked as fast as he'd been able to. But less than an hour later, Tanya had messaged to say she'd realised she had to get back to Cambridge, and not to worry – she'd catch him soon.

Reid had thought about that visit over and over since her death. About how he could just have broken off and gone for a coffee with her straight away. Because it was so abundantly clear that she'd needed him.

Now, though, he found a trickle of doubt creeping in. Because he'd assumed she'd needed him to talk through an emotional crisis. That she'd been reaching out for mental help.

But might she not also have been scared? And scared of something very real?

Trinity College porters' lodge called Reid as he was climbing onto the Cambridge train at King's Cross station.

Reid had felt a strong need to be moving and doing something after seeing Cordelia, and he knew that it was ridiculous to delay going to Cambridge any longer. Anna had been there when she vanished. The people she'd been with were there.

It seemed that the porters had been doing their due diligence on the CCTV, anyway.

'We've had a really good look through the footage from ten p.m. until four a.m.,' the woman he was speaking to said, and Reid was positive that she was ex-police. Something in the way she answered Reid's questions. She knew what she was doing. 'There's only one exit from the ball, but I checked the entrance, too, in case she managed to slip back out somehow. She'd be quite distinctive in that dress, and with her height, but there's no sign of her around the time you're looking. It gets harder from then on because a lot of people left as it started to get light and there was a big exodus after the survivors' photo.'

'The . . .'

'The photo of everyone who makes it to the end,' the porter said. 'It happened at six. So then there was a flood of people leaving after. I can have a proper look at them, or send it over.'

Reid knew it was just a name. That it didn't mean anything. But somehow it still hit him like a punch to the stomach.

She wasn't one of the survivors. She never made it to dawn.

'I'd be grateful if you could do both,' Reid said, mentally pulling himself together all over again. 'Sorry, I didn't take your name . . .'

'Trish,' she replied.

'Thanks so much, Trish. I appreciate that this isn't your job. It's just that we're early stage.' He hesitated for a moment, and then added, 'Guessing none of my junior colleagues has asked you for this in the interim? Don't want to make you guys do it twice.'

'No, you're OK,' Trish said. 'And honestly, you're all right. Just give me your email.'

Reid read it out as the train started to pull out of the station. He knew that if nobody else had asked for this it meant Cambridgeshire Constabulary had decided Anna wasn't high risk. It was getting towards 7 p.m. now and they hadn't even looked into the basics.

They're going to leave her in danger, he thought with a feeling of anger.

'Anything else you need?' Trish asked.

'That's OK,' Reid said, and then, with a sudden thought, he added, 'I'm guessing there were no weird events last night? Nobody hurt?'

Trish gave a half-laugh. 'Nope. The usual handful who drank too much, one of whom needed the St John's Ambulance guys, but no fights.' There was a pause, and she said, 'Nothing like last year, thank god.'

Reid found himself breathing out slowly, knowing this was what he'd really been asking. He'd been horribly afraid that the reason they hadn't found Anna on CCTV at the exit yet was that she'd drowned.

He hung up, thinking about what Trish had told him. James Sedgewick had told Seaton he'd seen her leaving at eleven, walking with someone he didn't recognise. So why hadn't she appeared on CCTV? Had they not actually walked to the exit?

If she hadn't, why hadn't anyone seen her after that?

He thought about all the things Cambridgeshire Constabulary could be doing right now that they weren't. They could put an urgent authorisation through to the phone provider for the mobile she'd been carrying. The one she used for her Aria identity. They could track her location.

With a jolt, he remembered the phones in his pocket. He might not have the phone she'd been using, but he had her real one.

He pulled it out, and out tumbled another handful of memories with it. Memories of Anna laughing over a video. Anna saying, 'Just a second.' Anna frowning as she read with concentration.

This phone had so often been the focus of Anna's attention as she thought of something to look up or as she read something out to him. Or equally when she lost herself in what she liked to call 'side-quests' but which were really just a series of distractions.

Seaton hadn't known the code, but surely Reid should be able to work it out. He'd spent so much time with her. He'd understood her . . . or thought he had.

He sat holding the phone as the train moved out into open countryside. He watched occasional reflections play across it as he tried to get into her head. It was creeping towards evening now, the sun low and mellow.

He remembered catching sight of Anna punching her code in while she'd been curled up against him on his sofa. He'd asked with a laugh if she'd actually, genuinely, set her passcode to 1111.

'I have not!' she said. And then, after a pause, said, 'It's just not *that* far off. In an emergency, I want to be able to get into it quickly even if my face isn't available.'

He'd shaken his head at her. 'I don't even know what that means.'

'I might not be able to use face ID sometimes,' she'd explained. 'What if someone's gagged me? Or what if I have a prosthetic on for a job? What if my hands are tied behind my back and I can only get the phone out but not see it?'

He'd found it impossible not to grin at her half-earnest, half-laughing reply. 'So you think you could do it behind your back?'

'Uhhhh, like, without question,' she said. 'I've *practised* it.'

And she'd sat up fully, leaned forwards with the phone behind her, and performed a few manoeuvres with her thumbs and one finger.

'See?' she asked, holding it up to him, triumphantly. 'And look, I've even worked out how to get it out of my pocket if my hands are tied or cuffed behind me.'

She stuffed the phone into her jeans pocket and then repeated the manoeuvre with her hands crossed over as if tied. This time she twisted to tug the phone out with her fingers, turned it expertly and then unlocked it.

Reid remembered with a flush of warmth that he'd found the whole manoeuvre both impressive and a huge turn-on.

'What if . . .' he'd said, lifting the phone gently out of her hand. 'What if your hands were tied over your head . . .'

He'd lifted them, crossing them back over until they were held above her.

'Oh,' she'd said with a flare of heat in her expression, 'I see where this is going.'

'It's important research . . .' he'd told her, releasing one hand to pull her closer in towards him.

He closed his eyes. This wasn't what he was supposed to be thinking about. Not now.

Not ever.

But instead of feeling angry at himself he felt a strange sense of regret that he'd pushed all this away for so long.

God, I miss her.

It was such a simple thought, but it was one he'd been adamant he'd never let in.

It was almost as an afterthought that he realised he probably knew Anna's code. That she wouldn't have changed it. She still had the same battered phone in its bright, star-patterned case eighteen months on. She would have the same code, too.

He'd seen her thumb sweep up and down, and then up and down again.

He let go of the memory with a sigh and woke the phone up then typed in 4141.

It opened in a moment, and Reid suddenly, fiercely, felt like crying.

Find her, he told himself. *Get it together and find her.*

He started with her WhatsApps, that being her favourite method of communication. But there was nothing there in recent days except a breezy chat with Imogen from the *Ensign* about a company's tax returns. It was clearly about the other job she should have been doing, and the messages had stopped the day before the ball.

Her iMessages were even less revealing. She'd barely sent any in weeks. Most of her incoming ones were automatic notifications from her GP, gas engineers, or the people who did her eyelash extensions.

He turned to her emails next, trying her inbox and sent folders, and was beginning to feel real disappointment when he thought to look in her drafts folder. He wasn't even sure, afterwards, what made him look there.

But right at the top, right there, was an email addressed to him. An email she'd never sent.

It was titled *Help*, and it began

Hi Reid,

So if you're reading this, it's just possible you might be the only person who can save my life.

19. Anna

It's rare, in this job, that you feel like you've really screwed up. I mean, I'm careful about what I say in front of people.

But somehow, I'd managed to have a whole, open conversation about *everything* only yards away from Philip Sedgewick. The father of one of the most likely suspects.

And the way he was looking at me, with a knowing smile, I felt a sick certainty that he must have heard.

It made me jump when his expression changed to one of recognition and he said, 'Aria! Goodness. Twice in two nights. Everyone will think we're doing it on purpose.'

I still felt fully nauseous as I gave him my best attempt at a return smile and stood up. Had he not seen or heard anything, then? Or was this a facade?

He hadn't been there when I arrived. That much I was sure of.

I also hadn't seen him when I watched Cordelia leave. But I hadn't been paying attention. I'd been busy freaking out. I could easily have missed him, and if so, who knew when he might have arrived?

'Mr Sedgewick,' I said, coming to kiss his cheek. 'I thought it was you.'

There was no sign of obvious threat or anger as he said, 'And this is my friend Max, who's all right, even if he *did* go to Oxford.' He gestured to his companion, who looked like a slightly less good-looking version of himself. 'This is Aria, a friend of James's from Cambridge,' Philip went on as I held a hand out.

'Great to meet you,' I said. 'Even with the Oxford thing.'

Max laughed, but then looked towards the door. 'I'd better go and find Clarisse. I'll already be in trouble. Hope to meet you again soon,' he added to me.

'Oh, you, too,' I said, and then said quickly to Philip, 'I'm just meeting a friend who's a member. I'd . . . better go up to the room.'

It was supposed to be a neat excuse for being there, and to distract him in case he'd seen Cordelia. But the moment I'd said it I realised how much it must have sounded like I had a sugar daddy staying there. The kinds of people who had rooms at the Caledonian were generally older guys, and going up to the room implied . . . yeah. That.

It was excruciatingly awkward, and I saw Philip's expression change.

'Of course, of course,' he said. And then he cleared his throat, and said, 'Look, if you ever need anything, in London . . . you don't have to be a stranger. Any friend of James's.' He pulled out a business card and gave me a troubled look. 'I know a strange country probably feels a bit daunting, but you're not on your own.'

'Thank you,' I said, finding myself blushing in spite of every effort not to. 'That's kind. I've got – I know Seaton's there in a pinch, too.'

'Of course,' Philip said again. 'Of course. But if there are things you . . . can't tell him.'

He gave another clear of his throat, and I ducked past him with a nod of thanks. On the one hand, I felt hugely relieved that he clearly hadn't connected me to Cordelia Wynn, or heard anything we were saying. I was sure he'd have asked me questions if he had.

On the other hand, there was a real threat he might tell James not to get close to me because I was the wrong kind of girl.

I turned up the large staircase as if going to someone's

room – I had to follow up what I'd said, regardless of the subtext – and then proceeded to hide in an empty conference room for the next forty-five minutes until I was sure I could sneak out unobserved by both Philip and Cordelia.

On my wincing, heart-thumping way out to get an Uber to King's Cross, I remembered my promise to Dad that I wouldn't embarrass him, and I hoped that he never, ever found out about tonight.

I was still reeling from every part of the evening by the time I made it back to Cambridge. I was fully into unhealthy loops of anxiety as I cycled through what was thankfully still a warm night.

I had to stop before the lights changed on the junction of Hills Road and Gonville Place to adjust my wide-legged trousers, which were getting caught on the chain. The road was mercifully low on traffic so I had an extra moment once I'd pulled into the bike box. Another cyclist came to join me a second later, doing that kind of annoying thing of going further right and further ahead so they could get round the corner in front of me when the lights changed, but I figured it wasn't a race, for once. You know. Unlike the rest of the time, when it *clearly is a race.*

I straightened up and was only really conscious of a noise behind me just before the accompanying impact. It was a confusing, dizzying combination of sensations that involved a hard shove to my bike wheel and me trying frantically to keep from cartwheeling over the top of the bike.

I didn't quite manage it. With my legs braced either side, I was essentially tripped up by the bike itself. After multiple staggering steps I fell forward, throwing my left arm out to save my face and then feeling the lancing pain of the bike landing heavily across my left leg.

'Hey!' I heard a woman shouting. 'What the hell are you doing?'

It's the other cyclist, I realised, as I lay there stunned for a moment.

'Jesus, are you OK?'

The cyclist again.

I dragged myself upright, almost tripping again as I did it, and saw her concerned face a few feet from mine. She'd backed up a little but hadn't climbed off her bike to help.

'I . . . yeah,' I said, trying to assess the slightly numb pain in my leg. The bruised feeling in my arm. 'I think I'm OK.'

'He just didn't stop,' she said, looking out left towards Lensfield Road and the Fen Causeway. 'Fucking idiot.'

I twisted round, but whatever vehicle had clipped me it was no longer visible past the curve of the road.

'Don't suppose you have a bike camera, do you?' I asked.

The cyclist grimaced, glancing up towards where the lights had now changed for cyclists to go. She looked impatient to be gone. 'Sorry. I didn't see the reg, either. It's not lit properly.'

'No problem.'

The lights changed again so the cars could go, and of course there was now an impatient motorist pulling up behind us and pipping at his horn. Thanks, hon.

I walked my bike off to the side, out of the way, while the woman on her bike left with a wave. A not particularly helpful, if sympathetic, interaction.

I could feel that weirdly disconnected pain in my leg that tells you you're probably going to have some swelling there later, but I decided after some stretching that I was OK to cycle. I chose to head back across Parker's Piece, then stick to the pavement down the side of Christ's Pieces and Midsummer Common from there. No more roads.

All the while, I was looking ahead for assailants jumping

out at me or over my shoulder for cars in pursuit. But nobody else troubled me on the way home, and even though I was shaking slightly as I locked my bike up outside I began to feel a strange sense of triumph.

Because I was sure that the car must have been following me deliberately. The impact had been a warning.

I just had no idea what had triggered it.

Having managed to get to sleep by midnight, I woke bolt upright at 3 a.m., disturbed by a noise outside. I'd been dreaming about someone pursuing me, and I was on my feet at the window in a moment with thoughts of a masked intruder and a shock of pain through my injured leg.

The noise turned out to be just a couple of drunk guys who'd presumably been at a late-night lock-in at the Maypole pub. One of them had tripped over the kerb and the other was now laughing at him. It was the kind of thing I'd grown used to over the last couple of weeks, and I was on the verge of going back to bed when I realised that there was something attached to my front gate. Something that hadn't been there before and was now flapping in the light breeze off Jesus Green.

I think I must have sat in that window trying to peer at it and also in every direction for at least ten minutes. It looked, by the light of the street lamps, like it might be mid-brown in colour. It could have been just a flyer or poster, but there was nothing attached to anyone else's gate, and something in the way it was banging into the wrought iron made me think it was heavier than a single sheet of paper.

It looked a lot like an envelope with something inside.

I felt the strangest inability to decide what to do. Part of me was convinced it was there to lure me out so someone could finish what they'd started.

Another equally strong part was desperate to find out what was in there. Because if it was a friendly warning instead of a threatening one, or better still information about Holly, I couldn't risk it being stolen by the time I got up in the morning.

In the end, my inability to let things go won out. I crept downstairs without turning on any lights and fetched the rolling pin that generally did little except jam the cutlery drawer. I stayed standing inside the door with my hand on the latch for a good minute, psyching myself up.

And then I opened it and put it on the latch in one movement and ran down the three steps to the gate as fast as I've ever run anywhere. All the while I was conscious of the corner of the house to my right and the fact that someone could be hiding round there.

The moment I got to the gate it became clear that I'd been right. The flapping attachment was one of those card-backed certificate envelopes made from waxy brown paper. It had been fastened to the top of the open gate using duct tape.

I tugged at it, eyes flying wildly around. In my fear, I was frantically imagining human shapes in the bushes. Each breath of wind made my heart skitter.

It took three efforts to pull it clear, and by the time I'd done it nobody had emerged from any shadows. No real enemies had come to get me. The expanse of the green was quiet, lit in pools of white light by wrought-iron lamp posts.

I felt every part of me flinching as I turned my back on that big, empty space and ran back to the house. It was like every time I'd ever run away from the dark as a child, only without the privilege of being able to dismiss my fears as imaginary.

By the time I was back inside, with the door slammed shut behind me, my heart was in my throat. I almost felt like throwing the envelope away in anger at having been scared like this.

But the curiosity was too strong. And so I took a deep breath and peeled it open.

Inside was just one A4 photographic sheet, and I tipped it onto my hand. Someone had laid out three images in what could have been an attractive little triptych: only they were all images of me, taken without my knowledge or consent.

The first was of me heading into the station earlier that night, dressed for my meet-up with Cordelia in London. The second: me climbing into my Uber outside the club, on my way home.

And the third, Reid, was of me locking my bike up right outside the house as I'd arrived home, my stance uneven after the impact of that car, and my head half turned to look for any assailants.

I was looking out for people, I thought, all the hairs standing up on my arms. *I was looking out for people, and I never saw them.*

They'd been close enough to get my anxious expression as I'd bent down. Close enough to capture the way I'd tucked my trousers into my socks.

And worse than that were the words. There was one underneath each image, making up a single message in Arial typeface:

RUN AWAY HOME

And somehow all the triumph I'd felt evaporated. I didn't feel like I was on the right track any more. I felt out of my depth, and scared.

I tried to shut out all the more painful thoughts and work out, rationally, who might have been driving that car. None of the group had so far mentioned having a vehicle in Cambridge, and it would be extremely unusual for an undergrad to have one. But that didn't mean they hadn't hired one for the night.

I also thought about Philip Sedgewick again. He'd apparently heard nothing at the Caledonian Club and wanted to help me, but had that been a pretence?

The only thing in his favour was the difficulty of him managing it. I couldn't see how he could have ended up in a car in Cambridge at exactly the right time when he'd been going to a dinner. Unless he'd left the dinner and hung around the entrance somewhere without me seeing him.

But it was a big thing to do for a small pay-off, wasn't it? Wouldn't it have been easier to wait until a night when he was free and then follow me? Though maybe I was thinking too rationally and not like someone who thought their son's secrets were under immediate threat.

It was while thinking over his possible guilt that I processed something his friend Max had said in the bar.

I'd better go and find Clarisse . . .

That had been it, hadn't it? I was sure he'd said Clarisse.

And I was equally sure that Clarisse was the name of Esther's high-achieving mother who worked for the UN General Secretariat. The sort of woman who could probably brush anything she wanted under the carpet and have me chased down and threatened by a driver if someone tipped her off. Maybe this Max had, or maybe she'd been in the bar earlier on, when I'd been talking to Cordelia. Maybe she'd heard way too much.

I hadn't yet discovered a reason why Esther might have wanted Holly dead, but I was willing to bet that a woman who'd had Clarisse's kind of career would not want her daughter going down for murder. I wondered if she might even be able to convince the police not to look into it too closely.

I'll admit that this might have been a little *big conspiracy* for daylight hours, but it was 3 a.m., and I was wired with anxiety by this point. It *could* have been a totally different Clarisse, or a similar name, but I couldn't go back and check. I hadn't had my voice recorder on because I'd been there to see Cordelia, not to spy.

The worst thing was not having anything I could immediately do. Not about this new threat, and not about Cordelia, either.

I'd had no reply to my message to my former ally, and I had no idea whether she'd already contacted Gael to complain. By morning, I might be pulled off this story, or I might be staying, and in more danger than I'd bargained for.

I must have spent a full half-hour pacing the house, going over all this in my mind, jumping any time I caught sight of my reflection in anything, despite having pulled the curtains firmly over every window. I needed someone to talk to, and in the end I realised that the only person I really wanted to talk to was you, Reid.

So I did the only vaguely rational version of that I could think of and started writing this down. It wasn't exactly comforting to write to you but for a couple of hours I felt a little less totally alone. Imagining you reading it was . . . not comforting exactly. But it wasn't the same as having nobody, either.

With at least most of it down, I scraped a little sleep – more out of exhaustion than anything else – and hauled my ass onto the river to work out some nerves in the scull. My leg was hurting like hell just walking there, having swelled further overnight, and it looked bruised and ugly where it was displayed by my Lycra one-piece. But I could move up and down the slide, at least, and as I worked it got easier to put pressure down.

I was obviously on the lookout for someone throwing a brick off a bridge onto me the whole way, or even for someone firing something off the bank. It did nothing to improve my already questionable steering on the bends, and when combined with background pain from the leg I ended up seething with frustration at myself, reliving snippets of what Cordelia had said to me, and on the point of tears at my inability to just do something right.

It was humiliating.

I made it the five kilometres up to the lock and then back down to the comparative straight of the Reach before I'd had enough, and then pulled over close to the bank and lay back in my seat with the blades over my chest, trying not to feel like everything was falling apart. It was at least quiet enough to do that, out here beyond the city and on a day when few crafts were out.

The mantra of *You just need more sleep* didn't seem to be working as well as it should have done, and I had a moment of wishing I could just abandon the boat, and Cambridge, and the whole investigation, and walk off somewhere.

During this admittedly pretty self-indulgent sulk someone yelled my name – well, Aria's name – and I almost jumped out of my skin. I sat up, wobbly as hell, and was looking wildly for the threat when I realised that it was a cheerfully waving figure. Kit Frankland's cheerfully waving figure, in fact, dressed in shorts and a T-shirt, his face flushed and a pair of AirPods in his ears. It was clear that he'd been running.

'Oh,' I said, trying to give him a smile. 'Hey.'

He came to the edge of the bank, so I checked for traffic and pulled in all the way, lifting my left oar so I could glide in on a tilt.

'I've been looking out for you down here,' Kit said, coming to crouch next to me. 'Towpath is my favourite run.'

He didn't seem to have a problem with admitting he'd been checking up on me, but maybe that was the point. To make sure I knew he was keeping an eye out.

I thought of those photographs, and I shivered. Though

when his eyes went to my very bruised leg I saw them widen. Was he really surprised? Or had he wanted to see exactly how much he'd hurt me?

'Nobody should have a favourite run,' I told him, doing my best to pretend I hadn't noticed. 'Running is insanity.'

Kit shook his head. 'I know, but they won't let me have a boat on the rugby pitch, so . . .'

I had to give him that.

'How's it going?' he asked, nodding towards the water. 'That looks painful.'

'Oh, it's not as bad as it looks,' I said. 'Drivers around here really need to work out the size of their vehicles.'

'You got run into?' he asked with what seemed like simple concern.

'Yup! I was properly in the right place in the bike box, too. But they were in a hurry and didn't see me.' I shrugged. 'It's OK, I'm still getting the miles in.'

And then two things occurred to me: the first was that Kit was a sportsman and would probably recognise only too easily the signs of someone who was having a crisis of self-confidence. The second one was that I didn't *have* to lie about how I was feeling and it would be nice to just be able to tell one of these guys the truth, even if he *had* come to revel in my injured state.

So I let out a long breath and said, 'Actually, I'm having a crappy time of it. I didn't sleep well because my leg hurt and so I was off my game from the start, and I've been steering like a total moron, and kind of lost all belief that I'm good enough to even sit in this boat, never mind achieve what I want to.'

I gave a shaky laugh and leaned down to pick up my water bottle from beneath my feet.

'Ahh, sorry,' Kit said, and despite listening for any delight,

I heard nothing but sympathy in his tone. Though sympathy wasn't really what I wanted right then, either. 'I'm . . . I have a lot of days like that.'

'No, you don't,' I said, in what was, to be honest, a snappy voice.

Kit laughed. 'Don't buy into my positivity bullshit. A lot of it's about trying to convince myself.' I looked up at him, wondering whether this was an effort to manipulate or the honest truth. 'I have to work pretty hard not to have my dad's voice in my head. And it's worst if I take a knock during a game.'

'Oh.' I took a chug of the water, considering this. 'I kind of figured your parents were the nice kind.'

'Dad's not the worst,' Kit said. 'He just comes from the school of "you have to push kids to get them to achieve their potential". So he's spent a lot of my life telling me what I'm doing isn't good enough, which . . . It doesn't help, actually.' He half straightened from his crouched position but, instead of leaving, he sat himself down properly on the bank. 'But I have ways of shutting it out.' He nodded at the blades. 'It's probably the same as what you do. I have little ritual movements that make me feel Zen, like crossing my arms onto my shoulders and breathing. Doesn't matter if anyone thinks I'm a prick, I do it anyway.' He gave me a lopsided smile. 'And I ignore the pressure or what I feel I *should* be achieving and focus in on one tiny thing. Like dropping my shoulder an inch further on a tackle. Or being a fraction more on my toes in the sprint. It stops anything else getting in, like beating myself up about a bad pass or anything.'

I looked out at the water, thinking that beating myself up is actually one of my default states. I'd definitely been doing it over the rowing. And over Cordelia, too. Telling myself over and over that I shouldn't have overshared with her. That I'd been unprofessional. That I was messing everything up.

Kit's style of doing things sounded so much . . . kinder on himself. Not letting in the self-laceration, or the rage, or the guilt.

'I get told I shouldn't dwell on things a lot,' I said with a laugh. 'By coaches and academic supervisors. But I guess I haven't really developed any methods for *not* doing it.'

'Maybe it's worth finding a movement that makes you feel calm,' he said. 'Something that lets you feel like you're washing all the anger away. And then going from there.' Kit shrugged. 'But this is just me talking. I'm not a sports psychologist.'

'Oh, I've seen plenty of those,' I said. I looked out at the water and found myself thinking suddenly of Tanya. Of how she used to smooth her headband just before a match. How totally calm she'd looked doing it.

Weirdly, ritual movements had never occurred to me as something that might help me. I mean, I obviously fiddle with my nails or my hair or whatever's around all the time, but I don't have anything particularly conscious.

'I might give it a try.'

I closed my eyes and put my hands up to where one of Tanya's bright blue headbands would have been, up on the centre of my forehead. I should have felt stupid, doing it in front of Kit, but picturing Tanya, it actually felt almost like *she* was touching my head. Like it was her hands moving over my skin and hair, and brushing everything away.

And it was the strangest thing. It was like all the anger and self-loathing just slid away with them.

I blinked my eyes open and looked up at Kit with genuine surprise.

'OK, I think I see the point.'

'It's awesome, isn't it?' he said, his expression full of delight.

When he took my blade and pushed me back out into the river it was a whole new me who began rowing again. A me who was able to zone in on the feel of the water and the connection of the catch and wasn't worried about the pain in my leg or whether I was about to get fired.

Kit ended up running back alongside the boat, beaming at my enjoyment. And I think, also, enjoying that I was grateful to him.

It was some great sports psychology, Reid, and a genuinely enjoyable row home. But after I'd got back and Kit had watched me lifting my boat out and onto the racks he said something else. Something that made it all . . . less good.

It was as I was sliding the rack away, and he'd been telling me to come to King's Bar again that night to keep him and Ryan company.

'Esther'll be locked away working for her second exam,' he added.

'Oh,' I said, walking to pick my blades up from the hard. 'I could maybe come. I mean, I probably should be working . . . but . . .'

Kit gave me a grin, trailing alongside me. 'You definitely need to come. Guilt-free living starts here.'

I laughed at him. 'I think some of the guilt is probably reasonable.'

'I honestly think guilt is one of the least healthy emotions in the world,' Kit said, more seriously. 'All those parents who use it all the time . . . It's honestly abusive. I mean, sure. Learn from your mistakes. Think "I could have done that better". But don't torture yourself. It doesn't help anyone.'

It was so compelling, the way he said it. For a moment, I actually believed he might be right. Why *was* guilt necessary? All it meant was making yourself miserable instead of learning and moving on.

It was only after he'd gone that I started to remember that there were things people genuinely should feel guilty about and try to make amends for. Really terrible things.

And I wondered whether Kit would be able to do the worst things and just put them behind him. Because it sounded to me like he would.

20. Reid

The train was pulling into Cambridge and Reid had to put the phone away and stop reading. And although it felt jarring to stop, he knew he should.

He needed to walk out into the breezy evening air. To stop reading about Anna. About the weird student life she'd been living.

About Kit Frankland.

About Tanya.

And about how they'd failed each other.

He'd meant to skip ahead after the beginning. It made no sense to follow the story through and not go straight to the conclusion.

But somehow he'd found himself unable to stop reading, despite how painful some of it had been. Maybe *because* of how painful it had been. And because every word of it had been so warmly, unmistakably, infuriatingly Anna.

He wanted to be angry with her about Tanya. It had taken him such a lot to come to terms with his sister's overdose, and it hurt badly to have Anna unpick his work on that.

And yet he understood, now, why she hadn't been able to leave it. That she'd been grieving, just as he had. That this was how she had coped: by refusing to back down until she'd disproved, beyond all certainty, that Tanya had died as a result of violence.

It had never been about her career. He'd been so, so wrong. Anna had genuinely risked her career to try to find out the truth.

She wasn't a cold-hearted careerist. She was a driven, emotional, caring but also obsessive woman who would sometimes get so consumed by something that she stopped noticing the collateral damage.

What had gone wrong between them had been an enormous clash between her grief and his. And he'd been the one who'd been too blind to see it.

He realised that he was standing outside the station now, unmoving. It was gone 9 p.m. and he needed to rush if he was going to make it to see James Sedgewick and get back before the trains got extremely sporadic. Assuming, that was, that he could actually find James.

At least there were six taxis waiting in the rank nearby, and nobody piling into them. He walked as purposefully as he could to the first one and told the driver to take him to St John's College.

And then, as soon as he was in the back, he opened the phone up again and scrolled to the end of Anna's account.

Tell me what happened, he thought.

But with a bitter sense of inevitability, he realised that it didn't give him the answers he needed. That it told him what she'd been about to do, but that she hadn't worked everything out by the time she'd stopped writing.

Which meant if he was going to figure this out and find her, he needed to read the rest. Every staggeringly painful part of it. And to do it not as a hurt ex-boyfriend or a man who ached to put things right but as a detective. With the analytical part of his mind alone.

But before he could do that he needed to do something else. As a gesture, if nothing more.

He pressed the reply button on the email he'd forwarded to himself, and he wrote back to her.

I'm so sorry. I'm so, so sorry. This was all my fault, not yours.

I'm going to find you. I promise.

X

Once he'd sent it he took a very deep breath and then scrolled backwards. It took him a minute to find where he'd been. And then he read on.

21. Anna

There were three of them already gathered at a table in busy King's Bar when I rocked up (late, obviously). My calf was now hurting a lot worse where the bike had landed on it – it seemed as though the rowing hadn't been *such* a good idea – but a lot of ice had taken the swelling down some and I'd picked out a jumpsuit from the wardrobe that successfully covered it up.

I'd felt weird doing that alone, without messaging Cordelia first. But I'd also felt a sense of independence. I could learn this stuff, if slowly.

I watched for a reaction when I arrived, waiting to see if Kit had told them about my accident and whether any of them might be looking out for an injury. Though if they were, they were hiding it pretty well.

There was no sign of James tonight, which was a shame, and Esther had her most-dreaded exam the next day, so it was just Ryan and Kit and Sarah.

I was glad to see Sarah there. She'd been the one to actually talk about that night with Tanya, and Kit's guilt. I hoped I could draw her out on the subject once she was drunk or high. Or both.

'How's the leg feeling?' Kit asked as I sat down gingerly.

'A little unhappy with me,' I admitted. 'But hey, it was a good row in the end.' I turned to Sarah and Ryan to add, 'Kit had the joy of witnessing me having a full-on meltdown on the river, did he tell you?'

Ryan looked between me and Kit. 'What was the meltdown about? And what happened to your leg?'

He didn't look quite happy. He didn't *sound* happy, either. His voice was too tight, and it made me wonder if he knew something.

But when I said, 'Oh, the leg was just me falling off my bike because someone clipped me,' there wasn't a particular reaction. 'As to the meltdown, I basically hated rowing, myself, the water, boats and the whole concept of sport. It's a fairly common occurrence.'

Ryan grinned at that. 'How many times during the row did you quit sport forever?'

'At least five,' I said, laughing.

'Some of us had the sense to quit it in first year,' Sarah said, lifting her glass. 'Novice term was enough.'

'Oh, did you row?' I asked her, genuinely surprised. She was totally not the build to be immediately recruited for rowing, but that said, I've known smaller women become hugely strong.

'I learned quickly that it wasn't for me,' Sarah said. 'Hours of sitting freezing in queues of traffic . . .'

I shook my head. 'See, that's a Cambridge problem. There are no queues at Columbia, and when it's cold we row indoors. We're seriously pathetic.'

'Yeah, I was thinking exactly that,' Ryan said, shaking his head. 'Real rowers do it stationary in sub-zero.'

'With weights, obviously,' Kit chipped in. 'Cambridge novices always carry at least a hundred kilos of weights, too. And they have to be blindfolded.'

'Yeah, so this is sounding more like a fetish than a sport,' I said, narrowing my eyes at him.

'Why can't things be both?' Ryan asked. 'Kit only does rugby because of the other guys in shorts.'

'True, that,' Kit agreed.

I couldn't help laughing at all of this. And you know what

I hated about that moment, Reid? It was the thought that I really liked these people. That, in any other situation, we could so easily be real friends.

It wasn't the kind of thought I usually have when working. Most of the people I have to buddy up to are deeply into criminal activities or loathsomely elitist.

I tried not to let the fondness in. I'd come here for a reason and I knew that I needed to talk to Sarah while I had the chance.

I'd decided to be teetotal again tonight, both to keep supporting Ryan and in order to keep my head in the game. I'd taken a bunch of co-codamol, too, and that was enough head-altering substances for me. So when Kit and Sarah offered to go to the bar I asked for a tonic and bantered with Ryan for a little while in the background, thinking about how to approach Sarah.

But when the two of them returned and I tried to strike up a conversation I realised that Sarah was no longer keen on talking with me *at all*. She gave me snippy replies and there was something frosty and guarded in the way she was looking at me.

I found my pulse rate climbing. Why had this change happened? She'd been OK with me when I'd arrived.

But then she'd gone to the bar with Kit. Was it possible that he'd told her I couldn't be trusted? Had he seen through me this afternoon?

Unless Sarah doesn't trust me for her own reasons? I thought.

I realised only then that I didn't know whether Sarah had been at the ball when Holly died. Whether she'd even known this group back then. She hadn't appeared in their photos, and I knew she'd only been dating Kit for the last three months. But that didn't mean she *hadn't* been involved, did it?

What if she'd wanted in on the group for a long time?

People could get obsessive. She could have been watching them all for ages. Could have seen Holly as an obstacle, for some reason.

I felt something close to guilt. I should have known more about this by now. Cordelia's angry exit at the Caledonian Club rushed back to me and I wondered whether I was letting Holly down. Was it possible that in allowing my thoughts to slide too often towards Tanya, I was failing her? And failing Cordelia, too?

I'm not going to fail, I thought to myself as I looked between Kit, all cool smiles, and brittle, angry Sarah. *There's something going on between them all, and I'm going to figure out what it is.*

Ryan, at least, seemed to be on good form. He jumped up to help with drinks and insisted on getting my round for me.

'You're injured,' he told me, firmly. 'You're not carrying anything, and you're not paying, either.'

I couldn't help feeling relieved. As good value as student drinks were, I was starting to worry that the credit card was going to hit its limit. Every part of this cost money, and it was, frankly, astonishing watching this group spend as easily as breathing.

I decided that I should push the conversation in a direction that wasn't selfish: the topic of who did and who didn't have a car. That wasn't about Tanya: it was about who might have wanted to warn me off. It was what I *should* be asking.

'Anyone feel like driving me to London tomorrow?' I asked, once Ryan had returned. 'I need to show my coach and physio the damage and work out a plan, but after today I honestly can't face the train and the tube.'

Ryan shook his head with a grin. 'Americans. Always assuming people drive everywhere.'

'I do not!' I protested, slightly surprised that he was being harsh. 'I've been cycling all year like I'm Scandinavian or something. But if anyone could let me pay them to drive me, it would be kind of helpful.'

Kit gave me a thoughtful look. 'Let me see if I can get out of something.'

'Oh, like, don't move anything,' I said, immediately. 'I could just woman up and take the train.'

'No, it's cool,' he said. 'Just depends on how flexible this revision supervision is.'

I gave him a crooked smile. 'Thanks. I guess James doesn't have a vehicle, if that doesn't work out?'

'Save-the-planet Sedgewick?' Ryan asked. 'No way. He thinks owning a car is morally wrong.'

'Oh.' I gave a short laugh. 'I mean, I guess he kind of has a point . . .' And then I broke off, seeing a possible advantage. 'Oh. That wasn't . . . that wasn't how his girlfriend died or something?'

'No, nothing like that,' Kit said after a momentary silence. 'Holly . . . it was the May Ball. We were all there, but she – wandered off and – and drowned.'

I saw him look over at Ryan with what might have been an expression of concern but might also have been a brief reminder to keep his mouth shut.

He said they were all there, I thought. *Including Sarah.*

'I'm so sorry,' I said. And then, addressing Sarah directly, I said, 'It must be really hard, losing a friend like that.'

Sarah gave a sniff and turned her head away. 'Not me. When Kit says "we were all there" he means the Pitt Club crowd. The ones who count. I wasn't friends with anyone back then, and I went to St John's ball instead.'

Now that, Reid, was interesting. It sounded like there *was* something significant about membership of the Pitt Club after all.

Kit blinked and gave Sarah a squeezing hug. 'I'm . . . what

do you mean, the ones who count? I don't like half the Pitt Club, and you count the mostest.'

The cuteness was unexpected, and it jarred with the situation as well as with Kit's personality. Did Kit ever really, truly talk to his girlfriends like that?

Sarah didn't visibly melt into his squeeze, but she did turn and give him a peck on the lips.

'Hey, I'm with you,' I told Sarah. 'Non-Pitt Club member and proud. I hear they only let you in if you hate puppies, anyway.'

She gave me a half-smile, one that didn't look at all happy.

'Kittens,' Kit said, deadpan. It was a shame. I was hoping he'd get offended and argue. 'And they've relaxed the rule a bit.' He glanced at Sarah. 'You're both too cool for the kitten-haters, you know.'

A little later Kit pulled a small tissue-paper packet out of his pocket and slid Ryan and Sarah each what I guessed must have been a tab of MDMA.

'Pick-me-up time?' he asked, quietly.

Ryan looked over at me, a clear question in his expression. Evidently he wasn't willing to go totally off the party drugs to support me. But I hadn't been teetotal at the wine tasting, either.

I gave him a nod and a smile, thinking that there were benefits to him being a little out of control. He'd taken it within seconds, so quickly it was hard to see it happen. And then he washed it down with what must have been another soda water.

Sarah took hers with a swift, almost angry movement. I hoped it might loosen her inhibitions enough to get her talking about what was bothering her. She might not have been there on the night Holly died, but *something* was clearly up. All I needed was for her to get halfway to high and go to the bathroom alone so I could follow.

With the tabs handed out, Kit raised a questioning eyebrow at me.

'Still fine,' I told him with a shake of the head. 'Still a boring killjoy.'

Kit gave me an odd little smile.

'As long as you don't mind if I do.'

'Not at all,' I told him.

He nodded and glanced down at the little tissue-paper pouch. He hesitated, and then surprised me by sliding it back into his pocket. He held my gaze for a moment as he drank from his glass instead.

I felt suddenly profoundly uncomfortable under that gaze. What was he saying? That he wouldn't get high around me? That he knew not to trust me?

Sarah stood and pulled Kit upright. 'Come outside for a minute,' she said. She was speaking to him, but her gaze was on me.

Fuck, I thought, trying to keep my face deadpan. *Whatever Kit thinks, Sarah thinks something worse. And maybe she's done a little research and worked out more than he has.*

I watched them retreat outside, the music rising as they went. It was time to dance, apparently.

'Come on!' Ryan said, reaching for me with a smile. The MDMA was clearly hitting fast. Or at least his brain was telling him that it was, and that was enough for Ryan.

I went with him to a clear space on the floor and started off enjoying it all. Ryan was a good, enthusiastic dancer and his commentary between songs made me laugh. He insisted on getting us more hydration after a little while, and it was only as he was walking back over towards me carrying a couple of mostly full glasses that I realised he was unsteady on his feet.

He's drunk, I thought, light dawning.

He hadn't been drinking soda water all evening: he'd been

drinking alcohol. That was why he'd insisted on going to the bar for me.

He gave me a huge, beaming smile as he returned and held a glass out to me.

'I got you a proper one,' he said.

'Oh, that's . . . thanks,' I said. 'I guess I can have the one.'

We clinked glasses, but when I went to drink mine it was horrendously strong. It must have had more than two shots of gin in there, which meant he'd probably added multiple drinks together.

I watched him empty his glass, and then he was pressing himself up against me, one hand on my backside and the hand with the glass in it round my shoulders.

'Hey, Ryan!' I said, loudly. 'This is invading my space!'

'I just wanted . . . You know, you're amazing,' he said.

'Thanks,' I told him, trying to peel his arms off me. 'But you know you can tell me from further away.'

He let me move away a little but then looked soulfully into my eyes and said, 'We'd be amazing together, you know. You don't need any of these other guys.'

I remembered, suddenly, Cordelia's comment about Ryan's history of being a womaniser. His worry after the first time we'd met that he'd been an asshole.

This is what he does when he's drunk, I thought with dawning comprehension. *This is what he's been avoiding.*

I felt the inevitable consequence of everything Gael had asked me to do rushing in on me. I'd set out to seduce Ryan, hadn't I? Only now here I was, surrounded by strangers and realising that I wanted nothing more than to get away from him.

'That's – you're great,' I said. 'But I'm not looking for any guys. I need to row and study.'

'You know it'd work,' he said, trying to put a hand up to touch my face.

'I need to go to the bathroom,' I said, a feeling of panic rising in me. 'Why don't you get us another drink? Maybe Kit and Sarah want one, too.'

I felt huge relief as he processed this and then nodded and let me go. I almost ran out of there to the ladies' toilets, and then spent a while in front of the sink, thinking through how to handle this. Maybe the best thing was just to leave. Ryan, I was confident, would feel really bad about this tomorrow. It didn't need to get difficult.

You've got this, I thought.

But as I emerged into the corridor Ryan was right outside, his strawberry-blond head not far off the low-hanging light fittings.

It didn't matter that I'm a tall, strong woman or that I'd been doing a shit-ton of weight training. I was never going to be able to fight off a fully grown man of his size. Still less one in training.

'There you are,' he said, and closed the short distance between us unsteadily.

I looked past him up the corridor, hoping that someone else would come along and make it awkward for him. But the short stretch was currently empty all the way up to the stairs. There'd been nobody else in the bathroom, either. I was absolutely on my own with the guy.

'I'm just going back to dance,' I told Ryan, trying to move round him.

He grabbed hold of me, by one arm and my waist.

'Please don't go. Just stay here,' he said.

'I really need to go,' I told him, pulling away.

Ryan didn't seem to be able to hear me. He pushed me back against the closed bathroom door and used his weight to press into me. I suddenly couldn't see anything beyond him and my nose was full of the reek of beer.

'Not until you give me a kiss,' he said.

'Ryan . . .'

I tried to push against him, but he was immovable. Utterly solid beneath the tight green T-shirt.

He laughed, a very out-of-control laugh. 'I know you want to as well,' he said. 'We're so made for each other, it's unreal.'

I tried to make eye contact with him. To show him that this was Not OK using my expression. But his eyes were barely focusing.

Inebriation did nothing to make him weaker, though. As I pushed harder, he pressed in closer, and it was genuinely painful where he was shoving his leg against my pelvis.

'I've wanted to have your body against mine since the first time I saw you,' he said. 'You're so strong.'

I thought, in a horrible jolt, of Holly Moore. She'd been his friend's girlfriend, but maybe that hadn't mattered to him. She'd been an athlete, too. He'd probably wanted the feel of her body against his, no matter what *she* wanted.

And Tanya. Tanya had been strong, too.

Is that why they died? I thought. *Was it all about what one out-of-control man wanted?*

The thought turned me from being keen to get away to being seriously, honestly afraid. I started writhing away from him, and I screamed at him to get the hell off me.

I was still mostly pinned, but I got an arm free and started pushing and shoving at him, sensing freedom.

And then Kit Frankland's voice said, 'Ryan, get off her!'

There was a second while I continued to try to slide out from behind Ryan, and then he pivoted away, as if pulled. With his weight released, I staggered, and crashed straight down onto one knee on the stone tiles of the corridor.

'For fuck's sake, Ryan,' Kit said, his voice low and angry.

I felt hands on me, on my arms and shoulders, but it wasn't

clear to me just then whose they were. I pushed them off and scrambled to my feet. My knee was numb in that way that told me it was going to really hurt later, a perfect addition to my already sore calf and shin from the fall off the bike, but I breathed in and gave Kit a nod as I straightened my hair. 'I'm OK.'

I walked past him down the corridor. I found my unsteady way out to the front quad of King's and stood in the chilly June moonlight. I turned away from the road and found myself looking past the bulk of the Gibbs' building towards the gleaming river. Then raising my head to look at the moon as I breathed in and out. In and out.

I couldn't quite seem to catch my breath out there. Not for minute after minute.

Come on, Anna, I thought. *Toughen up.*

But I couldn't seem to find the tough version of me.

I probably should have expected Kit to be the one to come and find me. I could hear steps coming hesitantly towards me, but I was still watching the moon, which was just on the point of touching the roof of the building ahead. I felt like I'd be OK if I could just watch it until the two shapes met.

'Are you . . .?' Kit cleared his throat. 'I know you said you're . . . but that was shit. I'm . . . I'm really sorry.'

I gave in and turned to look at him, trying to read what he really thought from his expression. Because Ryan was Kit's friend, and I knew he must – *must* – have known what he was like. He must on some level approve of this bullshit. This apparent concern . . . it must be fake.

But he just looked sad. And a little horrified.

'Is this what he does?' I asked. 'Is this . . . how Ryan treats girls? Because I don't think I . . . I don't feel like I did anything to encourage him.'

'No,' Kit said, quickly. 'It wasn't you. He just gets out of control when he's drunk sometimes. It's like, I don't know, he just starts thinking someone wants him. I think maybe all the inside imaginary situations take over and he stops taking in that someone's saying no.'

I shook my head. I knew the best thing would probably be to shrug it all off and pretend to be fine. It would give me a chance to ask Kit about the other times Ryan had done this. I might have found out, right then and there, whether Holly could have been a victim.

But you know, Reid, I was so far from OK just then. I was afraid, and not just for myself. For other women.

'He needs to be talked to,' I said, a shake to my voice that I hated. 'He's going to end up . . .'

Kit nodded. 'I know. I've talked to him . . .'

'No,' I said, and I stepped towards him, failing to keep my thoughts and feelings in real check. 'He needs proper therapy. Or a warning from the police. Or for you to tell him that you're going to report him for this, right now. He needs more than a little speech about behaving himself. I know there are reasons he is the way he is, but there always are. He *has to stop*.'

There was a pause while Kit gave me a very long look, and then he said, 'I know that, too.' And I guess I must have let more of my feelings show than I was aware of, because he said, 'There's a hug here if you . . . if you want.'

He opened his arms, and somehow it made perfect sense to step forward into them.

And weirdly, despite having just been pinned to a door by one rugby player, that non-sexual, comforting hug was exactly what I needed just then.

I guess part of Kit's power is knowing that kind of thing. What people need. Where all our weaknesses are.

After a moment, it occurred to me that Sarah might come out and find us like that. The last thing I wanted was that kind of a reputation.

'Is . . . do you think Sarah would mind you hugging the new girl?' I asked into his ear, without letting go.

'Well, that's . . . Um, we just broke up,' he answered, with his voice rumbling into my shoulder. 'So I guess maybe this hug is for me, too.'

It really was only then that it dawned on me that Kit might have weaknesses, too. And everything changed at that point. The dynamic. All of it. It was suddenly clear what Kit wanted, and why Sarah had been so angry with me.

You know what really saddens me, though, when I write this? It's knowing that at that moment, the one person I really wanted there, to comfort me, was you, Reid.

And it sucks.

22. Reid

Reid climbed out of the taxi feeling pretty much as bad as he'd ever felt.

On the surface of it, what he was reading now confirmed everything he'd believed about Anna. The manipulation. The willingness to seduce. The way she'd put the story above everyone's feelings.

And yet the truth underneath it all was so different. Anna had been sent in there to capture the interest of an undergraduate, and then had done her best to be a friend to him, even if her motives hadn't been totally pure. What she'd said to Kit had been right: she'd done nothing to encourage Ryan Jaffett.

But that hadn't stopped him from assaulting her. And something much worse could so easily have happened, too. Which made Reid want to track Ryan down right now and haul him to the police station himself. Worse, it made him want to ignore everything he was supposed to represent and go and beat the guy senseless.

He felt wretched that she'd been put in that position, and worse that he hadn't been there for her when it had happened. Instead, it had been up to Kit bloody Frankland to save her.

Reid had been ahead of Anna in understanding that Kit had fallen for her. Of course he'd fallen for her. How could he *not* want someone so sparky and smart and out of his control?

But the single worst thing was what else Reid could see: that despite what she was actively saying, Anna had fallen for Kit, too. For his clever, manipulative, charming ways.

It had been plain as day from the way she'd walked straight into that hug of his, but from before that, too. From every description of him. There had been a connection there from the start.

And if she'd fallen for him, it meant she wouldn't have been able to see Kit clearly when she'd needed to. That she would have been vulnerable to him, and to anything he told her about the others.

Reid felt like emailing her back again, trying to somehow warn the Anna of two and a half weeks ago not to trust that feeling. But obviously that was useless. He couldn't send something back in time.

Thrumming through all this worry was a growing sense that he was going to find out something about Tanya soon. Something that might be worse than what he'd already come to terms with.

If one of them killed her, he thought, *I could have stopped it. I could have stopped it, if I'd got her to talk to me.*

As he climbed the stairs to James Sedgewick's third-floor room he had the dark, heavy thought that he might even be about to come face to face with Tanya's killer in the flesh. And he felt almost glad to see James's handsome face drain of colour as he opened the door to Reid and his badge.

'DI Reid Murray,' Reid said, his voice flat. Professional. 'I'd like to have a quick word.'

'Are you . . . definitely with the police?' James asked, his voice tight with anxiety.

'That's what the badge is for,' Reid said, smiling but without much humour.

'Only . . .' James glanced into the corridor behind him. 'You messaged, didn't you? And I tried to call the station to see if I should come in, and they'd never heard of you.'

Reid felt momentarily wrongfooted. It had never occurred to him that James wouldn't just call him back on his mobile. 'Was that here at Cambridge?'

'Umm . . . yeah, it was,' James said. 'I called 101, so . . .'

Reid sighed. This could spell trouble if his DCI got told he was overstepping the mark. 'That's because I don't work for Cambridgeshire; I'm with the Metropolitan Police in London,' he explained, knowing there was nothing else for it. He held the badge out to James. 'Here.'

James nodded, slowly, looked at him anxiously again, and then let him into a large, slope-ceilinged room.

'Sorry,' James said, handing the badge back and perching on his desk chair. 'Always worry about things being scams and . . . I didn't know the Met would do a missing persons here.'

'There's some suggestion that the missing person in question might be in London,' Reid said. He sat himself on the edge of James's bed, as there was nowhere else to sit. Despite being large, the student room was remarkably empty.

'Are you talking about Aria?' James asked, looking at him intently.

'The young woman you knew as Aria,' Reid agreed. 'Her real name is Anna Sousa.'

James gave a slow nod. 'Is she police?' he asked.

Reid tried not to show that he was taken aback by this. He'd expected James to either be surprised that she had a double identity, or pretend to be. But instead, James had reacted as though this wasn't news to him at all.

'She's . . . a civilian,' Reid said. 'You don't seem surprised that she had another name.'

James gave a shrug. 'She was trying to work out who killed Holly. I knew she probably wasn't who she said she was. I was . . . glad she was doing something about it, at first. But then it didn't seem to go anywhere . . .'

Reid scrutinised James's face for a few moments. If he'd known about Anna, that would have given him a possible motive to wish her harm. 'So you were aware of what she was doing before she went missing?'

'Yes,' James said. 'It took me a while to work out. But the questions she was asking and the way she suddenly appeared . . .' He sighed. 'I got there in the end.'

'What makes you think she didn't uncover anything?' Reid asked.

'Some things she said at the May Ball,' James replied. 'She said she was sorry for letting me down. And I got the impression she was saying goodbye to us all.'

Reid felt a flash of something at that. If Anna had acted like she was going somewhere, maybe she'd left of her own volition. Or had she realised something bad was coming her way?

If she said any of that at all, he thought, watching James's face. It was hard to read anything there except worry, and James had plenty of innocent reasons for that.

'Can you think of anyone who might have found that behaviour a threat?'

There was a pause, and James said, 'Yeah, well . . . whoever killed Holly might have done.' He swallowed, looking slightly sick. 'But I don't think anyone got to Anna. I hope not. I think she meant to go wherever she's gone. She left with someone.'

It sounded true. But then, James was supposedly a decent actor, wasn't he? Though there was a big difference between student Shakespeare on stage, and lying under pressure.

'You're sure?' he asked.

'Yes,' James said. Reid saw his eyes going back to the badge in Reid's hand and wondered if he *was* lying after all. Was that little tell because he was afraid of saying something false to an officer of the law?

'Can you describe them?'

James looked into the distance, and Reid watched intently. It seemed as though the young man was genuinely trying to recall something. 'Definitely a guy. Older than we are, I thought, but I was seeing him from the back. I think her height in heels, maybe?'

'Hair colour?'

James let out a huff of air. 'It was pretty hard to . . . Light brown? Cut quite short?'

'And what time did you say they left?'

'Straight after the fireworks,' he said, immediately. 'So that's . . . just before eleven?'

Reid pulled his iPad out and, opening up notepad rather than an official form, wrote all that down.

'The trouble I have, see, James,' he said as he was finishing up, 'is that I've been sent the CCTV at the exit and Anna doesn't appear anywhere on it at around eleven. We've checked right up until the survivors' photo, and nothing.'

He looked up at James and gave him a very flat smile.

For the first time James's certainty seemed to slide. 'I . . . well, I don't know how . . . That's weird,' he said. And then he added, 'Look, I . . . I don't know. But she's a really nice person, even if she had to lie to us. I hope she's OK.'

'So do I,' Reid said, quietly.

James rose to open the door, and Reid noticed that his hands were shaking on the latch. A shake that ran right the way through him.

23. Anna

It's taken me a while to come back to this. It . . . wasn't the most comfortable thing, telling you about Kit Frankland, and I felt like I wanted to stop right after I started.

To be honest, it's not the most comfortable thing to think about, either. The whole situation makes me feel like I'm almost what you thought I was.

I'd seduced him. By accident, sure. But when I realised what had happened, I didn't back away. I felt weirdly triumphant, because now maybe he'd tell me things that he really shouldn't.

You'd do anything, wouldn't you? Charm anyone, sleep with anyone, betray anyone . . .

I remember your face when you said that. I don't know if you remember. It was in a whole slew of stuff you slung at me before you left.

But honestly, Reid, I don't think anyone else has ever managed to hurt me that badly. Not the high-school boyfriend who casually told me he was sleeping with someone else; not the probable narcissist I met on a job who love-bombed me and then ghosted me.

I didn't understand how you could be saying any of those words. When what I was telling you was that I was going to keep fighting for you, and for Tanya. When I was being absolutely honest with you, and always had been.

And I want to tell the truth about this, too. Or at least write it down.

What's happened with Kit has felt like the only thing I could do. Because as much as you'll have trouble believing this, it isn't *the story* that I want: it's justice. For Holly and Tanya's killer to be jailed, and for no other girls like them to die.

OK. I guess if you're still reading, then that's something.

Though maybe you'll stop kind of soon. Because the next part might actually be . . . worse.

In the three days since Kit rescued me, I haven't had to see Ryan once, which has been a relief.

The day after it happened, Kit drove me, as promised, to London. I'd worked hard to make sure I knew exactly where he should take me to meet up with the other Olympic rowing hopefuls, and that I had exactly the right equipment with me to look like someone who was injured but was hopeful I might still be able to train.

I left him at the entrance to the boathouse and walked in as if I belonged there, promising I'd call if I needed picking up. I then brazened it out, heading up the staircase and in, and sat on my phone for a good twenty minutes amid an increasing number of rowers going in and out for a weights session until somebody asked me if I was OK. I grinned at her and said I was there for physio, and nobody seemed to pay me any attention after that.

Forty-five minutes later, I messaged Kit to tell him that I was on light duties but cleared to at least train and asked if he wanted to hang on for an hour or head home. He immediately replied that he was happy to wait and so I dumped my bag in the gym and went for a hobbling, uncomfortable run down the bank until I'd built up enough of a sweat to look like someone who'd been erg training for an hour and then hung around outside until he came to pick me up. Aside from a couple of athletes commenting on my bruised, swollen leg in a curious and sympathetic way, now that it was extremely obvious under my rowing

Lycra, nobody accosted me, and I was able to get back into his ridiculous silver Bugatti and tell him a load of fabricated nonsense about the physio session on the way home.

It made me feel weirdly guilty to do all this when he was putting himself out for me, squeezing the trip in before his own training when he really ought to have been studying. But any time I started to feel bad I'd remind myself about Holly and Tanya, and then about the reason my leg was swollen and bruised, and then about the photographs someone had taken of me.

I'm not the one with the biggest secrets, I told myself more than once. *And if lying to Kit helps me work out who killed them, I'm willing to do it.*

Since then, Kit has arranged to meet me alone several times, or with Esther and James. He has also avoided the topic of Ryan entirely in each and every formation. Which has been welcome, but has also made me start to suspect that he hasn't actually *done* anything, despite promising to. I'm beginning to think he's just avoiding an argument until everything blows over, as if Ryan and I had just had a falling-out instead of him committing a major sexual assault.

Esther's response has been, in contrast, both kind and touching. I didn't see her until she'd finished her final exam on Friday, the day after the attack, but she still took the time to message me the morning after it happened.

> Kit told me what Ryan did. I'm really, really sorry, darling. I don't give a shit that he's my friend, that's so not ok. I'm here for you if you need me. Xx

It was a lot less diplomatic than I would have expected, and when I saw her in person she had every reason to be full of post-exam distraction, but she still hugged me fiercely and asked, 'Are you doing OK?'

'I'm OK,' I told her, and gave her a squeeze back. 'Thank you.'

When she let me go it was to look searchingly at me for a long moment. Then she said, 'They get away with so much, don't they?'

It was a strange, startling thing to say. I wanted to ask her what she meant – ask her if she meant Ryan and Kit and James, or someone else. But Kit arrived at that point, fresh from his training for the summer's big rugby tour to Japan, and Esther assembled her face into a flawless smile as she caught sight of him.

I realised that I needed to talk to her properly. After what happened with Ryan, I'd lost sight of Esther, and of the secret boyfriend I'd guessed she had. Of her own secrets beyond that.

It occurred to me, suddenly, that of all of them, Esther was the one I'd most easily believe would leave photographs like that, and a note. She was the patient, watchful, sometimes unnoticed one.

I felt myself drawing back from her at the thought.

'Hey, you,' Kit said, coming to hug me, too. Despite the fact that he'd only seen me three hours before when he'd dropped me home from London, it was a long, lingering hug that ended on a held gaze.

'Hey,' I said, feeling blood rush to my face in a not-that-professional manner.

I realised that Esther was watching us with that same polished smile but that one of her hands was rhythmically clenching and relaxing.

Kit turned to her at that point and slung his arm round her. 'How was it?'

Esther stopped squeezing her hand closed and tucked her hair behind her ear. 'Honestly, I'm not sure. For now, I'm just glad it's done. I'll have all of tonight to relive everything I did wrong.'

'I stan that,' Kit said. 'Picnic at the Mill Pond?'

'Perfect,' Esther said.

It turned into a strange evening, where I felt like I was the central point in some bizarre triangle. Kit was so clearly hyper-aware of me and finding every excuse possible to be near me or touch me or make me laugh. It was an electric, zinging kind of flirtation that made me feel I had to be on my toes.

What was stranger, though, was the way Esther seemed to want my attention and touch, too, in a softer, more comfort-craving way. She would sit with my arm drawn round her or her shoulder leaning into mine. At times she even lay with her head on my legs, looking tired and kind of sad.

Although there were two of us there and Kit was her long-term friend and flatmate, she often seemed like she was talking exclusively to me. It felt that way when she asked, 'Were you nervous the whole way through your finals? Just terrified?'

I laughed. 'Hell, yes. And I had more reason to be. I'd screwed up on the work side. Too much rowing . . . and I didn't cope very well with all the crap that went with rowing.' I squeezed her arm. 'You've got this so much more under control.'

'I don't think I have,' Esther said, and there was no trace of the cool, together young woman I'd first met at that party. She sounded vulnerable. Lost. 'I'm not clever enough for this stuff and I . . . I find my brain just sliding off it.'

'You're plenty clever enough,' Kit said, firmly. 'It's just not what you wanted to do. This is what happens when you force someone into a subject that doesn't suit them.'

I looked at Esther. 'What did you want to do?'

'Biology,' she said, quietly. 'Nat Sci. It's . . . I've never been good at essays. But I love lab time, and even programming and modelling's OK.'

It's weird how, in that moment, I felt really sorry for her, Reid. That rich, beautiful young woman who seemed to have it all.

'Could you do a postgrad?'

Esther grimaced. 'Mummy would . . . Honestly, there's no way. I need to find a job, as soon as possible.'

'Oh,' Kit said. 'I . . . so the one you were looking at . . .?'

'I didn't get through the last round,' Esther said, tightly.

'Well, they're idiots,' Kit said, then added, squeezing up close on Esther's other side and putting an arm round her, 'Sorry, E. You'll get something amazing. And you know, someday soon, you're going to be free of that woman, and you're going to fly.'

'Thanks, Kit,' Esther said. But she had the dull expression of someone who didn't believe it.

'Have another gin,' he said after that, and got to his feet. We'd brought food and a few cans with us from the central Marks and Spencer, but had then been taking it in turns to go to the Mill pub and bring drinks out. It was only once Kit had crossed the grass and gone out of earshot that Esther suddenly said to me, 'I really don't want Ryan to ruin anything. It's the best having you here. Things have been so shit.'

She started studying the grass, as though embarrassed to say this to my face, but she still kept one hand twined through mine.

'You mean since Holly?' I tried.

Esther nodded, and then said, 'I've had literally nobody to talk to.'

'I'm sorry,' I told her. 'Tell me stuff. I'm here.'

'I . . .' She looked away from me. 'It's hard to . . .'

I nodded, gave her a moment, and then asked, 'What was she like? As a person?'

'She was . . . a ray of light.' She laughed. 'She always, always saw the best in everyone. I . . . sometimes I used to find it frustrating, actually. She had a close friend who wasn't that good for her.'

'Oh, like, a bad influence?' I asked.

Esther pulled a face. 'Kind of. I mean, more controlling, maybe? They'd been at school together.'

Oh, shit, I thought. *She means Cordelia.*

'It's really hard,' I said, tentatively, 'seeing someone controlled by someone else.'

'It was,' Esther said, picking at the grass. 'She used to try to tell Holly how to live. Tell her she shouldn't be going away on holiday, or seeing us all. She thought it was immoral to spend money, for god's sake, as if there shouldn't be an upside to having the parents we all have.' She gave a snort of derision. 'Holly would sometimes end up cancelling on us to keep her happy, even when it was stuff she really wanted to do.'

I felt like everything was twisting around on me. Had I got both Holly and Cordelia wrong? Had Holly been caught between these people?

'Did you feel like you had to share her with this friend?'

There was a pause, and Esther said, 'Yes. Though Holly gradually realised that it wasn't OK, I think. She'd got a bit better at standing up to her, but . . .' She shook her head. 'She never really got free, and now she's dead, and Cordelia blames us, because we were there. Even though Holly went off alone and we would have done anything to stop it happening.'

'God, Esther, I'm sorry,' I said. 'I can't even imagine how hard it must be.'

There was a brief silence, and then Esther said, in a voice full of emotion, 'It was so hard, but it . . . I feel so selfish, because it's not what I keep thinking about.'

'It's OK to have other stuff that makes you sad,' I told her. 'And to want to talk about it. You're a human being.'

There was a pause, and then Esther said, 'I can't get over this – this relationship I had which . . . It wasn't even good for me. I know that.'

'The guy you saw for breakfast?' I asked.

'Yes,' she said, miserably. 'But I want him back so badly. I shouldn't have seen him. It's made it all so much worse again.'

I *clearly* needed to know more about this guy, particularly as he seemed to be linked to Holly in her mind. I swung round so I could lean on the grass next to her, and I had a glimpse of proper tears pouring down her cheeks. I felt another uncomfortable rush of real, honest sympathy.

'It's really hard to let people go,' I said, acknowledging inwardly that this was profoundly true for me, too. 'I had this relationship a while back. I thought it was perfect, but then it all went wrong. I've worked so hard to get over him, but then stuff reminds me of him, and I just . . . I end up writing these stupid emails . . .'

There I was, giving her a real part of myself once again. The weird honesty that sometimes surfaces in this job. It can mess with you a little.

But however messy it was, it worked to get her talking. Esther gave a sobbing laugh and said, 'I do that. I message him sometimes. And then I feel so stupid, because I always think when he replies that it means something . . .'

'Because it's kind of . . . a little interested?' I asked.

'Yes,' she said. 'But it never amounts to more.'

'He sounds like he's stringing you along,' I said with a frown. 'At least my ex has made it clear he is *not* keen. Is he – does he have someone else, maybe?'

There was a long pause, while I felt like maybe that had been too blunt, and then Esther said quietly, 'He does. I actually know he does, but I still . . . I just keep thinking I can win him back.'

I gave a sigh. 'I so get it. We're always wired to feel like we have to win them, aren't we? But you are so, so great, Esther.' I leaned in close to her, not quite sure what I should tactically be saying to her, but positive the moral thing to do was to tell her she was better than this. 'I know that's a platitude, but you are *intimidatingly* wonderful. Smart and beautiful and this incredible friend. If he's too stupid to see that and to put you first, then he doesn't deserve you.'

I saw her lift a hand to wipe her eyes. 'I don't know.'

'Truly,' I said. 'Plus, he's dicking you around, which is *not* nice. What's his name, this guy?'

There was a pause, and then Esther said, 'I . . . I actually can't tell anyone, because it . . . We shouldn't be doing anything at all. Both of us would be in so much trouble.'

I felt a real zing of interest at that, as you can imagine, Reid. Was this a supervisor or a tutor? Because one of those might have been at Trinity May Ball in his own right without appearing on Cordelia's list.

I glanced up and saw, across the lawn, that Kit had emerged from the Mill with our drinks. Clearly a short queue, just when I could have done with it being longer.

'Well,' I told her, 'if you ever want him taking out, just let me know. All the weight training has to be good for something.'

Esther laughed at that, but I found myself thinking much more deeply about her than I had. If she'd talked to Holly about all this, which she'd implied she used to do, then was it possible that Holly had worked out who her illicit lover was? And had this been the thing that had gotten her killed?

If so, how had that connected with Tanya?

I found myself wondering whether Esther could really have had enough of a motive. If she'd had a relationship with someone teaching her, it would be frowned on, and really not great if he was married, but it also wouldn't be enough to get her kicked out or in serious trouble.

But, I thought, *it could well be enough to ruin a diplomatic career. And Esther might be desperate enough to stop her mother finding out that she'd do something drastic.*

I hoped I'd get to see Esther alone over the weekend, but the next times I saw her Kit and James were there, too. The first time, we went punting, all crammed in one boat, and the second we visited a tiny coffee house in the centre of town named Indigo. There was no space to talk privately at either, and all the while I was aware that Kit was watching me in the way that people do when they want to be more than friends.

It interested me that James was in better spirits at these meet-ups. He stayed longer, and seemed much more relaxed, even though he was now diving head first into his exams.

'I need something to do that isn't sitting in my room,' he said when I expressed surprise at seeing him out instead of studying.

But as I watched him interacting with the others I wondered suddenly whether the difference in him was because Ryan wasn't there. And that interested me as much as Esther and her secret boyfriend. Because if James found Ryan's presence stressful, there were two possible reasons I could think of that were very relevant: that James suspected something bad about Ryan, or that Ryan *knew* something bad about James.

The idea of having to talk to Ryan again to find out more made my stomach tie itself in horrible knots. But, in fact, I haven't faced him yet, Reid, and I think all this might be done. Because the bad stuff that came out tonight is . . . I'm not sure I can get past it.

*

So. It's Monday, and I had my check-in with Gael. I told Kit I had to be in to see my coach, and had lunch with him first.

The two of us drank too much, and he told me a lot about his difficult relationship with his dad, and then made me laugh about his weird dissertation supervisor.

I was still kind of drunk by the time I got to the *Ensign*, if I'm honest. Kit always wants to order alcohol with everything, and daytime drinking hits hard. I'd only managed to keep it reasonable by telling him I'd have to get on a rowing machine later.

I'd promised Gael an update at 6 p.m., and actually made it by quarter past, which wasn't so bad. I arrived feeling anxious that Cordelia had spoken to him, but there was no sign of it. When I told him all about the hit-and-run and Ryan's awful drunk behaviour he looked pleased as punch. And then when I went into how Kit was now really into me, he looked totally delighted. He was *all over* that particular development in a way that made me feel weird. And you know, I do sometimes wonder if Gael understands how it feels to do what I do.

He barely even commented on how Ryan forced himself on me, you know. And I wanted to ask him why not. It's not a small thing, and it could happen again. I so often have to get close to men who make my skin crawl, or who I think might have done something terrible.

And you know, I've been finding it hard in a lot of ways, getting close to Kit. I mean, he might have killed someone, but he's also handsome and generally kind and I might just be really hurting him for no reason.

'Have you made any inroads on the club itself?' Gael asked, after all that.

This was the one point that made me feel genuinely worried. Because the truth was, I'd made none. I hadn't been invited to any Pitt Club events yet, and I'd heard virtually nothing about it. No stories about anyone there, and not even any mentions of the others going along.

'I'm working on it,' I told him, brightly. 'I think I should have my foot through the door soon.'

Gael seemed to accept that, and I was free to hand over my receipts and talk practicalities for the rest of the meeting. At some point, a message arrived from Cordelia. She said she was in Cambridge and wanted to see me.

I genuinely didn't know what to make of it. It sounded like it might be a peace offering, and yet I wasn't too sure. I felt like she'd been genuinely angry with me.

And on top of that, I'd been really, *really* looking forward to a night in my London flat. A night back being Anna instead of Aria.

But I agreed. Of course. I was too curious not to, and to be honest I missed her.

An hour later I was back in Cambridge and cycling to my temporary home. My leg was hurting with every turn of the pedals, but I could still ride, and I was determined to keep it moving. Plus, I was sure as all hell not going to let someone scare me out of cycling around the place.

I didn't have time to mentally ready myself for Cordelia. Ten minutes after I made it home, she was there, at my door. And she'd brought someone with her. A tall, skinny guy in his twenties sporting a long-sleeved top, round glasses and a tightly trimmed moustache.

Natural sciences student, I thought, narrowing my eyes at him. Don't tell me I haven't picked up some of this fashion stuff, Reid.

'Hi,' I said, more than a little wary.

'This is Anthony,' Cordelia said, meeting my eye with a look that was . . . what? Excited? Firm? I wasn't sure. 'Can we come in?'

She has something, I suddenly thought, light dawning. *She really has something, and she's too pissed off at me to say it straight out.*

'Sure.' I took a step backwards, and then realised I should be making a proper effort to welcome them in. I kicked a pair of shoes out of the way, hastily hung up a coat and then waved them into the little sitting room.

'You want tea? Wine? Gin?'

'Umm . . . Gin, actually,' Anthony said, sitting down shakily on the sofa.

'Right.'

I went to find ice and glasses with a strange feeling in my chest. I understood what I was seeing. This guy had come with a confession. A hard one. The alcohol was his coping mechanism.

They weren't the best-made gin and tonics ever, though I did at least remember to use the alcohol-free stuff for me and Cordelia. But the drinks had ice, and a kind of slice, even if it looked like it had been hacked rather than cut.

'OK,' I said, handing them out and sitting in the armchair at ninety degrees from them. 'I . . . Do you want to talk first, or . . .?'

'We can chat properly later,' Cordelia said, tersely. 'First of all, I have photos to show you of the night Tanya died. It turns out I persuaded Holly to come into London to see me. She wasn't in Cambridge at all.'

This gave me a little dip of disappointment. If Holly hadn't seen something incriminating that night, it was maybe less likely that she'd been killed to keep her quiet.

But there was still the fact that she'd come to whatever revelation she'd come to six months later. So it might actually have been something she had been told, or overheard.

'OK,' I said. 'Thank you. That's helpful.'

Cordelia's expression told me she could see *exactly* what I was thinking. But she didn't argue. She just said, 'And now you need to hear what Anthony has to say.'

She turned to Anthony, so I did as well. He was involved in drinking half the gin in one go, and he put it down shakily. I noticed, inconsequentially, that his nails were painted a really nice shade of sparkly green. For some reason it felt better to focus on that than the twisting fear of what was coming.

'Right. Soz.' He sniffed, and then said, 'Cordelia approached me because I – I was the one who gave Tanya the . . . the Ritalin and the modafinil that she took.'

I felt . . . I don't know, Reid. Cold. Detached. Not quite right.

'Sorry?'

'I'm ADHD and I have a brother with narcolepsy,' he said, his voice shaking. He looked miserable. Guilt-ridden. 'Tanya was . . . your sister-in-law?'

I glanced at Cordelia, thinking that 'sister-in-law' wasn't quite the right way of saying it, and yet . . . in some ways maybe it was true. Cordelia just held my gaze, so I nodded. And then I cleared my throat and said, 'Yes.'

'So she – Tanya got put in touch with me by someone else I – I supply things to. Sometimes.' His lips were moving in a way I recognised. He looked like he was on the verge of tears. 'I never . . .' He took a very deep breath. 'The friend of mine said she was behind on a few essays and needed some help. That she'd had a shit break-up and the training schedule was too much and she needed me. I thought . . . I thought I was helping.'

I was looking for the lies, Reid. I was looking for all the tells I knew. And I was hating him, too. Hating him and disbelieving and wanting him to get the fuck out of my house.

'You . . . talked to her?' I asked. 'In person?'

Anthony nodded. 'We met up on the – on the day before

she was found.' He shook his head. 'I'm so sorry. I know it was my fault.'

'Tell me,' I said, sharply. 'Tell me what she said. What you said. Where did you meet?'

'She came to my room,' he said. 'She – she looked really together. Not like someone who was going to . . . take too many.'

I turned my head away from him. 'And?'

'She said I was saving her life,' he said with a bitter laugh. 'She said she was about to get kicked out and it was going to be the end of everything. I . . . I actually asked her if she'd, you know, talked to her tutor. Anything like that. But she said she couldn't afford to. She'd already had a lot of warnings, and if they told her she had to stop playing hockey . . .'

I couldn't help looking at him again, then. He was pale. Sick-looking. Haunted. God, I hated him. And also. Also. I felt . . . so sad for him, Reid. I felt so, so sad for him.

'It . . . she reassured me that she knew what she was doing,' he added. 'She said she'd been taking both of them off and on for over a year, when needed. Never too much. She just needed a batch for the week.'

I felt my heart squeeze, thinking of what you'd told me: that the coroner believed she'd made a habit of it. I wanted to protest again, but I couldn't this time.

'So what did you give her?' I asked him, my voice barely working.

'She said she needed a solid week of work and two late nights,' he said. 'So I gave her three modafinil tablets and seven capsules of the ADHD medication I take. It's – it's called Medikinet XL. It's a continuous eight-hour release that's like Ritalin, only more sustained. It's half my dosage. I really only need thirty on most days, and take a few days off, you know. That's why I can sell the rest . . .'

‘How? How do you sell it?’

I knew I’d asked the question aggressively, but this mattered. It mattered because I wanted so badly to catch him out in a lie.

‘Oh, yeah,’ he said. ‘I have migraine tablets, too. I empty them out because you can take them sprinkled on food. I empty them and then I use the empty capsules. Then they just look like migraine pills, so . . . Yeah.’

I had to get up then and move away from him. Because I knew something that wasn’t on the coroner’s report. I knew from that police officer I’d flirted with that the Ritalin pills left over had been in empty topiramate capsules. It’s an epilepsy drug sometimes used for migraines.

He wasn’t lying.

I left the two of them there in the sitting room, opened the front door and went out on to the expanse of Jesus Green alone. Still a tiny part of me was fighting. Wondering whether Cordelia could have paid him off, somehow. Whether she could have set this all up to stop me looking.

But she didn’t want me to stop, I thought. *She wanted to know if Tanya’s death was the cause of Holly’s. She just somehow pulled a fucking miracle out of the bag.*

It wasn’t Cordelia’s fault that everything – *everything* – had been resting on what she’d just disproved.

I realised that I needed them to go. That I couldn’t talk rationally to them right now. That I might cry. Might fly at Anthony and try to stab him with the knife I’d used to cut the limes. Or just break apart.

I charged back inside and tried not to let them see that I was crying because screw that.

‘I’m – thank you so much for coming to tell me. It means a lot. I . . . I just need to take some time to adjust to it all.’ I looked at Cordelia, who was already getting to her feet, a complex expression on her face. 'Can I . . . call you tomorrow?' I said.

'Sure,' Cordelia replied, with a sympathy I hadn't expected. 'I'll . . . Just let me know what I can do.'

I almost lost it then. The worst thing when you're on the edge of breaking down is sympathy, right?

'God, I should be the one saying that.' I gave a really not-cheerful laugh. 'Peak unprofessional. I'm really sorry.'

Anthony looked like hell as he left. But I wondered for just an instant whether this had been the exorcism of a demon for him. And I feel so sad and resentful and angry over that. Because how am I supposed to exorcise mine, Reid? If I can't find a killer?

I didn't really do anything after the door was shut. There was nothing to do, was there?

Because I was wrong. I was so, so wrong about everything, Reid. Wasn't I? I hurt you when I should have been there for you and I fucked everything up.

Everything.

24. Reid

It could have felt like a victory.

The Reid of yesterday – even the Reid of this morning – would probably have been triumphant that Anna had been wrong.

But he'd let her back in now, and accepted who she really was. So all he felt was the pain of it.

As dark as the thought that Tanya might have been killed had been, it would at least have meant the possibility of justice. It would have meant someone to blame.

Someone except himself.

And he felt Anna's pain, too. It was so blindingly clear to him now that she'd been coping with Tanya's death by hanging on to her theory. And then it had all been pulled away.

It was physically painful that he couldn't reach back in time and console her. And that feeling was enough to drive him to his feet again, off the hard stone wall outside St John's College and back onto the paved street.

Trinity College is just next door, he thought. *Surely you can at least find this man she left with if you make them show you the CCTV. James sounded totally sure about him. So find him.*

He slid Anna's phone back into his jacket and began to walk the few dozen yards along the pavement to Trinity College. The entrance was oddly similar: a near-carbon copy of the turreted brick-and-stone gateway that he'd been through to get into St John's.

A few yards from the little pedestrian gate he faltered as another thought hit him.

Maybe the reason they couldn't find her on CCTV was that she didn't leave last night. What if she went to a room in the college? Or was taken to one?

He made his way into the porters' lodge with more determination, and pulled his badge out to show the female porter on duty.

'DI Reid Murray,' he said. 'I think it was you I spoke to on the phone? Trish, wasn't it?'

'Oh, yes,' Trish said, tucking her short blonde hair behind her ears. 'I'm still going through the CCTV for you, double-checking, but I haven't found her leaving. I did go back and find her arriving, if you want to see.'

Reid knew that this wasn't the priority, but the thought of seeing Anna as she had been only last night was impossible to resist.

'Sure,' he said, trying to sound as though it meant nothing more than any other missing persons case.

Trish let him through a flap in the counter into the porters' area, which was largely taken up by a couple of office chairs, the computer, and an assortment of packages that were presumably waiting to be picked up by students or fellows.

'This is ten to eight, when she arrived. VIP queue, so they got in early.'

The screen was suddenly filled with a black-and-white but thankfully clear image that must have been taken from just outside the porters' lodge. On the left was a table where a couple of students in black suits were presumably checking tickets. To the right of the frame was the expanse of the court, a huge space that had a queue of people dressed in evening wear snaking round it. In the corner of the screen Reid could see what looked suspiciously like a hot-air balloon.

He had a moment to think that this whole May Ball thing

was madness before a figure appeared at the ticket table and it made the breath catch in his throat.

'There she is,' the porter said, tapping the screen.

But Reid didn't need the comment. Of course it was Anna.

She was wearing the dress he'd seen in the photograph Seaton had sent, her hair elaborately curled and pinned up. Despite a serious pair of high heels that made her taller than most of the men around her, she moved smoothly as she stepped back from the table slightly.

Even in black and white, she looked like she had the sun on her. And god, it hurt to see.

Reid saw her head tip back slightly as she laughed at something, and he knew exactly how it would have sounded. He was vaguely aware that a few students trickled through the porters' lodge entrance while he was watching, and that Trish went to see to them, but he couldn't look away.

The student at the desk handed Anna something – a programme, maybe – and she slid it into her handbag and then put the bag onto her shoulder. And then she turned and moved away, until she was out of range of the camera. And that was all. The video carried on without her in it, seeming blank. Empty.

Trish returned, and he asked, 'So you didn't pick her up anywhere else?'

'We don't have a huge number of cameras,' she replied. 'She's not on any of the feeds I've looked at. Scanning through the crowds leaving is taking a while. I'm being careful. But nothing so far, and I'm most of the way through.'

'Can students book rooms for the night?' he asked. 'I mean, I'm wondering if she stayed with someone here after the ball.'

'Well, Trinity students have their own rooms already,' Trish told him.

'But students from other colleges?'

'No,' Trish said. 'They don't have room rights here. Just alum members.'

Reid opened his mouth to ask something else and then remembered that most of these kids had parents who'd been to Cambridge, too. If those parents had gone to Trinity, they'd have the right to book rooms as alumnus members.

'Can you check some names for me on your booked rooms?' he asked.

'Sure,' Trish said, and he thanked his stars that he'd happened on an amenable porter. If he'd had to argue over all of this, it could have taken a long time.

'The surnames would be Jaffett, Frankland, Sedgewick and Thomas.'

Trish wrote those down and then brought up a new screen. She scrolled and checked between it and the names, and then said, 'There was a Roland Frankland booked in last night, but none of the others.'

Reid straightened up, adrenaline flooding through him.

Kit's father had a room.

'Was it just for one night?'

'Actually, two. He extended it today.'

And that might mean everything. Why extend a room booking if it was just for his son, who had his own room a ten-minute walk away?

What if she's being held right here in the college?

And then the fact that twenty-four hours had gone past hit him like a train.

They might want something from her, he thought, trying to convince himself that it was all going to be all right. *If they need something from her, they'd hold her. They wouldn't do anything else.*

'Will you be able to show me the room?' he asked.

'Well, we can't let anyone in without good reason,' Trish said. 'First thing I'd say, you have to go over there and knock.

If there's no answer, we can maybe look at getting in there once Peter's back from doing the rounds.'

'OK, thanks.'

She gave directions to a room on Nevile's Court further towards the back of the college. He tried to slow his heart to the point where he could listen and then stepped out into the twilit college proper. He was caught briefly in a moment of startled surprise at the huge scale of the open front court. It was much larger than he'd realised from the CCTV. Acres of space. And in what was now almost total darkness the lights of the central fountain and the windows around it made it seem like some immense fortification.

You could build a village in here, he thought.

He hadn't got any further than that thought before rapid steps behind made him swing round. He was still night blind from the lights in the porters' lodge and could do nothing to protect himself against an oncoming rush.

His assailant hit hard and didn't just drive him backwards but diagonally, so that his back struck the wall of the nearest tower with crushing force. Above the thoughts of *What the hell?* Reid felt a few rusty instincts kick in. He hadn't had to out-and-out fight for years, but his body still knew how to go for his attacker's weak points.

He raised his knee sharply into the assailant's bent torso and then immediately brought his foot down hard onto where he guessed an instep must be. He got it just about right by the feel of it.

The form flinched backwards, and he tried to make out the face even in the backlighting from the courtyard, but it was near impossible. And then the guy – he was at least sure of that – straightened slightly and produced a swift, vicious roundhouse that connected squarely with Reid's chin.

Reid felt his head snap back and into the stone wall,

and it was all he could do to keep his legs from collapsing. Momentarily afterwards, pain exploded in a line between his jaw and the back of his head.

Breathe, he thought, as his vision became a pattern of diamonds.

He tried to straighten. To get ready for another attack. But nothing came. There was only the sound of running footsteps and then the quiet of the great empty space.

25. Anna

I'm back writing to you, even though I'm not sure why.

I think maybe this is more about having somewhere to put it all down than anything else. You – or an imaginary version of you – have just become the person I'm addressing it to.

After what I learned about Tanya, I felt a lot like giving up. On Holly and Cambridge and all of this. Realising I'd been just so, so wrong about Tanya was . . . it kind of unravelled me.

I don't know if believing she was murdered had kept me from feeling that she was dead, but suddenly I felt like she was really gone. Never coming back.

I didn't know what to do after Cordelia and Anthony left. The Jesus Green house felt so wrong and empty and stifling.

I walked out of the front door at eleven with no real plan and found myself wandering until I arrived on Dad's doorstep.

It was a weird impulse, you know. It wasn't like Dad had ever been the one to comfort me – except maybe, in dim memory, when I'd grazed a knee as a very small child. He isn't, as you know, wired for comfort.

But after you and I broke up he wasn't so bad. I refused to leave my flat for a full week, so he eventually just came and picked me up and drove me to his house without talking. In his own, weird way, he was there for me. And it was that quiet, awkward looking-after that I was craving just then.

Though when he opened the door and saw my expression I genuinely wondered whether he was going to close it again. I was clearly freaking the hell out of him.

But after he'd nodded a few times he let me in, and said, 'I'll run you a bath. Come and sit by the fire.'

He even, to my almost amusement, asked me if I wanted to talk about it. He waited until I'd emerged from the bath and been fed seafood linguine and champagne (of course). And then he forced the words out, looking so uncomfortable that I shook my head, and said, 'I'd rather just . . . watch a Bond movie and get quietly drunk.'

It was gone midnight by this point, and it wouldn't have been unreasonable for him to just go to bed. But Dad cleared away, set up the TV and sat with me to watch.

And I did feel better by the time I crawled into bed. But I don't know how easy it would have been to pick myself up again if Cordelia hadn't refused to let me ignore her.

She messaged first thing asking me to talk, but I didn't even open it. I ignored every other message, too. I'd WhatsApped Kit saying I'd got a horrible bug and was stuck in London festering, then turned both my phones off entirely and spent the next two days lying in bed watching crap on Dad's guest television.

But Cordelia was not going to let me get away with that. At four on Thursday, she rang on the doorbell of Dad's house. It became clear that she'd called him in advance, because I heard him asking how the journey had been.

Traitor, I thought. And then I dragged myself out of bed, feeling like a worse traitor for ignoring all her calls and messages. I owed her more than that.

She was still in the hall when I turned the corner of the stairs, and she looked up at me with what I thought was probably anger. I couldn't help flinching.

'I'm really sorry,' I told her.

I saw her look me over – pyjamas, unbrushed hair and inevitably horrible skin – but the bright, hard energy in her expression stayed. And I realised it wasn't actually anger.

'Come on,' she said. 'Your dad's making us tea.'

I followed her to the sitting room, with a brief stop-off in the downstairs cloakroom to use the toothbrush Dad had insisted on lending me. It was definitely the first time I'd used it, which is admittedly pretty gross.

Dad did his tea-maid bit and gave me an assessing look as he handed me the mug. I could tell he was wondering if I was up to this.

'It's OK,' I said. 'And thank you.'

With the ghost of a smile, he turned and left us to it.

'Right,' Cordelia said once he'd closed the door. 'You look like death, and I think I understand why.'

'Look,' I said. 'I . . . I know this probably makes it look like I only ever cared about Reid's sister –'

'I did think that at first,' she said, cutting me off. 'But luckily for you, you've told me a lot of things, and I realised there was probably more to it. I think you dealt with Tanya's death – or *didn't* deal with it – by cleaving to the idea that she was murdered. And it's only now all that's been taken away that you're finally having to process it properly, and it's shit.'

I took a breath, reeling from how much she'd hit the mark. But it turned out she wasn't finished.

'I also think,' she bulldozed on, 'that all of this is why you found it so hard to get over Reid. Who, let's face it, was pretty crap to you. He messed you around once, then turned on you without warning when he was upset. After which he blocked you completely so you never had a chance to fix things.' She gave me a wry headshake. 'I would have binned the whole man, personally, and I don't get the impression you're someone who refuses to let go normally. I think how you felt about Reid was tied up with loss. And, you know, a break-up is a form of grief, too. So you're having to grieve all of that as well.'

God*damnit*, that was painful to hear. I wasn't ready for it, and I wanted to protest. I wanted to tell her that you and I were different. That what we'd had was special, and had been worth hanging on to.

But it suddenly hit me that I'd had these conversations with people from the other side. With college friends, and once with Imogen over a rich asshole. With some of the women I'd ended up alongside when I was undercover.

And for the very first time I found myself wondering if the anger I'd felt at you might be more justified than the hurt or the empathy.

Whether, actually, you'd just been . . . not that great.

I couldn't think of anything to do except laugh. 'I . . . maybe. Maybe a lot of that. I . . . you're good at this whole reading-people thing.'

Cordelia shrugged. 'It's not too hard to imagine the first half. I just asked myself how I'd feel if I found out Holly had simply overdosed. And then I imagined how I'd feel if I'd been dating her brother and he'd treated me like that.'

I nodded, and then felt . . . awful.

I don't know why, but the quiet logic of what she'd said made me feel a wave of desolation that was genuinely worse than what I'd been feeling before. Was *every single thing* I'd been hanging on to a mirage?

Instead of comforting thoughts, I found myself remembering one of those times you'd been rigid and unbending about something. It was that time I left my stupid recording device in the bathroom while I was pretending to be a political aide because it had a bare wire and started electrocuting me. I'm sure you remember. I'd had to quickly take it off and hide it, and then the people I'd spent three days trying to get the dirt on had a whole incriminating conversation *right next to it*.

I remember telling you about it in absolute wonder, and

the way, instead of marvelling and giving a single moment of thought to how it could still be used, you immediately said, 'You need to delete it.'

I was crushed at the time, however much I knew you were, technically, right. It's illegal to record someone by bugging them, and however much I'd never meant to do it, I should have been *with* the device at all times. I'd come round to thinking that you were a man of morals, and I'd kind of respected you for it.

But after what Cordelia had said I found myself remembering other parts of what you'd said: how you'd told me you'd report me if I even thought about using what I'd found out. How you'd been unbelievably fucking cold and acted like the law mattered more than everything, including me.

And you know what, Reid? I realised that it probably *did* matter more, and always would. And that makes you far from the hero I thought you were. It makes you someone who was always, one day, going to let me down.

I found myself having to try incredibly hard not to cry as all that hit me. Which would have been pretty humiliating to do a second time in front of Cordelia.

I took a very unsteady breath, made proper eye contact with her and asked, 'What if that *is* the answer about Holly? I mean, I was completely wrong about Tanya for a year and a half. What if we're both wrong about Holly, too?'

Cordelia shook her head, but slowly. 'I don't think we are. And either way, you need to keep pushing until you actually know. Because not knowing will drive me genuinely insane. And you, too, I think.'

I nodded, feeling a tiny little rekindling of that burning need to get at the truth.

'How the hell did you find Anthony, anyway? In two days. I mean, I tried for *months* . . .'

Cordelia gave a sigh. 'This has to be between us, all right? My brother Luca . . . the reason he still gets invited to undergrad parties and the reason my mother *thinks* he's financially more successful than he actually is . . . he's sort of a dealer.'

That surprised an actual laugh out of me, and somehow that made Cordelia smile, too. 'Seriously?'

'He started while he was here, and then carried on.' Cordelia shrugged, still smiling. 'Which makes him connected. And it also means people owe him. So when he asked some of his regulars who people were buying Ritalin and modafinil from, it was a fairly short list. And only two of them were dealing at the time Tanya died. So I came up here with Luca as backup and pretended I wanted a supply. Anthony was the first one I asked, and he broke down when I mentioned what had happened to Tanya. Then, with a little persuasion from Luca, he told us everything. Obviously, I had to promise that it wouldn't go any further.' She studied my face, more seriously. 'It won't, will it? Luca was in the car outside the other night, by the way. Just to keep Anthony honest. He's not so bad, sometimes.'

I was silent for at least five seconds before I said, 'Jesus. I . . . Can I hire you? Both of you?'

Cordelia gave me a full-wattage grin. 'I'll consider it if medicine gets boring, but Luca might prefer not to repeat the experience.' Then she took a breath, and said, 'Luca is why I was so sure about Holly. He asked his users about who was selling ket. And these are people who are reliant on him. To be honest, they're probably slightly scared of him, too. He told them he heard there was a ket dealer at the ball and he'd like to partner up.' She shook her head. 'But *nobody* bought any there. There just wasn't anyone trading on the night. Luca knows all the dealers in town, too. None of them – like, genuinely, nought per cent – were stupid enough to give some first-time user five grams of the stuff. So that was reason number four why I knew it was bullshit.' Cordelia gave me a very piercing look. 'And you know it's bullshit, too, underneath all the grief.'

I found myself nodding at her, slowly.

'I just . . . what if I'm not up to it?' I asked her hoarsely. 'I mean, I hope that on a good day I'd be . . . I'd be fine. But . . .' I swallowed, and then said, 'As well as everything else, I had an incident with Ryan. And to be honest, I never want to have to see him again.' I shook my head. 'Even though it shouldn't bother me.'

'An incident?' Cordelia said, absolute fire in her expression. 'What happened?'

'Oh, he just – pinned me up against a bathroom door and tried to . . .'

At that point, all my attempts at looking professional deserted me and I turned into a pathetic, snivelling mess. Cordelia reached over and pulled me into a proper hug.

'I'll fucking kill him, Anna. I'm really sorry.'

It took me a while to get it together enough to say, 'I feel like I'm falling apart.'

'Of course you do,' she said, letting go of me in order to look at me. 'But you believe in this, and you'll have to pull it together in order to make it work. And that'll be enough to get you through. I can see that so clearly.'

I wasn't sure how to feel about that. It was huge pressure, when I felt like I wanted – needed – to just let all the sad stuff I'd blocked out hit home. But it was also such an amazing declaration of faith from someone I barely knew. And as lame as it sounds, I really needed to hear it right then. Dad was never going to say it, and there really wasn't anybody else.

'OK,' I told her, nodding. 'Back in the saddle.'

'Tomorrow?' she asked.

'Tomorrow,' I agreed. 'For the last Pitt Club dinner of the year, which Kit is *determined* for me to go to.'

And for the first time since he'd invited me I actually felt like this was a good thing. That I was finally getting the chance I'd wanted for almost three weeks.

'Oh, perfect,' she said with a grin. 'You have to let me help you choose an outfit.'

After she'd left I found myself thinking over and over again about what she'd said about you: about the fact that you'd maybe just been a bit of an asshole, who I'd built up in my head because of grief.

When I'm being really honest with myself, there were times I was shocked at your lack of empathy for another person. At your willingness to judge them. It occasionally made me want to shake you.

And I guess I've spent so long feeling like you were the absolute moral authority and I had to prove myself to you that I lost sight of the fact that you were just a flawed human being, and maybe not the love of my life after all.

Dad has just given me a little lecture about respecting your decision, by the way, having seen me writing to you. Which is funny, considering I'm now thinking of stopping writing to you entirely. I've realised I no longer have any intention of sending you this, either.

I'm writing for me, now. Just for me. For somewhere to put this all down, and I guess so that there's a trace left if everything goes really wrong. Dad'll know it's here, at least.

I obviously updated him on a few things after Cordelia left. I mean, I didn't tell him what I believed about Tanya, or anything about the situation that had developed with Kit Frankland. There was no way I was ready to tell him that the son of Philip Sedgewick's good friend was pursuing me; and that I was letting him.

But I did, actually, manage to tell him about the motorist

who'd hit me, and in a very few words about Ryan Jaffett. And I saw a tightness in his expression that made me think Cordelia wasn't the only one who might want to kill the guy.

'What do you want to do?' he asked me.

I sighed. 'I think, ultimately . . . stop Ryan. If he's the killer, get him arrested,' I said. 'And if it's not him, get the murderer arrested, and then stop Ryan somehow, too. By reporting him, I guess.'

'Good,' Dad said, and squeezed my arm. Which I figured was as close to an emotional display as I was going to get. Though he surprised me by adding, 'I wondered, ahhh, whether I might . . . buy your dress. For the May Ball.'

I blinked at him. Dad had never offered to buy me anything before. I mean, except dinner with him, which I always saw as a bribe to get him out of being bored.

'I . . .'

'You don't have to feel like you owe me anything,' he added, hastily. 'I just thought it would help with the budget. If you wanted to get something a bit more . . . extravagant than the paper allows.'

I felt knocked sideways by this, but also profoundly grateful. 'That would be awesome. I . . . There was one I found, but it's too much. So . . .'

And then, as I was getting ready to go to the dinner in the clingy Rasario silk-and-net evening gown Cordelia had picked out (which had, luckily, been a second-hand purchase), Dad surprised me by calling out, 'Do come back here after the dinner. I'll want to hear how it went!'

I didn't know how to answer for a second. I was both surprised that he *wanted* me to stay longer and confused about his motivation. Though, of course, it made sense when I thought about it. He wanted to make sure I hadn't been attacked by a predator or a motorist with a vendetta, though I'd assured him that Ryan was not attending the dinner. Kit had already confirmed that.

The problem with staying at Dad's was Kit himself. I suspected he'd want to walk me home and – yeah. Anyway. I wasn't sure how the whole going-to-my-apparent-godfather's might work. Though playing hard to get was a good idea in *many* ways.

'Thank you,' I said to Dad, in the end. 'I'd – I thought I should go back to my flat, but maybe that's a nicer idea . . .'

'Well, up to you,' he told me. But I could tell that he was eager.

'OK, you're on. I'll get a cab.'

26. Reid

Reid was back in a taxi now, and this time was heading straight back to London. It was going to cost him a fortune, but by the time he'd made it out of Trinity College he'd barely been holding it together enough to stand, never mind navigating onto the right train.

He'd had to argue with the porters about going to hospital, and eventually persuaded them that it was more important to check the room Roland Frankland was using. But when they'd forced access, it had been to find the place empty of life, a fact that hadn't surprised Reid at all.

He'd made a few desultory checks for signs of restraints or other indications that Anna might have been held there and then called DC Kav Rohin at Finsbury Park and asked him to look into the whereabouts of Roland and Kit Frankland.

'Is this a live investigation?' Kav had asked.

'I'm pretty sure it will be,' Reid had told him. 'If you can kick off, I'll bring you up to speed once I'm back.'

But for Reid to make the investigation live he was going to have to find evidence that Anna could realistically be in London. And at the moment he wasn't even sure that she'd been here at the college, though the idea that he might have missed her by minutes made his heart squeeze.

He'd left the porters with false promises of going to A & E and instructions to check if anyone in surrounding rooms had seen or heard anything.

'I need CCTV for the whole site for the last twenty-four hours, too.'

The two male porters who'd arrived at the lodge after their rounds had looked at him with something between concern and irritation, but Trish had settled in at the computer to get to work. Reid had felt profoundly glad that she'd been on duty tonight, even if he'd had to argue with her over treating his injuries first.

He'd pulled Anna's phone out again the moment he'd made it into an Uber, and forced his alarmingly blurry eyes to focus on the screen.

Give me something, he thought. *If not something to point to where you are, at least a definite excuse to take this to the Met.*

But instead of finding that, he'd been hit by the double gut-punch of Cordelia's words about him and Anna's conclusion that she might have been right. And as angry as it made him to be judged so harshly by his ex-girlfriend, some part of it rang a deep and resounding bell within him.

He *had* put his vision of right and wrong ahead of Anna. Not once, but repeatedly. He remembered other occasions when she'd told him with excitement about a story and he'd reacted with dislike over a sensationalist element. Times when they'd worked together and she'd suggested doing things her way and he'd shut her down. Other moments when he'd become angry with her for an action he'd seen as crossing a line.

It made him feel unanchored and dizzy to wonder why he'd done it all. What it was about those small rules – not even laws, but his little definitions of right and wrong – that had been important enough to make him hurt her.

And here he was, genuinely worried about procedure, when Anna's life was in danger. When she might be injured or worse than that already.

He looked down at her phone, and said, 'Fuck it,' just loudly enough that the Uber driver glanced at him in his rear-view mirror.

He called Kav Rohin again and said, 'Can you do a phone trace for me, too? Urgent one,' and reeled off Anna's burner phone number.

27. Anna

I was on fire with excitement over the Pitt Club dinner. By which I mean I was equal parts curious and terrified.

The building was, as I'd already worked out, really close to my little house on Jesus Green, though of course I was coming from Dad's. It was a neoclassical concoction of pillars with a broad frontage that was just *made* to impress.

Only the building isn't actually all theirs any more. All those elite members who once owned a whole palace are now consigned to the first-floor rooms. The grand entrance and big chambers are now, in fact, owned by a pizza chain.

Not even an individual restaurant. A chain, Reid.

I decided, on balance, that mocking them about their changed fortunes wouldn't be a good thing. But let it be known that I was incredibly tempted.

These thoughts were much better than the ones that had been crushing me for the earlier part of the week. I had others keeping me together, too. Thoughts of getting a look inside the place and of finding out who the movers and shakers were. Of working out who Esther's boyfriend was; what Ryan had done in the past; and why James seemed to have trust issues around his friend.

Kit was waiting outside for me and looked uncomplicatedly happy to see me. Not to make a point out of it or anything.

'You look totally great,' he told me, giving me a brief peck on the cheek. 'And only a little bit plaguey.'

'You, too,' I told him. 'You always look a tiny bit plaguey. It's part of your charm.'

There were none of his usual complex stares. He simply grinned and took my arm to go into the club itself.

'Are you sure this will actually be fun, though?' I asked him, quietly. 'I mean . . . the Pitt Club . . .'

He raised an eyebrow. 'You mean, is it full of horrible right-wing misogynistic snobs who are going to give you rage?'

I laughed. 'Yeah, that.'

Kit shook his head. 'I think, in my dad's time, it probably was a lot like that. But the whole place has had to change. I mean, students aren't really like that any more here, any more than they are in the US.'

'Uhhh, there are definitely students like that in the US,' I told him.

'OK,' he amended. 'There aren't many people like that at Cambridge.' He paused at the top of the stairs. 'Because of this move towards being less elitist, the Pitt Club membership shrank like crazy over time and then they realised they had to adapt and let in women.'

'My god,' I said. 'End of the world.'

'Exactly.' Kit gave me a gleaming smile. 'And obviously, once that happened, it was only going to change further. They're mostly good people now, and the rest are just a bit boring about money.'

I studied his face for a moment, wondering whether this was his attempt to justify joining but feeling a worrying suspicion that it wasn't. That he really meant it.

Which was great for tonight's conversation but seriously bad for my efforts at finding a backup scandal here to write about.

'OK,' I said. 'You've convinced me. But I'm holding you responsible if anyone mansplains anything to me.'

'Fair,' he said.

He squeezed my hand, but then let go of it as we entered the dining room, as if to avoid giving off too many relationship vibes. I couldn't help feeling relieved about it. The fewer people who saw us in public looking like a couple, the better, for the long-term good of my career and my sense of guilt.

Inside, the place was thickly carpeted enough to make walking in heels treacherous, and decorated ornately. The lighting was well done, I thought, and although the portraiture was heavy on the moody men, it was tasteful.

James was hovering in a corner with a glass of champagne, his handsome face looking a little drawn this evening. He was fiddling compulsively with a vape when we arrived and jumped slightly when Kit greeted him.

'Hey, we all need a glass,' Kit said, reaching out to where a waiter was standing with a silver tray of bubbles. 'One more exam to go! Here's to oncoming freedom!'

I took the glass Kit had handed me and lifted it. There was a beat before James copied us and replied, 'Freedom!'

Was James just tired? Or was there something else going on?

'Oh my god, you're all so close!' I said, trying to cover the momentary pause. 'When is the last exam?'

'Wednesday,' James told me.

'When are you finished?' I asked Kit, realising he hadn't actually told me, despite sharing about his family and his hopes for his rugby career. It was like the academic stuff didn't matter to him.

'Tuesday.' Kit gave me a grin. 'On Tuesday night I'm going to become a walking Vice documentary.'

'Will I know the difference, or . . .?'

'Oh, you'll know,' he said, and gave me the kind of look that told me he wasn't just talking about drinking and taking MDMA.

Crap.

'Oh, I didn't know we had Clarisse here tonight,' James said at that point, cutting through the sexual tension.

I turned to see Esther standing next to a woman who was such a carbon copy of her that she could only have been her mother. From Clarisse's sleek dark hair in its French pleat (the same colour as Esther's) to her perfect cheekbones and complexion; from her large, long-lashed eyes to her cool smile. Even the *clothes* were basically the same: Esther's knee-length beaded dress the match of her mother's silvery number.

Seeing them together struck me as important. It was so clear that Esther was different around her. That veneer of control had descended, and it was like seeing the stranger I'd first met all over again. The flawless, unassailable, *cold* human who I'd only later realised was really a fragile, warm thing.

I was both fiercely curious to meet this woman and aware that I was absolutely not on my game. I deliberately hung back, turning a little away. I had Kit to talk to at first, and then James after Kit vanished to the bathroom.

James was still looking pale, tired and out of sorts. But he managed a brief conversation until his parents emerged at the top of the stairs and snagged his attention. The Pitt Club family, of course. He left me alone to go and talk to them.

Esther was at my shoulder a moment later. I wondered if she'd been waiting for a chance.

'Would you like to come and meet Mummy?' she asked, her voice containing that alabaster-smooth quality she used for greeting strangers. It made me pity her, but it also made me uneasy.

'Sure,' I said, trying to smile. 'I'd love to.'

Clarisse's expression was curious beneath her social smile as Esther introduced us, but she was far from hostile, as I'd feared she might be as an over-controlling mother. I guessed she was wondering whether I was an appropriate friend for her daughter, but she seemed inclined to think I was.

'This is Aria, Mummy,' Esther said, still perfectly poised,

and I couldn't help finding it weird that she still called her mom that at the age of twenty-one.

'It's a delight,' Clarisse said in an accent that was a perfect balance between English, French and East Coast American. She leaned in to offer her cheek. 'I've heard a lot about your rowing.'

I pulled a self-deprecating face. 'Sorry. It's a rower thing. We're basically incapable of having normal conversations.'

Clarisse laughed. 'Not from what I hear. Esther tells me you're a wonderful friend.'

I gave Esther a smile, and then said, 'She's honestly way too kind to me. I've spent most of the year being seriously anti-social and your daughter's actually forced me to make some friends at last. I owe her a lot, but I'm kind of sad I left it so late. They're all about to leave, and I'll be back to just rowing and studying.'

'Oh, I'm sure you can keep in touch,' Clarisse protested. 'Particularly with so much of your training in London, where Esther's first two years will be.'

I couldn't help looking very sharply at Esther. Hadn't she said she was looking for a job? To hear that her career was mapped out was . . . surprising.

'Well, that sounds OK then,' was all I said.

'Will you go back home to your family over the summer?' Clarisse asked. 'Or will they visit you here?'

'A little of both,' I answered. 'I mean, I doubt Mom and Dad will make it over here, but maybe my bro.'

Clarisse's smile grew imperceptibly brighter, and I realised that it was Aria's senator brother who was the real draw here. I was being seen as a networking opportunity.

Though actually, I realised, it might be more that Aria's brother was deemed an eligible match for Esther.

Clarisse didn't say anything further because her attention

was caught by someone across the room, and to my horror I heard her say, 'Ryan, my darling. Are you not coming to say hello?'

There was movement, and suddenly Ryan Jaffett was being welcomed into the circle.

I felt my chest tightening, and I turned in blind panic to look over at Kit, whose expression was slack-jawed and horrified.

I saw his mouth move as he said, 'What the fuck?'

I felt like leaving, but I knew I couldn't. I had a week and a half left to figure all of this out, and if I made no progress, the *Ensign* could pull the story at any moment.

It's all right, I told myself. *You're all right.*

And then I remembered what Cordelia had said, about being committed enough to this that I'd *have* to be all right, and it helped.

'I . . . Hello, Ms Thomas,' Ryan was saying. 'It's . . . you look great.'

He sounded awkward. Wretched. But he wasn't making an excuse and leaving, which would have been the kind thing to do.

I decided to look anywhere but at him. I wasn't going to be chased away when I was trying to learn things. It wasn't fair.

But I also couldn't focus on anything they were saying any more, and at one point Ryan moved towards me and I flinched backwards.

It was Philip Sedgewick who intervened and essentially rescued me. I don't know if James had told him about what happened, or if he just saw that I was looking panicked. He stepped in and said, 'Oh, I meant to ask you something about James. Could I borrow you for a minute?'

I let him draw me away, feeling a flood of huge relief as well as a bitter feeling of disappointment. It was pathetic, and it was getting in the way of my job. And worse still, it was clear that other people could see something was wrong. James's mother, Marcie, was looking after us in concern, too.

I caught her eye and gave her a slightly unsteady grin.

It's OK, I tried to telegraph.

And Marcie nodded at me before moving to talk to Clarisse. James's parents were genuinely sensitive, I realised. And I wondered how that had affected him: whether it made him more or less likely to be a killer.

Because everything still came down to that, in the end.

When I glanced back at Esther, I realised that she was looking after me, too, her expression questioning. Worried. Her guard finally down once again. And it made me feel a rush of guilt.

She gave a faint smile when I rolled my eyes at her, and that only made it all worse.

You can't let yourself like these kids, I thought sternly to myself, after that. *Esther might be a killer as easily as James or Ryan.*

Once we were a distance away, Philip said, 'I just wanted to know what present to get James for exam results day. He usually seems disappointed or morally offended by what I choose. I have a suspicion you might be better at finding out what he'd like than the rest of them, and I wondered if you might like a little mission.'

I narrowed my eyes at him. 'Are you calling me nosy?' I asked, as a slight challenge.

Philip laughed. 'Not in the least. I'm accusing you of actually listening to people.'

I glanced towards James himself, who I'd barely exchanged a word with all evening. 'Not as much as I should. But I'm on it. I won't let you down.'

It was a while later, once the dinner had started – with Ryan mercifully seated a long way from me and the starters eaten – that I excused myself to the bathroom and spent a while breathing out some tension. I'd managed to hold it together and even to tell a few humorous rowing anecdotes, but I hadn't made any actual progress and I needed to get my head back in the game.

It was after I'd finished pep-talking myself and was returning to the dinner that I stumbled on Kit and Ryan having a hushed conversation in the corridor outside. They were round the corner from the bathrooms, huddled in a doorway, and they clearly hadn't heard me closing the door or walking across the thick carpet towards them, so I ducked back behind the corner and listened.

The part of it I caught was Ryan saying, unclearly, '. . . off, Kit. Stop fucking interfering.'

'You need someone to interfere,' Kit said, his voice low and intense. 'If you don't stop it –'

'Do you really think you can threaten me?' Ryan was so clearly drunk and, with it, belligerent.

But when Kit replied it was with a greater level of anger than I'd heard from him. 'It's not even a threat,' he said. 'I'm telling you what's going to happen if you keep doing this.'

'What's that then?'

'You're going to ruin your life,' Kit said. 'And there won't be anything anyone can do to help you.'

Ryan gave a harsh laugh. 'I'm helping myself.'

There were padding steps, and one of them retreated. I thought, from the unsteady steps, that it must be Ryan. I waited a few moments and then made my way round the corner, feeling a rush of fear that it would be Ryan waiting there for me. But it was Kit who was still there, staring into space as he leaned against the door. He looked . . . I don't know, Reid. Furious. Desolate. Done with it all. A mixture of all of this.

'Hey,' I said. 'You OK?'

Kit blinked and looked up at me.

'I . . . yeah, I'm OK.' He sighed. 'Are you? I'm – Ryan shouldn't be here. I'm so sorry.'

He held a hand out to me and I came to stand beside him, our arms intertwined.

I nodded. 'I'm all right. I'd . . . prefer him not to be here, but I'm going to have to see him sometime, right?'

'You don't have to,' Kit said, immediately. And he gave me a very open, earnest look. 'I will support you in whatever you decide to do, and no matter what Ryan does, I'm not going to let him hurt you ever again. All right?'

And you know, as crappy as I'd been feeling, I felt a sense of genuine reassurance wash through me for the first time in days.

28. Seaton

There was a huge relief to this all being official now. To the fact that Reid had asked him to go to Finsbury Park station and talk to a DC, instead of making him wait, interminably, for something to happen.

There was something even better about sitting once again in an interview room, ten hours after he'd sat in the last one, but this time being listened to. The officer was young and bright-eyed, and wearing a suit instead of a uniform. And Seaton felt instinctively that he could trust this man.

The only thing that made it a little uncomfortable, in fact, was having to remember Reid's concocted story about Ryan Jaffett's phone. Luckily, the DC seemed to be nodding along to that, too.

'So you handed that to DI Reid Murray, along with your daughter's phone?' the DC asked, once Seaton had explained the rigmarole about the phone being posted through his door with a note.

'Yes,' Seaton said. 'By that point I was very concerned for my daughter's whereabouts and beginning to suspect that she was no longer in Cambridge.'

The DC nodded.

'It looks as though this is now a Met Police investigation,' he said. 'Your daughter's phone last pinged at a location on the outskirts of London.'

Seaton felt his heart twist. Reid hadn't told him this. Had he known? Or was this new information?

'Where?' he asked, immediately.

'Not far from South Mimms services,' he said. 'Which would be on a driving route from Cambridge.'

Did someone take her? Seaton thought, immediately. *Or did she run?*

He was opening his mouth to ask what day and time this had been when Reid entered the room, with more presence than he'd seen the man ever exhibit before. And along with the surprise of seeing Anna's usually rather uninspiring ex arrive as if he'd brought all the energy in the place with him, there was a further surprise in seeing a huge, swelling bruise on the left side of his jaw and a half-closed eye on the same side.

'Reid,' Seaton said, getting to his feet hurriedly. 'What on earth . . .?'

DC Rohin was rising, too. 'Boss, do you need . . .?'

'I'm fine,' Reid said, waving a hand at both of them. He came in and sat a little carefully in the other chair opposite Seaton, but then immediately went on, 'I've asked for this to be made a priority missing persons investigation with possible risk to life. The team's updated me that Anna's phone was last traced to the outskirts of London last night, at midnight, but has been switched off since. In addition, I've received an email from your daughter's account with a lot of information that suggests she was involved in a high-risk situation, very much as you thought.' He gave Seaton a very serious look. 'I need you to tell us everything you know about Kit Frankland and his father.'

29. Anna

It's funny how there are things I'm still finding hard to put down, even now that I'm no longer writing it for you. And when I'm no longer really trying to convince you of anything, either.

But I have to record it somewhere, because some of it is really important. And some of it led me to change my mind about everything and everyone.

So here we go. The Rest of the Pitt Club Dinner.

The moment of calm that happened talking to Kit was pretty much washed away when I walked back into the dining room. I was confronted by Esther pulling Ryan over towards me with a determined look on her face.

What are you doing? Stop it! I wanted to shout.

'Ryan . . . has something to say,' she said, her voice unsteady.

Ryan met my eye for the first time that evening, and I don't know if the clearly tearful eyes were worse than if he'd looked unrepentant. It felt unfair; like he was demanding sympathy from me.

'I'm sorry,' he said, quietly. 'I'm so, so sorry. I did . . . the worst thing. I've got to stop.'

'So why are you here?' I asked him, coldly. 'If you know you need to stop, why are you here, drinking, and making me feel worse?'

He gave me a desperate look, and then said, 'Because my dad made me come.' He breathed in on what was almost a sob. 'He told me I had to come and talk to the old boys, or . . .' He shook his head and looked away for a moment.

I watched him, wondering whether this same man had wanted Holly Moore enough to kill her when she tried to say no. To drug her and drown her. Whether his dad had told him he should get himself a girlfriend and not take no for an answer.

I wanted to ask him how many times he'd done what he did to me before. If anyone had stopped him. To tear into him with questions. But I couldn't do that and stay for the rest of the evening. I had to be smart, and I hated it.

'You need to sort this shit, Ryan,' I said to him in a low voice. 'You can't be drinking. No matter what somebody offers you or how bad you're feeling. Trust me, I know how tempting it is. But you can't.'

Ryan nodded, mutely. There was sweat standing out on his skin and I felt such an odd mix of things. I felt revolted by him and scared of him, and weirdly sorry for him, all while wondering whether he even felt remorse for what he did or was just panicking because he'd got caught.

I should be reporting him right now, I thought, for one clear, sharp second.

But instead, I turned away from him and went to sit down once again. Kit followed me and sat sideways in his chair, using his back to block Ryan from view, something I was profoundly grateful for. Though James was still in view, and I could see him watching Ryan with something approaching loathing.

'He's . . . done it before, hasn't he?' I said, on instinct, to Kit. 'Ryan. He's done this to people you care about.' I glanced at Kit's face and said, knowing what the answer would be, 'Was it Esther?'

Kit blinked. 'No, it . . . No, not to Esther. He's never seen her that way.'

But I saw the way Kit's eyes slid to James, and I knew, Reid.

I knew that I was right. That, at some point, Ryan had tried to force himself on Holly. And maybe she'd laughed it off, to try to avoid causing trouble. Maybe Esther had talked her into letting it go. Forced him to apologise, because she couldn't bear not to have these people around her.

I looked over at James's beautiful face and soulful eyes, wondering whether I could imagine him blaming Holly. Whether he might be capable of killing his girlfriend in a jealous rage. And I felt strangely sure that he would be.

I was emotionally drained by the end of dinner. Even after Ryan left – which was not long after I spoke to him – I couldn't relax. I wanted nothing more after it was done than to crawl to bed.

But just as I was going to order a cab to get to Dad's, Kit leaned towards me and asked if I'd like to go for a late-night walk. He was close enough to me that I could feel the breath as he spoke into my ear, and it made me shiver.

I was torn. It was clearly a bad idea from the point of view of things going too far, but it was *also* a perfect opportunity to ask Kit some probing questions. He was drunk, and expansive, and I think a little worried that Ryan was going to scare me away for good. He kept looking to see if I was OK.

So I went with him, subtly so that nobody saw us leave. I pretty quickly abandoned my heels, which was a relief to my still-painful leg, and walked in bare feet on the warm paving stones, trying not to think about the substances that had been spilled on them on other nights.

We ambled and talked, and found ourselves at the river. Kit led me up onto the steeply sloping Garret Hostel Bridge. (I just googled what it's called, by the way. I would have probably said 'Trinity Hall Bridge' since it's round the back of there, but it has a proper name that nobody ever uses.)

We'd been talking about life goals, and Kit was deeply involved in telling me exactly how he saw his rugby career going. But then, at the top of the bridge, he suddenly seemed to lose all focus. He was staring out in the direction of Trinity College, and he looked like he'd left the planet.

It didn't take me long to figure out why. This was the river where Holly had died. We'd stumbled across the clearest, most resonant memory of Holly's loss for him.

I followed him as he drifted to the railings. I'd hoped he might talk, but he stayed silent for an eerily long time. So I eventually asked, 'Whatcha lookin' at?'

'It . . .' He turned towards me in the end, eyes a hard-to-define murky colour under the warm yellow street lighting. 'I sometimes forget, and then . . . Holly. Our friend. James's . . . James's girlfriend. She died there.'

He nodded towards the river below us, and for some reason, looking out at it after he said it, I felt the sadness of what had happened harder than I had before.

'Oh, shit,' I said. 'I didn't realise it was . . .'

I stared down into the darkness of the water. There were punts tied up along the right-hand bank, and in the shadows of one of them I briefly imagined I could see a floating form. And I wanted to run down there and save that girl I'd never met, and tear into the person who'd done it, all at once.

But I had a job to do, and it was this. Here.

'How did it happen?' I asked Kit, quietly.

'I don't know,' he said. When I looked back at him he was frowning, his mouth twisted. 'We lost track of her. Which I suppose isn't *that* strange, but usually . . . I know where everyone is. Anyway, after the fireworks, we moved across the bridge to the music tents to try to find her. But I heard some kind of commotion going on, and I saw a St John's Ambulance guy just *running* back towards the river . . . and . . .'

He looked straight at me. 'You know how you sometimes think an ambulance must be for someone you know?'

I nodded at him, shivering. 'Yes,' I said. 'I know exactly.'

'Well . . . I followed him, and – it was. It was for her. I saw them trying to give her CPR . . . I had to call James and – and tell him.' He rubbed the back of his hand over his eyes.

I didn't have to pretend to feel a rush of sympathy. He looked so *raw* over it. I found myself reaching out to touch his arm.

'I'm . . . I'm really sorry. I knew it must have been the worst for James, but it sounds . . . awful for you, too.' I squeezed his hand. 'I don't know how your friendship has survived so well after trauma like that.'

There was a beat, and then Kit said, 'It wasn't great for a bit. James was pretty angry.'

I wanted to ask him *who* he was angry with. Whether it was all of them, or just one of them. But I couldn't.

Kit looked away from me, towards the river again, so I asked, 'The article said she'd taken something?'

It took him a moment to shake his head. 'I don't even know how or why she would. She was such a square.' He gave a sad, unsteady laugh, and I realised that there was a gleam of tears in his eyes.

And before you ask, I wasn't being a total credulous dumbass about it all. I was thinking and analysing; trying to weigh up whether he was telling the truth.

'I've felt like . . . I let her down, you know? I should have been there. Not – not super into my new girlfriend, or trying to drink every single thing they had at the ball to get the full experience.'

'But . . . Holly was . . . James's girlfriend. She was with him, right?'

Kit stiffened, and for a nanosecond I worried that this had

been a step too far. Something that made my real interest too obvious.

But after a pause, Kit said, 'No. Before the fireworks, I wanted a photograph in this classic car they had on the lawn. I hassled James to go and queue for the champagne bar so we had enough for the fireworks.' He grimaced. 'We were taking it in turns to get drinks. So it was sort of his turn. I didn't see Holly go anywhere, but when James came back, she'd vanished, and he couldn't find her. I did try to help. But then it was the fireworks . . . And I actually prioritised watching the fucking things. Seriously. While she was out there, dying . . .'

It's strange, isn't it? The urge to ease someone's guilt, even when you don't really know whether or not they're guilty. I found myself taking his hand, and saying, 'I can't tell you not to feel bad. I've . . . I've spent years of my life wrapped up in guilt about the people I didn't help. But you only knew what you knew.'

And maybe this is true for us, too, Reid. Maybe this is the truth about Tanya; that we both did the best we could.

I probably don't need to tell you that he kissed me after that. I know you'll be angry at me for letting him. But I hope it makes sense to tell you that it was Aria doing the kissing, not me.

It didn't last long, anyway. Because there were hurrying steps on the bridge, and when we broke apart to see why, we were confronted by James Sedgewick, his beautiful face contorted with rage.

'You fucking prick!' he said, shoving Kit hard enough that he banged into the railing of the bridge. I'd found it hard to believe before that James, all slim and actorly, had that kind of strength in him, but he was more than just angry now: he was raging. 'How can you stand here? *Here?* And do that? When she died below you?'

Kit looked totally shell-shocked. 'James, mate –'

'It's so easy being you, isn't it?' James spat at him, taking a step back that looked like the preparation for a charge. 'You can just find yourself another girl. While I lost my – my – and it's *your fucking fault*.'

Kit blinked at him for a second, his head moving slightly in denial.

'I don't . . .'

'She trusted you!' James yelled. 'And you let her down!'

Kit was staring at him now, his mouth slightly slack, his hands out but unmoving.

'James,' he said with what sounded like profound hurt in his voice. 'James. I couldn't find her.'

For a second, I wondered whether the shorter, slighter man was going to go for him. Whether he was going to try to tip him into the river. But instead, James looked towards me with a roiling, angry look, and then he turned and walked back the way he'd come, towards town.

I was left in the cooling night air with Kit, feeling suddenly very alone, and not sure Holly's death hadn't been his fault after all.

30. Reid

Reid didn't want to admit to anyone, including himself, how much his head and jaw were hurting, or how hard he was finding it to concentrate. He kept finding himself drifting off midway through conversations and then jumping back to himself in confusion.

He'd managed to read a little more of Anna's email in the cab, but increasing nausea had eventually stopped him. He'd fallen asleep for a while despite the way the bumps in the road were sending lancing pain through his head, and had woken groggily when he'd arrived at Finsbury Park.

He'd now forwarded the email to the DCI, anyway. It had been shared with Dom Davies and his team. It was brutally embarrassing to have his colleagues read it, but it was also something that needed to happen, especially while his faculties weren't working properly. They all needed to read it, and to take it seriously.

He'd thought about trying to edit out some of Anna's more humiliating observations, and more urgently about deleting everything that might cause her professional issues later – the segments about Kit in particular. But in the end his unfocused vision and the huge difficulty of editing anything on a phone had made him realise he just had to send it as was and deal with the consequences later.

Dom was now in charge of finding Anna. He hadn't hesitated over taking it all on and had called them in for a briefing with his usual cheerful energy. Reid had watched his almost triangular form – stacked with muscle from years of MMA training – move around the briefing room and had felt both guilt and gratitude. He owed Dom a conversation, and probably an apology for the way he'd shut him out for the past two years. He needed to explain how hard he'd found it, accepting that he'd overlooked those WhatsApp messages from his colleagues. And maybe, just maybe, that he'd been too black-and-white about it.

But right now they had to work together because, as Anna's ex-boyfriend, Reid was too closely involved to be senior investigating officer.

If Reid was honest, it was a relief to have someone else taking control. He knew he wasn't with it enough to drive this thing forwards, but he had to be here. The alternative was to walk away from Anna all over again, and he wasn't willing to do that.

Kav Rohin let himself into the briefing room at a point when Reid had drifted off again, and Reid blinked in an effort to focus as the DC said, 'Got location info on Roland Frankland. He's in Madrid.'

Reid took a moment to remember that finding Kit's father had been his request, back when he'd been the only one doing this. Because of the room at Trinity. And the attack.

'Madrid?' he asked.

'Yeah, ANPR caught his reg going towards Stansted,' Kav said, 'so I checked with passport control. He got on the three forty this afternoon.'

'Thanks,' Dom said. 'Nothing on the son?'

'I've left him a message asking him to come in urgently,' Kav said. 'But his friends haven't seen him and the college porters say he's not in his room.'

'OK, I want someone to head round to his dad's house,' Dom said. 'That's, what, Kew?'

'Yeah, I can get the address,' Kav agreed.

'Someone needs to be chasing the urgent authorisation on Anna's phone records. It shouldn't be taking this long. And let's pursue one on Kit Frankland. I want eyes on James Sedgewick as soon as possible. And I want CCTV from South Mimms, too. It's possible that ping was before or after Anna pulled in there.'

Between one blink and the next, they were scattering, presumably to do what Dom had asked. Reid got to his feet and was alarmed to find the room tilting and his vision closing in on him for a good few seconds while a ferocious pain shot through his head.

The moment it had cleared he staggered out to his desk and sat heavily, leaning down to rifle in the drawer.

'Are you all right, mate?'

It was Dom's voice, and when he looked up Reid realised that they were the only two still in that section of the building. Kav and the other DCs had left and there was nobody else still working.

It must have been late, he thought, trying to focus on the clock on the far wall. Did it say eleven thirty? Or was it half twelve?

He closed his eyes, suddenly unable to stand the brightness of the room.

'Reid?' Dom asked.

'I'm just . . . looking for painkillers,' Reid said, making an effort to open his eyes again.

'Stay there,' Dom said, reaching into his own desk. 'I've got tramadol and ibuprofen. You OK with opiates?'

Reid felt wretched with guilt, even through everything else he was feeling. Here was Dom, helping him when he least deserved it.

'I would . . . actually love some opiates.'

He saw Dom give a slightly strange smile and then nod,

but he was too weary and in too much pain to do any more than sit back in his comfortable desk chair and shut his eyes once more.

He had the unsettling sensation from that point on of only being kept awake by Dom bustling around. But when he felt a hand on his shoulder he managed to force his eyes open and take the offered three tablets and glass of water.

'The packets are there for another dose in four hours, then another in the morning. Just make sure you take some laxatives tomorrow,' Dom added, 'or you won't shit for a week.'

'I . . . thank you,' Reid said. And he did suddenly feel a rush of gratitude, both that Dom's MMA career meant he was now a walking pharmacy and that he was willing to ignore all of Reid's behaviour towards him over the last two years and help when he needed it.

He swallowed the pills and tried to focus on Dom's concerned face.

'Are you sure you should be here, mate?'

'I'm . . . I really need to be.'

He felt a sense of relief as Dom nodded.

'OK. But you know I'm not going to let anything happen to her if I can avoid it, right?'

'Thanks, Dom.'

Once Dom had returned to his desk, and presumably to reading or checking what he'd been sent about Anna, Reid opened his own phone and loaded up Anna's email. But he couldn't seem to focus on the screen. Even unlocking the keypad was difficult, and then the tiny email font was next to impossible to decipher. Plus, the screen started to do weird things. Like locking itself.

Every time it did, the time seemed to have jumped forward by five minutes without warning, and Reid felt like the phone was messing with him. He wanted to hurl it to the floor, but part of him remembered that this was important.

He was feeling too hot. Suffocated by the shirt and tie. Why had he put them on?

He pulled at his collar and then realised in a rush that he was going to be sick. So he lunged for the waste bin and vomited a stomach full of bile into it.

'Jesus,' he heard Dom say. Reid could hear him moving over but felt unable to lift his head. 'Reid, mate, are you . . .?'

There was a sudden painful, sharp sensation on his cheek, the only signal to Reid that he'd fallen sideways onto the wiry carpet. There was noise behind him and then the sound of Dom muttering, 'Fuck,' before, closer by, he heard, 'OK, mate. We're going to the hospital.'

'You can't,' Reid said, though it was a loose-lipped blur of sound. 'Need to find her.'

'It'll take an hour to get you through A & E, tops, the state you're in,' Dom said, 'and I've got the team on this. I can be on the phone.'

Reid pushed himself up to his knees and shoved the phone into his pocket. At least if he had that, he could do something, too.

And then he was sick again. It was a thin dribble of liquid this time, but his body still wanted to keep retching for a while. He tried to straighten up once he was done, before feeling a strong grip under his arms.

He was more glad than he'd ever been that Dom was six feet of muscle-bound, trained-up MMA fighter. His legs felt like snakes somewhere beneath him.

'Come on, mate,' Dom said, and in strange little bursts of awareness Reid found himself moved into the lift and then down to the underground car park.

He did his best to help Dom bundle him into the car and

felt overwhelmingly relieved when he was finally sitting down with the door closed and his seat belt on. The headrest felt like soft bliss behind him.

It was only as he was drifting off into a strange sleep that he thought of the tablets Dom had given him. The sickness. The fact that nobody else had seen him leave.

Dom, who he couldn't really trust. Who was corrupt.

Forcing his eyes open, he picked up his phone to try to send a message, but the screen was a shattered mess in front of his eyes. Moments later, his eyes had slid shut and there was nothing he could do to save himself from the blackness.

31. Anna

These last few days. I'd actually kind of like to forget them. To pretend that Aria Lauder really was a whole other person and that none of this involved me at all.

But I have to write it all down. There are a lot of reasons why that's more important now.

The pressure on me stepped up three days after the Pitt Club dinner, during my Monday check-in with Gael. I'd expected him to be happy about the big confrontation between James and Kit, but I could see frown lines building as I went on talking, and after I'd finished he was silent for quite a while. His brooding expression was out in full force.

'Maria is concerned that you're not really achieving anything there,' he said. 'Your main story is slow to come together, and her comment on your notes is that you don't seem to be finding actual scandal about the Pitt Club to write about. There's nothing to justify the outlay, which is . . .' He gestured at one of the expense forms I'd submitted, and I wanted to tell him that I *knew* it was ridiculous. It included my newly submitted ticket to the May Ball for almost £300; enough for a minibreak. I hadn't even mentioned I was going to need my hair and nails done, and I had a dinner coming up to pay for, too.

As I opened my mouth to answer, he held up a hand.

'I told her you were on to something here, so don't think I'm hanging you out to dry,' he said, and my heart rate slowed a little. I know you aren't a fan of Gael's, but that's one of his good sides. He has my back when I need it. 'From my point of view, I'm just worried you're not going to get there in time.'

'Hey, come on,' I said, trying to keep it light. 'It takes a little while to gain people's trust, but I'm there now. I can feel I'm close to getting to the heart of it. I've set up a webcam outside my house in case anyone leaves any more weird notes, and I feel like I'm on the verge of things opening up.'

'But you need to push harder,' Gael said. 'We don't have time to go gently now. You have ten days left, assuming we let you stay until the end of May Week.'

'I'm pushing!' I said.

'But, look. This dinner was on Friday, right? It's Monday now. And you haven't found out why Kit said that to Ryan, or gone to confront James Sedgewick about the big argument yet?'

I grimaced, feeling a sense of genuine shame. I *had* wanted to confront James, but it had been difficult to find a way of seeing him without Kit getting to hear about it. James hadn't appeared at any of our socialising at the weekend, allegedly because he was working, though I could tell from Kit's tight, hurt expression that it was more than that.

The truth was, I was anxious Kit might have found out I'd seen James behind his back after their row. More so now that Kit was expecting us to have stepped up into an official relationship. And I couldn't really explain why I was letting that anxiety get the better of me, but it was complex and I think had something to do with already having felt like I'd betrayed Cordelia along the way.

'James has his final exam on Wednesday,' I said, as convincingly as I could. 'I figured . . .'

'You need to get in there before that,' Gael said, not unkindly but firmly. 'You need to push him on this. And find out who Esther Thomas was dating.' He paused for a second. 'And Ryan Jaffett's history. Have you made progress there?'

I felt my heart sinking. 'I . . . no, but I think Esther might tell me.'

'Get her to talk to you,' he said, 'and if that doesn't work, confront Ryan.'

I could feel a shake running through me at that idea, but I gave him a bright smile.

'Sure,' I said. 'I'm on it.'

There was a pause, and then Gael said, 'I know what you can do. So go and do it.'

I stood up with the apparent air of someone who's feeling fully motivated, all the while feeling as though my previous low-level anxiety had just skipped all the middle gears and hit fifth.

I realised that Gael was basically right, though. I was running out of time before term and the week of partying ended and everyone scattered. I needed to confront James today.

I decided to go and see him straight off the train, before I could let any guilt about interrupting his study time hit me. He lived in a large attic room in the Third Court of St John's, I knew, though I'd never been there. Chances were he'd be buried in his books right now.

True to my prediction, he was in when I knocked at a little after midday. When he opened up he looked both surprised to see me and as though he was in a really bad way. His eyes were pits of shadow and he couldn't seem to summon so much as a polite smile. Over his shoulder I could see some kind of essay on his laptop, and what looked like an ordered-in breakfast from Dessert Co.

Is this about that argument? I thought with fizzing curiosity. *Has he made up his mind that Kit killed Holly?*

I gave him a smile. 'Sorry, I know you're working,' I tried. 'Could I just come in for, like, five minutes?'

'Um . . . sure,' James said, backing away to let me in and running a hand over his mouth as if to wipe away any dessert. 'Just can't promise to be . . . with it, you know.' He cleared his throat. 'I've been pretty out of it with all the work. Not really . . . myself.'

I wondered if that was supposed to be an apology for what had happened on the bridge. Obviously, I wasn't going to leave it there.

I gave him a sympathetic grin and then deposited myself on the edge of his bed. The bed is basically *the* place to sit in one of those student rooms. Your host takes the desk chair, and you take the bed. Unless, of course, the student you're visiting is lucky enough to also have a sofa, which James was not. His room was pretty much just empty floor and hand-woven rugs, made more cheerful by the sunlight streaming in through the dormer windows.

'Would you like tea?' he asked, ducking his head slightly.

'Sure.'

I watched him make it, in real teacups with a lot of very hesitant fuss, and I marvelled again at his lack of self-assurance. What was it that he was lacking, this boy with good looks and brains and money?

Though, for a moment, I remembered how he'd been on the bridge: definite and furious, his expression so enraged that he'd cowed his taller, stronger friend . . . and I wondered whether there were two sides to James.

'I don't want to distract you too long,' I said when he eventually handed me the tea, 'but I feel like . . . like I'm trampling all over really important stuff without meaning to, and I wanted to say that I'm really sorry, and to find out how to . . . not.'

'Oh, don't,' James said, giving a half-laugh that at least had a trace of energy. 'I should have messaged a proper apology. None of that was your fault.'

'No, it is,' I said, insistently. 'You've all been through this huge thing, and I haven't. You more than anyone have . . . grief.' I watched him as he lowered himself slowly into his chair, his expression distant. 'None of them talks about Holly, really,' I went on. 'And I don't blame anyone for that. But it sounds like there's a lot to say. And if Kit was to blame for . . . what happened, then I want to know that. Because I can't just ignore it.'

It took James a long time to look up at me. He seemed to find a lot to stare at in the surface of his tea.

But when he did look, I could see that expression in his eyes. The one that said he was burning to say something.

Tell me, I thought with every fibre of myself.

'Look, I . . . I don't know if I'm totally right or . . .' He made a frustrated sound and then went on as if he'd planned on saying this many, many times. 'She went to see him, on her own, the afternoon she died. The afternoon of the May Ball. Without telling me. Even though she usually told me everything.' He shook his head. 'She said she was going to get her nails redone. And instead, she went to see him. Which I know because I happened to drop in on him, and I saw her. She was coming down his staircase.' James looked up at me again. 'It was brutal, realising she'd lied to me.'

I put out a hand towards him, not so much in protest as trying to soothe him. 'Could it have been for, you know . . . an innocent reason? Something to do with the ball?'

'I think it *was* to do with the ball,' he said, bitterly. 'I think Kit gave her the drugs. He'd been in this party mood all week. The moment exams were out, he was into everything. And somehow he talked her into it, too.'

I looked at the raw anger in his eyes – at the hurt – and I felt terrible for digging this up. But I knew it all had to come out into the open. All of it.

Because whatever Kit had met Holly about that afternoon I was certain it hadn't been about the supply of drugs. I was sure it had been about that same concern she'd mentioned to Cordelia.

Just not sure what to do about some stuff that's gone down and I don't want to put anything down in writing until I've had some advice. Got someone in mind to talk to . . .

That was what Holly had messaged Cordelia.

It occurred to me, then, that it could have been Ryan that she was talking about. Ryan, who would get drunk and then assault women. If something had already happened to Holly and she'd seen him assault someone else she could easily have wanted to seek advice.

But she never told Cordelia about that, did she? I thought with a chill. *She never told her best friend that Ryan tried to assault her.*

I realised that my suspicions about Holly had probably been right: she was someone who didn't want to rock the boat. If she'd told Cordelia about Ryan assaulting her, it would have given her friend more ammunition. It would have proved Cordelia right about her rich friends not being good for her. And Holly had wanted to hang on to her friends, and her lifestyle.

Unless Esther was right about Cordelia, I thought with a wince. *And Cordelia was actually being controlling, so Holly was having to hide things.*

I knew I had to allow for that possibility. Although it didn't tie in with what I thought of Cordelia, or how I'd seen her behave, I did acknowledge that she had an obsessive side.

But whichever way I looked at it, I had to assume that Holly had learned to hide the bad stuff. That made me wonder how much else she'd been willing to hide for them. She'd known about Esther, hadn't she? About this older boyfriend. But maybe she'd messaged Cordelia because she'd figured out who he was and there were legal ramifications to it.

She might have hidden other secrets, too. Even Kit's secrets. Maybe she'd gone that day to confront him.

The big question was whether talking to Kit had got her killed.

With Gael's voice ringing in my ears, I decided I was going to have to ask Kit about Holly's visit. There was no time to be careful or wait for things to fall in my lap.

I still had to wait twenty-four hours, because he had his final exam the next day and needed to focus on it. But that left me free to focus my attention on Esther instead, who was free of exams now and eager for company.

Knowing that my spending on the company card was under fierce observation, I still asked Esther to come into London and help me find a dress for the upcoming Tribal Barbecue that marked the start of May Week. (It's no longer actually called Tribal Barbecue, by the way, but Cambridge students seem to hold onto names for decades.) Wincing, I paid down some of the company credit card using my own bank account, and decided this was just going to have to be something I funded myself. Though with that in mind, I asked Cordelia to tell me exactly where to shop before I did it.

It was a great bonding experience for me and Esther, but it produced frustratingly little in the way of firm information about this boyfriend of hers. Esther opened up quite a lot about her mother and the way she had Esther's whole life mapped out for her, and also about her fear of standing up to her. But on the subject of this lover's identity, she was silent.

The only thing I learned wasn't something she intentionally told me. Late in the afternoon, once we'd finished spending on clothes and switched to spending on alcohol at a French-styled bar off Oxford Street, I came back from the bathroom to witness Esther sending a message.

It's a little gross, I know, but I hung back to watch from behind her. And it turned out she was editing and then sending an image of herself she'd clearly taken in one of the fitting rooms. In it, she had a finger in her mouth and was posing in a sultry, incredibly un-Esther-like way.

Just underneath, I could see that she'd written the words:

Dress shopping in London today with A. xx

I got as close as I could to try and work out who the guy she was messaging was, but there was only the name Beau, and his photograph was of a dog. The name could be his actual name, or it could well just be a nickname for a boyfriend. Unhelpful.

I realised I couldn't hover there until he replied without risking getting caught, so I took a few steps back and then pretended to arrive noisily. Esther quickly blanked the screen out and put her phone down on the table.

She had her defences up as she talked to me, and I heard the phone buzz a short while later. I looked at it when she did: a banner that said 'Beau' but no message content.

I was itching to see that response and realised the best way of doing it was probably to seem like I was distracted. So I found an excuse to google an eating place and then, while apparently engaged with my own phone, I covertly watched Esther pick hers up and open it.

She went straight to WhatsApp, and I could see it was the same chat. Luckily for me, she left his reply up for a few beats while she stared at it, giving me plenty of time to read:

You look beautiful, as always. But aren't there any of the two of you together? x

I'd just finished reading when Esther clicked her phone screen off again and put it quickly away. Despite the smooth facade, I could tell that she was upset. More than upset.

I felt my heart squeezing for her. Whoever this guy was, he was a sleaze who didn't care about hurting her feelings. What kind of an asshole gets a sexy picture of a woman and then asks to see their friend? It was even worse considering he was already in a relationship.

He's someone who thinks he can have whatever he wants, I thought.

But that horrible interaction was all I was able to learn about this Beau of hers, and I couldn't find any university lecturers or people connected with her named Beau when I googled later on. A frustrating lack of progress.

So, by Wednesday, I was seriously desperate to find something – anything – out. I promised to meet Kit late afternoon to catch a little Bumps racing (an insane set-up, by the way: hugely expensive rowing eights all lined up in a row down the river with the intention of crashing into each other. It's just as chaotic as it sounds) and then to dinner with the whole gang to celebrate the end of everyone's exams.

It was desperation that led me to suggest that Ryan should come to the dinner, too. I wanted *so badly* to say the opposite: to tell Kit I wanted Ryan nowhere near me, but I had eight days left here at most, and I was facing total failure. If getting Ryan into a room was what it took, then I needed to do it.

I'd hoped to talk privately to Kit on the riverbank before the dinner, but the moment we arrived we saw a whole group of people he knew and had to sit in a group and make generalised conversation. Luckily, none of them were actual rowers, which meant I could relax a little. I held my composure and chatted nicely to them, bantered with Kit and gave commentary on everyone's technique as they rowed past.

So the dinner was going to have to be it. Kit had booked us a private room at Restaurant Twenty-Two. 'I can't be bothered with other people tonight, and bollocks to having to dress up for Midsummer House,' had been his breezy comment. 'But let's get a drink in first, before the others come, hey?'

Dressing up was, I realised as I arrived, all relative. There were folks in the downstairs room of Restaurant Twenty-Two dressed up more than I would have been for a cocktail party. There was also a seriously expensive wine list, which made me wince when I thought about Gael's comments. But Kit was *dead set* on paying for everyone tonight, and I thanked my stars. The food was going to be in the hundreds, too.

Cordelia and I had chosen one of the Zimmermann silk minidresses Imogen had donated for me to wear, benefiting from the fact that the plunging neckline was made a lot more so by Imogen having breasts a good two sizes smaller than mine. I felt dressed up just enough, and I could see that it was working from the way Kit kept reaching out for my hand or my leg as we sat alone together over our pre-dinner champagne.

I knew I had seriously limited time to talk to him in private and that I'd just have to jump in. Even so, my heart was pounding as I pulled big, sympathetic eyes and asked, 'How are you feeling about the stuff with James the other night?'

'God, I'm . . . sorry,' he said, leaning down to kiss my hand. 'That was a pretty crap start to things, wasn't it? And it wasn't even James's fault,' he went on. 'We're all pretty messed up over Holly. I don't expect him to be . . . you know. Totally chill. And it's pretty natural to blame the people who should have looked out for her.'

I gave him a sympathetic smile, and then I hit him with, 'He thinks you gave her the drugs, you know.'

He didn't move his hand, but his eyes snapped up to my face. 'What?'

'He saw her coming out of your room earlier on that day,' I told him. 'She lied about where she was going, so he thinks she went to get drugs from you and didn't want to tell him.'

Kit looked, to do him credit, completely horrified. 'What the hell . . .? Why would he think that?'

'You're often the guy with the gear,' I said with a shrug. 'And he said you never mentioned her visiting.'

Kit looked dumbstruck for a good few seconds. His eyes were moving as if he were trying to work something out, or remember something, or, I don't know, fabricate something.

'I didn't think to . . . She came to pick up her cardigan from me,' he said. I was looking for anxiety, but he looked sad, actually. Really sad. 'Her . . . bolero, she said it was. Because she needed it for the ball and had left it at my room the day before. That was the only thing I gave her.'

I looked past him for a second, then said, 'You don't think it was an excuse?'

'What do you mean?'

'I might deliberately leave something behind if I wanted a private conversation,' I explained. 'Did she try to talk to you about anything while she was there?'

Kit looked genuinely startled, and then he said, 'She kind of – I mean, yeah . . .' He frowned and then let go of my hand to rub his forehead. 'It seemed like a side point. Not her main reason for being there. But she asked . . . yeah, about what I'd do in a dilemma.' The rubbing at his forehead faltered. 'She said her friend was having a crap time. And she asked . . . what would I do if I'd worked out something really bad about two people I cared about. Something that might ruin people. Was it my duty to tell everyone, even if it meant a huge amount of hurt?' He stopped, and took my hand again. 'Something like that.'

I could feel my heart doing strange things, and I was afraid he'd be able to feel it in my pulse.

'Oh. Weird,' I said. 'What did you say?'

'Well, I said I'd need a lot more specifics to be sure,' he said with a tight laugh. 'I mean, even from a legal perspective, there's a huge difference between something that might affect a financial situation and something really criminal. I . . . kind of suggested we should talk about it when we had more time.'

I was trying to find the right thing to say; the thing that Aria would have said on hearing this for the first time, instead of any of the questions I now desperately wanted to ask.

Aria wouldn't have been thinking, *Cordelia was right. One of them did something bad enough that they killed her for finding out.*

'What would that even have been about?' I tried, in the end. 'She didn't say anything else?'

Kit frowned and then briefly kissed my hand. 'I don't know. I figured if it was *that* important, she wouldn't have brought it up when we were all rushed to get ready . . .'

I paused for a second, and then said, 'I guess it could have been nothing. It's so . . . weird. That nobody might ever know what it was.'

I watched him so, so carefully for a reaction, Reid. I watched for a moment of satisfaction, or of fear. A desire to change the subject.

But instead, he just looked desolate. Like I'd made him realise all over again what had been lost.

James Sedgewick turned up then, so of course the conversation stopped right there. And James looked . . . well, unhappy to see us both. But he tried to give me a smile of some kind.

This is weighing on him, all of it, I thought, with the sense of satisfaction that comes from knowing things are unravelling. *I just need to give him a push.*

There was little room for private conversation that night, though. Esther and then Ryan slid their way round the table, and the chat got very cheerful and annoyingly group orientated. A bad situation for dark confessions. It was annoying, too, that there was no bar to go to. Everything was ordered right there at the table.

But even so, I could read tension in all of them. And the moment I packed away my own feelings about Ryan Jaffett – who was trying very hard to get me to acknowledge him while I breezily talked to everyone else – I started to see that there was something weird going on between him and the others, too.

It was after we'd started eating the main course, and Ryan had once again tried to get me to speak to him, that Esther said to him, quietly and urgently, 'Give her some space, for god's sake, Ryan.'

There was a beat, in which Ryan looked both hurt and guilty, and then something twisted in his expression.

'How was your night yesterday, Esther? Nice little jaunt into London?'

And Esther's face froze. She was suddenly white. Sick-looking.

'I . . . yes, I went to see one of Mummy's friends. Possible work, you know.'

'Oh, right.' Ryan gave her a strange smile. 'Must have been before I saw you. Don't think you were with anyone Mummy would have approved of . . .'

'Ryan,' Kit said sharply. 'Whatever you're doing, stop it.'

Ryan looked back at Kit and reached over to pick up his glass of water. He drank it very deliberately.

'I'd forgotten you were the judges of good behaviour,' he said once he'd swallowed. 'The two of you . . .'

I found myself looking between Kit and Esther, trying to read their expressions. And for the first time I wondered whether I'd been wrong about this secret boyfriend of Esther's.

Could it be Kit? Kit had declined to do anything post-exams, claiming exhaustion. He could easily have been in London. *Had Esther been trying to tell me that her ex-boyfriend was actually . . . my new one?*

I remembered the message asking for a picture of us both and I felt a roiling sense of nausea. There was so much lying going on, the lies I was telling included. I should understand them all by now, but I didn't.

'I'm happy to judge your behaviour when you won't do it yourself,' Kit said to Ryan. 'Every time you get like this you start trying to drown it in drink, and then you regret it. I'm the one who ends up dealing with your self-loathing the next day, Ryan. So go home now. Go home, and wake up tomorrow feeling all right about yourself.'

Ryan stared back at him for a long time. I felt the threat of actual physical violence in the air and was bracing myself to back Kit up, even without being sure I should.

But something in Ryan cracked, and he rose quickly.

'Fuck it, I don't need this.'

He walked to the door and then left.

There was a silence in the wake of his exit, during which time I was thinking back over every interaction between Kit and Esther.

Is Kit playing the two of us? I thought.

But then why was Esther so happy to have me in the group? It didn't quite make sense.

I felt Kit's arm go round me after that, and he murmured, 'In case you're wondering, none of this bullshit is your fault.'

Which, I have to say, did a lot to dispel the idea of him as nothing but a player in my mind. But I still felt uncertain, somehow. Almost like I had to convince him all over again that I was worth something. Almost as though Esther and I were in competition for his affection.

It's so messed up, when all I was there to do was work. I don't know why people and situations like that have the power to get under my skin, but they do.

And, Reid, even if I'm not really writing this for you any

more, I feel like I don't want to tell you this, and that it hurts to say it. Things happened later with Kit that are . . . not right. I don't even know why I let them happen. But I have to write it out anyway.

The truth, in all its horrible glory.

32. Reid

Reid's last seven hours had been a nightmarish blur. He'd woken to Dom shaking him, and reflexively readied himself for some desperate kind of struggle.

Only to realise that they were at Guy's A & E.

Dom had half carried him out of the car to the entrance, where a nurse had told him it shouldn't be long as it wasn't that busy.

'Not that busy' turned out to be a packed waiting room and snippets of conversation overheard about people having been there hours. *The state of a health service chronically underfunded for over a decade*, Reid had thought, at a moment when he'd managed to gather his thoughts together.

During another of those moments he'd looked sideways at Dom and realised that he'd been imagining phantoms back in the car. Dom had brought him here to save his life.

Just because he did the wrong thing once doesn't make him a bad person, he thought, and as he looked the other way he briefly imagined he saw Anna there, giving him a crooked, approving grin.

It had been impossible not to slip into sleep once he was settled in the high-backed chair Dom had managed to requisition for him. And then to be repeatedly brought out of it by his colleague's voice. Sometimes he'd thought he heard Dom talking to someone else, but then he realised that the other voice was a wizard's, and then a dragon's, and he thought that probably wasn't quite happening.

He knew he'd definitely told Dom to go and get on with

the case at some point, only to realise that it was no longer Dom sitting next to him but Seaton Laws.

'I've got this under control now,' Seaton had told him. 'The reg will be seeing you soon.'

Aside from wondering how Seaton had ended up there, Reid had felt a strange sense of peace at the man's presence. It felt as though Seaton was a father figure, despite all the messy history between Reid and Anna.

At some unidentifiable time, Reid had at long last been summoned to a cubicle, where he'd been so out of it that he'd been convinced for a while that the registrar worked for the accounts department. He wasn't quite sure why. But Seaton had been able to explain drily that this was a doctor and that Reid needed to answer his questions.

Reid had done his best to answer, though most of the questions had seemed to be about the Eurovision song contest, for some reason he couldn't fathom, and which he'd told him seemed a bit silly. The registrar had next taken a good, blinding look at his pupils with a light and then suggested that it might be worth him having a CT scan, though he was fairly confident that there was no haematoma.

'You're probably all right, but I'm just a little concerned by your confusion,' he told Reid.

'What confusion?' Reid asked him.

'You said he was given tramadol?' the doctor asked Seaton.

'His colleague gave him some, but he vomited it up about ten minutes later,' Seaton replied. 'And he's been worse since.'

'All right,' the registrar said. And then seemed to suggest that Reid should go on the red-eye.

'Can't fly anywhere,' Reid mumbled. 'My girlfriend . . . ex-girlfriend . . . she's missing.'

'No flying. It's a CT scan, Reid,' Seaton said with a sigh. 'You're having your head scanned.'

The CT turned out to be an exceptionally large cylinder, which he was slid into. He was a little confused as to whether he was being launched into space or was going to hibernate, but somewhere in there he found himself in a room with Ryan Jaffett and Esther Thomas. Esther was posing in front of a mirror, and Ryan was taking a video of it.

And then Esther suddenly saw Reid watching and looked horrified.

'Shhhh, you can't tell anyone,' Esther whispered to him, her face pale and her voice urgent.

He half woke, full of a sense of urgency, only to find himself in that tube once again. The loud hum of it was intensely soporific, and in spite of himself he slid back into an all-consuming sleep.

He only woke again properly when a female nurse pulled up a set of metal bars on the bed next to him with a loud clang and he realised that he was now on a ward. The extreme confusion of the last few hours seemed to have receded.

His head and jaw now felt horrifically sore, and when the nurse asked, 'Would you like any painkillers?' he immediately said, 'All of them, please.'

The nurse laughed and padded away on flat shoes. Reid moved his head fractionally and felt as though it was being squeezed by something massive and relentless. He closed his eyes, but as he did he realised that his dazed subconscious mind had solved something for him.

He knew what was on Ryan Jaffett's phone.

He opened his eyes again and located his own phone, which was sitting on his folded-up jacket on a unit next to the bed. He sat upright just enough to reach it and felt like swearing at the throbbing pain in his head, but made it back to where he'd been without actually dying.

The phone was on 8 per cent battery, which wasn't ideal.

There were ten WhatsApp notifications from Dom Davies on it, and he opened them with a feeling of mixed fear and optimism.

What if he's found her?

But the most recent message was an update to say that they'd only just found Kit Frankland, who was on his way to Finsbury Park now. Previous messages were, when he read them, to say that there was no sign of either Anna or Kit at the Frankland house in Kew, which they'd forced entry to, and that their CCTV search at South Mimms had come up with nothing.

Another message sent Reid's heart rate up a notch, even though he probably should have been expecting it.

> Mate, we've had a reply this morning from Anna's editor at the *Ensign*, and he said she wasn't supposed to be on this Cambridge story any more. He says they pulled it on Monday, before the ball, so there wouldn't have been anyone to take an emergency call from her. But we've got lots of other possible avenues, and we could well have found her by the time you're awake.

Reid sighed. Of course Anna would keep going when she'd been told to stop. It was what she did. And of course it had got her into trouble. But not having the newspaper as backup didn't mean everything was lost.

Reid messaged him back as succinctly as he could, telling him they should be looking on Ryan Jaffett's spare phone for videos and images showing Esther Thomas with an older man. And then he sat back, trying not to think about the fact that it had been thirty-five hours and that they might no longer be looking for a kidnap victim but for a body.

Seaton appeared in the gap between the curtains just after the nurse had visited again with three hefty tablets, and Reid gave him a small smile.

'I think I might owe you one for last night. Was that . . . did you pull a few strings to get me seen quicker?'

'I didn't want you dying on me,' Seaton replied, slightly acerbically. 'It wouldn't have helped at all with our efforts to find Anna.'

Reid couldn't help smiling properly at that. 'Well . . . thank you.'

'You don't have a bleed on the brain, anyway,' Seaton told him, coming to sit on the plastic-covered padded chair next to him. 'But you clearly did get a serious concussion. Did your attacker use a weapon?'

Reid tried to think back to the night before. 'I don't think so. I think he just hit me really hard, and then I hit my head on the wall, too.'

Seaton nodded. 'Do you still think it was Kit Frankland?'

'I . . . maybe.' He frowned, and then regretted it. Anything that moved the muscles of his face and eyes was a mistake. 'I might have freaked someone else out. It . . . I need to be there when they talk to Kit.'

Seaton gave him a long look, and then said, 'I'll get hold of the reg. You'll need to be seen again before they discharge you.'

He returned to wait with Reid while the wheels were set in motion – Reid reflecting all over again what a different life it must be when you were Seaton Laws and always knew someone who could help you jump the queue. They fell into an awkward silence in which neither of them seemed to know what to say next.

Reid tried for a little light conversation after a minute.

'So . . . how have things been, since I saw you last? I didn't . . . get the chance to ask.'

Seaton gave a short laugh. 'Oh, they're fine. Much as usual.'

Reid nodded, and then asked, 'Garden going well?'

Seaton blinked at him. 'Yes. Ahhh . . . it's fine.'

'How are the gladioli coming on?'

'Yes, very well. Very well.'

'The colour must be wonderful at this time of year,' Reid added.

'Indeed! Quite varied.' There was another short silence, and then Seaton said, 'Want a coffee or anything?'

33. Anna

After that, Reid, everything went to shit. And I think it might have been my fault.

Two days after we'd all dined at Restaurant Twenty-Two, with exactly one week left on the clock, James turned up at my door. I'd been hoping to see him in private but was struggling to find any excuse to be away from Kit. So the fact that James came by a few minutes after I was back from a rowing session (you have to keep up your cover in this job, Reid, even when your body is crying out for a rest) seemed like a godsend.

I quickly realised that he'd timed it on purpose, possibly even by hanging around near my house until I returned. There was something big that he needed to talk about, and it was coming off him in waves.

The downside to his timing was that I was both tired and sticky, and I didn't want to sit inside with him and worry that I reeked of sweat.

'Let's sit on the green,' I said instead. 'While it's not raining.'

It was a humid, cloudy day, and a lot warmer than the last few. June has been pretty hit and miss in Cambridge this year. I guess it's probably the same in London. I haven't kept track so much.

'Look, I don't want to put you in a difficult position,' James said, once we'd sat on the grass. His voice was tight. 'I'm not asking you to – well, you know. Betray Kit or . . . or any of the others. I don't think Kit's a bad person, even if he did what I think he might have done. Or even if he covered for someone else . . . It's just . . . the *not knowing* is really . . . it's the worst.' He shook his head. 'It's the worst.'

'You want me to find out if he gave Holly drugs?' I asked him, bluntly. 'Or if he knows who did.'

James winced. 'I know it's . . . maybe it's ridiculous.'

I watched him for a minute. The clear sadness. The awkwardness. 'Have you tried asking the others?'

'They literally don't want to hear it,' James told me, a clear vein of anger running through his voice. 'They tell me they loved her, and I think . . . maybe they did. But Kit is so . . . I don't know. Central to their lives, I suppose.' He shrugged. 'They don't want to confront the reality of who he might be. The bad as well as the good.'

I nodded, slowly, and watched a couple of guys throwing a Frisbee around for a moment. 'I did . . . talk to Kit,' I said. 'I really wanted to know, too. And I don't think he gave her anything.' I looked back at James. 'He says she came to pick up a bolero, but then asked for advice as well. It seemed like random advice, about a friend. She wanted to know what he'd do if he found out something bad about someone. Holly said, if she knew something that might ruin people, was it her duty to make it known?'

James looked at me blankly. 'Ruin people?'

'Yeah,' I said. 'She was talking about someone close to her.' I gave him a moment, and then I asked, 'Do you think she witnessed something? Something that made someone want to hurt her?'

His head jerked back and then he looked away. I could see this working its way through his thoughts. There was clearly a lot to process.

'You think she saw . . . some kind of crime, or . . . or what? A betrayal?' he asked, eventually.

'Maybe,' I said. 'If somebody knew she was thinking of going to the police, like Kit suggested, maybe they decided to kill her before it could go any further.'

'Fuck,' James said, very quietly. 'Fuck.' And then, with real emotion: 'I knew it. I knew she wouldn't have taken those bloody drugs. It didn't matter what everyone kept saying. Oh my god.' He put a hand up to his head, looking sick.

'What could she have seen, though?' I asked him, knowing full well that he needed to think of the next steps himself. Or think he had. 'I mean, this must have been someone really close to her if they knew she was going to the police. Can you remember anything happening?'

I could see him trying to gather his thoughts. 'I don't . . . I need to work this all out.' He stood, shakily, and then said, 'Thank you. I . . . needed to know this.'

And as much as this was exactly what I'd been angling for, to have someone else looking into this, I felt a rush of worry. Because James – who wasn't a big, rugby-playing type and who also wasn't the calculating kind who'd be on the look-out – might now be in as much danger as Holly had been.

'Please be careful,' I told him. 'If she was . . . you know . . .' I gave him as meaningful a look as I could. 'You're messing with someone who reacts badly to threat.'

James didn't really focus on me. He was sickly white with the shock of it all. But he nodded. 'Yes,' he said. 'OK. OK.'

I failed him, Reid, didn't I? I should have tried harder. That's what I think now. That the first of the things that went wrong was totally my fault.

Two days later, on the horribly named Suicide Sunday, James Sedgewick was found unresponsive in one of the college shower rooms. He was extremely lucky he'd collapsed when there was another student waiting to use the bathroom. The student used a spoon to open the lock when he'd had no response after twenty minutes.

The porters called an ambulance, and when they checked

his room to try to work out what had happened they found a glass of Diet Coke and next to it a bottle of phenobarbital with the prescription label scrubbed off. Ground-up remains of multiple tablets were next to it on the desk, making it look to all intents and purposes as though James had decided to overdose.

James hadn't ingested enough to kill himself, probably because he'd thrown up in the bathroom. With medical intervention, he regained consciousness after a few hours.

I don't know if I need to tell you how fucking terrified I was during those hours of waiting. How terrified, and how much I felt the weight of responsibility. For this to happen shortly after I'd revealed that Holly was murdered – that couldn't be a coincidence. He must have asked the wrong questions, and it was obviously my fault that he'd started asking them.

A few hours after he woke up, James messaged me himself. It was a simple message:

Please come and see me. On your own. X

It was only then that I wondered whether he might have seen his killer, and I hoped beyond hope that he'd already told the police if he had. I didn't want him lying there, the only witness, while I cycled my way through slow Sunday-evening traffic towards Addenbrooke's Hospital.

I was still wearing the dress I'd put on late in the morning to go to Tribal Barbecue, the big event that kicked off May Week. It was the dress I'd laboriously picked out with Esther in London.

We'd none of us ended up going to Tribal, and Kit had never even come as far as picking me up. As soon as he'd heard about James he'd apparently run straight to St John's to try to help, and then followed the ambulance to Addenbrooke's.

By the time he'd called me he'd been heading back home

to get food and supplies for James. That was good. It meant he wouldn't be there when I talked to James. But there would still be James's parents to face.

I felt an awful, crushing fear as I let myself into the three-bed ward in the treatment centre that James was now on. The only other patient in there was unconscious, which made me even more aware of how serious a brush with death this had been.

I'd already scared myself half out of my mind looking at the possible long-term effects of a barbiturate overdose, including respiratory issues, cardiac issues and cognitive ones, as well as possible long-term kidney damage.

Seeing James sitting up and talking to his family was a relief, but I still felt like a piece of absolute crap. Like the worst human being.

Philip Sedgewick was sitting close to the bed, telling James something clearly hilarious about a neighbour, while Marcie – laughing, too, but with a finger to her lips – attempted to get him to talk more quietly.

I realised with a note of surprise that Marcie was wearing a lanyard over her neat white shirt. I'd never stopped to wonder what she did, but clearly it was a job in the hospital. I guessed that must be one of the reasons the Sedgewicks lived in Great Shelford, which was just out of Cambridge on this side.

It was strange seeing James and Marcie together again. Both were so strikingly beautiful, and both somehow afraid of taking up space.

James saw me first, and gave me a rueful grin. 'Hi, Aria.'

His dad stood, quickly, and greeted me warmly. Which probably meant James hadn't told them I'd almost gotten him killed.

'It's lovely to see you,' Philip said. 'You've met Marcie, haven't you?'

'Yes, it's so nice to see you again.' I was given a brief but wonderful-smelling hug by James's beautiful mother. How could she be in the middle of working at an overheated, disinfectant-laden hospital and still look and smell amazing? 'I didn't realise – you're a doctor here?' I added as she released me.

'Ah, ish,' she said. 'Radiology consultant.'

'OK. Scanning people, right?'

'Exactly,' she said with a smile. 'But luckily not James.'

'Yeah, wouldn't want to see the mess I am underneath it all,' James said with a trace of dark humour.

I saw the way his parents both reacted. It was as if the joke had cut through their cheerfulness and let a bleak, awful fear for their son ooze out.

'Absolutely,' Philip said. 'Hey, we should go and find coffee. James must want a break from us.'

They were out of the room by the time James said, tiredly, 'Their determined cheering me up is exhausting.'

I sat a little shakily in the chair next to the bed. 'Do they . . . think you did it to yourself?'

James gave me a slightly sardonic laugh. 'I honestly don't know. Dad's talking about bodyguards for the foreseeable, and I don't know if that's to save me from outside threats or . . .'

'I'm so sorry,' I said, reaching out to squeeze his hand. 'This is all my fault.'

'Of course it isn't,' James said.

'It really is,' I insisted. 'I was the one who told you about what Kit said. I pretty much suggested trying to find out what happened.' I took a wobbly breath. 'Jesus. You could have ended up dead.'

There was a long pause before he said, 'But I wanted to know. I felt like I needed to. Like I owed it to Holly.' He paused again, and said, 'But honestly? Now? I'd rather nobody ever knew if it meant not putting them in danger. I can't let this bullshit happen to anyone else.'

I wished I could tell him the whole truth, but I didn't think it would help anyone right then. So I did the next best thing I could think of and asked him who he'd spoken to before this happened.

'Aria,' he said, forcefully. 'Please don't. Please don't try to find answers. I didn't even see it coming.'

'But if you only spoke to one person . . .'

'I spoke to all of them,' he said, helplessly. Angrily. 'The whole gang. Kit, Ryan, Esther . . . even Esther's mum . . . I was on a mission.' He looked at me steadily. 'I thought it was worth it, but I don't any more. And it's definitely not worth it for you. You didn't even know her.'

I was trying to reply, persuasively, when a series of footsteps on the lino flooring announced that James had more visitors. I probably should have guessed that it would be some of the others, but it was actually all three of them. I flinched slightly as Kit stopped in his tracks.

'Hey,' he said, shifting a bag in his hands. 'I didn't know you were coming.'

'I couldn't stand waiting at home,' I told him. 'I figured I'd get here the same time you did if I cycled hard.'

It was at that point, though, that I realised Kit must have asked the others to come with him. They hadn't all arrived coincidentally at once.

Which meant he'd deliberately excluded me.

Why? I thought. *Why keep me out?*

I rose to kiss him, feeling all over again the strangeness of the situation. Somehow Kit was both my boyfriend and absolutely not my boyfriend in any way. I was going to act like he was everything I wanted for as long as I was Aria, and then

I was going to leave Cambridge and never see him again. It was increasingly messing with my head.

I saw the surprise and discomfort in his expression relax in the face of my warmth, though he made no move to explain why he hadn't asked me along. Soon after that he was focused on James, and on cheering him up.

He did it sensitively but jokily. Whereas Ryan came in with banter so harsh about fainting in the shower that it made me actually wince. Though, weirdly, James seemed to find it funny as well, which made me think this was just how it worked between them.

They still default to being friends, I thought. *Even when one of them tried to kill him.*

Watching them, I realised with a sense of disappointment that Kit seemed to have made up fully with Ryan. Despite what he'd done to me. Despite their big stand-off at dinner.

I couldn't get a handle on their friendship. It was like Kit was an indulgent parent and kept finding reasons to forgive him.

Even when he's done terrible things to the woman you say you care about the most, I thought.

At one point Ryan looked up at me and caught me watching him. And for a split second, his broad grin fell away. He looked like a sad, angry, messed-up kid. And then he made an impatient gesture with his hand as if trying to wave all of that away, and looked down. Then he smiled again at something Kit was saying.

Esther spent most of the time with her arm threaded through mine, and I thought she seemed anxious, too. But I found it impossible to tell whether this was guilt, worry for her friend, or her inability to cope with an emotionally complex situation without the help of MDMA. She'd brought a couple of books and a box of macarons for James in a fairly practical style of offering help.

'I'm so sad you'll miss the ball tomorrow,' she said to James at one point in a low voice. 'Do you want us to sell our tickets, too?'

'Don't be ridiculous,' James protested with a crooked grin. 'I'll totally be there. Just as long as Dad can sort a ticket for my brand-new bodyguard, it's all fine.'

I thought, once again, how strange it was that they were all so keen to go. To the same event that had claimed the life of their friend. It wasn't like there weren't a dozen other May Balls they could have gone to. But Kit had told me there would be a minute's silence in Holly's memory, and maybe that was as much a reason to go as any.

We were all chased out not much later when James's parents returned, pushing us over the visitor limit.

Once we were out in the hall, on our way to the exit, Ryan let out a long breath.

'I'm no good at this stuff,' he said, suddenly. 'I don't know how . . . How am I supposed to know what to say? I was trying to be funny, and I kept thinking I should shut the fuck up, but it was . . . I couldn't help it. And now I'm worried I might have pushed him to feel suicidal all over again.'

'He wasn't suicidal,' Kit said, tersely.

'Look,' Ryan said, holding up a hand. 'I know I . . . He's a friend, but . . . We all know that stuff about someone else poisoning him is bullshit, right? Like, how would anyone know his room was empty?' He caught Kit's eye and clearly picked up on a dangerous look there, but he went on, 'I mean, it's really understandable. It's almost a year since Holly. This time of year must remind him . . .'

We'd all come to a stop outside the treatment centre now, alongside the bike racks. But nobody was making any attempt to unlock anything. Kit and Ryan were facing each other, and Kit looked . . . coiled. On the verge of lashing out.

Ryan himself looked somewhere between scared and defiant. As though he knew he didn't want this but couldn't quite stop himself.

This is how he is, isn't it? I thought. *This is what makes him wreck things, and then drink.*

'Someone attacked him,' Kit said, deliberately. 'And here you are, trying to play it all down. Why is that?'

Ryan looked genuinely horrified. 'What the fuck, Kit?'

I could see Kit's jaw working, as if he were poised on the edge of saying more, or backing down and conciliating. And it occurred to me that if I pushed things just a little, the truth might fall out.

'Maybe it was a friend who did it,' I said, folding my arms over myself as if worried. 'Because he got all hung up on what happened to Holly, didn't he? He was going around to everyone. Asking weird questions . . .'

Kit looked caught off guard. He turned to me with a frown. 'What do you mean?'

'He told me about it,' I said. 'He had big questions about how she died and he was going to ask you all.'

I saw Kit glance over at Esther, who gave me a shake of the head. 'He didn't ask any of us anything, darling.'

Somehow the remaining anger seeped out of Kit all at once, and Ryan backed off a few steps. He reached into his pocket for his bike key and then started attacking the D-lock on his Scott.

'Yeah, he must have changed his mind about asking,' Kit said, watching him blankly. 'Didn't come to anything.'

He came to put his arm round me after that, but it did nothing to dispel the sense of cold I felt. Because it was clear that they'd all joined ranks now, and had decided James was on the outside.

Though not just James. I was on the outside, too.

*

I emailed Gael to update him as I made my way into London. We were due to meet the next morning for our check-in, and I'd decided to stay over at my own flat before it. I'd need as much sleep as I could get the night before Trinity May Ball.

I also emailed Imogen, asking her to find out anything she could from Cambridgeshire police about the attempt on James's life. Despite it being Sunday, I got an immediate, enthusiastic response. I could tell that Imogen was desperate to be involved in this as more than a dogsbody. I added a message to tread very carefully, which she at least acknowledged.

Having heard nothing more from either of them, it was a shock when I arrived on our floor of the *Ensign* at nine to find Gael waiting for me with a heavy expression. I know him well enough that I immediately realised this was not good news. I knew he might be about to tell me James's near-death was all my fault.

It's difficult to rally your arguments against something you basically agree with, but I tried to think of a few anyway.

I needn't have bothered. The moment I sat down in Gael's office, he said, 'Maria is pulling the plug.'

I stared at him, dumbfounded.

'But . . . come on. I know it's taking time, but everything is *moving now* . . .'

Gael nodded, his expression full of sympathy. 'I know. And I know it's a rough deal when you're in the middle of things. But as well as little progress over several weeks, she's extremely concerned that our actions – however careful – have caused a student to try to attempt suicide.'

I couldn't help making an outraged sound. 'He didn't! I talked to him today. Someone tried to poison him.'

Gael pulled a doubtful face. 'Imogen got the attending

officers' report. It seems incredibly unlikely there was outside involvement, whatever he's now saying.'

'Well, there was,' I insisted. 'And we owe it to him to work out who and how, otherwise we're leaving him in greater danger.' I stood up. 'It was asking questions that triggered the killer to move. Seriously, Gael.'

He rubbed his hand across his head. 'I don't think they're going to budge, Anna.'

'They? I thought this was Maria.'

He sighed. 'I got hauled in by her and the editor. They're both declaring themselves horrified by our casualness with student welfare.'

'God,' I said. 'That's not – that's not fair.'

Gael gave me a wry smile. 'Never expect fairness.'

I shook my head, feeling a surge of huge frustration.

'I can't leave all this unfinished. There's James's safety to think about, and Cordelia Wynn –'

Gael held up a hand. 'You explained to her at the beginning that there might not be enough for us. You and she are going to have to accept that.' And then he added, 'I'm really sorry about this, but with the two of them saying no there isn't a lot I can do.'

I gave him a last, desperate, pleading look. 'But what am I supposed to do to protect James Sedgewick?'

He let out a sigh. 'If you really think he was attacked, I'd say the best thing you can do is convince him to report it all to the police and then walk away. Let them look at this their own way, without you.' He nodded. 'In terms of practicalities, we can give you a reason to vanish. A sick relative. A drug relapse.'

I thought of Esther and James all being told that I was an addict. Of Kit and Ryan, the ones who thought they knew this already, being told that I'd given in and relapsed. Somehow the thought made everything inside me churn almost as much as the idea of walking away from the case itself.

'I'll sort it,' I told him in a dull voice.

And then I left the office for Cambridge again, knowing that I wasn't going to walk away at all.

34. Reid

Dom's team looked somewhere between concerned and happy to see Reid as he made his way to his corner of CID.

'All right, mate,' Dom said, going to give him a shoulder squeeze. 'Kit Frankland should be here in fifteen, and he's our main person of interest at the moment.'

Reid gave him as much of a grin as his face currently allowed. The painkillers had at last started to do something, so while his jaw wasn't fully mobile, it at least didn't feel on the point of rupture.

'I'd like to be in on the interview.'

'Let's discuss,' Dom said. And then he drew Reid aside to say, 'Overnight we got phone records back from the burner phone Anna was using as Aria Lauder. The last call she made was to her father, which didn't connect.' He cleared his throat. 'Just before that, she tried to call your old number.'

Shit.

Reid still couldn't explain exactly why he'd felt the need to change his number after the break-up. He could easily have blocked Anna. But somehow the fear that she would call him from another phone and trick him into talking to her had been heart-pounding.

Looked at now, in the cold light of day, it had been a mad thing to do. Why had he been so afraid of her contacting him?

But he knew the answer. He'd been afraid of experiencing all the feelings he'd had since yesterday afternoon. He'd been afraid of having to accept that he'd been the one in the wrong, and that he'd ruined everything.

If he'd just kept his bloody number she'd have been able to ring him. She'd been calling from a totally different phone.

'I have to ask,' Dom said, his expression apologetic. 'With the email to you, and the call . . . You definitely haven't seen her since her disappearance?'

Reid suddenly understood why Dom had wanted to tell him this in person. He needed to make sure that Reid wasn't involved in his ex's disappearance.

'No,' Reid answered. 'Not at all. I changed that number eighteen months ago, which is why she had no idea I wouldn't answer. If I hadn't, she might not be missing.' He gave Dom a very steady look. 'I really let her down, Dom. I can be a judgemental prick sometimes, as you know. And the fallout of that was not being there for her when she needed it on Monday night. But when her dad came and asked for my help, I realised he was right. She was in danger.'

'All right. Thanks.' Dom blew air out, then nodded. 'I'd appreciate your help with Kit Frankland. We've found out something about him we think might be relevant.'

'What's that?' Reid asked.

'Holly Moore was the second young woman whose death he was peripherally involved in,' Dom said. 'There was another girl, back when he was at school. She was sixteen, and she apparently hanged herself.'

Reid felt a wash of cold. Whatever Anna had said about being wary of Kit, there was no question that she'd been caught under his spell. She wouldn't have wanted to believe he was a killer. Not really.

He could see in Dom's expression that he was thinking the same, and realised that he must have read all of Anna's email by now. He might even know more than Reid did, and that made Reid feel a strange pang of jealousy.

It had been written for Reid, at least at first. It was his to understand.

'If someone can make me a coffee, I'll be ready in ten,' he said, and went to find a quiet corner to read the rest.

35. Anna

The train ride back to Cambridge was an anxious one. With the *Ensign* credit card now handed back, I had only a whisker of a gap between me and my overdraft, and a host of things that needed to be paid for.

I knew I'd have to find the money for hair and make-up for tonight's ball somehow. It was either that or arrive looking like someone who didn't fit in. The rest of May Week is shaping up to be horrifically expensive, too. Unless I solve it tonight and can just go home, obviously.

Which I'm going to. I'm going to.

But cashflow is still important.

I realised I was going to have to ask Dad for help, however much the idea made me cringe. And I was going to have to do it at the same time as admitting to him that I'd been the cause of his friend's son ending up in hospital.

I messaged asking if I could drop in on him at eleven fifteen, which would just give me time to get off the train from London and cycle over to see him, before making it home to shower. Hair and make-up was booked for 1 p.m. until 3. Honestly, this dressing-up stuff is pretty much a career.

Dad messaged a 'Great idea' back, and I spent the cycle over rehearsing how to both tell him about James and ask him for money without admitting that I'd been kicked off the story. I wasn't willing to actually lie to him, so it was all going to have to be about obfuscation.

(And I can already hear you snorting to yourself about me using that word. I basically put it in on purpose for you because

I know it'll remind you of that ridiculous defence lawyer in the sex-trafficking case, not that you'll be reading this, of course.)

I hadn't really thought much about whether Dad had anything to tell me in return, but I realised he might as I parked my bike and saw him waiting for me on the porch with a troubled, closed-off look on his face.

Just then, something about him – the gleaming blue waistcoat, illuminated by the warm yellow sunshine – made him look like some kind of a lord, waiting to judge his subjects. Like he was a class above. Unassailable.

'I had a phone call with Philip Sedgewick this morning,' he said, immediately, before he'd even let me inside. 'It was . . . well, it was a pretty uncomfortable experience.'

'Oh.' I felt like I was suddenly standing on something slippery. 'You mean . . . because of what happened to James?'

'Of course because of what happened to James,' he said, slightly impatiently. At that point he stood back and let me in, but then walked ahead of me without turning round until he said, 'We . . . everything we talked about early on . . . the care you were supposed to take over him . . .'

It was a horrible feeling, Reid. I'd come looking for support and now felt as though Dad was the personification of all my guilt over James. And on top of that, I was sticky from cycling and standing there with my helmet in my hands in his perfect kitchen feeling as though I didn't belong.

'I have been taking care, Dad,' I said, not sure who I was convincing. 'I told him to be super careful. You know what Holly said to Kit? The stuff I told you? Well, that was what tipped James into getting involved, and I didn't – I didn't think that it would.'

'Well, it was bound to, wasn't it?' Dad said, his irritation stepping up. He paced over to the cupboard and pulled out a couple of champagne flutes, and then went to the wine fridge.

Despite the stress of the situation, I couldn't help admiring the fact that he was still offering me champagne. 'How else was James going to react when you told him his girlfriend might have been murdered by one of his friends?' He gave me an anguished look while he grabbed a bottle of Taittinger off the shelf and started pulling the foil off. 'It was awful, Anna. I had to sympathise and pretend to know nothing, while I felt as though I'd been complicit in hurting my friend's son. And all because I'd helped you do this for your own reasons.'

It felt like a slap across the face. Like he was standing in front of me and telling me that these old friends of his were *his* people and I was just the grubby little interloper who couldn't be trusted.

'My own reasons?' I asked him. 'Holly is *dead*, Dad! She deserves to still be alive! That's my reason!'

'But James deserves to live, too,' he said, his voice full of emotion and the bottle of champagne only a mildly ridiculous addition as he held his hands out in appeal. 'And I became a part of risking his life.'

'You said you were happy to help,' I told him, trying to remind him how much of this had been his idea while he battled with the cork. 'I didn't think there were limits on that. Do you want me to . . .?'

'I've got this!' he snapped back. 'I've got this.' He managed to actually get the cork out, which at least meant I was safe from it being fired into my face. 'And of course there were limits! There were always going to be limits. If you'd . . . I don't know, threatened someone with violence, you wouldn't expect my unwavering support, would you?'

'Honestly?' I asked. 'Logical, but not exactly a fair comparison. I'm trying to bring a killer to justice, not threaten anyone, and James Sedgewick was almost a victim of whoever they were because they are *still dangerous*.'

'Because you got him involved,' Dad said heatedly, handing me a full glass of fizz. 'And although I understand Philip's willingness to believe otherwise, it seems very unclear whether James didn't . . . well, do it to himself.'

'Oh, come on, Dad,' I said, loudly, and then – because it's my rule not to waste good alcohol – had a mouthful of champagne. That stuff is so good, honestly, I wish I had the money to drink it every day. 'Holly was murdered, and someone tried to kill James for asking too much. It's pretty straightforward. And do you think his family really, truly, if they were asked, would want him hanging around with a killer?'

'But you *didn't ask*,' he said, stiffly. He picked up his glass, and drank the bubbles like they were water. It only made me feel more like an outsider. 'And Philip doesn't believe that any of James's friends is capable of it. He's known them since they were knee-high.'

I laughed at that. 'Do you have any idea how many people have been protected by that feeling? By the "but my child couldn't have" defence? Nobody ever thinks the people they know are capable of violence, until they're confronted with it.' I tried to step back. To appeal to his sense of logic. 'Look. Those three are the only ones who fit. When I started talking to them, someone tried to warn me off, for starters. We *know* that whoever killed Holly reacts badly to feeling threatened. We know it was her friends she was considering confronting. I think those three are the only people on this earth she'd have hesitated over naming, too. She'd have given them a chance to hand themselves over to the police or explain themselves. She would have cared about them and, to be honest, not wanted to rock the boat and destroy the life she'd managed to win for herself. Plus, for what it's worth, they all have issues a mile wide.'

'But there were better ways, Anna,' he said, almost slamming his glass down onto the counter. 'You didn't need to push until James was in danger. And to find out from Philip that you've been having a – a relationship with Kit Frankland,' he said with something in his voice I'd struggle to describe as anything other than disgust. 'For a grown woman to take advantage of a student like that, all to try to wheedle out a story. It's – I'm going to be the one left mortified by all this, Anna. I'm going to be the one trying to explain that I had no idea about any of it.'

And there it was. Full proof that he thought as badly of me as you do, Reid.

I think it might have been all right if he hadn't hit exactly – exactly – the same anxieties that you did when you left. Though maybe it would have been less awful if he hadn't also hit all the points about this that were making me feel confused and uncomfortable and like I wasn't sure if I should just walk away.

I didn't have anything to say to him in response. I felt so hurt and anxious. Even though all I was trying to do was *the right thing.*

So with a pang of regret about more than just the wasted fizz, I placed the glass carefully down, turned round and walked out of his beautiful granite and grey-paint kitchen. As I headed back into the sunny morning I heard him calling, 'Look, Anna,' after me, but I didn't go back. There was no way I could bear to let him see me cry. I just grabbed the bike I hadn't locked up anyway and cycled away as quickly as I could.

I understood, at that point, that I was going to have to do this on my own. That even dragging Cordelia into it any further while I no longer had newspaper backing wasn't fair.

And as I cycled back through sun and then clouds, I realised that all of it came down to doing the right thing and ignoring anyone who thought I was in the wrong.

*

Dad's tried to call me twice since. He accompanied these calls with a text message apologising for losing his cool and asking if I was going to be all right for money in the short term.

I have no idea how he guessed money might be an issue, but I was obviously not going to tell him what I needed. Or, in fact, reply to him at all. I'd decided I would just have to use the last of my overdraft on the hair and sell some things on eBay to make it to the end of the month. The dress might make something second-hand, at least, if I could avoid wrecking it.

In spite of my non-responsiveness, midway through the make-up session at Ricci Rizzo (a salon brilliantly only a five-minute walk from my house) my phone chimed with a notification that £500 had been credited to my bank account. Another message came shortly afterwards.

> Look I've sent something in case you need it. I know you don't usually want my money, but it might be useful for the job this week. X

I have to admit that I ruined a perfectly good application of eyeliner by crying it off at that point. I don't know if it was the relief or the shame of it, or the fact that nobody has ever in living memory sent me that much money without it being my salary.

But at the same time, there was nothing in any of Dad's messages that said he'd been in the wrong or that I wasn't a terrible person. I just didn't feel as if we were on the same team. Not any more.

So I kept quiet and let the wonderful make-up artist redo my eyeliner. I had my Aria Lauder mask back on a short while later, and it was a good thing I did, because James Sedgewick walked along Hobson Street, right past the window where I was sitting. I saw him catch my eye, do a double-take and then give me a grin.

He mouthed something and gave a wave to someone behind him, and then opened the door to come inside the salon.

'Wow, look at you,' he said, coming to stand behind me. He looked pale, but whole, and if I hadn't known to look for it, I might have missed the desolate look behind his smile.

My amazing make-up artist Alia (whose name was ALMOST the twin of my fake one. Weird, hey? Or maybe not. Maybe just a meaningless thing.) had gone to make me a cup of coffee so it was just the two of us in front of the mirror.

'Aren't you supposed to be resting up?' I asked.

'I was in bed twenty-four hours,' he said. 'I was going mad, being stuck inside.' He turned his head as another figure entered the shop. 'Besides, I had to give Ned something to do.'

'Oh, the bodyguard? Nice.' I'd forgotten that James would now be shadowed, though now that I got a look at the aforementioned Ned, it was pretty obvious what he was. He was probably mid-forties, had sunglasses on under the brim of his cap despite now standing inside, wore a black hoodie with a generic logo and had the kind of stillness I'd come to recognise in the ex-military men I'd met during my career. I gave him a brilliant smile. 'Nice to meet you.'

Ned gave me a small nod, and I got the impression that he was trying hard not to smile back.

'You, too,' he said, his voice deep and reassuring.

'This is Aria,' James said, quickly. 'She's a friend of mine.'

Ned nodded, but I could see his attention moving away. He'd clocked that there was another door to the place and a flight of stairs leading downwards, and without another word he paced over to the top of the stairs and peered down with that bent-kneed gait of someone used to holding a gun steady.

'He takes it seriously,' James said, quietly, under the cover of a hairdryer going on elsewhere. 'But he's all right.'

'Does he follow you everywhere?' I asked, just as quietly, as Ned paced over to the other door now, and looked out.

'Yup. Even stands outside the toilet,' James said with resignation.

'Oh my god,' I said, delighted. 'Can we mess with him? Like, get him to follow you to some really weird places?'

'Only if you want me to mess with you back,' Ned said from across the room.

James laughed, a momentary lightening of his gloomy mood, and it was good to see.

'Busted,' I muttered.

'What can I say?' James asked. 'He's a pro.'

All in all, I feel better about James's safety now. I trust Ned to stop anyone trying to kill him again. Or at least, to stop them succeeding.

Which brings us up to date. I'm back in my little house, and with two hours until showtime I only have nail polish, my recording device, dress and shoes to put on, and a final last-minute brush of my teeth and spritz of perfume, of course. Which has left me with a lot of time to write all this down. And overthink, obviously.

Threaded through all my thoughts about tonight is a sense of excitement. Because it feels like everybody's emotions have worn them thin. Like they could crack open at the smallest breath of wind.

More than that, I feel as though the May Ball, where Holly died, is the right place to see it happen. They'll be remembering it all, reliving it. They'll also be drunk and high. It's a golden opportunity.

But if I'm being really honest with myself, I'm also afraid. I keep thinking back to that car hitting me, and those photographs stuck to my gate. To the feeling that I've been watched throughout this. And if everything does erupt while they're drunk and high and emotional, then there could be repercussions.

It hasn't escaped my notice, either, that if they could get to Holly at Trinity May Ball, they could so easily get to me.

The other overthinking I've been doing is about you, Reid. Because I found myself wishing you could be there tonight, and it felt like a stupid thing to wish after all the times you let me down badly.

But then I found myself reflecting for the first time on the aftermath of that incident with my recording device in the bathroom. The part I'd forgotten.

I remembered that after it happened I stormed out and told you to butt out because I was doing it anyway. I was furious with you for thinking I was immoral.

But at midnight that same night, when I ended up stranded after screwing up an attempt to sweet-talk a banker, you came to help me without question. It didn't matter that you'd been angry with me, or that you'd already gone to sleep after a long day. You climbed into the car and drove to my rescue.

The weird thing is that you still help the people you think badly of, don't you? That's what I realised. You just do it, without question.

Like when Tanya's awful ex, Matt, called you because he'd been mugged, and you raced to help him. And when that asshole neighbour of your parents' who'd been making their lives hell sliced his leg open, you ran over there and sacrificed your nicest shirt to make a bandage.

For all my anger over how you treated me, I have never once seen you turn your back on someone who needed you. Not knowingly, anyway.

And that's why it's your number I've saved into my phone

under my coach's name, in case things go wrong. And why if I have to write this to anyone, it will always be you.

I mean, I won't be getting drunk, Reid. I'll be staying largely sober and watching my back. So you really don't need to worry about me.

Though, actually, I guess you'll only be reading this if you *should* be worried. Schrödinger's worry.

So . . . if this email finds its way to you, you have to promise to figure this crap out, OK? I think I can ask that much of you, at least.

36. Reid

Reid had to sit still for a few minutes after finishing the email. There was something so strangely hopeful in being judged worthy, but it fought with a bitter weight of guilt at having let Anna down.

Because he hadn't been there for her. He'd made it impossible for her to contact him, which was basically as bad as turning his back.

Dom tapped on the door as he was trying to gather himself together again.

'Kit Frankland is here,' he said. He waved a file at him. 'You'll need a scan of these. I'm coming in with you, but I want you to take the lead.'

Reid gave him a crooked smile. Letting him lead the interview was a serious mark of trust when he must have looked like hell.

'Thanks, mate,' he replied. 'I'll gesture for help if I stop being able to form words.'

He scanned through the notes and felt a heavy sense of worry at the similarities he was seeing. Another young woman in Kit's friendship group who'd wandered off during a party. Another apparent display of grief from Kit.

He got to his feet and made his stiff way over to the interview suite. He tried to prepare himself for the person Anna had described. For the measured, intelligent man who saw and controlled everyone around him.

It was more than a little surprising to find himself shaking hands with an extraordinarily posh, slightly over-cheerful young man with a babyishly handsome face.

'I understand you have a few question about . . . Aria,' Kit said, his gaze roving over the interview room as if committing it to memory. Reid could imagine how he'd relate this already, telling all of it as a fascinating anecdote to his equally posh friends.

'We do,' Reid said, settling down alongside Dom. He had to move his chair a few inches away to make room for Dom's beefed-up arms. How the man found shirts that fitted him Reid had never understood.

Reid unfolded his notes, trying to mentally rehearse his plan while a large part of him was stuck on how this – *this* – was the young man Anna had been so mixed up over. This pompous, overbred *boy*.

He'd been bracing himself not just for an intellectual battle but for a feeling of complete inadequacy in the face of a superior male. And now here he was, sitting opposite a wall of designer aftershave and smugness, wondering what the hell Anna had seen in the guy.

'OK,' he said, getting himself together. 'I think you know we're now quite concerned for the whereabouts of Ms Lauder.'

Kit nodded, earnestly. And then, with a sudden drop in the cheerful act, said, 'I . . . should we call her Anna?'

'Why would you call her Anna?' Reid asked.

Kit's expression didn't shift as he said, 'I'm assuming you know who she really is, if you've been asked to find her. Was it her dad who raised the alarm?' Reid felt momentarily unsettled, and then reflected that he might need to reserve some of his judgement on Kit Frankland after all.

'I should have raised the alarm myself,' Kit said, quietly. 'But when I found out . . . I just thought she'd played me for a fool and then left.'

Reid sighed, with a trace of fellow feeling for Kit Frankland. Perhaps that was what Kit wanted. For Reid to sympathise.

But it was impossible not to recognise what he was seeing. It was so very much like Reid's own confusion over Anna. The questions over whether he'd really known her at all.

'Before we go on, can you tell me how you found out who she really was?' Reid asked.

'My father,' Kit said, simply. 'Who says he was tipped off by a friend.' He gave the ghost of a sigh. 'But it seems to be fairly widely known. By the time I spoke to Esther, her mother had already told her.'

Reid scrutinised him. 'And how did that make you feel?'

Kit's mouth twisted into a smile. 'Like an idiot. But in some ways . . . in some ways it was better than what I'd been thinking before.'

'Which was . . .'

'That she'd gone home with another man,' Kit said. 'James was pretty sure he saw her leaving with someone, and that was a bit . . . shit, actually.'

'It's a little strange, that,' Reid said. 'Because we haven't yet identified this guy she left with and we haven't found her leaving on any of the CCTV. Which implies that she may have fled in some covert way, or that someone smuggled her out against her will.'

Kit looked totally confused at this. 'What . . . do you mean by "covert"? You mean over the wall or something?'

'Do you have any reason to think that?' Reid asked.

'No,' Kit said, looking slightly frustrated. 'I just . . . I don't understand what you mean.'

'Did anything happen that could have made her feel threatened?'

Kit looked off to one side, and then said, 'I don't . . . well . . .' He shook his head. 'I guess maybe what Ryan said spooked her.' He glanced back at Reid. 'Ryan told us she wasn't on the high-performance rowing programme at all. Or at least he didn't think so. He met the coach, who apparently had no idea who Aria was.' He gave another slightly twisted, humourless smile. 'Which makes perfect sense, when you think about it.'

'And Anna knew this?'

'Yes,' Kit said. 'I . . . told her about it. But nobody actually accused her of anything and she was pretty convincing about it being a mistake. I ended up thinking Ryan had got it wrong. And I . . . Look, I don't think she would have thought me a threat.' He pushed a lock of hair out of his eyes and said seriously, 'I would have protected her.'

Is this what she liked about him? Reid thought, realising that he wanted to believe Kit. Though unlike Anna, he had a strong reason not to.

'You had a room booked, didn't you?' Reid said. 'Is that where you took her?'

Kit looked slightly off balance. 'I didn't – I never used the room.'

'Then why extend the booking for a night?'

He felt satisfaction as Kit's discomfort visibly increased.

'You talk about protecting her,' he said, quietly. 'But you aren't very good at protecting the young women in your life, are you? Holly died. And Chloe . . .'

Reid saw the change in Kit's face. The way the muscles in his jaw went momentarily slack and then very tight.

'Why are you bringing that up?' Kit asked, his voice slightly hoarse. 'That's . . . seriously harsh.' He shook his head. 'I would have done fucking anything to protect the two of them. All three of them.' His jaw worked for a moment. 'I don't even give a shit about Anna lying to me. I've still been trying to find her. I went to the police and waited for bloody hours for them to see me last night.'

'You also ignored our calls asking you to see *us*,' Reid shot back.

'Seriously,' Kit said, somewhere between indignant and earnest, 'I had no idea you weren't the same people. I was *waiting* to see the police, so I didn't think I needed to do anything, and then this morning I got asked to come here instead. Fucking hell,' he added in a mutter. 'This is a shitshow. You're wasting time splitting hairs when she could be –'

'We're all working to find Anna,' Dom said, interrupting in a cheerful but firm voice. 'This has been our priority since yesterday evening.'

Kit's gaze went to Reid's face. 'Did you get beaten up over this? Is there . . . does somebody not want her found?'

'It happened when I went to look at your room in Trinity,' Reid said coldly. 'Do you want to explain?'

That silenced Kit. He opened and closed his mouth, and then looked down at his hands.

'You gave that room to Ryan Jaffett, didn't you?' Reid said.

Kit looked up at him and, this time, there was a pleading expression on his face. 'Look. I'm sorry you got caught in the middle of it, but it has nothing to do with any of this.'

'Regardless, you're currently shielding someone who attacked an officer,' Dom said. 'I'd start talking if I were you.'

Something broke in Kit then, and he sagged. 'All right. All right. Ryan . . . he has a problem. When he's drunk, he gets . . . he doesn't take no for an answer.' He looked up at Reid. 'A few weeks ago, before we knew Anna, he did something really stupid. The girl he . . . The next day, she was telling him she was going to go to the police and the college.' He gave an angry look. 'I thought it would be enough to stop him. But then he did the same fucking thing to Anna. But, by then, it was like I was complicit in all of it.'

'Complicit how?'

'I should have gone to his college and told them what he told me,' Kit said, miserably. 'I, like, justified to myself not doing it because I didn't have enough details. And then nothing seemed to happen and I thought maybe it hadn't been that bad. Maybe the girl had been upset but not . . . harmed.' He bunched his fist and then flexed his fingers out on the table, his eyes only on them. 'But yesterday, the shit hit the fan. It turned out Ryan had kept her quiet. He'd fucking *filmed* some of it and threatened to share it online if she reported him. And then, during the May Ball, apparently someone went into his room and stole the footage. So Ryan was freaking out and accusing everyone. And now he's hiding somewhere, convinced he's about to be lynched or arrested and, to be honest, he probably deserves both.' Kit let out a long breath. 'I don't know who I'm angrier with. Him, or me. I've been letting him get away with this shit. Even gave him the room, which he's basically been hiding in for two days.'

Reid was thinking a lot of things at once: that the footage had been taken by Seaton and was not, in fact, in some student's hands but hopefully already being accessed by the cyber team. And that he was sure it wasn't the only footage Ryan had on that phone.

'OK,' he said. 'Tell me about Esther, then. Do you know who her secret boyfriend is?'

Kit looked startled. 'Beau? I never met him . . . but I don't think he can have anything to do with this. He's someone she met on holiday. I think he's probably an Italian waiter or something, but she won't say. Apparently they meet up sometimes for fun. I think she probably wants to be with him but can't be because she's too desperate to please her mum.'

Reid already knew that Kit was wrong on this. Anna had witnessed enough to be sure the boyfriend was an older man in a position of authority. Esther seemed to have kept this from Kit, despite living with him.

But Ryan *had* known about it. He was sure that was why Esther had supported his presence at the Pitt Club dinner, and why he'd made the dig about Esther being in London with someone her mother wouldn't approve of. And Esther had been desperate for Kit not to find out the truth.

Which meant it could only be one of three people, didn't it? The three older men who Kit would go ballistic about her seeing.

'You weren't aware it was someone known to you?' Reid asked him, as though he hadn't just put all this together. 'Someone much older than Esther?'

Kit's expression went slack once again, for a moment, and it was almost satisfying. Kit was clearly – despite initial impressions – in the loop about a lot of things, but this was a total shock to him.

'I . . . what?' Kit gave a short laugh. 'She said it was nobody I knew. Seriously. Why would she lie about it?'

'For good reasons, I think,' Reid said, quietly, to himself. He got to his feet. 'Thank you for all the help, Mr Frankland. I'd appreciate it if you'd stay here and not contact anyone just for now.'

Once Dom Davies had followed him through the door Reid said, 'We need to look at all the images on Ryan Jaffett's phone asap. And if that's not going to be possible in the next half-hour, I need Anna's father back here.'

37. Seaton

Monday, 23 June – two hours before the ball

Seaton raised the knocker with a feeling of almost out-of-body anxiety. This was the kind of situation he dreaded beyond almost any other: a situation where he put himself at risk of humiliation, rejection and an emotional scene.

He'd almost convinced himself that he could leave it, letting Anna go to the ball without making any effort to fix this. He had, after all, only been reacting out of shock when he'd said those things.

But Seaton was familiar with the sense of shame that had descended on him after his daughter had left. It was one rooted in having let his family down over and over.

It was the shame of not being capable of proper familial emotions. Of being cold or judgemental when he should have been warm or loving. And onto this shame piled the increasing wretchedness of hours passing without being able to tell her the right words, even in a message.

He'd tried to salve his guilt by sending her money, but he knew it wasn't enough. That it would probably revolt her. He'd found himself pacing around his big, immaculately cared-for garden, wishing he knew what to do, so that at least he'd feel he was caring for something. Tending to something.

He'd found himself halting in front of the big, pink peonies close to the tennis court he rarely used.

Albert Crousse, he thought with a sudden smile.

They were the only flowers he knew the name of, and that

was down to Anna. She'd buried her face in one of the wide-open blooms what must have been three years before and told him peonies were her favourite flowers on earth.

'What kind are they?' she'd asked. 'I want to get some for my balcony.'

Seaton, of course, hadn't known and had gone to fetch ever patient Martin, who actually cared for these living things. And Martin had told her.

'Oh my god, Albert Crousse? They sound like a curmudgeonly next-door neighbour,' Anna had said, delighted. 'How can they look so pretty? I love it.'

They were almost in bloom once again now, those big pink peonies. They always flowered late in their shaded position. All those pale pink Alberts just waiting to burst into flower, but Anna not here to see them. And maybe never here to see them again, because he'd been inexcusably vile to her.

You need to fix this, he'd thought, and hurried to the shed to find a pair of secateurs. *You can't keep avoiding all the hard parts of being a father.*

He'd cut five of the blooms and wrapped them in paper towel. And then, as an afterthought, he'd gone to the kitchen and pulled a bottle of Roederer out of the fridge. They'd probably need a drink if they were going to talk about the tough stuff.

He'd packed them both into a bag (with the champagne in an ice pack) and set off for Anna's house before he had time to give in to his anxiety. Though it had plenty of time to hit him as he waited for her to answer the door.

He was taken aback by the sight of her. She was already dressed for the ball, her hair curled and piled up until it looked like there was twice as much of it, and the black-and-silver dress he'd bought for her fitting her brilliantly. Though, in many ways, it was the make-up that was the most striking. It changed the shape of her face, somehow, making her seem untouchably glamorous. No longer quite his daughter.

The two of them looked at each other for a beat, and then she gave a small nod and a smile.

'Would I . . . be able to come in?' he asked.

He held the flowers out, and she gave a half-smile as she took them.

'Sure,' she said, and let him through into the kitchen. The house smelled overwhelmingly of nail polish, but Seaton was too relieved that she'd let him in to say anything. 'These are amazing . . . thank you,' his daughter added, and he felt a strange note of pleasure in having given her something that she actually liked.

'Look,' he said, hovering awkwardly while she retreated to the kitchen to fill a vase with water. 'I understand why you've not wanted to talk to me. I just wanted to make sure you knew how . . . how sorry I am about what I said.' He cleared his throat. 'I should probably explain why I did. It was more about Philip than anything else.' He couldn't help the pleading tone that crept into his voice. 'He's always been so incredibly supportive of me, in every way. At difficult times in my life. And we're . . . close. We've always been close.' He gave a frustrated sigh. 'I felt like I'd let him down. And I was so busy thinking about that that I then let *you* down, and much more badly.'

Anna fiddled with the flowers. He found himself wishing, intensely, that he knew her better. That he could read the nuances of her expressions. He didn't know whether she was angry with him, or sad for him, or just taking this in.

It felt like a long time before she said, 'I guess I understand. It's . . . sometimes there are people who get under your skin.'

Seaton found himself skewered by the reality of that, and wanting to tell her that it was true of family, too. Not just of

Philip Sedgewick. But in the end, he said, 'Yes, I suppose so.' Then he cleared his throat and added, 'You know, I really don't think – at all – that you're doing this for yourself. I think it's admirable, trying to find out the truth about Holly. It's the right thing to do.'

Anna nodded at him and took a small breath. 'Thanks, Dad. And for the dress and the hair and the make-up.' She pulled a face. 'I was about to have a breakdown about affording everything, and you saved me.'

Seaton felt that same sensation he'd felt when this had all started: the unique, aching joy of being able to do something for his daughter. 'I . . . I know you don't like to accept things from me, after I wasn't there for you . . .'

Anna blinked. 'I . . . what made you think that?'

There was a long moment in which they stared at each other, and then Seaton said, 'After . . . your mother told me you didn't want my help. She said it was a pride thing. I . . .'

Anna turned away from him. 'I have honestly no idea where she got that,' she said with a choked laugh. 'Maybe she said we shouldn't take things from you and I agreed with her because I'm a people-pleasing idiot, but . . . I will tell you now I have zero pride when it comes to you feeling like you want to help out.'

It felt as though he'd been struck. Or as though he'd discovered that the sky was the floor and the floor the sky.

He could have done so much . . . for all this time.

'I always wanted to help,' he said. It was all he could find to say.

'That's good,' Anna replied.

Seaton felt keenly aware that they could have hugged. That any other father and daughter would have done and that it was probably the healthy thing to do.

Also, that the idea of actually doing it made him want to run right out of the door.

The two of them managed to nod it out, instead, and Seaton realised he could cover the awkwardness by pulling out the Roederer.

'I thought . . . we might as well have a glass. To toast everything you're doing, and have done.'

Anna grinned at him and ran for the cupboard with what looked like relief. 'I guess it'll be good for the nerves,' she called over her shoulder.

'Is there . . . anything I could help with in practical terms?' he asked as he removed the foil with care. 'Over the next few days?'

Anna paused on her way back to the table with the glasses. 'Well, there's one thing you *could* do, if you don't mind a little breaking and entering . . .'

They spent twenty minutes planning a heist on Ryan Jaffett's room, fuelled by pre-dinner champagne.

By the time Seaton left it was with a feeling of buzzing warmth that was only in part down to the champagne. By far the greatest part of it was feeling that he and Anna were finally going to be a proper father and daughter to each other.

38. Seaton

Wednesday, 25 June – two days after the ball

The relatives' room was deathly quiet. Seaton had been here for an hour and a half now, waiting uselessly for something to happen. For something to do.

Right up until eleven thirty, he'd paced fractiously around, trying to think of some way he might make himself useful and wanting to rail against the lack of communication from any of the officers here since his initial interview.

But then, having checked his phone for the hundredth time or more, he suddenly realised what the time meant. That more than thirty-six hours had now passed. More than thirty-six hours since anyone had seen Anna alive.

And something in him untethered itself.

They aren't going to find her, he thought.

He felt as though his legs had lost solidity. He grabbed for one of the chairs and sat in it, but it felt like sitting on the deck of a boat. The whole room seemed to be heaving and rolling.

Why didn't you love her like you should have done?

Nineteen wasted years. More than that, really. Anna's whole lifetime wasted, barely knowing her, when he might have been a real father to her. And that tantalising hope that he might finally have her in his life . . . it had been all there was. All there would be.

He pulled his phone out and through the fractured lens of tears he found the photo album he'd saved. The one titled 'Anna'.

He searched through the photos he'd kept of her. Those last images of her May Ball dress. Of the two of them at the cricket match. Of lunches and dinners.

Images that she'd sent him to show him what she was up to. Sometimes in the clothes of her assumed characters, sometimes at work events, and, going back, some with Reid. And then, beyond that, photographs of Anna back in the US. Images of her dorm room and of her on campus at Columbia. Images of her at regattas and, before that, at high-school proms and barbecues.

The images grew sparser as he scrolled back. Her mother hadn't liked sending him photos, though he had persisted in asking. And back when she'd been in Cambridge with both of them, as a child, the photographs had been on his big digital camera instead. Photographs that he'd printed and framed or put into albums.

The very last photograph he had of Anna on here was of her as a six-year-old. He knew the date it had been taken: 14 August 2006. Eight days after Carina had fled to Coney Island with her. He knew, because he had been frantic with fear for his daughter and unable to believe that she was well until he saw it.

But there she'd been, six-year-old Anna, grinning agreeably at the camera, with a smudge of chocolate frosting on her cheek from the doughnut she was in the midst of consuming. Carefree and happy and, by the looks of it, missing him not at all.

You could have gone straight out there to see her, he thought, now. *You could have asked her what she wanted and fought for her.*

But he hadn't. He hadn't been that man. He'd been too willing to feel rejected, and ashamed, and as though he deserved for his daughter to move on.

He was still looking at that photo and willing himself to

somehow have been a different man when Reid opened the door to the relatives' room and said, 'I need your help.'

Seaton straightened up, startled all over again by the force of this man; this man who he'd thought dogged and slow and unimaginative. How was he so determined? So energised? When he must, of all people, know that there was no hope now?

But Seaton found himself putting his phone away and pretending to be just as positive. Just as energetic.

'Of course,' he said. 'What do you need help with?'

'I need to find Esther Thomas,' Reid said. 'Urgently. Her college tells us she's here in London with her mother. And I thought you might be the man to tell us where the two of them would go.'

Urgently . . . The word cut through to Seaton, and he wondered whether there was some chance for Anna after all. If there was the tiniest chance, then he was going to step up.

'I have a friend at the UN,' he said. 'Give me a moment.'

Five minutes later he hung up the phone with a ghost of a feeling of optimism.

'She's at the Francis Crick Institute,' he told Reid, who had been pacing in the hallway. 'Her mother is on a visit there and dragged her along. Bizarre thing to do on May Week, but Clarisse is renowned for being a tiger mother.'

'You're an absolute marvel,' Reid told him. And then, after a beat, he said, 'I'd like you to come along to see her, if you don't mind.'

'It'd be a pleasure,' Seaton said, gathering up his briefcase and phone as though this were simply a favour to a friend and not about the life of his daughter.

They were at the Francis Crick Institute within twenty minutes. Reid had chosen an Uber over the tube, a choice Seaton was inclined to agree with. The man was looking quite unsteady again, and Seaton asked him quietly as they climbed in whether he'd taken another dose of painkillers.

'I'll . . .' Reid began to protest, and then stopped. 'No, I should. You're right.'

He reached into his jacket pocket, and Seaton pulled his insulated water bottle out of his briefcase and handed it to him. Reid gave a small smile of thanks and took the tablets quickly. It didn't seem to have done much to improve his focus by the time the Uber spewed them out at the Crick, however. Reid had spent the whole journey staring into space. But Seaton had hopes that things would improve as they worked their way into his bloodstream.

He's worked something out, he thought.

Though for some reason he couldn't bring himself to ask, directly, what it was, or whether it meant Anna was alive.

Seaton took the lead as they approached the reception desk. He explained that he was joining Clarisse Thomas for part of her trip, and the two receptionists bent over backwards to help him work out where to go.

'She's currently with Dr Langton,' one of them said, as their two visitor passes emerged from the little photo printer on her desk. 'Up on the South Side.'

Seaton smiled at her, feeling less of a failure at least than he had at the police station twenty-four hours ago. This was his domain, a place where he was both known and respected. He wasn't going to be told not to be ridiculous and ejected onto the street.

Seaton took the two neatly encased passes. 'I know where that is. Many thanks.'

He led Reid over to the lifts, trying to look businesslike.

'That was . . . smooth,' Reid said, appreciatively, as they waited for the lift. 'Glad I brought you along.'

'I suppose I have the equivalent of a badge here,' Seaton told him, with a small smile.

They were up on the third floor in less than a minute. It was hot up here. Sunlight was streaming in through the windows of most of the South Side offices. A few others had their blinds closed, presumably so their occupants could escape the heat and the glare.

Seaton walked ahead down the hallway until he found a door marked Dr Manisha Langton and was gratified to see that both Clarisse and Esther were inside. They were with a young woman who was sitting behind the desk, and a young man who was presumably PR for the Crick.

Seaton had yet to meet Esther Thomas in person, though he'd met her mother a few times. He was taken aback by how much she was the mirror of her mother: the tailored trousers; the dark hair in a very French haircut; the subtle lipstick; the glowing skin. A mirror in every way except for her expression. Where Clarisse was smiling with absolute poise as she listened to something Manisha Langton was saying, Esther's expression was quietly, soulfully sad.

He might have felt for her if he hadn't been here about Anna.

If you've dared to hurt her . . . he thought.

Seaton tapped on the door and opened it, feeling a strange little quirk of satisfaction at the way Clarisse's smile dropped at the sight of him.

'I'm so sorry to interrupt,' he said, earnestly, 'but the police here just need a quick word with Esther about when she last saw my daughter.'

He gave Esther a small, encouraging smile, for everyone else's benefit, and let Reid come in and shake everyone by the hand.

'Ah . . . of course,' Clarisse said. 'So sorry about this. Seaton is – his daughter went missing on Monday night. Anna is a very good friend of my daughter's, so Esther is hoping to help them. It's been incredibly worrying for everyone, but we hope she'll turn up very soon.' She slid an arm round Esther and then said, 'Do go and talk to them, darling. I know how much it means to you.'

'Thank you,' Esther said, and to Seaton's surprise, Esther looked, if anything, relieved.

With the door closed behind them, Seaton led them to one of the vertiginous walkways across the lobby which had clusters of low, grey, almost spherical chairs. As soon as the three of them were sitting, Esther asked, 'Has anyone heard anything?'

'Not from Anna, as yet,' Reid said.

'She's . . . your daughter?' Esther pursed her lips slightly and looked towards Seaton.

'That's right,' Seaton said.

'We have a few very important questions for you,' Reid said. 'Which are . . . related to Anna's disappearance.'

'I'd still like to help,' Esther said after a moment. 'Even if she wasn't really a student or . . . well, a friend.'

'Thank you,' Reid said. 'I actually wanted to ask you about your secret relationship last year.' He gave her a steady look. 'When did Holly Moore find out that you were dating your friend's father?'

Seaton hadn't been ready for this question. He was aware that he was now staring at Reid and had to consciously turn towards Esther again. She looked white. Sick. Awful.

'How did you know?' Esther asked. And then she looked towards Seaton, desperately. 'Did he tell you? He told me he'd never, never say anything.'

'I'm sorry that this is so uncomfortable,' Reid said, saving Seaton from having to admit he'd known nothing about this.

That he still wasn't sure who they were talking about and didn't want to admit to himself the thought that was creeping into the back of his mind. 'This isn't about exposing you or making you feel bad. It's about establishing why Holly died.'

Esther's look went from anxious to openly horrified.

'I . . . You don't think I hurt her? I didn't! I didn't do anything!'

'Please,' Reid said. 'Just tell us how she found out.'

Esther's head drooped. 'All right. It . . . it was probably only a week before she died when . . .' She cleared her throat. 'I never meant to get in the way of their marriage. Really, truly. I just . . . I fell for him.'

'It had been going on for a while, hadn't it?' Reid asked, quietly.

'Yes,' she agreed, almost inaudibly. 'For a year. Since the summer at the end of first year.'

'And you'd been careful,' Reid said.

'Yes,' Esther said. 'We only met up when Marcie was away. But then I managed to lose my necklace somewhere in the bed, and as I was trying to find it James arrived back home and I had to just run and hide until Philip could smuggle me out.'

No, Seaton thought. *No, no, no.*

Esther sighed. 'We were incredibly lucky, actually, when it happened. It wasn't actually *my* necklace. So when Marcie got back later and *did* find it she was confused, and went to ask James whose it was. He recognised it as Holly's, so Marcie just assumed they'd been . . . you know, borrowing their room.' She swallowed, very noisily. 'But when he returned it to Holly . . . well, obviously Holly figured it out. She wore the necklace out on the Friday night and when she caught me looking at it she gave me a look like . . . like she knew, and she thought . . . I don't know. Terrible things.'

Esther closed her eyes, and Seaton had a fierce wish for that to be it. For Esther to stop talking entirely. But Reid seemed to want to push for more.

'Were there . . . particular stakes, for Philip, if Marcie found out about it?' he asked.

Esther looked startled. 'Yes, of course there were. Philip would have left her if . . .' She looked between them. 'The money is all hers. Her working-class dad sold his dotcom company for a hundred million and set her and her brother up for life, while Philip's line of ancestors had run the family fortunes dry.' Esther blinked a few times and said unsteadily, 'She owns almost all of the property he runs. If he'd been caught with me, he'd have been destitute, and . . . and I'd have been disinherited. The two of us would have had nothing.'

Seaton turned away from her. How could any of this be true? How could Philip, his friend, who had for so long seemed absolutely loyal to Marcie, be . . . this person?

'Did Philip find out that Holly knew?' Reid asked.

'Yes,' Esther said, and her voice came out like a sob. She glanced around, as though someone might be watching her. Judging her. 'I – I was an idiot, and I told him Holly had worked it out. He – he went so quiet . . . and then he said we needed to end it. Us. That he couldn't do that to his family.' She paused, and tried to wipe at her face, but big, fat tears began escaping from her eyes to roll down her cheeks. 'So although we still . . . he still loves me, we haven't . . . been together.' She looked away, suddenly. 'You know, I . . . I actually don't know if he does love me. I thought he did. He still messages when he's alone, and he calls me sometimes . . .' She drew a shaky breath. 'But actually, I don't know. Because sometimes I feel like it's all just a game. He'll say things that are just . . . cruel.'

Reid was nodding, slowly, while Seaton was trying to imagine his friend – his oldest, oldest friend – doing any of this. It was hard not to tell Esther to stop. Not to hate her a little. All while a huge part of him felt heartbroken for her.

'But then Ryan Jaffett found out?' Reid asked.

Esther jolted out of her sadness. She looked at him with wide, frightened eyes and then she took a breath and nodded. 'Yes. It was at the ball, last year. We were both drunk and Philip suddenly asked me if he'd made the right decision. Of course, the moment he was sober he was back to telling me we couldn't be anything to each other.' She gave a twisted, bitter smile. 'Ryan was being photographed in that stupid car with Kit, so that one moment of regret ended up being caught in the background. I didn't know he'd captured it until last week, when he turned up at my room and told me I had to support him or he'd show everyone. Ruin my life and Philip's.' She closed her eyes, and added in a whisper, 'It's all going to happen now anyway, isn't it? What will James think? Oh my god.'

'I'm sorry,' Reid said with feeling. 'But I don't think you're the one who should feel any shame.'

Esther gave him a very cynical look, and Seaton understood why. It didn't matter that Esther had been eighteen and a vulnerable student when this had started; she would be judged as The Other Woman anyway.

As Seaton watched she sat back and seemed to start processing some of this beyond her own guilt. 'Why are you asking me about all this? What has this got to do with . . . Anna?'

'Anna was trying to find out why Holly died,' Reid said. 'Finding out what she knew is vital to finding her.'

'But why . . .?' She faltered, and then stared at him 'It can't have been Philip.'

'If Philip is involved in what happened to Holly, and what's happened to Anna,' Reid said, 'we need to know.' He paused, and then said, 'Sometimes people do things that seem crazy to protect the people they love.'

Seaton finally felt as though he'd caught on.

Reid wasn't accusing Philip of having murdered Holly.

He was accusing James.

39. Trinity May Ball

Monday, 23 June

The path Anna Sousa trod on the night of the May Ball was witnessed by dozens of people. Hundreds, in total, from all those present on the street or at the event. So many chances to stop what happened. To step in.

But many of those people barely noticed her. They had no real reason to dwell on a tall young woman in a black-and-silver dress amid so many glamorously dressed young students.

Others did notice. Their paths intersected at moments when the glamour of the evening had worn thin. Tiny points of time when things could have tipped in another direction, if they'd said something.

If they'd stepped forwards.

One of those was a first-year Pembroke Student named Dora Hu. Her boyfriend, a second-year Trinity maths student named Nicky, had bought them a pair of VIP tickets to the May Ball, and she had been nervously excited about this night for the last four months.

Dora spent five hours getting ready and in that time reapplied her make-up twice and took the blue silk dress off once to steam creases out of it. In the end, she felt beautiful enough to go. In fact, she felt more beautiful than she'd ever felt. Which might just be enough.

She walked through streets that had been transformed: between scatters of students wearing tuxedos, cocktail dresses and huge, princess ballgowns, as if a series of ghosts of bygone ages had been resurrected for the evening. All these fairy-tale figures were walking with an only slightly self-conscious air across flagstones and cobbles, and between eclectic buildings; past sweet shops and bollards, and gargoyles crafted hundreds of years ago. It seemed to Dora like they didn't need to touch the ground. Any of them.

Well, any of them except her.

Because although Dora at first felt part of it, she quickly began to feel the tightness of her strappy heeled shoes. Less than halfway to Trinity they were digging into her feet hard enough to hurt and she had to stop and sit on the wall of King's College to try to loosen them a little.

By the time she'd arrived at the ball, where the VIP queue was ready to enter, Nicky already in place close to the front, she was ready to cry. How could she last a whole night with this pain?

But Nicky was waiting for her with a smile of huge pride, and she couldn't ruin his night. So Dora kissed him and moved inside as if she didn't hurt at all, past the ticket desk and into the wide expanse of the Great Court. And she nearly forgot her painful feet at the sight of a huge, red-and-gold hot-air balloon sitting stationary at the centre, its basket tied down but with the balloon lifting to strain at the ropes.

The very first students in the queue were being ushered into it to take photographs, and Dora beamed up at Nicky.

'That is so cool.'

But she was drowned out by another voice close by.

'Hot-air balloon! Fuck yes,' a very tall, very muscular red-haired student just ahead of them was yelling. Dora felt Nicky – who was slim and shy – edge towards her a little.

She found herself watching the red-haired student after that, on high alert for signs that he might get rowdy. She was still, a year into being at this place, heart-thumpingly scared of drunk, boisterous men getting out of control. The redhead's little group had that aura. They'd brought bottles of champagne and were opening them and commenting on everything loudly.

But a little later, as the queue moved on and the redhead decided to throw a cork at another student, the other tall boy with them drew him aside. He seemed to be trying to calm him down. To tell him not to behave like that.

'Yeah, well,' the red-haired guy suddenly said, 'I'm not the one dating a fucking liar.'

Nicky started trying to talk to her then, clearly not listening to the conversation as she was, but Dora put a finger to her lips and leaned in. She caught only a low, intense, snippet: '. . . serious, Ryan . . . chance to actually talk to her and stop judging her.'

But then one of the others was waving, and the one talking to red-haired Ryan turned and was smiling at a newcomer: a blonde in a dramatic black-and-silver dress, wearing heels much higher than Dora's but with a pair of hot-pink flats poking out of a handbag slung over her shoulder.

I should have brought some of those, Dora thought, and then she found herself watching, transfixed, as the blonde girl put her arms round the peacemaker and kissed him. And although the two of them looked beautiful, in a Hollywood-perfect way, Dora saw a drop of sadness on the boy's face and a look of worry on the girl's.

Maybe she cheated, Dora thought. And she kept close to them and tried her best to find out if that was true while they slowly moved towards the entrance to the ball itself. But the group spoke only about plans for the night, and how beautiful the girls looked, and then – at the gateway – they drifted off into the night.

Dora realised that she'd been ignoring Nicky and that his expression was hesitant. Hurt.

'Sorry,' she said. 'I thought I knew one of them. I don't think I do.' And then she slid her arm through his. 'Let's go and find something to drink.'

And then there was Patrick Offerly, a part-time psychology student and Bao Bun caterer who might have said something. Might have reached out.

At a little after nine Patrick witnessed a conversation between Anna and the bodyguard, Ned. The conversation took place right outside Patrick's Bao Bun van during a quiet patch. Most of the ball's attendees were at that point jumping around to the Miley Cyrus tribute act in the main tent, so Patrick had tidied up a bit and was now leaning on the counter to people-watch for a while.

It was the first time Patrick had really had any downtime, but he'd already noticed an older man in Ray-Bans. The guy had spent the last few minutes standing back watching a group of students on the dodgems, his hands folded in front of him and his head moving back and forth. He was close to the van, but his back was turned to it. He was definitely not a student or a fellow, and definitely not interested in food.

He looked, to Patrick, like a security guard, but he wasn't wearing the black top and radio mic that the security guys were all wearing tonight. Patrick wondered whether he might be there to watch someone in particular.

While Patrick was trying to work him out a student in a striking black-and-silver dress who'd been standing close to the dodgems walked across the black matting in their direction. She looked relatively sober still. She came to stand alongside the Ray-Bans guy, moving out of his sightline – it was restricted by the serving hatch – but still only a few feet away.

'How's it looking, Ned?' she asked him, clearly audible over the van's generator. She was American, he thought. East Coast. It gave him a pang of nostalgia for the gap year he'd spent running youth camps over in Saratoga. Great kids, time outdoors and no bullshit food van to run. 'Any murdery people about?'

'That's the trouble,' the Ray-Bans guy – Ned – answered. 'Murdery people look like anyone, because pretty much anyone could murder.'

Definitely personal security, Patrick thought.

'Huh,' the girl with the silver-and-black dress answered. 'I don't know about that. I don't think *I* could.'

'You could,' Ned said, firmly. 'Given enough of a reason. Nobody finds taking a life easy, but if enough people are depending on you . . .'

That interested Patrick. It sounded like this guy had served. Didn't a lot of special forces guys become bodyguards?

He wondered whether he was this girl's bodyguard, but he seemed to be watching the dodgems still.

'Oh, I get you,' the girl said, lightly. 'I just meant I actually couldn't. Like, zero competence at fighting and a high likelihood of stabbing myself instead of the target.'

The bodyguard – Ned – sounded like he was smiling as he said, 'That's a fair point.'

There was a loud laugh from the students at the dodgems, and something in the security guy's expression changed. He could see it even from a fragment of his profile.

One of them, then, Patrick thought. *He's looking out for one of them. Is it a celebrity?*

'You like him, don't you?' the girl said next.

There was a pause before Ned said, 'He's my responsibility, but he's also easy to like. Which is nice.'

Patrick studied the group on the dodgems. There were

three boys, one watching and two riding around who were clearly part of the same group. Patrick found it hard to make their faces out, but he didn't immediately recognise any of them. Maybe he should take a photo. Ask some people later.

There should be a Shazam for celebrities, he thought. *Tap on their face and it tells you what they've been in.*

He found himself jumping slightly when the girl said, in a suddenly really intense tone, 'I'm scared something's going to happen tonight. Nothing feels right. Don't let him get hurt.'

Patrick could feel his heart in his neck. Was there really some threat? Was this guy Ned here because something might happen?

The dodgems were stopping now, and the girl moved off towards the friends piling out of them. Patrick saw the security guy, Ned, watching her intently.

Three of the other students from the dodgems approached the van, and Patrick realised he needed to straighten up and start serving them. But he could feel sweat on his skin as he filled their orders.

Are the rest of us safe? he thought, looking at the wide-eyed, inebriated faces below him. *Should I be telling someone?*

But when he tried to spot Ned or the girl again there was no sign of them. They'd moved off somewhere and his queue of customers built steadily after that to the point where he had no time to worry about anything.

By the time he thought of the girl again it was almost dawn and no threat had emerged. None that Patrick had seen, at least.

A while later, there was Nicola.

She was a thirty-year-old oncologist who'd come with a group of former student friends who she wasn't sure she really liked all that much any more. It was an uncomfortable realisation.

While she felt as though her life had been thrown into stark relief by her work, her priorities winnowed down to the big ones, these former friends seemed impossibly frivolous and melodramatic. They still talked about the same things they had as undergrads: about shagging and drinking and holidays, and when they weren't doing that they'd make glancing, judgemental remarks on other women's outfits or sex lives that were, frankly, just spiteful.

Nicola had escaped them all with the excuse of needing a soft drink and was now standing in the queue for the bar closest to the music tent. She'd decided she'd string the experience out for as long as she could stomach it and then maybe just feign an emergency and run away home.

It was a shame, though. The place was beautiful, and there were music acts she wanted to see. She'd hoped it would feel freeing, this night away from work and her small background worries about what her sister was doing with her life.

Maybe she'd just lose the friends. Try experiencing the ball on her own. It wouldn't be the first thing she'd managed alone.

Turning to watch the Ferris wheel, she saw a tall girl in a black-and-silver dress escorting her clearly very drunk friend in her direction.

'I don't want to,' the smaller, dark-haired girl was saying, pushing her friend away.

'Well, we need to hydrate so we can keep going,' the taller one was saying as she brought them both to a stop close to Nicola. They were clearly joining the queue.

Nicola gave the taller one a sympathetic grin. She'd always been the sober one at parties. Somehow always the mum.

In that strange way of very drunk people the other girl

suddenly went from angry to affectionate, putting her arms up round her friend and pulling her close.

'You need to stay here,' she mumbled.

'Of course I will,' the tall one said. 'Are you having fun?'

'No,' the smaller one replied, truculently. 'Everyone I like turns out to be a fucking arsehole.'

She lurched away, almost colliding with a couple trying to join the queue behind her.

The tall one started to apologise to the other couple, but her friend hadn't seemed to notice. She was readying herself for a tirade.

'You're not my friend, are you?' she said, her eyes glittering in the fairground lights. 'The others think you're just lying about your rowing stuff, but it's not that, is it? You're a fake. A total fake.'

Nicola found herself staring at the two of them, realising it was socially unacceptable but absolutely unable to look away.

The tall one gave her a slightly panicked look before stepping towards her friend, and Nicola tried to grimace in a way that said she wasn't believing any of it. All the while wanting the dark-haired girl to keep going, because this sounded *a lot.*

'Esther . . . why would I lie about rowing?' the tall one said, sounding confused.

'Fuck knows,' brunette Esther said, unsteadily. 'I guess because it's part of the act? Whoever you are, you aren't Aria Lauder.'

'Why . . .?'

'Don't side-step,' Esther snapped. 'Mummy decided to engineer a meeting with Aria's brother, and his sister is in fucking Maine. In rehab. Not here, and not you.'

Jesus, Nicola thought.

It was like watching reality TV.

There was a pause, and then the tall woman said, 'I'm sorry, you're right. Have you . . . worked out why I'm here?'

The smaller one – Esther – laughed, and then faltered. 'I . . . what are you . . .?'

'I'm here because of Holly,' the girl who wasn't Aria said, quietly. 'I came to try to work out what happened to her. Why you lost your friend.'

Esther gaped at her, and Nicola knew she was gaping, too. 'What do you mean?'

'There are reasons to think she was murdered,' the tall one said, her face – when Nicola glanced at it – strangely calm in the colourful lights from the dodgems and the music tent. 'If you know anything that could help . . .'

Esther looked as though someone had pulled all the supports away from her. She swayed and her hands reached out to try to find something to hold on to. Nicola instinctively lifted her hands, but Esther took a few steps to grab the edge of the bar and lean against it.

What is going on? Nicola thought. Fleetingly, she wondered if this was some kind of an immersive experience. But she knew – *knew* – that it wasn't. That this was real.

The two of them were now talking in lower voices that were too quiet for her to make out, and Nicola took a small, subtle step towards them, then smiled at the couple behind her in the universally recognised sign of someone giving up their place in a queue.

God, this is pathetic, she thought.

But she couldn't *not* hear the rest of this.

The next thing she heard was Esther shouting, 'What the fuck is wrong with you? You're just here to hurt all of us. When we – when I – when all we did was try to be your friend.' Her voice was shaking with rage and she shoved herself upright, away from the bar.

'Esther,' the taller girl said, trying to calm her.

'Don't talk to me,' Esther spat. 'Don't fucking talk to me. You're a blood-sucking ghoul.'

And she rushed away, into the crowds on the bridge.

Nicola thought, fleetingly, about going after her. About offering her comfort. She wasn't sure whether she wanted to help, or whether she just couldn't bear not to find out more.

But it would be hard to catch her, and she didn't look in a mood to trust anyone. Whereas maybe the taller girl would tell her more.

She watched the expression on the blonde one's face and then felt as though *she* was the ghoul here. The young woman just looked . . . lost. Stricken. Awful.

And Nicola felt her curiosity collapse under the weight of simple empathy. Because whatever that had been about, it had clearly left this girl feeling wretched.

She was on the verge of offering to get the girl a drink when a couple appeared and her expression shifted.

She knows them, Nicola thought.

They must have been in their forties or fifties: clearly well moneyed and well preserved. And there was an aura of warmth and comfort about them that made even independent Nicola feel a draw towards them.

The woman stepped past Nicola, leaving a scent of roses behind her, and wrapped the tall girl in a warm hug.

She's got support, Nicola thought, nodding to herself. *She doesn't need you.*

And she turned her back on them and began to queue once again for her mocktail.

At 10.21 a Trinity English fellow named Martin White extracted himself from the main music tent, where the Chemical

Brothers were playing their headline set. He'd rushed away from his slow-moving group of academic friends to make it to the front and raised his arms as they'd entered the stage, full of nostalgia for his teenage years.

It had taken him probably fifteen minutes to remember that he'd never actually liked jumping around to music, and after twenty-five minutes of gritting his teeth and trying not to swear when his feet got stamped on he'd decided it was time to leave it to the more energetic.

He was now clammy with sweat, his white shirt soaked through and his tux prickling at the neck. It was barely any cooler out here, but it was at least quiet. Most people were either in one of the tents or on the rides, or clustered at the various bars.

Martin pulled his phone out to message his little group. They would probably be up on the lawn already, waiting patiently for the start of the fireworks. They none of them liked to rush.

He glanced up as another figure emerged from the tent, this one hurrying, and he found himself watching her. There was something particularly frantic in the way she was walking, one arm across her body and her head lowered towards her phone screen.

He watched her lift the phone to her ear, her feet moving compulsively, and then saw an unmistakable drop in her expression. He heard her swear before she hurriedly scrolled on the phone again and made another call.

Lost her friends, maybe? he thought. *Or something valuable?*

She kept holding on, phone to her ear, clearly listening to it ring. He heard her say, quietly, 'Come on, Reid.' And then her face fell and she looked . . . bereft.

Hmm. Maybe an argument with a lover, he thought.

But then a baby-faced young man a little taller than she was appeared out of the tent and put a hand on her arm in what looked a very relationship-type move.

'Hey,' the boyfriend said. 'What's up?'

'I . . . Nat isn't answering,' the girl with the phone said, turning to him. 'My fucking coach is ghosting me. Why did he tell Ryan he doesn't know me? He's dropped me, hasn't he? He's fucking dropped me.'

'I'm sure it doesn't . . . Ryan probably got confused,' the boyfriend said, soothing her.

'I can't do this again,' the young woman said, her voice raw. 'I can't fail at all this again.'

Martin felt more than a little uncomfortable at how emotional she was, but curious, too. It felt like a puzzle he wanted an answer to, so he kept listening.

The young woman pulled away from her boyfriend and started scrolling on her phone once more.

'Hey,' the boyfriend said, gently, tugging on the arm that held the phone. 'In the unlikely event that he's been stupid enough to drop you, you'll fight back. You're Aria Lauder. You're not going to let some guy tell you what you're worth.'

And in spite of his former cool interest Martin felt an ache at that little speech. It reminded him immediately and powerfully of Fionnan, and how he'd once been there to comfort him. How he'd once been right by Martin's side, against the world . . . before work opportunities became more important.

He found himself watching with a sense of nostalgic jealousy as the girl – Aria – looked up at her boyfriend, her eyes very wide and very trusting. The young man reached out and gently prised the phone off her.

'Let's put this away, huh?' he said, and tucked it into the handbag she had over her shoulder. His gaze moved past her then, towards Martin, and Martin looked away. He felt like some kind of a voyeur, despite their decision to play out their little scene in front of him.

He found himself thinking about that speech of the boy's as he walked away. Memories of Fionnan took the place of his brief concern for the young woman, and he was too busy yearning for someone to look out for him to worry that the young man might have been controlling her.

The person who came, perhaps, the closest to doing something – to stepping in – was a waitress named Rachel Skoulding. She'd been working for four hours by the time the crowds started assembling along the riverbank for the fireworks display and she was really ready for a break.

Handing out champagne at the start had been fine. She'd actually kind of enjoyed smiling at everyone and welcoming them to the event – even when she had to keep going and refilling her tray or holding it steady when people grabbed at glasses and spilled some.

It was all this clearing up of glasses she didn't really like. Trying to squeeze past students while they seemed oblivious and pick up the sticky, half-empty glassware from the weird places everyone had stashed them.

She'd thought there would be more glamour to the job, if she was honest. Everyone had told her it'd be 'an experience', including her older sister, who worked for the college. She just hoped getting to wander around and eat stuff on her break would make it worth it.

She was clearing glasses from the cabaret tent when she caught sight of Anna. She didn't know her, of course, and she never heard her real name spoken.

To Rachel, Anna was at first just the silent one standing between a jubilantly affectionate brunette girl and a ridiculously handsome guy with floppy hair.

'Will you be OK, James?' the brunette was asking the handsome guy, her head against the blonde girl's arm. The brunette looked, Rachel thought critically, off her face on MDMA. 'With the minute's silence and . . . everything?'

Rachel was listening in at this point because she wanted an excuse to talk to the handsome guy. To this James. But after she'd positioned herself for a proper look she found herself staring. And not at him.

The tall blonde woman in the silver-and-black dress looked . . . terrified.

She was sheet-white, and standing absolutely stock-still between them, looking like she wasn't on the same planet. The person she was looking at – *staring* at – was an older guy across from them.

Rachel retrieved the glass she'd been bending to get and turned to look at the other guy. He looked . . . odd. Like he was in a film instead of just being one of the guests. He was maybe forty, but not bad-looking either, and clearly buff. His way of standing advertised that he worked out. And even though it was dark, he was wearing sunglasses.

Why's she scared of him? Rachel thought, her skin prickling.

But while she was trying to make sense of it two other guys came over. They were student age, and not threatening-looking, but they looked like they could handle themselves in a fight. She felt better, seeing them arrive.

If she's worried about this guy, they can look after her, she thought.

The blond newcomer slid his arm round the girl in the silver-and-black dress and said, 'OK, all set. Time for some fireworks.'

The group moved, blocking the silver-and-black figure from view. But Rachel could still hear it when the girl said, 'Is this how it happens? Is this how you murder someone in public?'

She felt her heart jerking at that. Why was she saying that? What was going on?

'What . . .? Are you OK, Aria?' It was the guy who'd put his arm round her. 'You look seriously out of it. Did you take something? Fucking hell, your pupils . . .'

Rachel glanced back towards the man with the sunglasses. He took a step forwards, and then stopped.

Did he . . . give her something?

'She needs some water, that's all.' It was a loud, firm comment. Surprisingly so, coming from James, the super-hot guy she'd first caught sight of. He'd seemed kind of shy, before. Her type. 'Come on, Aria,' he was saying now. 'I'll get you sorted out. You guys find us somewhere to stand.'

Rachel found herself frowning at them, watching as James looped the blonde girl's arm round his shoulder and started steering her away. She looked barely able to walk. She was leaning heavily against him, and when she briefly glanced back towards the guy in sunglasses it was with wide, terrified eyes.

She's definitely taken something, Rachel thought, feeling a shudder run down her spine. *Not party drugs, though. Unless she's just taken too much?*

She thought about stepping in. About telling them this woman needed help.

'Look, I should be the one taking care of her,' the blond guy said.

'Honestly, I want something to take my mind off the sodding fireworks,' James shot back. 'It'll take me five minutes to take her to get some water. Please.'

The blonde girl turned and grinned at the other guy. 'I'm OK. Don't need looking after. Just need a little H2O. See you in a second, Kit.'

OK, Rachel thought with a feeling of intense relief. *She's OK.*

The taller guy, Kit, seemed torn for a moment, but then gave her a nod and a smile.

'OK. Bring me back a champagne, will you, James?'

'On it,' James called, already leading the girl away.

Rachel watched them weave away across the grass, illuminated by the fairy lights and orb lights around the bar. And then they crossed the boundary of the lit area, and the two of them vanished into shadow.

40. Reid

Reid could tell that Seaton was both hurt and angry, but he wasn't sure whether it was aimed at him.

He knew he could have explained about Esther and Philip earlier to soften the blow, but he'd been afraid of what might happen if he'd started throwing accusations around without any proof. At the worst end of the spectrum, Seaton might have warned Philip. And if Anna was still alive, then the last thing he should do was to make Philip feel under threat.

Reid also hadn't been *completely* sure about Philip. There had still been a chance Esther had been having an affair with Kit's father, Roland. There was even a tiny chance of her boyfriend being Marcus Jaffett, who was apparently a known womaniser. Though he'd pretty much counted that out, given Ryan had been the one blackmailing everyone.

A very small part of him had even wondered, fleetingly, if the older man might be Seaton himself But every instinct he had about him had fought with that, and his instincts had been right.

So Seaton had ended up hearing the stark truth from Esther herself. Which had been undeniable proof, if not exactly kind.

But Reid didn't really have time to worry about the man's feelings, any more than he had time to worry for Esther Thomas. All Reid needed to know for sure was that neither of them would warn Philip about any of this.

And at that thought, he realised that somehow he'd ended up acting like Anna: putting a single objective above all the collateral damage. And strangely, the idea didn't trouble him at all.

He should probably still try with Seaton, though. As the lift doors closed on them, he said, 'I'm . . . sorry if this is all quite difficult.'

Seaton turned his head sharply away. 'Whatever there was between Philip and Esther . . . that doesn't mean he killed anyone. And it doesn't mean James did, either.'

Reid took a moment to gather himself as he stepped out of the lift at the ground floor.

'If you were James,' he said in a quiet, non-confrontational tone, 'and your mother found your girlfriend's necklace in her bed . . . what would your first thought be? If you *knew* that you'd never been in there with her?'

Seaton was silent for a moment and then said, 'I wouldn't assume anything. I'd ask her what it was doing there. And if he did, Holly would have just told him.'

'But we know from Cordelia and Kit that she didn't tell anyone,' Reid countered, still gently. 'Holly understood what it would have meant to tell. She understood the ramifications and the hurt it would cause. And maybe also what it would mean to the lifestyle she was getting to live.' He glanced at Seaton. 'She went to get advice from Kit about it before she said anything. Which means even if James did ask her, she hid the truth from him, and unintentionally let him think the very worst of her.'

Reid watched him. He could tell that Seaton was thinking all this through. And he was an intelligent man. He would inevitably think about James's attempts to stop Anna investigating. The apparent poisoning in his room, which must have been staged to make James seem innocent.

He can't have done any of it alone, Reid thought.

Which meant that Philip had to have known. He'd been trying to protect his son, perhaps in part out of overwhelming guilt for what he'd caused. And he was still trying to protect him now.

Seaton said nothing in reply. He walked ahead of Reid through the security barrier and out onto Midland Road. And then, without turning or waiting, he walked away.

Reid watched him go with a momentary feeling of sadness. It would have been good to have Seaton's help for the next stage. But it didn't really change anything. He knew where he needed to go.

41. James

Monday, 23 June

Aria was out of it. Really out of it. Muttering to him about dragons chasing her down before turning to him with huge eyes and promising she'd never tell anyone anything. Whatever they'd given her had done its work.

They stumbled and swayed their way away from the group, darkness coming down over them like a cloak.

James gave a half-smile. *Almost home and dry.*

But then there were jogging footsteps and a call came from behind him.

James rounded on his bodyguard with a sigh and waved a hand towards him as if he were drunk, and not inwardly screaming with tension.

'Sod off, Ned,' he said. 'We're only going five feet that way.' He pulled Aria – or whatever it was she was really called – closer towards him and gave Ned an appealing look. He dropped his voice. 'Can we have a couple of minutes of space, you know?'

Ned blinked at him, clearly surprised by this turn of events. It made James cringe, seeing the reaction. He hated the idea that he was being seen as some kind of a cheat, but it was better than the alternative.

So much better.

Tomorrow, he'd just have to convince Ned that he'd been drunk and confused. That the anniversary had made him emotional.

Ned started to back away, and James gave him a grateful grin and then turned Aria's stumbling form round once again. He knew where he needed to take her. He'd thought this through hours ago, because sometimes you had to plan for everything going to shit.

He was leading her past the edge of the college, between the buildings and the river. They passed the platform for the punts – the last few people were cramming themselves into boats to watch the fireworks display from the river – and drew her onwards.

He saw the cobbles in front of him light up in flickering red, and a moment later an explosion sounded.

The fireworks, seven minutes late and absolutely when he needed them.

In the sudden illumination he could see the unglamorous side exit to the college: the big refuse bins and the gate beyond. It was flanked by two security guards and the St John's Ambulance crew. All there, ready and waiting for disaster.

He felt his heart thumping as he approached, remembering walking down here a year ago. How they'd wheeled Holly's lifeless form towards the open gates.

'James,' Anna said, 'there are snakes in the grass.'

'No snakes,' he said as soothingly as he could. 'And no grass. It's just the drugs. Look. We're on paving slabs.'

They were within clear sight of the four staff members – two security and two ambulance – when Anna turned and said, 'You can't take me to Addenbrooke's. They'll find me. You have to hide me, James.'

'It's all right,' he said. 'I've got a plan.' And he turned and looked at her with a level gaze. 'I just need you to be quiet and go along with it, all right? Just act normal, and I'll get you out of here.'

Anna's pupils were huge in the explosions of light from

above. What the fuck had they given her? Was she going to be able to hold this together?

But she nodded at him, and he smiled.

'OK. Here we go.'

He wrapped a steadying arm round her and approached the first of the St John's Ambulance crew. A bubble of hope rose in him as he realised he recognised him. He'd been here the year before. He'd seen Holly. Spoken to James.

He'd remember him, wouldn't he? People remembered tragedies like that.

'I . . . I'm sorry,' James said, giving him a shaky smile. 'I'm really sorry, I . . . I don't know if you remember, but my – my girlfriend drowned last year. While the – the fireworks were on. I thought I could do it, be here and remember her . . . but I can't. I need to go. We need to go. Now.'

The sympathy and understanding in the man's eyes made him feel a little sick. What kind of a person was he? Really?

But he felt nothing but relief as the first-aider went to talk to the security team, who nodded and opened the gate for him.

'Thank you,' James said, doing his utmost to hold Aria upright.

They smiled at him as he walked through the gate; all four of them smiled, with the kind of expression he'd got used to over the past year. Sympathetic. Pitying. Ultimately helpless.

And James responded with his own carefully crafted expression of long-suffering pain as he led Aria out into the night.

42. Seaton

Wednesday, 25 June

Seaton was trying to outpace the feeling of sick sadness that was threatening to overwhelm him, but he was failing. He'd been walking the streets of London for a good half-hour, at speed, and yet it was all right there with him.

How was he supposed to outrun this? The possibility that he'd not only lost his daughter but also the one person who'd been there for almost forty years?

Philip isn't a murderer, he thought, furiously. *He hasn't got a violent bone in his body. And neither has James.*

But at that second thought he found himself floundering. Did he really *know* that about James? He knew that he was sensitive. That he felt things deeply. That he had loved Holly with a fierce intensity and that he'd been in pieces ever since she'd died.

Could he really have killed her that night? Out of bitter hurt and humiliation?

Seaton imagined James dwelling and dwelling on the necklace. Waiting for Holly to explain it. He imagined that intense love turning into a form of hatred.

And if James *had* done it, what might Philip have done to protect him? Could he have helped James kidnap Anna, to find out what she knew? If he'd thought of her as a snoop?

And what if he'd needed to silence her? Would he have done it?

As everything in him was crying out against this thought his phone buzzed with a number he didn't recognise. Could it be Reid on another phone? He hesitated and then picked up.

'Seaton Laws,' he said.

And into his ear came a warm, achingly familiar voice. A voice that in equal parts frustrated him and made him want to hug her as tightly as possible.

'Hey, Dad,' Anna said. 'Sorry for the radio silence.'

And Seaton embarrassed himself entirely by starting to cry.

43. Anna

Anna called her father the first moment she was able to. Which was a full two hours after she'd first demanded to make a call.

The delay had been largely her own fault. Well, her fault, with the mitigating factor of having been drugged out of her mind at the time of the bad decisions she'd made.

It had been her idea to go to a hospital in London, and James had obliged, perhaps because he'd believed his mother might find her, but maybe also to stop her freaking out completely. She'd felt almost able to cope with her fear as he'd helped her into the Uber, but then had descended into a shivering pit of terror.

That terror had only got worse. The cab had seemed to grow inwards at her and passing cars had seemed like monsters. She'd been convinced that everyone was trying to kill her and, midway through the cab ride, she'd opened the window and hurled her phone out of it, to the distress of the driver.

Luckily, the payment for the trip was being made through James's account. More luckily still, the driver had been a decent human being. Having arrived at North Middlesex Hospital and realised Anna had slid into unconsciousness he had run for help and had her stretchered inside. He'd also handed them the note James had given him: a note explaining she'd taken some kind of injectable drug and was overdosing. The note had, she'd discovered later, even helpfully listed her symptoms of hallucination and rapid heart rate.

Anna hadn't known any of this until much later, obviously.

In fact, she'd only begun to understand anything at nine something this morning when she'd finally woken up out of the comatose state she'd been left in. And even then her attempts at interrogating one of the health-care assistants had been largely unsuccessful. She hadn't even remembered that she'd *asked* to come here for a good hour.

It hadn't helped her confusion that everyone had kept calling her Alice, which had been the name James had written on his note. She'd then recalled, with a rush of embarrassment, telling him to write a pseudonym. She'd leaned in to hiss to him that her enemies were everywhere and she had to go undercover.

By the time she'd eventually been shown the note and fed both fluids and food she'd felt not only a lot more on top of the situation but also crushingly aware that her dad would be freaking out right now. She'd been unconscious for almost thirty-six hours. She'd *missed lunch.*

She was in so much trouble.

But when she'd demanded to get in touch with him she'd hit a major snag. She had zero idea what his phone number was, and when she'd asked them to look him up they'd drawn a blank. Dad was clearly either ex-directory or no longer had a landline. Assuming, of course, the long-suffering staff had actually bothered trying to find him and hadn't decided to do the more urgent work of dealing with patients.

So it was gone twelve by the time she was at long last discharged and could make her shaky way out of Ward T5. She'd followed the maze of corridors until she reached the ground-floor shops. A WHSmith supplied her with a mobile phone and SIM card, but after she'd made it out front and into a cab back to Cambridge, she'd collapsed in a dizzy heap for a good while.

She was still at a loss to understand how her body could

be affected so badly. She'd assumed that with no more drugs in her system for thirty-six hours she ought to be functioning just fine. But the serious overdose of scopolamine she'd apparently been spiked with hadn't miraculously cleared from her system after she'd woken up. It was still making itself known.

She'd started the fiddly process of putting the SIM in the moment she'd felt like she could stay conscious doing it, her coordination frustratingly bad. It didn't help that she kept catching sight of her sheeny dress and now appallingly messy hair in reflections from the window and wincing. She was still wearing her ballgown, the Jimmy Choos swapped for her pink flats and with the beautiful hair and make-up turned to ruin.

The frequent flashbacks to the night of the ball weren't helping, either. With them came all the abject terror that had hit her as they'd assembled for the fireworks. Moments when she'd been convinced that James was made of shadow. Others when he'd been a monster with a gaping maw about to swallow her.

But he'd been none of those things. He'd been trying to save her from his family in the only way he could think of.

'I didn't know,' he'd whispered to her before turning to her with those huge, sad eyes. 'I didn't know about Holly until what you told me. They . . . I'm not going to let them hurt you, too, I promise.'

And he'd made good on that promise: paying for the cab, and presumably not telling anyone where to find her.

Should probably have told him to tell Dad, actually, she thought now.

At least she had all her contacts saved into the Outlook app. Now that she had a phone she was able to sign into it.

The moment the app opened it began downloading emails,

and she sat back to watch them come in. New ones popped up as notifications and, of course, in spite of the urgency of everything, Anna found herself reading each banner alert. Emails from Imogen about the drugs James had been given, because Anna had forgotten to stand her down. One from Gael called *Finances* that made her heart squeeze with worry. A bunch of spam.

But then there was one that wiped everything away. It was titled 'Re: Help' – and it was from Reid.

She felt like she was barely breathing as she opened it.

She read that he was sorry. That he was going to find her.

And then she had to stop and wipe tears out of her eyes as she said under her breath, 'Reid, for fuck's sake. What have you been doing?'

Lacking any immediate way of getting in touch with him, owing to him having changed his number, she realised she still had to call her dad. And so she did, bracing herself for a lacerating earful about disappearing without warning.

But when she got through, Dad instead made her emotional situation that much worse by crying audibly down the phone.

'It's OK, Dad,' she said, hushing him. 'The fuckers tried to drug me with scopolamine, but I'm all right, and I've worked it all out.'

'Reid went to arrest them,' Seaton said, a note of worry in his voice even through the tears. 'Philip and James. Though I'm not sure they're at home. Philip's just messaged me.'

Anna felt something in her chest drop.

'He what?'

'Reid realised Philip was in a relationship with Esther,' her dad said, sounding tired. Heartsick. 'But James thought it was Holly, didn't he? Reid thinks he killed her and Philip kidnapped you to cover it up. He tried to, didn't he? Or was it

Ned? Reid went to rescue you, anyway. He came through in the end, you know.'

'Shit,' Anna said, her heart squeezing like mad. 'Shit, shit, shit. I need to get over there. He's got it wrong and he's going to get himself killed.'

44. Reid

There was only one car parked outside the huge sprawl of Philip and Marcie Sedgewick's house.

Reid had readied himself for no one to be home. For Anna not to be here and for the backup squad car he'd requested to be as pointless as his visit.

He'd had some hope, though. He'd managed to put through an urgent authorisation to access Philip Sedgewick's phone location at the start of the journey and the last ping had been here, at his home, only two hours ago. Yet the Jaguar that Philip usually drove, according to Kav's careful research, was not here.

He climbed out of the Uber and looked over the house itself. The red-brick building had strangely shoved-together sections that must have been built at very different times, and every one of them looked empty. There was no sign of movement at any of the windows.

But the place was vast. Multiple people could be hidden away inside.

The driver left as he was walking towards the door, and Reid hoped he wouldn't have to wait long for the squad car, for a number of reasons. He was out in leafy Great Shelford now, on the ultra-expensive side of Cambridge where cottages and ordinary houses vied with a few massive piles. Philip and Marcie lived on what seemed to be the most expensive and manor-house-heavy road of them all.

And all of it paid for by Marcie, Reid thought, darkly. *While Philip fools around with students.*

He rang the bell and was relieved when a figure appeared behind the slightly crazed glass. It was Marcie's tall, slim form, he realised. He recognised her from the photographs he'd been sent during the drive here.

Ryan's phone had proved to have exactly what he'd suspected: a mine of images from the ball last year, including several that showed a very significant interaction between Esther and Philip.

Marcie looked, Reid thought, almost as glamorous in her lightweight fitted top and trousers as she had in the ballgown she'd worn in some of Ryan's other photos. Though her hair had been longer a year ago. Her face perhaps a little rounder.

Reid readied a professional smile for her. She looked unflustered as she opened the door, perhaps expecting to see a neighbour. But something changed the moment she saw his swollen jaw. The bruising.

'Oh, are you . . .? Are you all right?'

'I'm DI Reid Murray,' he said. 'I was hoping to speak to Philip. Your husband, I think?'

'Yes. Oh. Sorry.' She shook her head, glancing behind him at the driveway. 'He's whizzed out. Had to pick our son up.' She looked over his jaw again, her forehead knitting. 'That looks recent. I've got ice. It'd probably still help.'

'That's very kind,' Reid said, remembering that Marcie was a senior medic. 'Sorry, am I interrupting? You must be working.'

'I'm on paperwork for now,' she said with a faint smile. 'I can spare a little while.'

She turned and led him down the hallway.

'Do you think he'll be long?' Reid asked.

Marcie glanced at her watch, a delicate, silver thing with diamonds set into it. 'I'd guess a quarter of an hour or so?'

On the inside, the house was expansive and beautiful. Marcie led him into a huge room that must have consisted of at least four original rooms knocked together. It was now an enormous open-plan sitting room that became a vast kitchen, with floor-to-ceiling windows at the back showing off a sweeping lawn. They stood open, and through them came an intoxicating smell of jasmine. These people had serious, serious money.

'Can I help?' Marcie asked, settling herself into one of the sitting-room chairs.

'You might be able to,' Reid said, thoughtfully. He took a perch opposite her and tried not to sag too obviously into the cushions of the sofa. 'I'm investigating a missing person. She vanished from Trinity May Ball.'

Marcie looked startled and Reid felt a moment of pity for her. It was clear that Philip had kept her out of all of this, just as he'd kept his affair from her. He wondered what else Marcie didn't know about her husband. And how much more there *was* to know.

That had its downsides for Reid: Marcie may well not know enough to help him. But there was also an upside. If he could seed doubts in Marcie now, he might get her talking to him and giving away more than was good for her husband.

'Her name is Aria,' he began.

'Aria Lauder?' Marcie asked. She sounded both alert and anxious. 'She's *missing*?'

'I'm afraid so,' Reid said. 'Though of course that isn't her real name, as your husband has no doubt told you by now.'

Marcie's large, dark eyes stared at him with a troubled, soulful, desperate look. She looked so much like James. 'I don't . . . He must have . . .'

'Philip has kept a lot from you over the years, hasn't he?' he said, gently but relentlessly. 'Did you realise? That there were things everyone knew about except you?'

She turned away from him and he realised that she was trying not to cry.

Some part of her guessed, he thought.

Reid saw a box of tissues on a bookshelf and rose to get them. They were placed artfully in front of a display of photographs. Multiple prints were laid out in each frame.

Several of the photographs featured a man he didn't immediately recognise, but Reid found his gaze lingering on him. He was brown-haired and had the same large, dark eyes as Marcie and James. But unlike them, his hair was cropped close. In two of them he had an arm slung round a younger James. And in one of the photos he was wearing military uniform and being presented with a medal.

She'd said she had a brother in the forces, hadn't she? She'd told Anna about him.

Reid was slow turning to hand Marcie the box of tissues. And slower still to sit in the armchair again. God, his headache needed to go. He needed to work out what was bothering him about the photos.

Marcie took a tissue with a terse 'Thank you'. And he realised that she had pride, as well as a softer side. He could use her pride.

'I'm surprised he didn't tell you about Aria,' he said. 'Wouldn't it have been useful to know that she was really an undercover journalist? I mean, Roland Frankland, Marcus Jaffett and Clarisse Thomas all know. Everyone else.'

He saw Marcie's expression harden slightly. 'What are you talking about?'

'Aria was never a student, though she does a good job of playing the part,' Reid said with a half-smile. 'She's a very good journalist. And she's also the kind of person who doesn't let go once she's realised an injustice has happened.' He broke off for a moment, suddenly sure he heard a sound somewhere else in the house.

She's here, he thought. And he got to his feet and started to move towards the doorway to the hall, drawn irresistibly towards the possibility of Anna being here. Of her being alive.

'Where are you going?' Marcie asked.

Reid paused at the doorway, listening, and then turned to her. She'd followed him and was now standing in the big kitchen, her feet in sunlight but her face shadowed. Hollow.

'Have they asked you to help them?' he asked Marcie, quietly. 'Did they explain why?'

Marcie's jaw tightened. 'I honestly don't know why you think it's all right to come in here and throw out . . . *spite.*'

'That necklace of Holly's you found,' he said, deliberately. 'Did you ever realise that it wasn't Holly who'd been wearing it?'

Marcie's face changed completely now. It lost all its colour and half its structure. But Reid couldn't stop to feel guilty.

'Is she here?' he asked. 'Did they ask you to help hold her? Or did they lie to you about that, too?'

'Hold who?' Marcie asked, her voice full of a startling, extraordinary rage this time. 'That – *whore*? Why would I let her through my door?'

Reid blinked at her, stunned. There was another sound behind him, but he couldn't even spare a thought for it because the woman he was seeing was so wholly different to the one he'd walked into the house to talk to.

'Anna is a journalist,' he said. 'She's never been a whore.'

You thought she was a whore, too, a tiny voice told him, and with it came profound shame. Here was his absolution, the moment where he proved that he'd been wrong.

'She came to Cambridge to find out what had happened to Holly Moore,' he said.

'Maybe she did,' Marcie spat, as though struggling to hold firm. 'But it was just an excuse. I knew. All the signs were there. The calls, the overnight stays, the lies . . .' Her mouth twisted. 'It was her. She was all over him from that first night, and I could tell it had been going on for months. A perfect set-up with her godfather's friend. I could see it all, so I followed her. And I saw her – I *saw her* – at the Caledonian Club with him. I tried to warn her off but that fucking bitch just *smiled* at me and went right on.' She took a long, shaky breath. 'I wanted the truth from her. I wanted the truth, this time. I missed my chance with Holly, and I regretted it. I wanted her to tell me how she did it. How she tempted him away.'

Marcie was standing in front of him, shaking with fury and a pain so apparent that it made him wince.

It was then that Reid understood that Esther had been totally wrong.

James had never convinced his mother that he and Holly had been using their bedroom; he'd told her the necklace was Holly's, and Marcie had assumed that Holly had been in there with Philip. Marcie had known Philip was cheating with someone; she'd just been waiting to find out the other woman's identity.

She killed Holly for it, he thought, numbly. *And she believed Anna was the same. Marcie thought she was sleeping with Philip.*

'That isn't . . .' he said, and then, in a hoarse voice, he asked, 'What did you do to her?'

Marcie's eyes slid past him and, maybe on another day, he might have been quick enough to turn and pull out the baton he carried. Though perhaps not. Ned had trained for years and was not likely to be troubled by an out-of-practice DI with a stick.

In a blur of agonising movement he found himself spun round and shoved against the kitchen wall by his neck. In an enraging, horrible echo of the night before, his head banged straight into the wall.

Reid thought he might pass out. He closed his eyes and tried to breathe, almost relieved at the painfully tight hold on his arm. It gave him something to focus on.

Ned, he thought. *It's Ned. Why didn't you ask where he was?*

At that point he realised what had bothered him about the photographs: Marcie had an ex-special forces brother, and James's bodyguard had come from the special forces. Something he should have put together before.

'This has all gone wrong,' Marcie said, her voice high and tight. 'He knows about Holly.'

Shit. Shit, shit, shit.

Reid had one free hand. His only available weapons were a phone and a baton, in two different pockets of his jacket.

But even as he had the thought Ned reached into each side of his jacket, finding first the phone then the baton and flinging them both away.

Great, Reid thought. *That's . . . great.*

'You have to get rid of him, Eddie,' Marcie said, her voice all but hysterical. 'He's – it's all going to come crumbling down. Please, Eddie. Please. You can't let this happen to James.'

'That's . . . that's madness, Marce. You know it's madness.' Ned's voice was not quite calm. 'We don't even know what the journalist has told people.'

'Then we deal with her, too! What else can we do?' Marcie asked, her voice sharp, and Reid opened his eyes, trying to turn enough to see something. He could only see half of Eddie's arm. Ned's arm. Whatever his real name was.

Reid tried to speak but the hold on his neck made it strangely hard, totally aside from the wicked pain still flooding his head.

'There's – squad car – coming,' he said.

There was a pause and then Marcie said, 'That's a bluff. He was totally wrong about everything. He doesn't have any evidence . . .'

Reid wanted to swear. She was almost entirely right, except for the squad car not being a bluff. Assuming they actually turned up at some point. He just needed to keep everyone talking until then.

'Lots of – evidence,' he said. 'Email from – Anna. Sent on to – lots – people.'

'*Anna* didn't have a clue,' Marcie said. What had happened to the kind, caring woman he'd thought he'd met? The one Anna had written about? 'She walked straight into that ball and let me stick a bloody needle full of scopolamine into her. She thought she had nothing to worry about.'

Reid felt a tearing sensation inside him. He couldn't believe it. Wouldn't believe it. That she'd done to Anna what she'd done to Holly.

There was rage in him, but, above all, despair. He'd let her die. He'd let it happen.

'Marce,' Ned was saying, and Reid could feel his grip slackening ever so slightly. 'We can't do this.'

'I am *not* going to let my son suffer,' Marcie said, her voice shaking. 'And if you can't do what you need to – what James needs you to – then please, please just hold him. Hold him while I do it. I will fix this.'

Ned's grip on him tightened to the point where it was hard to breathe. Reid didn't need to look round to know that Marcie had gone to get a medical kit. It was how she operated, wasn't it? The swift needle to the arm. Clinical. Professional. Quiet.

And Reid wondered how he'd ever thought anyone else responsible.

'Eddie,' he said, his voice still half choked. 'Ned. This isn't – going to help.'

There was absolute silence from Marcie's brother, and his grip remained wickedly tight. Even through Reid's frantic, panicked thoughts, he understood that Ned would do anything for his family, and that his sister knew how to use that fact in her favour.

There were footsteps, and then Marcie's voice again.

'Hold his arm out. Please.'

Ned hesitated, and Reid used the moment to kick back as hard as he could in the direction of Ned's shins. Some remnants of his training were still there, and he twisted just afterwards, seeking to break Ned's hold.

But Ned wasn't the kind of amateur Reid had been trained to fight off. He never even loosened his grip. He just kicked Reid on the side of the leg so hard that it collapsed under him, leaving most of his weight hanging agonisingly off his neck and arm.

He felt his twisted arm being straightened and pulled outwards and scrambled to get his other hand against the wall. To get his feet under him. Anything.

And then he heard another voice, one he'd genuinely believed he would never hear again.

45. Anna

It had taken the cab another twenty-one minutes to charge down the M11 towards the Sedgewick family home in Great Shelford. Halfway through that time, Anna had realised she should call the police, too. She gave them Philip and Marcie's address, deciding to tell them there was a violent altercation going on at the house for good measure. Which was possibly even true; a thought that she tried not to let in.

They had slowed to a stop on the road outside, and Anna asked the driver to drop her next to the gate, unsure about what she would be walking into. She shoved an extra twenty-pound note she'd found in the purse at him and asked him to wait and be ready if she needed him. He'd looked a little alarmed at this but seemed willing to hover.

There had been no sign of any activity as she'd stepped quickly and quietly up to the front door, but it had been locked, an eventuality she hadn't thought about.

They could be killing him, she thought, numbly.

And without any more thought, she'd started running round the side of the house, out towards the beautiful, pristine lawn. She ran until she heard voices floating out through the French windows, and then she slowed rapidly and flattened herself against the nearest wall.

It was Marcie's voice she'd heard. Marcie's shrill words, calling someone a whore.

Oh, she thought, just afterwards. *That must be me.*

How had Marcie understood that her husband was a cheat, and been clever enough to kill a young woman and almost get away with it, and yet been stupid enough to misidentify his mistress *twice over*?

Though maybe it wasn't so hard to understand. Anna herself had been wrong; looking at every man with suspicion and letting sweet Marcie jab her with a syringe full of scopolamine and laughingly apologise for her spiky sequins making her hugs uncomfortable.

Anna almost gasped as she heard Reid's voice in reply. Reid, actually him in the flesh, for the first time in eighteen months. Reid, saying loudly and clearly that she wasn't a whore.

About fucking time, Anna thought, while, in spite of herself and the circumstances, she was smiling about as broadly as she'd smiled in months.

She was just on the point of wondering where Ned was when she heard the unmistakable sounds of a struggle. Anna abandoned stealth and turned to peer in through the open French window.

None of them were looking her way. Ned had Reid pinned up against the far interior wall with his back to her, the two of them locked together painfully. And Marcie was fixated on them, her back almost entirely to the French windows, too.

Fuck, fuck, fuck, Anna thought as she ducked down and crossed the threshold into the room. She scooted across the floor until she was behind the kitchen counter and out of sight.

Marcie had gone full nuclear. Obviously. She didn't seem to have a middle ground. And Anna was going to have to do something, because there was no sign of the police yet. Why hadn't she pulled up loudly with the taxi driver and banged on the door? Maybe that would have stopped them.

Or maybe it would have panicked them.

Anna wasn't *dressed* for this. A crumpled ballgown wasn't good combat gear, even with the flat shoes. And she had no weapons. The spiky Jimmy Choos were in the Uber, and the most she had in her handbag was a phone, a May Ball programme and a wallet.

Come on, Anna, she thought, as behind her the conversation went on. *You can improvise.*

This was a kitchen. And kitchens had knives. In fact, there was a great big wooden block of them on the counter across to her left. She only had to be quiet enough to get to them.

The process of scooting across the floor again, standing up and sliding out a knife at random – inwardly thinking, *please, please, not a cheese knife* – was the most heart-pumpingly, spine-crawlingly awful thing she could remember doing.

Well, it was the most awful right up until Marcie came back and she had to stand up and creep up behind her until she was close enough to do some damage, all the while wondering what she'd do if it turned out that Ned had a gun.

Neither of them was looking at her. They were both too focused on Reid, and his arm, just waiting for the syringe in Marcie's hand.

Even Anna struggled to look away from Reid. He was really here. He'd come to try to save her.

But now she needed to save him right back. And fast.

Anna took another step, until the knife was touching Marcie's back, enough for her to stiffen slightly.

'You'd better let go of him, Ned,' Anna said, loudly, 'or I'm going to stick this knife into your sister's kidney.'

There was a moment of absolute silence and then Marcie suddenly jabbed backwards with the syringe towards Anna.

'No!' Anna yelled, because she was *done* with this woman. She grabbed Marcie's arm with her free left hand, blocking it.

Marcie twisted round to face her and pushed hard against her grip. She was trying to shove the syringe into Anna's body, clearly not caring where it went as long as it hit her.

But Anna wasn't going to let that happen, whether Ned got involved or not. She might not be at her best, but she hadn't spent all those hours at the gym to be overpowered by a forty-something woman who looked like she might break in a strong breeze.

Or to let Reid die at the hands of an ex-military psychopath, for that matter.

She held Marcie's wrist back and started to twist it. The expression on Marcie's face was extraordinary. It was like every ounce of civility had been peeled back. She just kept trying. Pressing forwards with her whole body.

'Fuck – you!' Marcie yelled, her arm now in an impossible position. 'You and that little slut Holly can die!'

Anna gave a roar and dug her fingers into the tendons of Marcie's arm. The syringe clattered to the ground.

'You know what?' Anna said, staring her down with her grip still in place. 'I am *so* tired of women blaming other women for their husbands being cheating assholes! Go and talk to Philip and stop killing innocent girls!'

She zoned back in on the fact that Ned could take her down in about ten seconds. But James's uncle was staring at them both, his face strangely blank. He was still holding on to Reid, but his grip had finally slackened and Reid was getting his feet back under him.

'It wasn't Philip's fault!' Marcie spat.

Anna was still holding Marcie's arm, while the woman tried to tear it free.

Does she just not give up?

Anna looked past her, to Ned. 'OK. You need to let him go now,' she said. 'Do it! Or I really will . . .'

It was only at that point that she realised she'd basically lost track of the knife. It was still in her hand, but it wasn't loosely held out in the air. In trying to force the syringe into Anna's flesh, Marcie had driven her abdomen onto the blade. It had sunk into her somewhere above her hip. Anna could even half remember feeling it happen, but she'd been so fixated on Marcie's arm and that needle.

The weirdest thing was that Marcie didn't seem to realise it had happened, either. She was still staring at Anna with her eyes full of rage. Was still trying to twist her wrist free.

Even as Anna faltered and stumbled slightly backwards, Marcie didn't wince.

'Crap,' Anna said. 'Just . . . stay there. We need to keep the blade in and get you some bandages.'

But instead of staying there Marcie pulled backwards, away from the blade. Anna *felt* the horror of it sliding free, but Marcie just turned to her brother like nothing had happened.

'You have to stop them,' she said, her voice shaking. Pleading. 'Please, Eddie. She's just as bad as Holly. She's just as bad. She's been sleeping with Philip, too.' She began crying, while Ned's wide eyes went from her stomach to her face and back again. 'Please stop them.'

There was a momentary pause while Anna thought frantically about what she could do. And then Ned said, quietly, 'You told me it was James.'

Marcie rubbed her eyes, roughly. 'It . . . doesn't even matter.'

'You said he'd killed her by accident,' Ned said, more loudly. 'You killed her? Deliberately?'

'Wouldn't you have wanted to help, even if you'd known?' Marcie asked, pleading.

Ned shook his head. And then he stepped away from Reid completely. Reid slumped the rest of the way down the wall to the floor.

'Reid!' Anna ducked past Marcie and skidded to her knees on the floor next to him.

'I'm OK,' he said, making an effort to push himself off the

floor, and she half turned to see whether Ned was about to punch one or other of them. But he was still staring at his sister.

She saw Marcie shudder slightly and look down at her abdomen, and then slowly fold towards the floor as her brother tried to catch her, as if it was only now she saw it that the wound had become real.

Later, Marcie's health would probably matter to Anna a lot. Anna had, after all, been the one wielding the knife. But right now, she couldn't seem to care.

She was here, and Reid was Reid. She levered him as gently as she could into a sitting position against the wall. He'd closed his eyes and there was sweat along his forehead.

She saw the full glory of his bruised face now, and it made her ache.

They beat the shit out of him, she thought. *All because of me.*

'God, Reid,' she said.

He opened one eye, blearily, and gave her a half-smile. 'I've never been so glad to see anyone in my life,' he said. And he reached out clumsily and grabbed her hand. 'Though I may love you more if you can find me some fuck-off-strong painkillers.'

Anna was smiling and crying at once as she answered. 'So you're saying you love me even without the drugs?'

'Yes, I am,' he said. 'And I do.'

And Anna leaned in and kissed him, accompanied by the highly romantic sound of sirens approaching – finally – at speed.

There was, of course, no easy resolution to what had happened that day. As Reid and Anna were helped to sit in the back of one ambulance Marcie was already being loaded onto another. The doors weren't yet shut when a Jaguar slewed into the driveway and disgorged Philip and James, the two of them white-faced with fear.

With perfect timing, Ned was brought out of the house at this point, wearing handcuffs, the result of Reid having explained his role in covering up Holly's murder.

'Shit,' Anna said, half rising to her feet.

'Stay here,' Reid said, gently but firmly. 'You don't need to do anything else.'

And despite his wobbly gait and what must have been a terrifically painful head, he hobbled over to Philip and explained that his wife was about to be taken urgently to hospital, where she would be under a state of arrest for the murder of Holly Moore and the attempted murder of himself and Anna Sousa.

Philip took three running steps towards the ambulance, and Anna wondered whether he'd taken any of that in. But it was at least good to see that he cared a little for the woman he'd cheated on persistently.

James was staring at Reid, his face slack with shock. 'I . . . you're an actual police officer,' he said.

Reid gave him a confused look. 'I . . . yes. We met yesterday.'

'I know, I . . . I thought you were a fake,' he said, and his eyes travelled to Ned. 'I'm . . . I'm sorry. I didn't trust anyone.'

And then he sat heavily on the ground, on what must have been viciously uncomfortable gravel, and he started sobbing into his hands in a way that all but broke Anna's heart.

There was more, too, later. When Anna had climbed into the back of a squad car with Reid and used her replacement phone to call Gael at last.

'OK,' she said as he answered. 'I've done some stuff and I want you to listen and try to be OK with it, because I really need your help right now.'

'Jesus, Anna,' he said, in a voice that was far warmer and more steeped in relief than she'd expected. 'I thought you were dead. You can . . . Just come and tell me everything and we'll work it out. OK?'

And actually, he basically did, though much of it made her uncomfortable. He listened while she explained that this had never been about a group of kids killing their friend, but about a woman filled with rage at the student her husband had taken advantage of. 'Only she got the wrong girl,' she added, with an empty feeling of sadness. 'She killed Holly Moore instead of Esther Thomas. One innocent girl instead of another.'

She told him that her brother Eddie had been her only confidante, but that she'd twisted the truth to manipulate him. Told him it had been James, in a moment of rage when he realised she'd cheated, and that they would have to rally together if anyone found out.

'So James Sedgewick didn't know?' Gael asked her.

Anna sighed then, long and loud. 'Not until I gave him enough information to make it click. I was wrong and Maria was right. I think he tried to kill himself that day. He realised that this all came back to that necklace, and Esther's affair with his dad. Which meant someone in his family killed her. She died because of him and he didn't even have anyone to confide in.'

Gael nodded, slowly, and then said, 'But you were right, too. There *was* danger. Esther Thomas would not have been safe. Nor would whatever young woman Philip chose to move in on next.'

He listened while she told him about Kit Frankland and Ryan Jaffett too, and his expression was nothing but understanding. Understanding, and maybe a little sad.

Once she'd finished, he sat back with a sigh. 'What you have, it's . . . it's going to be some goddamn story.'

'It is,' Anna agreed.

'We've . . . had an email,' he said after that. 'From Roland Frankland. It arrived while you were on your way back. He's threatening us with legal action.'

'Shit.' She felt her heart twisting and then said, 'I don't have any defence.'

'That isn't true,' Gael replied. 'It sounds like there are a lot of things I can say in reply. Like the fact that his son basically left you with a known abuser to be sexually assaulted. The fact he covered up for other assaults.' He nodded. 'I don't think you were the only one manipulating, there.'

She felt a sense of wrongness rising up in her. 'No. I did the wrong thing, Gael.' Her voice was shaking as she said, 'There was obviously a line, and I shouldn't have crossed it.'

'No,' he said, 'you shouldn't, but I think . . . I should never have pushed you to cross it, either.' He frowned and then said, 'Just because the easy way of getting to a story is seduction, that doesn't mean it's right for me to push you into it. I'm . . . sorry. About all of it.' He gave her a look that was full of pain. 'The things that happened with Ryan Jaffett, they're my fault. After I thought you were dead, I had time to feel a lot of guilt over this, and it's . . . well.' He cleared his throat. 'I'm going to support you over this, and try to sort something out with the Franklands. If anyone stands to be in trouble, I think it should be the *Ensign*. Not you.'

Anna wasn't sure how she felt about that. How she *should* feel about that. There was obvious relief, but there was a grimy feeling of taking the easy way out, too.

You'll have to make this better, somehow, she thought. *And own what you did, too.*

There was another feeling that hit her as she left the *Ensign*: a feeling that things had changed for the better. And that they had a good chance of staying changed. So it was with a shaky smile that she messaged Reid to tell him she was on her way to him.

46. Anna

From: Anna.Sousa@fleetfoot.com
To: rmurray@met.police.org.uk
05/07/2026 16:12
Subject: Trial!!!

I just saw the news about Ned's evidence. Oh, my god, it was incredible. Cool, calm facts about all the terrible things she told him to do. It's so confusing, knowing he covered up Holly's murder and almost let her kill you, but now getting to watch him to do the right thing. And I know it's weird that I sort-of like him still. I guess there's something appealing about the folks who will do anything for the people they care about.

Don't worry, you are now firmly in that camp, in case you wondered.

How did Marcie take it, anyway? Was Philip there today, too? Was he on Ned's side or Marcie's? Can you please answer your goddamn phone?

I can't even share my sad/mad excitement and horrible moments of guilt about this with anyone. I messaged Dad but this is obviously all still painful for him. They were his friends for decades. I can't even imagine. But he still wants lunch once I'm back. A good sign.

Over here in Coney Island, my little brother is at least a little excited on my behalf, though obviously he's still worried about his dad. Frank is doing OK, by the way. He's not out of the woods, and he's going to have to change his lifestyle pretty profoundly, but they're talking about discharging him tomorrow. Mom is more positive but – weirdly – is kind of clingy. Even with me. She keeps saying how glad she is I flew out to support them and how I should come more often. I guess it's understandable when you almost lose someone to a heart attack you never saw coming. And maybe she's thinking about what she'll do if she really does lose Frank. How she'll only have me and Ben.

But honestly, it's the first time in years she's seemed like an actual mom to me. I'm not sure if I like it or hate it.

The other weird thing that happened today was getting a message from Esther Thomas, who I thought I would never hear from again. She sent me a link to an article about Aria Lauder, the real one. Looks like Aria broke out of another stint in rehab, stole a car and then crashed it while incredibly high. No injuries, but she came close to taking out a pedestrian.

Esther sent it with this single message that said, 'She sounds worse than you xx.' And it was maybe a dig, but in some ways I wondered if it might be a kind of olive branch. Obviously, I have immediately replied because I have zero cool. I've not had an answer yet, but I guess it doesn't matter as long as she's OK. Of everyone in this I think I probably feel the most sorry for Esther.

I mean, I feel sorry for Kit as well, if I'm honest. What I did . . . it wasn't right. It was bound to hurt him.

It sits badly with me, too, that Gael shut his dad up like he did. And it worries me that there's now a pretty hotshot lawyer out there who would happily see me dead. Maybe two hotshot lawyers, depending on whether Kit sticks it out as a lawyer or really does pursue rugby as a career. Is it wrong to still be rooting for him to do that? You could tell me to stop talking about him. Only you can't, because you *haven't picked up your phone*.

Anyway, I'm looking forward to getting back and seeing you. And also to doing my bit in court. I've already been thinking about exactly what I'm going to wear (the D&G suit, obviously. Because I look hot in it, and you've now agreed with that assessment so it's a *fact*). Secondary to that, I've been thinking a lot about what I'm going to say. Though I know I'll get *trained* in how to say it. But it's kind of exciting, getting to be a witness instead of writing everything up. And also good practice for when Ryan's trial finally gets to court.

You're still not answering, *REID*, which is unacceptable. I'll just have to keep writing this stream of consciousness in an email instead.

I want to know, actually: has it felt to you like this is kind of . . . justice for Tanya, too? I don't know why it feels like that. Maybe because we got to the real truth, and maybe because the university is taking responsibility for overlooking both Philip Sedgewick and Ryan Jaffett preying on vulnerable students. Maybe partly that. But I guess also because every young woman with a promising future deserves to have their story told.

Anyway, that may all just be in my weird brain. I'll ask Cordelia and she'll tell me bluntly that it's all displacement for my own feelings of failure.

But I'm looking forward to seeing her again, regardless. Almost as much as I'm looking forward to seeing you. Pick up your stupid phone so I can repeat all of this at insane speeds that way.

Anna

xxx

Acknowledgements

There are so many people needed to bring a book to life, and my first standalone took more of everything: more discussion, more support, and definitely more patience.

So I want to thank every last person in the brilliant team at Penguin Michael Joseph, but particularly Joel Richardson and Beatrix McIntyre. And I equally want to thank the utterly wonderful team at Curtis Brown, and most particularly Felicity Blunt and Rosie Pierce.

I want to thank, too, the incredible Jennie Roman and Chris H, who were guides of two brilliant and different kinds at key points. As well as my wonderful author friends who so often have to listen to my wittering, including the fabulous LKs and the voice note gang.

There were also many people who offered fabulous advice on Cambridge University life as it is now. Thank you all, and particularly AW and Sarah Cain who provided in-depth, brilliant thoughts on how student life has changed.

And I suppose I should add my family in here, who are pretty supportive and OK between the brutal roastings they provide. This book was written across some tough times for my little family unit, and I'm secretly hugely proud of you for getting through it.

And finally, to all the readers who kept badgering me about when the next book was going to be out. It probably did actually help me through that difficult time, in a weird sort of way. Imagine your mum repeatedly asking when you're going to get a job until you give in and start applying: it was like that. So thank you.